Sushi for Beginners

ALSO BY MARIAN KEYES
FROM CLIPPER LARGE PRINT

Angels
Further Under the Duvet

Sushi for Beginners

Marian Keyes

W F HOWES LTD

This large print edition published in 2010 by
W F Howes Ltd
Unit 4, Rearsby Business Park, Gaddesby Lane,
Rearsby, Leicester LE7 4YH

1 3 5 7 9 10 8 6 4 2

First published in the United Kingdom in 2000
by Michael Joseph

A CIP catalogue record for this book is available
from the British Library

ISBN 978 1 40745 450 4

Typeset by Palimpsest Book Production Limited,
Grangemouth, Stirlingshire
Printed and bound in Great Britain
by MPG Books Ltd, Bodmin, Cornwall

FSC
Mixed Sources
Product group from well-managed
forests, controlled sources and
recycled wood or fiber
SA-COC-1565
www.fsc.org
© 1996 Forest Stewardship Council

For Niall, Caitríona, Tadhg and Rita-Anne

ACKNOWLEDGEMENTS

Thank you to my fantastic editor Louise Moore and all at Michael Joseph and Penguin for their hard work and enthusiasm.

Thanks to all at Poolbeg.

Thanks to Jonathan Lloyd and all at Curtis Brown.

Thanks to Caitríona Keyes, Mammy Keyes, Rita-Anne Keyes and Louise Voss who read this book as it was written and kept demanding more.

Thanks to Eileen Prendergast and especial thanks for giving me the name for the book!

Thanks to Siobhan Coogan for insider info on being a mammy.

Thanks to the Simon community for generously giving time and information about homelessness.

Thanks to Morag Prunty and everyone at *Irish Tatler* for revealing the world of magazines to me.

Thanks to all the stand-up comedians I know, none of whom are anything like the ones in the book!

Thanks to the Clarence hotel.

The following people also helped greatly with advice and enthusiasm. If I've forgotten anyone, please forgive me: Suzanne Benson, Jenny Boland, Susie Burgin, Ailish Connelly, Gai Griffin, Suzanne Power, and Annemarie Scanlan.

Thanks, as always, to my beloved Tony, for everything.

PROLOGUE

'*Dammit,*' *she realized.* '*I think I'm having a nervous breakdown.*'

She looked around at the bed she was flung in. Her well-overdue-for-a-bath body was sprawled lethargically on the well-overdue-for-a-change sheet. Tissues, sodden and balled, littered the duvet. Gathering dust on her chest of drawers was an untouched arsenal of chocolate. Scattered on the floor were magazines she'd been unable to concentrate on. The television in the corner relentlessly delivered daytime viewing direct to her bed. Yip, nervous-breakdown territory all right.

But something was wrong. What was it?

'*I always thought . . .*' *she tried.* '*You know, I always expected . . .*'

Abruptly she knew. '*I always thought it would be nicer than this . . .*'

CHAPTER 1

At *Femme* magazine, something had been in the air for weeks, a feeling that they were living on a fault-line. Speculation finally burst into flames when it was confirmed that Calvin Carter, the US Managing Director, had been sighted roaming around the top floor, looking for the gents'. Apparently he'd just arrived in London from head-office in New York.

It's happening. Lisa clenched her fists in excitement. *It's actually finally, bloody happening.*

Later that day the phone call came. Would Lisa pop upstairs to see Calvin Carter and British MD, Barry Hollingsworth?

Lisa slammed down the phone. 'Too right I would,' she shouted at it.

Her colleagues barely looked up. People slamming phones down, then shouting, were ten a penny in the magazine game. Besides, they were trapped in Deadline Hell – if they didn't get this month's issue put to bed by nightfall, they'd miss their slot with the printers and would be scooped once again by arch-rivals *Marie-Claire*. But what did Lisa care, she thought, hobbling to the lift, she wouldn't have a job here after today. She'd have a much better one somewhere else.

Lisa was kept waiting outside the boardroom for twenty-five minutes. After all, Barry and Calvin were very important men.

'Should we let her in yet?' Barry asked Calvin, when he felt they'd killed enough time.

'It's only twenty minutes since we called her,' Calvin pointed out, huffily. Obviously Barry Hollingsworth didn't realize just *how* important, he, Calvin Carter, was.

'Sorry, I thought it was later. Perhaps you'd show me again how to improve my swing.'

'Sure. Now, head down and hold still. Hold *still*! Feet steady, left arm straight, and swing!'

When Lisa was finally granted admission, Barry and Calvin were seated behind a walnut table approximately a kilometre long. They looked frowningly powerful.

'Sit down, Lisa.' Calvin Carter inclined his silver bullet head graciously.

Lisa sat. She smoothed back her caramel-coloured hair, showing her free honey highlights to their best advantage. *Free* because she kept plugging the salon in the 'Ones to Watch' section of the magazine.

Settling herself in the chair, she tucked her Patrick Cox-shod feet neatly around each other. The shoes were a size too small – no matter how many times she asked the Patrick Cox press office to send a size six, they always sent a five. But free

4

Patrick Cox stilettos were free Patrick Cox stilettos. What did an unimportant detail like excruciating agony matter?

'Thank you for coming up,' Calvin smiled. Lisa decided she'd better smile back. Smiles were a commodity like everything else, only given in exchange for something useful, but she reckoned in this case it was worth her while. After all, it wasn't every day that a girl was seconded to New York and made deputy editor of *Manhattan* magazine. So she curled her mouth and bared her pearly white teeth. (Kept that way by the year's supply of Rembrandt toothpaste which had been donated for a reader competition, but which Lisa had thought would be more appreciated in her own bathroom.)

'You've been at *Femme* for –' Calvin looked at the stapled pages in front of him. 'Four years?'

'Four years next month,' Lisa murmured, with an expertly judged mix of deference and confidence.

'And you've been editor for nearly two years?'

'Two wonderful years,' Lisa confirmed, fighting back the urge to stick her fingers down her throat and gag.

'And you're only twenty-nine,' Calvin marvelled. 'Well, as you know here at Randolph Media we reward hard work.'

Lisa twinkled prettily at this patent lie. Like many companies in the Western world, Randolph Media rewarded hard work with poor pay, increasing workloads, demotions and on-a-second's-notice redundancies.

But Lisa was different. She'd paid her dues at *Femme*, and made sacrifices that even *she'd* never intended to make: starting at seven-thirty most mornings, doing twelve, thirteen, fourteen-hour days, then going to evening press dos when she finally switched off her computer. Often she came to work on Saturdays, Sundays, even bank-holiday Mondays. The porters loathed her because it meant that whenever she wanted to come to the office one of them had to come in and open up and thereby forgo their Saturday football or their bank-holiday family outing to Brent Cross.

'We have a vacancy at Randolph Media,' Calvin said importantly. 'It would be a wonderful challenge, Lisa.'

I know, she thought irritably. *Just cut to the chase.*

'It will involve moving overseas, which can sometimes be a problem for one's partner.'

'I'm single.' Lisa was brusque.

Barry wrinkled his forehead in surprise and thought of the tenner he'd had to hand over for someone's wedding present, a few years before. He could have sworn it was for Lisa here, but maybe not, perhaps he wasn't as on-the-ball as he once used to be . . .

'We're looking for an editor for a new magazine,' Calvin went on.

A *new* magazine? Lisa was jolted off course. *But Manhattan has been published for seventy years.*

While she was still grappling with the implications of that, Calvin delivered the whammy. 'It would involve you relocating to Dublin.'

The shock set up a smothered buzzing in her head, as if her ears needed to pop. A numb, fuzzy sensation of alienation. The only reality was the sudden agony of her crumpled toes. 'Dublin?' she heard her muffled voice ask. Perhaps . . . perhaps . . . perhaps they meant Dublin, New York.

'Dublin, Ireland,' Calvin Carter said, down a long, echoey tunnel, destroying the last of her hope.

I can't believe this is happening to me.

'Ireland?'

'Small wet place across the Irish sea,' Barry offered kindly.

'Where they drink a lot,' Lisa said faintly.

'And they never stop talking. That's the place. Booming economy, huge population of young folk, market research indicates the place is ripe for a feisty new women's magazine. And we want you to set it up for us, Lisa.'

They were looking at her expectantly. She knew it was customary to make stumbling, tearful, over-whelmed noises about how she appreciated how much they trusted her and how she hoped to justify their faith in her.

'Um, good . . . thanks.'

'Our Irish portfolio is an impressive one,' boasted Calvin. 'We have *Hibernian Bride, Celtic*

Health, Gaelic Interiors, Irish Gardening, The Catholic Judger –'

'No, *The Catholic Judger* is about to fold,' Barry interrupted. 'Sales figures are way down.'

'– *Gaelic Knitting* –' Calvin had no interest in bad news, '*Celtic Car, Spud* – that's our Irish food magazine – *DIY Irish-Style* and *The Hip Hib*.'

'*The Hip Hip?*' Lisa forced out. It was advisable to keep talking.

'*Hip* Hib,' Barry confirmed. 'Short for *Hip Hibernian.* Young men's magazine. Cross between *Loaded* and *Arena.* You'll be setting up a women's version.'

'Name?'

'We think *Colleen.* Young, feisty, funky, sexy, that's how we see it. Especially sexy, Lisa. And nothing too clever. Forget downbeat features about female circumcision or women in Afghanistan with no freedom. That's not our target readership.'

'You want a dumbed-down magazine?'

'You got it,' Calvin beamed.

'But I've never been to Ireland, I know nothing about the place.'

'Precisely!' Calvin agreed. 'That's exactly what we want. No preconceptions, just a fresh, honest approach. Same salary, generous relocation package, you start two weeks Monday.'

'*Two weeks?* But that gives me almost no time . . .'

'I hear you've wonderful organizational powers,' Calvin glinted. 'Impress me. Any questions?'

She couldn't stop herself. Normally she smiled while the knife was being twisted because she could see the bigger picture. But she was in shock.

'What about the position of deputy editor at *Manhattan*?'

Barry and Calvin exchanged a look.

'Tia Silvano from the *New Yorker* was the successful candidate,' Calvin huffily admitted.

Lisa nodded. She felt as if her world had ended. Woodenly she got up to leave. 'When do I have to decide by?' she asked.

Barry and Calvin exchanged another look.

Calvin was the one who eventually spoke. 'We've already filled your current position.'

The world lapsed into slow motion as Lisa realized that this was a *fait accompli*. She had no choice in it at all. Fixed in a frozen screám, it took several long seconds to understand that there was nothing she could do except hobble from the room.

'Fancy a round of golf?' Barry asked Calvin, once she'd gone.

'Love to but can't. Gotta go to Dublin and interview for the other positions.'

'Who's Irish MD now?' Barry asked.

Calvin frowned. Barry should know this. 'A guy called Jack Devine.'

'Oh him. Bit of a maverick.'

'I don't think so.' Calvin strongly disapproved of rebels. 'Leastways he'd better not be.'

★   ★   ★

9

Lisa tried to put a gloss on it. She'd never admit she was disappointed. Especially after all she'd sacrificed.

But you can't make a silk purse out of a sow's ear. Dublin was not New York, no matter how you sliced it. And the 'generous' relocation package could have been sued under the Trade Descriptions Act. Worse still, she had to surrender her mobile. Her *mobile*! It was as if a limb had been amputated.

None of her colleagues were exactly devastated at her departure. She never let anyone else get a go of the Patrick Cox shoes, not even the girls with size-five feet. And her generosity with bitchy and untrue personal comments had earned her the nickname Slanderella. Nevertheless, on Lisa's last day, the staff of *Femme* were rounded up and press-ganged into the boardroom for the customary send-off – plastic glasses of tepid white wine that could have doubled as paint stripper, a tray with a desultory spread of Hula Hoops and Skips, and a rumour – never realized – that cocktail sausages were on their way.

When everyone was on their third glass of wine and could therefore be relied on to exhibit some enthusiasm, there was a call for hush and Barry Hollingsworth made his textbook speech, thanking Lisa for everything and wishing her well. It was agreed that he'd done a lovely job of it. Especially because he'd managed to get her name right. The last time someone had left he'd made a tear-jerking, twenty-minute speech lauding the unique talents and contribution of someone called Heather, while Fiona, the person who was leaving, stood by in mortification.

Then came the presentation to Lisa of twenty pounds' worth of Marks & Spencers vouchers and a large card with a hippo and 'Sorry to see you go' emblazoned on it. Ally Benn, Lisa's former deputy, had chosen the leaving present with care. She'd thought long and hard about what Lisa would hate the most and eventually concluded that M&S vouchers would cause maximum distress. (Ally Benn's feet were a perfect size five.)

'To Lisa!' Barry concluded. By then everyone was flushed and rowdy, so they raised their white plastic cups, sloshing wine and morsels of cork on to their clothing and, as they sniggered and elbowed each other, bellowed, 'To Lisa!'

Lisa stayed just as long as she needed to. She'd long looked forward to this leaving do, but she'd always thought she'd be surfing out on a wave of glory, already halfway to New York. Instead of being shunted away to the magazine version of Siberia. It was an utter nightmare.

'I must go,' she said to the dozen or so women who'd worked under her for the past two years. 'I must finish packing.'

'Sure, sure,' they agreed, in a clamour of drunken good wishes. 'Well, good luck, have fun, enjoy Ireland, take care, don't work too hard . . .'

Just as Lisa got to the door, Ally screeched, 'We'll miss you.'

Lisa nodded tightly and closed the door.

'– Like a hole in the head.' Ally didn't miss a beat. 'Any wine left?'

They stayed until every last drop of wine was drunk, every last crumb of Hula Hoop wiped off the tray with a licked finger, then they turned to each other and demanded in dangerously high spirits, 'What now?!'

They descended on Soho, swarming through the bars in a Friday-night, tequila-drinking, office workers' maraud. Little Sharif Mumtaz (features assistant) got separated from the others and was helped home by a kind man whom she married nine months later. Jeanie Geoffrey (assistant fashion editor) was bought a bottle of champagne by a man who declared she was 'a goddess'. Gabbi Henderson (health and beauty) had her bag stolen. And Ally Benn (recently appointed editor) clambered on to a table in one of the livelier pubs in Wardour Street and danced like a mad thing until she fell off and sustained multiple fractures to her right foot.

In other words, a great night.

CHAPTER 2

'Ted, you couldn't have come at a better time!' Ashling flung wide her door and for once didn't utter her most overused phrase, which happened to be, 'Oh shite, it's Ted.'

'Couldn't I?' Ted sidled cautiously into Ashling's flat. He didn't normally receive a welcome this warm.

'I need you to tell me which jacket looks nicest on me.'

'I'll do my best.' Ted's thin, dark face looked even more intense. 'But I *am* a man.'

Not quite, Ashling thought, regretfully. What a great pity that the person who had moved into the flat upstairs six months ago, and had instantly decided that Ashling was his best friend, hadn't been a nice, big, pulse-rate-raising man. And instead had been Ted Mullins, needy civil servant, aspiring stand-up comedian and small and wiry owner of a push-bike.

'First, this black one.' Ashling shrugged the jacket on over her white silk 'interview' top and magic lose-half-a-stone-in-an-instant black trousers.

'What's the biggie?' Ted sat on a chair and wound

himself around it. He was all angles and elbows, pointy shoulders and sharp knees, like a sketch drawing of himself.

'Job interview. Half nine this morning.'

'Another one! What for this time?'

Ashling had applied for several jobs in the past two weeks, everything from working on a wild-west ranch in Mullingar to answering phones at a PR company.

'Assistant editor at a new magazine called *Colleen*.'

'What? A real job?' Ted's saturnine face lit up. 'Beats me why you've applied for all those others, you're way overqualified for them.'

'I've low self-esteem,' Ashling reminded him, with a bright smile.

'Mine's lower,' Ted shot back, determined not to be outdone.

'A women's magazine, though,' he mused. 'If you got it you could tell that crowd at *Woman's Place* to stick it. Revenge is a dish best served cold!' He threw back his head and gave forth a hollow series of fake Vincent Price-type laughs. 'Nnnnyyyywwwwahwahwahwahwahwahwah!'

'Actually, revenge isn't a dish at all,' Ashling interrupted. 'It's an emotion. Or something. And not worth bothering about.'

'But after the way they've treated you,' Ted said, in wonderment. 'It wasn't your fault that woman's couch was ruined!'

For more years than she cared to remember,

Ashling had worked for *Woman's Place*, a weekly, unglossy Irish magazine. Ashling had been fiction editor, fashion editor, health and beauty editor, handiworks editor, cookery editor, agony aunt, copy editor and spiritual advisor all rolled into one. Not as onerous as it sounds, actually, because *Woman's Place* was put together according to a very strict, tried-and-tested formula.

Each issue had a knitting pattern – almost always for a toiletroll cover in the shape of a Southern belle. Then there was a cookery page on buying cheap cuts of meat and disguising them as something else. Every issue had a short story featuring a young boy and a grandmother, who were sworn enemies at the start and firm friends by the end. There was the Problem Page, of course – invariably with a letter complaining about a cheeky daughter-in-law. Pages two and three were an array of 'funny' stories starring the readers' grandchildren and the cutesy things they'd said or done. The back inside cover was a platitudinous letter, supposedly from a clergyman, but always scribbled by Ashling fifteen minutes before the printers' deadline. Then there were the Readers' Tips. And one of these was the unlikely instrument of Ashling's downfall.

Readers' tips were pieces of advice sent in by ordinary Josephine Soaps for the benefit of other readers. They were always about making your money go further and getting something for nothing. Their general premiss was that you needn't buy *anything* because you could make it yourself from basics already in the home. Lemon juice featured heavily.

For example, why buy expensive shampoo when you could fashion your own from some lemon juice and washing-up liquid! You'd like highlights? All you need to do is squeeze a couple of lemons over your hair and sit in the sun. For about a year. And to remove cranberry juice from a beige couch? A mix of lemon juice and vinegar would do the trick.

Except it didn't. Not on the couch of Mrs Anna O'Sullivan from Co. Waterford. It all went horribly wrong – the cranberry juice became ever more tenacious so that even a Stain Devil couldn't budge it. And despite magnanimous usage of Glade, the entire room stank of vinegar. On account of being a good Catholic, Mrs O'Sullivan was a woman who believed in bloody retribution. She threatened to sue.

When Sally Healy, the editor of *Woman's Place*, launched an investigation, Ashling admitted that she'd invented the tip herself. Readers' contributions had been thin on the ground that particular week.

'I didn't think anyone actually believed them,' Ashling whispered, in her defence.

'I'm surprised at you, Ashling,' Sally said. 'You always told me you'd no imagination. And Letter from Father Bennett doesn't count, I know you crib it from *The Catholic Judger*, which, incidentally – keep it to yourself for the moment – is about to go to the wall.'

'I'm sorry, Sally, it'll never happen again.'

'I'm the one who's sorry, Ashling. I'm going to have to let you go.'

'Because of a simple mistake? I don't believe you!'

She was right not to. The real reason was that the board of *Woman's Place* were concerned about the plummeting circulation figures, had decided that the magazine was looking 'tired' and were on the hunt for a fall guy. Ashling's cock-up couldn't have come at a better time. Now they could just sack her instead of having to shell out a redundancy payment.

Sally Healy was distraught. Ashling was the most reliable, hard-working employee one could have. She kept the entire place ticking over while Sally came in late, left early and disappeared for Tuesday and Thursday afternoons to collect her daughter from ballet lessons and her sons from rugby practice. But the board had made it clear that it was either Ashling or her.

As a sop to her long years of faithful service, Ashling was allowed to hold on to her job until she got another one. Which, hopefully, would be soon.

'Well?' Ashling smoothed out the front of her jacket and turned to Ted.

'Fine.' Ted's shoulder bones rose and fell.

'Or is this one better?' Ashling pulled on a jacket

17

that seemed to Ted to be identical to the first one.

'Fine,' he repeated.

'Which one?'

'Either.'

'Which one makes me look more like I've got a waist?'

Ted squirmed. 'Not this again. You're obsessed with your waist.'

'I haven't got one to be obsessed with.'

'Why can't you go on about the size of your bum, like normal women do?'

Ashling had very little in the way of waist but, as always with bad news pertaining to oneself, she'd been the last to find out. It wasn't until she was fifteen and her best friend Clodagh had sighed, 'You're so lucky, having no waist. Mine is tiny and it just makes my bottom look bigger,' that she'd made the shocking discovery.

While every other girl on her road had spent their teenage years standing in front of a mirror agonizing over whether one breast was bigger than the other, Ashling's focus was lower. Eventually she got herself a hula hoop and set to it with gusto in her back garden. For a couple of months she rotated and whittled, day and night, her tongue stuck earnestly out of the corner of her mouth. All the mammies from the neighbouring families looked over their garden walls, their arms folded, nodding knowingly at each other, 'She'll have herself hula-hooped into an early grave, that one.'

Not that the non-stop, obsessive whirling had made any difference. Even now, sixteen years later, there was still an undeniable straight-up-and-down quality to Ashling's silhouette.

'Having no waist isn't the worst thing that could happen to someone,' Ted encouraged from the sidelines.

'Indeed it isn't,' Ashling agreed with unsettling joviality. 'You could have horrible legs too. And as luck would have it, I do.'

'You don't.'

'I do. I inherited them from my mother . . . But so long as that's all I inherited from her,' Ashling added, cheerfully, 'I figure I'm not doing so badly.'

'I was in bed with my girlfriend last night . . .' Ted was keen to change the conversation. 'I told her the earth was flat.'

'What girlfriend? And what's this about the earth?'

'No, that's wrong,' Ted muttered to himself. 'I was *lying* in bed with my girlfriend last night . . . I told her the earth was flat. Boom boom!'

'Ha ha, very good,' Ashling said weakly. The worst thing about being Ted's favourite person was having to be the guinea-pig for his new material. 'But can I make a suggestion? How about, I was lying in bed with my girlfriend last night. I told her I'd always love her and never leave her . . . Boom boom,' she added wryly.

'I'm late,' Ted said. 'D'you want a backer?'

Often he gave her a lift to work on the back of

his bike, *en route* to his own job at the Department of Agriculture.

'No thanks, I'm going in a different direction.'

'Good luck with the interview. I'll pop in to see you this evening.'

'I don't doubt it for a minute,' Ashling agreed, under her breath.

'Hey! How's your ear infection?'

'Better, nearly. I can wash my hair myself again.'

CHAPTER 3

Ashling eventually decided on jacket number one. She could have sworn she detected a slight indentation roughly halfway between her breasts and her hips and that was good enough for her.

After agonizing over her make-up, she plumped for muted in case she came across as flighty. But in case she looked too drab she brought her beloved black-and-white pony-skin handbag. Then she rubbed her lucky Buddha, popped her lucky pebble in her pocket and looked regretfully at her lucky red hat. But just *how* lucky would a red bobble hat be, if worn to a job interview? Anyway, she didn't need it – her horoscope had said that this would be a good day. So had the angel oracle.

As she let herself on to the street she had to step over a man who was sound asleep in the front doorway. Then she pointed herself in the direction of Randolph Media's Dublin office and, walking briskly past the Dublin city-centre gridlock traffic, repeated over and over in her head, as advised by Louise L. Hay, *I will get this job, I will get this job, I will get this job . . .*

But what if I don't? Ashling couldn't help but wonder.

Well, then I won't mind, well, then I won't mind, well, then I won't mind . . .

Though she'd put a brave face on it, Ashling was devastated by the turn of events with Mrs O'Sullivan's couch. So devastated that it had triggered one of the ear infections that always showed up when she was under stress.

Losing one's job was embarrassingly juvenile, not the kind of thing that happened to a thirty-one-year-old mortgage holder. Surely she should be past all that?

To stop her life unravelling, she'd been job-hunting with a passion and putting herself forward for everything remotely feasible. No, she couldn't lassoo a runaway stallion, she'd admitted in her interview for the wild-west ranch in Mullingar – she'd actually thought the position they were interviewing for was an administrative one – but she'd be *willing to learn.*

At each interview she went for she repeated over and over that she was *willing to learn.* But of everything she'd applied for, the job at *Colleen* was the one she really, *badly* wanted. She loved working on a magazine and magazine jobs were rare in Ireland. Besides, Ashling wasn't a proper journalist: she was simply a good organizer, with an eye for detail.

The magazine arm of Randolph Media was on the third floor of an office block on the quays. Ashling had found out that Randolph Media also owned the small but growing television station, Channel 9, and a highly commercial radio station, but these apparently operated out of different premises.

Ashling came out of the lift and scooted down the corridor towards reception. The place seemed to hum with activity, people rushing up and down carrying bits of paper. Ashling thrilled with excitement that peaked into nausea. Just before the reception desk, a tall, messy-haired man was deep in conversation with a tiny Asian girl. They were speaking to each other in low tones and something in the nature of their exchange gave Ashling to understand that they wished they could shout. Ashling hurried on; she didn't like rows. Not even other people's.

She realized how badly she'd misjudged the make-up situation when she got a gander at the receptionist. Trix – that's what her namebadge said she was called – had the glittery, luscious-sticky look of a devotee of the more-is-more school of slapplication. Her eyebrows were plucked almost into non-existence, her lipliner was so thick and dark she looked as if she had a moustache, and her entire head of blonde hair was caught up in dozens of tiny, evenly spaced, sparkly butterfly clips. She must've had to get up three hours early to do it, Ashling thought, highly impressed.

'Hello,' Trix growled in a voice that sounded as though she smoked forty cigarettes a day – which coincidentally she did.

'I've an interview at nine thi–' Ashling halted at the sound of a loud yelp behind her. She looked over her shoulder and saw the messy-haired man nursing his first finger.

'You bit me!' he exclaimed. 'Mai, you've drawn blood!'

'Hope your tetanus is up to date,' the Asian girl laughed scornfully.

Trix clicked her tongue, flung her eyes heavenwards and muttered, 'Pair of gobshites, they never stop. Take a seat,' she told Ashling. 'I'll tell Calvin you're here.'

She disappeared through the double doors and Ashling wobbled down on to a couch, beside a coffee table which was strewn with all the current titles. The sight of them sent her nerves into sudden overdrive – she so badly wanted this job. Her heart was pounding and her stomach sloshed bile. Absently she rolled the lucky pebble through her thumb and finger. Through a gauze of trembling anxiety she was semi-aware of the bitten man slamming into the gents' and the little Asian girl stomping to the lift, her curtain of long black hair swishing to and fro.

'Mr Carter says go on in.' Trix was back and doing a bad job of hiding her surprise. For the past two days she'd been plagued by nervous interviewees who'd been kept waiting by her desk for up to half an hour at a time. During which Trix had had to hold off ringing her friends and fellas and deal with the interviewees' pleading questions about what their chances of getting the job were. And to add insult to injury, she knew for a *fact* that all Calvin Carter and Jack Devine were doing in the interview room was playing rummy.

But Calvin Carter had been deserted by Jack Devine, and he was bored and lonely. Might as well be interviewing someone as doing nothing.

'Come!' he commanded, when Ashling knocked timidly on the door.

He took one glance at the dark-haired woman in the black trouser-suit and immediately decided against her. She just wasn't glamorous enough for *Colleen*. He didn't know much about girls' hair, but he had a feeling that it was usually more elaborate than this one's. Wasn't it normal to have a kind of *interfered* look to it? Surely it shouldn't just hang there on her shoulders, being brown? And fresh-faced is all very well when you're a milkmaid, but not when you're an aspiring assistant editor of a sexy women's magazine . . .

'Sit down.' He supposed he'd better go through the motions for five minutes.

Breathless with the desire to do well, Ashling sat on the lone chair in the middle of the floor and faced the man who sat behind the long table.

'Jack Devine, the MD for Ireland, will be here shortly,' Calvin explained. 'I don't know what's keeping him. First up,' he turned his attention to her resumé, 'you better tell me how to pronounce that name of yours.'

'Ash-ling. Ash as in cigarette ash, ling to rhyme with sing.'

'Ash-ling. Ashling. OK, I can say that. Alrighty, *Ashling*, for the past eight years you've been working in magazines . . .'

'Maga*zine*, actually.' Ashling heard someone giggle nervously and realized helplessly that it was herself. 'Just the one.'

'And why are you leaving *Woman's Place*?'

'I'm looking for a new challenge,' Ashling offered nervously. Sally Healy had told her to say that.

The door opened and in came the bitten man.

'Ah, Jack.' Calvin Carter frowned. 'This is *Ashling* Kennedy. Ash as in cigarette ash, ling to rhyme with sing.'

'How's it going?' Jack had other things on his mind. He was in a foul mood. He'd been up half the night in negotiations with technicians at the TV station, while conducting almost simultaneous negotiations with a US network to persuade them not to sell their award-winning series to RTE but to Channel 9 instead. And as if his workload hadn't already reached critical mass, he'd been charged with setting up this stupid new magazine. The last thing the world needs is another women's magazine! But, if he was honest, the true source of his grief was Mai. She drove him insane. He *hated* her. He hated her so much. How had he ever thought he was mad about her! No way was he taking her calls. Never again, that was the last time, the very, very last time . . .

He swung himself behind the table, trying hard to concentrate on the interview – old Calvin got his boxers in such a bunch about them. In a moment or two he knew he'd be expected to ask something that sounded vaguely relevant, but all he could think about was that he might be bleeding to death. Or dying of rabies. How soon did the foaming at the mouth begin? he wondered.

Leaning back on the two hind legs of his chair, he held his wounded finger out in front of him, staring at it. He couldn't believe she'd bitten him. *Again*. She'd promised the last time . . . He pulled the twist of toilet paper tighter and bright red blood rushed through it.

'Tell me your strengths and weaknesses,' Calvin invited Ashling.

'I'd have to be honest and say that my weakest area is editorial work. While I can produce tag-lines, headings and short pieces, I haven't much experience of writing long articles.'

None, actually, if she was completely up-front.

'My strengths are that I am meticulous, organized and hard-working. I'm a good second-in-command,' Ashling said earnestly, quoting directly from Sally Healy. Then she stopped and said, 'Excuse me, would you like a Band-Aid for your finger?'

Jack Devine looked up, startled. 'Who, me?'

'I don't see anyone else bleeding all over the place.' Ashling attempted a smile.

Jack Devine shook his head violently. 'Nah, no . . . Thanks,' he added, surlily.

27

'Why not?' Calvin Carter intervened.

'I'm fine.' Jack gestured with his good hand.

'Take the Band-Aid,' Calvin said. 'Sounds like a good idea.'

Ashling lifted her bag on to her lap and, with the minimum of rummaging, produced a box of plasters. Lifting the lid, she flicked through them, lifted one out and handed it to Jack. 'Try that for size.'

Jack looked at it as if he had no idea what to do. Calvin Carter was no help either.

Ashling swallowed a sigh, got up from her chair, took the plaster from Jack's hand and ripped off the grease-proof paper. 'Hold out your finger.'

'Yes, Ma'am,' he said sarcastically.

With speed and efficiency she wrapped it around the bleeding digit. To her surprise, on the pretext of making sure the plaster was secure, she gave his finger a little squeeze and felt shameful satisfaction at the wince that fluttered across his face.

'What else have you got?' Calvin Carter asked curiously. 'Aspirins?'

She nodded cautiously. 'Would you like one?'

'No, thanks. A pen and notepad?'

She nodded again.

'How about – and this is a long shot, I'll admit – a portable sewing kit?'

Ashling paused sheepishly, then her entire demeanour lifted and lightened in a half-laugh of admission. 'Actually, I do.' Her smile was wide.

'You're very organized,' Jack Devine interrupted. He made it sound like an insult.

'Somebody needs to be.' Calvin Carter had revised his earlier opinion of her. She was charming and even though she had lipstick on her teeth, at least she was *wearing* lipstick. 'Thank you, Ashling, we'll be in touch.'

Ashling shook hands with both men, once more taking the opportunity to give Jack Devine's wound a good, hard squeeze.

'Hey, I liked her,' Calvin Carter laughed.

'I didn't,' Jack Devine said, moodily.

'I said I liked her,' Calvin Carter repeated. He wasn't used to being disagreed with. 'She's reliable and resourceful. Give her the job.'

CHAPTER 4

Clodagh woke early. Nothing new there. Clodagh always woke early. That's what having children did to you. If they weren't roaring to be fed, they were squashing into the bed between you and your husband and if they weren't doing that, they were in the kitchen at six-thirty on a Saturday morning, clattering saucepans ominously.

This morning they were on clattering-saucepans-ominously duty. She would subsequently discover that Craig, the five-year-old, was showing Molly, the two-and-a-half-year-old, how to make scrambled eggs. Out of flour, water, olive oil, ketchup, brown sauce, vinegar, cocoa, birthday candles and, of course, eggs. Nine of them, including shells. Clodagh knew from the quality of the racket that terrible things were taking place in the room below her, but she was too tired, or too something, to get up and intervene.

Eyes focused on nothing, she lay listening to chairs being scraped along the new limestone-tiled floor, month-old SieMatic cupboards being opened and slammed and Le Creuset pans being battered to within an inch of their lives.

Beside her, still deep in sleep, Dylan shifted, then threw his arm over her. She snuggled into him for a moment, looking for relief. Then froze in familiar reluctance and wearily moved away again as she felt his arousal unfurling and straightening against her stomach.

Not sex. She couldn't bear it. She wanted affection, but whenever she moved her body against his, seeking out comfort, he got turned on. Especially in the morning. She felt guilty every time she turned away from him. But not guilty enough to oblige.

He stood a better chance in the evenings, especially when she'd had a few drinks. She never deprived him for longer than a month because she was too afraid of what it would mean. So when the deadline loomed, she always orchestrated some form of drunkenness and delivered the goods, her enthusiasm and inventiveness in direct proportion to how much gin she'd consumed.

Dylan reached for her again and she slithered across the sheets out of reach, with a nimbleness borne of many months of practice.

A particularly hysterical bout of clattering wafted up from the room below.

'Little fuckers,' Dylan mumbled, sleepily. 'They'll knock the house down on us.'

'I'll go and shout at them.' It was safer to get up.

By the time Ashling arrived later that morning, the scrambled-egg débâcle was but a distant memory and had been superseded by the atrocities of the breakfast table.

When Clodagh went to answer the door, she was involved in some kind of complicated negotiations with the angelic-looking, flaxen-haired Molly, concerning the wearing of a cardigan. Molly was insisting on wearing her orange one.

'Hi Ashling,' Clodagh said absently, then thrust her face down to Molly's and insisted in exasperation, 'But you're too big for it, Molly. You haven't worn it since you were a baby. Why don't you wear this lovely pink one?'

'Nooooooo!' Molly tried to wriggle away to freedom.

'But you'll be cold.' Clodagh held tight on to Molly's arm.

'Noooooooo!'

'Come into the kitchen, Ashling.' Clodagh dragged Molly down the hall. 'CRAIG! GET OFF THE CAROUSEL!'

The equally angelic-looking, flaxen-haired Craig had clambered into the corner cupboard in the kitchen and was swinging himself backwards and forwards on the wire shelf, cushioned on bags of rice and pasta.

Ashling walked to the kettle and switched it on. Ashling and Clodagh had grown up two doors away from each other and had been best friends since the time when it was safer for Ashling to be in Clodagh's house than in her own.

It had been Clodagh who'd broken the news to

32

Ashling about her waistless condition. It was also Clodagh who'd enlightened Ashling on other aspects of herself by saying, 'You're so fortunate to have your personality. Me, all I have is my looks.'

Not that Ashling had ever taken umbrage. Clodagh wasn't malicious, simply candid, and it would have been a total waste of time to deny how singularly beautiful she was. Short and shapely, with Scandinavian colouring and long, burnished ropes of blonde hair, she was traffic-stopping. Not that that was saying much in Dublin, where the traffic rarely moved.

Ashling had momentous news. 'I got a job!'

'When?'

'I heard over a week ago,' Ashling admitted. 'But I've been at work every night until midnight tidying it all up for the new person at *Woman's Place*.'

'I thought it was funny you hadn't been in touch. So tell me all about it.'

But each time Ashling tried, Craig insisted on reading to her, from an upside-down book. When the spotlight moved away from him even for a second, he clawed it back.

'Go and play outside on the swing,' Clodagh cajoled him.

'But it's raining.'

'You're Irish, get used to it. Go on. Out!'

No sooner had Craig gone than Molly was centre-stage.

'Want!' she declared, pointing at Ashling's coffee.

'No, that's Ashling's,' Clodagh said. 'You can't have it.'

'She can if she wants . . .' Ashling felt she'd better say.

'WANT!' Molly insisted.

'Would you mind?' Clodagh asked. 'I'll get you another.'

Ashling slid the mug along the table, but Clodagh intercepted it before it reached Molly, which started a great caterwauling.

'I'm just blowing on it,' Clodagh explained. 'So you won't burn your mouth.'

'WANT! WANT! WANT!'

'But it's too hot! You'll burn yourself.'

'WANT IT. WANT IT NOW!!!'

'Oh all right then. Slowly now, don't spill it.'

Molly put her mouth to the lip of the mug, then pulled back and started screeching. 'Hot! Sore! Waaaaaaah!'

'Oh, for fuck's sake,' Clodagh muttered.

'Fuck's sake,' Molly enunciated, with crystal clarity.

'That's right,' Clodagh said, with a savagery that shocked Ashling. 'For fuck's sake.'

Dylan rushed into the room, in response to Molly's roaring.

'Ashling!' He smiled, using one big hand to shove his corn-blond hair back off his face. 'You're looking great. Any news on the job front?'

'I've got one!'

'Lassooing runaway stallions in Mullingar?'

'In a magazine. A young women's one.'

34

'Fair play! More money?'

Ashling nodded proudly. Not a huge increase, but better than the barely index-linked pittance she'd been getting for the past eight years at *Woman's Place*.

'And no more Letters from Father Bennett – just as well, did you see *The Catholic Judger*'s gone bust? There was a thing in the paper about it.'

'So it's all worked out for the best, really,' Ashling glowed. 'Mrs O'Sullivan from Waterford is probably the best thing that ever happened to me!'

Dylan looked amused – then alarmed, as a huge commotion erupted in the garden. Craig had fallen off the swing, and judging from his screeching and bawling was in considerable pain. Ashling was already rummaging in her bag for the rescue remedy.

For herself.

'Will you go?' Clodagh turned weary eyes to Dylan. 'I have them all week. And just tell me his injuries on a need-to-know basis.'

Dylan withdrew.

'Do you want me to check on Craig . . . ?' Ashling asked anxiously. 'I have plasters.'

'So do I.' Clodagh gave her an exasperated look. 'Tell me about your job. *Please.*'

'OK.' Ashling gave one last regretful look at the garden. 'It's a glossy magazine. Much more glamorous than *Woman's Place*.'

When she got to the part about Jack Devine

arguing furiously, then being bitten by the Asian girl, Clodagh finally perked up.

'Go on,' she urged, her eyes sparkling. 'Tell us! Nothing, but nothing puts me in better humour than overhearing people having a right old ding-dong. One day last week, I was coming out of the gym and there was a man and a woman in a parked car and they were *roaring* at each other. I mean, roaring! Even with the windows up I could hear them. Put me in great form for the rest of the day.'

'I hate that,' Ashling admitted. 'It's so upsetting.'

'But why? Oh, I suppose with your, um, background . . . But for most people it's nice. They feel they're not the only ones having a hard time.'

'Who's having a hard time?' Anxiety bruised Ashling's face.

Clodagh looked uncomfortable. 'No one. But I really envy you!' She suddenly exploded. 'Single, starting a new job, all that excitement.'

Ashling was speechless. To her, Clodagh's life was the Holy Grail. The good-looking, devoted husband with the thriving business; the tasteful, Edwardian red-brick house in the chi-chi village of Donnybrook. Nothing to do all day long except microwave Barney pasta, make plans to redecorate already perfect rooms and wait for Dylan to come home.

'And I bet you were out clubbing last night,' Clodagh almost accused.

'Yes, but . . . Only the Sugarclub and I was home by two. *Alone,*' she said with heavy emphasis.

36

'Clodagh, you've everything. Two gorgeous children, a gorgeous husband . . .'

Is he gorgeous? Surprised, Clodagh realized that this wasn't something which had occurred to her lately. Doubtfully she admitted that for a man in his mid-thirties Dylan's body wasn't bad – his midriff hadn't melted into a soft cone-shaped fold of pint-drinking flab like so many of his contemporaries' had. He still took an interest in clothes – more than she did these days, if she was honest. And he went to a proper hairdresser's, and not the local oul' fella barber, who sent everyone out looking like their dad.

Ashling continued to protest. '. . . and *you* look fantastic! Two children and you've a better figure than me – and I've had no children, nor am I ever likely to, if my luck with men doesn't turn soon. Ha ha ha.'

Ashling was keen for Clodagh to smile, but all she said was, 'Everything feels old. Especially with Dylan.'

Ashling desperately summoned some advice. 'You just need to recapture the magic. Try and remember what it was like when you first met.'

Where was she getting this stuff from? Oh yeah, she'd written it herself in *Woman's Place*, to a woman who was going mad because her husband had retired and was forever under her feet.

'I can't even remember where I met him,' Clodagh admitted. 'Oh no, of course I do. You brought him to Lochlan Hegarty's twenty-first, remember? God, it seems like a lifetime ago.'

'You have to work at keeping things fresh,' Ashling quoted. 'Go out for romantic meals, maybe even go away for the weekend. I'll babysit any time you like.' She experienced a surge of alarm at this rash promise.

'I *wanted* to get married.' Clodagh seemed to be talking to herself. 'Dylan and I seemed right for each other.'

'That's putting it mildly.' Ashling remembered the *frisson* that had passed through the party when Clodagh and Dylan first clapped eyes on each other. Dylan was the most good-looking man in the group that he hung around with, Clodagh was undeniably the best-looking girl in her gang and people always gravitate towards their equals. When Dylan and Clodagh exchanged that fatal eye-meet, Ashling was actually on a date with Dylan – her first and, as it transpired, her last. With that one look she was toast. Not that she held it against either of them. They were meant to be together, she might as well be a good sport about it.

Clodagh gave a tired chuckle. 'Everything is fine, really. Or at least it will be when I've changed the colour scheme in the front-room.'

'More decorating!' It seemed no time since Clodagh had got her new kitchen in. In fact, it didn't seem much longer than that since she'd done her front-room.

In the afternoon, on the way home from Clodagh's, Ashling ducked into Tesco to buy food.

She flung packet after packet of microwaveable popcorn into the basket, then went to pay.

The woman ahead of her in the queue had such a laquered, stylish look about her that Ashling found herself leaning back, all the better to admire her. Like Ashling, she wore sweatpants, trainers and a little cardigan, but unlike Ashling, everything looked touchable and lustrous. The way things are before they're washed for the first time and lose their sheen of perfect newness.

Her trainers were pink Nike ones that Ashling had seen in a magazine, but that you couldn't get in Ireland yet. Her pink, parachute-silk rucksack matched the pink gel in the heel of the trainers. And her hair was lovely – shiny and swingy, thick and glossy – in the way that you could never achieve yourself.

In fascination Ashling checked out the contents of the woman's basket. Seven cans of strawberry Slimfast, seven baking potatoes, seven apples and four . . . five . . . six . . . *seven* individually wrapped little squares of chocolate from the pick'n'mix. She hadn't even put the chocolate into a bag, she looked as if she was treating them as seven individual purchases.

Some irresistible instinct told Ashling that this paltry basketful constituted the woman's weekly shop. Either that or she was providing a safe house for Grumpy, Sneezy, Dopey, Happy and whatever the other three were called.

CHAPTER 5

It was pouring with rain when Lisa's plane landed at Dublin airport early on Saturday afternoon. When she'd taken off from London, she'd foolishly assumed that she couldn't possibly feel worse, but one look at the rain-soaked view of Dublin made her see the error of her ways.

Dermot, her taxi-driver to the city-centre, only added to her grief. He was chatty and amiable and Lisa didn't want chatty and amiable. She thought with longing of the psychotic, uzi-carrying madman who might have been driving her taxi, if only she was in New York.

'Have you family here?' Dermot asked.

'No.'

'A boyfriend, so?'

'No.'

When she wouldn't talk about herself, he talked instead. 'I love driving,' he confided.

'Whoop-de-doo,' Lisa said nastily.

'Do you know what I do on my day off?'

Lisa ignored him.

'I go for a drive! That's what I do. And not just down to Wicklow, either, but a long one. Up to

40

Belfast, over to Galway, or across to Limerick. One day I made it as far as Letterkenny, that's in Donegal, you know . . . I *love* my job.'

On and on he went, as they inched through the wet, greasy streets. When they got to the hotel in Harcourt Street, he helped her with her several bags and wished her a pleasant stay in Ireland.

Malone's Aparthotel was a strange new breed of hostelry – it had no bar, or restaurant, or room service or *anything* really, except for thirty rooms, each with small kitchen areas attached. Lisa was booked in for a fortnight and hopefully by then she'd have found somewhere to live.

In a daze, she hung up a couple of things, looked out at the grey view of the busy road, then flung herself out on to the damp streets, to inspect the city that now constituted home.

Now that she was actually here, the shock hit her with unprecedented force. How had her life gone so horribly wrong? She should be strolling along Fifth Avenue right now, and not in this drenched *village*.

The guide-book said that it would only take half a day to walk around Dublin and see all its important sights – as if that was a good thing! Sure enough, less than two hours was enough to check out the high spots – read shopping – both north and south of the river Liffey. It was worse than she'd expected: nobody stocked La Prairie products, Stephane Kélian shoes, Vivienne Westwood or Ozwald Boeteng.

'It's total pants! A one-horse town,' she thought, in mild hysteria, 'and the horse is wearing last-season's Hilfiger.'

She wanted to go home. She longed for London so badly, then through the mist she saw something that made her heart lift – a Marks & Spencers!

Normally she never went near them: the clothes were too dowdy, the food too tempting, but today she flung herself through the entrance like a pursued dissident seeking asylum in a foreign embassy. She resisted the urge to lie, panting, against the inside of the door. But only because the door was automatic. Then she immersed herself in the food department because it had no windows and didn't interfere with her fantasies.

I'm in the High Street Kensington branch, she pretended to herself. *In a moment I'm going to leave and drop into Urban Outfitters.*

She idled in front of the fresh fruit. *No, I've changed my mind*, she decided. *I'm in the Marble Arch branch. As soon as I've finished here I'm going to South Molton Street.*

It gave her a peculiar comfort to know that the melon salads in front of her were part of the diaspora of melon salads in all the London branches. She pressed slightly on a taut cellophane lid and felt a sense of belonging – faint but real.

When she was restored to calmness she went to an ordinary supermarket and bought her weekly shopping. A routine would keep her sane – well, it had certainly helped in the past. Home she traipsed, the hood of her cardigan up to protect her hair from the rain that had started to fall again. She unpacked the seven cans of Slimfast and placed them neatly in the cupboard, the potatoes and apples went in the little fridge and the seven pieces of chocolate went into a drawer. Now what? Saturday night. All alone in a strange city. Nothing to do but to stay in and watch . . . It was then that she noticed that there was no telly in the room.

It was such a big blow she cried a flashflood of hot, spurty tears. What was she going to do *now*? She'd already read this month's *Elle, Red, New Woman, Company, Cosmo, Marie-Claire, Vogue, Tatler*, and the Irish magazines that she'd be competing against. She could read a book, she supposed. If she had one. Or a newspaper, except newspapers were so boring and depressing . . . At least she had clothes to hang up. So while the streets below filled with young people *en route* to a night on the piss, Lisa smoked and shook dresses and skirts and jackets on to hangers, smoothed cardigans and tops into drawers, arranged boots and shoes into a perfect military parade, hung handbags . . . The phone rang, startling her from her soothing rhythm.

'Hello?' And then she was sorry she'd answered. 'Oliver!' *Oh, bugger.* 'Where did you . . . how did you get this number?'

'Your mum.'

Interfering old cow.

'When were you going to tell me, Lisa?'

Never, actually.

'Soon. When I'd got my own place.'

'What have you done with our flat?'

'Got tenants in. Don't worry, you'll get your share of the rent.'

'And why Dublin? I thought you wanted to go to New York.'

'This seemed like a smarter career move.'

'Jesus, you're hard. Well, I hope you're happy,' he said, in a manner that meant he hoped the very opposite. 'I hope it's all been worth it.'

Then he hung up.

She looked down on the Dublin street and started to shake. Had it been worth it? Well, she'd just better make damn sure it would be. She'd make *Colleen* the biggest success in magazine publishing.

She inhaled deeply on her cigarette, then went to light it again because she thought it had gone out. It hadn't, but it wasn't calming the pain. She needed *something*. The chocolate called to her from the drawer, but she resisted it. Just because she felt she was in hell was no excuse to go over fifteen hundred calories a day.

In the end she gave in. She coiled in an armchair, slowly removed the paper and ran her teeth along the side of the chocolate, shaving away tiny curl after tiny curl, until it was all gone.

It took an hour.

CHAPTER 6

There was a clink of bottles at Ashling's door, announcing Joy's arrival.

'Ted's on his way, leave the door on the latch.' Joy clattered a bottle of white wine on to Ashling's tiny kitchen counter.

Ashling braced herself. She was not disappointed.

'Phil Collins,' Joy said, with an evil glint in her eye, 'Michael Bolton or Michael Jackson, and you *must* sleep with one of them.'

Ashling winced. 'Well, definitely not Phil Collins, and definitely not Michael Jackson and *definitely* not Michael Bolton.'

'You must choose one.' Joy busied herself with the corkscrew.

'Christ.' Ashling's face was a twist of revulsion. 'Phil Collins, I suppose, I haven't picked him in a while. Right, your turn. Benny Hill, Tom Jones or . . . let me see, who's truly revolting? Paul Daniels.'

'Full sex or just . . .'

'Full sex,' Ashling said firmly.

'Tom Jones, then,' Joy sighed, handing Ashling a glass of wine. 'Now, show me what you're wearing.'

It was Saturday evening and Ted was doing the 'try-out' slot at a comedy gig. It was his first time doing his act for anyone other than friends and family, and Ashling and Joy were going along to hold his hand, then crash the party afterwards.

Joy – whose surname was, memorably, Ryder – lived in the flat below Ashling's. She was short, rounded, curly-haired and dangerous – on account of her prodigious appetite for drink, drugs and men, coupled with her mission to turn Ashling into her partner in crime.

'Come into my bedroom,' Ashling invited and they both edged in. 'I'm going to wear these cream cargo pants and this little top.' Ashling turned from the wardrobe too quickly and stood on Joy's foot, then Joy leapt up and banged her elbow on the portable telly.

'Ouch! Doesn't the crampedness of these shoe-boxes ever get to you?' Joy sighed, rubbing her elbow.

Ashling shook her head. 'I love living in town and you can't have everything.'

Quickly, Ashling changed into her going-out clothes.

'I'd look like a Diddyman in that get-up.' Joy admired her, wistfully. 'It's a terrible thing to be pear-shaped!'

'But at least you have a waist. Now, I thought I'd do something with my hair . . .'

Ashling had bought several coloured butterfly clips after she'd seen what a lovely job Trix had done with them. But when she stuck them into the front of her own hair, sweeping two strands off her face, the effect wasn't quite the same.

'I just look ridiculous!'

'You do,' Joy agreed, kindly. 'Now, do you think Half-man-half-badger will be at the party after the gig?'

'Could be, it was at a party with Ted that you met him before, wasn't it? He's friends with some of the comedians, isn't he?'

'Mmmmm,' Joy nodded dreamily. 'But that was weeks ago and I haven't seen him since. Where did he disappear to, that international half-man-half-badger of mystery? Get the tarot cards and we'll have a quick look at what's going to happen.'

They traipsed into the bijou sitting-room, Joy plucked a card from the deck, then turned it to Ashling. 'Ten of swords. That's a shite one, isn't it?'

'Shite,' Ashling agreed.

Joy grasped the bundle of cards and at high speed flicked through them until she found one she liked. 'The Queen of Wands, now that's more like it! Now you pick one.'

'Three of Cups.' Ashling held it up. 'Beginnings.'

'That means you're going to meet a man too.'

Ashling laughed.

'It's ages since Phelim went to Australia, no?' Joy interrogated. 'It's about time you got over him.'

'I *am* over him. I was the one who ended it, remember?'

'Only because he wouldn't do the decent thing. Although good for you, even when they won't do

47

the decent thing by me, I still can't give them their marching orders. You're very strong.'

'It's not strength. It was because I couldn't stand the tension of waiting for him to make up his mind. I thought I was going to have a nervous breakdown.'

Phelim had been Ashling's on-off boyfriend for five years. They'd had good times and not-so-good times because Phelim always lost his nerve at the last minute when it came to full-blown, grown-up commitment.

To make the relationship work, Ashling spent her life avoiding cracks in the pavement, saluting lone magpies, picking up pennies and consulting both her and Phelim's horoscopes. Her pockets were always weighed down with lucky pebbles, rosequartz and miraculous medals and she'd rubbed nearly all the gold paint off her lucky Buddha.

Each time they got back together the well of hope was further depleted, and eventually Ashling's love just burnt out from all his dithering. Like every break-up, the final one had been un-acrimonious. Ashling said calmly, 'You're always talking about how you hate being trapped in Dublin and how you want to travel the world, so go on. Do it.'

Even now a faint line of connection hummed between them, across twelve thousand miles. He'd come home in February for his brother's wedding and the first person he'd gone to see was Ashling.

They'd walked into each other's arms and stood, squeezing each other for minutes on end, tears in their eyes from the close-but-no-cigar air of it all.

'Bastard,' Joy said, energetically.

'He wasn't,' Ashling insisted. 'He couldn't give me what I wanted but that doesn't mean I hate him.'

'I hate all my ex-boyfriends,' Joy boasted. 'I can't wait for Half-man-half-badger to be one, then he won't have this hold on me. Now what if he's there tonight? I need to seem unavailable. If only . . . no, an engagement ring would be going too far. A love-bite might do the trick, though.'

'Where are you going to get one of those?'

'From you! Here,' Joy swept aside a mass of curls from her neck. 'Would you mind?'

'Yes.'

'Please.'

And because she was an obliging type, Ashling pushed away her reluctance, half-heartedly put her teeth on Joy's neck and gave her a hickey.

Mid hickey-giving, someone said, 'Oh.' They looked up, frozen in a pose that was somehow *sodden* with guilt. Ted was standing, looking at them. He seemed upset. 'The door was open . . . I didn't realize . . .' Then he gathered himself. 'I hope you'll both be very happy.'

Ashling and Joy looked at each other and roared laughing, until Ashling took pity on him and explained all.

He saw the tarot cards on the table and pounced. 'Eight of Wands, Ashling, what does that mean?'

'Success in business,' Ashling said. 'Your act will go down a storm tonight.'

'Yeah, but will I be a big hit with the goils?'

Ted had become a stand-up comedian for one reason and one reason only – to get a girlfriend. He'd seen the way women flung themselves at the comedians working the Dublin circuit, and thought that his chances of pulling were higher than at a dating agency. Not that he'd go to a *real* dating agency. The only one he'd have anything to do with was the Ashling Kennedy dating agency – Ashling regularly sought to matchmake all her single friends. But the only one of Ashling's pals Ted had liked was Clodagh and unfortunately she was unavailable. Very.

'Take another card,' Ashling invited him.

The one he picked was the Hanged Man.

'You'll definitely get lucky tonight,' Ashling promised.

'But it's the Hanged Man!'

'Doesn't matter.'

Ashling knew that if you put a man on a stage, no matter how plug-ugly he is – and be it strumming a guitar, lepping around in doublets and purple hose or observing that you can wait for a bus for ages, then three come at once – you can guarantee that women will find him attractive. Even when it's only standing on a dusty, foot-high

50

platform in a twenty-foot-square room, he assumes a strange, seductive glamour.

'I've decided to change my act, go slightly surreal. Talk about owls.'

'Owls?'

'Owls have worked for lots of people.' Ted was defensive. 'Look at Harry Hill, Kevin McAleer.'

Oh Christ. Ashling's heart sank. 'Come on, let's go.'

As they left the flat there was a little pile-up in the hall as everyone sought to rub the lucky Buddha.

The comedy gig was in a packed, rowdy club. Ted wasn't on until the middle of the show and though the proper comedians were clever and slick, Ashling couldn't let go and enjoy herself. Too worried about how Ted would go down.

Like a lead balloon, if the performance of the other first-timer was anything to go by. He was an odd, hairy little boy whose act consisted almost entirely of 'doing' Beavis and Butthead. The audience were unforgiving. As they booed and shouted, 'Get off, you're crap,' Ashling's heart twisted for Ted.

Then it was Ted's turn. Ashling and Joy clasped hands, like proud but justifiably anxious parents. Within seconds, their hands were so slippery with sweat that they had to let go.

Under the lone spotlight, Ted looked frail and vulnerable. Absently, he rubbed his stomach, lifting up his T-shirt, giving a brief glimpse of the waistband of his Calvins and his narrow, dark-haired midriff. Ashling approved. That might get the girls interested.

'This owl walks into a bar,' Ted started. The audience's upturned faces were lambent with expectation. 'He orders a pint of milk, a packet of crisps and ten smokes. And the barman turns to his friend and says, "Look at that, a talking owl."'

There were one or two nonplussed titters, but otherwise an expectant silence reigned. They were still waiting for the punchline.

Anxiously, Ted started into a new gag. 'My owl has got no nose,' he announced.

More silence. Ashling had almost gouged stigmata in her palms with tension.

'My owl has got no nose,' Ted repeated, laced with desperation.

Then Ashling understood. 'How does he smell?' she called, her voice quavering.

'Terrible!'

The air was thick with perplexedness. People turned to their neighbours, their faces twisted into what-the-fuck . . . ?

And on Ted laboured. 'I met a friend of mine and he said, "Who was that lady I saw you walking along Grafton Street with?" And I said, "That was no lady, that was my owl!"'

And suddenly they seemed to get it. The laughter started small, but began to swell and burgeon, until the audience were in paroxysms. In fairness, it was Saturday night and they *were* pissed.

Behind her, Ashling heard people wheeze, 'Your man's *hilarious*. Off-the-wall, completely.'

'What's yellow and wise?' Ted dazzled with a smile.

The audience were in the palm of his hand, their breath held, waiting for the gag. Ted smiled around the room. 'Owl-infested custard!'

The roof nearly lifted.

'What's grey and has a trunk?'

A giddy pause.

'An owl going on holidays. That's a grey owl, obviously.'

There went the rafters again.

'You're recruiting for a job.' Ted was on a roll and the audience were in floods of merriment. 'You interview three owls and ask each of them what's the capital of Rome. The first one says she doesn't know, the second one says it's Italy and the third one says that Rome is a capital. Which owl do you give the job to?'

'The owl with the biggest tits!' someone yelled from the back and once again laughter and applause rose and flapped like a flock of birds. The more established comedians, who'd only let Ted on as a favour to stop him pestering them, looked at each other anxiously.

'Get him off,' Bicycle Billy muttered, 'the little bollocks.'

'Gotta go,' Ted ruefully told the audience as Mark Dignan made an urgent throat-cutting gesture.

'AAAAAAWWWWWWW,' everyone complained in bitter disappointment.

'We've created a fucking monster!' Bicycle Billy whispered to Archie Archer (real name Brian O'Toole).

'I've been Ted Mullins, a comedian who tells a load of oul' jokes. Or should I say *owl* jokes?' Ted twinkled. 'And you've been an owl audience!'

Amid hysterical cheers, whistles, foot-stamping and thunderous applause, he took his leave.

Later, as everyone beat their way out, Ashling overheard person after person talking about Ted.

'What's yellow and wise? I thought I'd end myself laughing.'

'That Ted was fantastic. Sexy too.'

'I liked the way he lifted his –'

'– T-shirt. Yeah, so did I.'

'D'you think he has a girlfriend?'

'Bound to.'

The party was in a modern block along the quays. As it was Mark Dignan's flat, and loads of the other guests were also comedians, Ashling had expected to be kept in hysterics all night. But though the room was crowded and noisy, a bizarre atmosphere of gloom pervaded.

'They're all keeping shtum in case anyone steals their lines or ideas,' explained Joy, a veteran of such knees-ups. 'Without a paying audience you wouldn't get these fellas being funny to save their lives. Now where *is* he?'

Joy went on a Half-man-half-badger walkabout and Ashling poured herself a glass of wine in the galley kitchen where Bicycle Billy was rolling a spliff. As he was short and troll-like, she was able to smile at him and say, 'You were very funny tonight. You must get great satisfaction from what you do.'

'Ah, not really,' he said tetchily. 'I'm writing a novel, you see. That's what I really want to do with my life.'

'Lovely,' Ashling encouraged.

'Oh no, it's not,' Billy was keen to emphasize. 'It's very truthful, very depressing. *Very* grim. Ah, where's my lighter?'

'Allow me,' Ashling flared a match and lit his spliff. Seemed to her like he needed it.

Through the crowds in the sitting-room, she saw Ted enthroned on an armchair, an orderly queue of interested girls shuffling forward to make their case. Staring out the window into the oil-black waters of the Liffey was a broody figure, a thick stripe of grey through the front of his long, black hair. Aha, thought Ashling. International half-man-half-badger of mystery, I presume. Joy was nearby, energetically ignoring him.

Under the half-man-half-badger circumstances, Ashling decided to let her alone. Hanging around, swigging her wine, she spotted Mark Dignan. As he was almost seven-foot tall and had the poppiest eyes she'd ever seen on someone who hadn't recently been strangled, she was able to have a little chat with him too.

But he dismissed her praise of his act with a

cranky wave of his hand. 'It'll do until my novel is published.'

'Ah, you're writing a novel too. So, um . . . what's it about?'

'It's about a man who sees the world in all its *rottenness*.' Mark's eyes bulged even further. They'd fall out on to the carpet soon if he wasn't careful, Ashling thought anxiously. 'It's very depressing,' Mark boasted. 'Like, *unbelievably* depressing. He hates life more than life itself.'

Mark realized he'd said something vaguely witty and flicked an anxious glance to make sure no one had heard.

'Er, the best of luck.' *Miserable bastard.* Ashling moved away, and was buttonholed by an enthusiastic, bright-eyed man who insisted that Ted was a comedic anarchist, an ironic post-modern deconstructionist of the entire genre. 'He's taken the basic gag and completely subverted it. Challenging our expectations of what's funny. Anyway, d'you want to dance?'

'What? Here?' Ashling was completely thrown. It was a long time since a strange man had asked her to dance. Especially in someone's sitting-room. Although now that she looked, people – all female, of course – were kind of flinging themselves around to Fat Boy Slim. 'Ah, no thanks,' she apologized. 'It's too early in the night, I'm still too inhibited.'

'OK, I'll ask you again in an hour.'

'Great!' she exclaimed hollowly, taking in his

eager face. An hour wouldn't get her drunk enough. A *lifetime* wouldn't suffice.

Some time later, to her delight, she spotted Joy kissing the face off Half-man-half-badger.

She hung around a little longer. Though it was a fairly crappy party, she was surprised to find she was happy to be with a crowd and happy to be on its edges. Such contentment was rare: all Ashling knew was that she almost never felt whole. Even at her most fulfilled, something remained forever absent, right at her very core. Like the tiny, pinprick dot that remained in the wash of black when the telly used to shut down for the night.

But tonight she was calm and peaceful, alone but not lonely. Even though the only men who'd hit on her weren't her type, she didn't feel like a failure when she decided to go home.

At the door she met Mr Enthusiastic again. 'Going already? Hold it a minute.' He scribbled something on a piece of paper, then handed it to her.

She waited until she was outside before opening the twist of paper. It was a name – Marcus Valentine – a phone number and the instruction, 'Bellez moi!'

It was the best laugh she'd had all night.

The walk home took ten minutes – at least the rain had stopped. When she reached the front-door of her block of flats, there was a man asleep in the doorway.

The same man who'd been there the other day.

Except he was younger than she'd realized. Pale and slight, clutching tightly on to his thick grubby-orange blanket, he looked barely more than a child.

Rummaging in her rucksack she found a pound and placed it silently beside his head. But maybe it'd be nicked, she worried, so she moved it under his blanket. Then, stepping over him, she let herself in.

As the door clicked behind her, she heard, 'Thanks,' so faint and whispered she wasn't sure if she'd imagined it.

While Ted was going down a storm in the Funny Farm, Jack Devine was opening his front-door in a bleak, sea-facing corner of Ringsend.

'Why didn't you call me?' Mai demanded. 'You never have enough time for me.' She pushed past him and marched straight up the stairs. She was already unbuttoning her jeans.

Jack stared out at the sea, the nearly-black of the night-time water as impenetrable as his eyes. Then he closed the door and slowly followed her up the stairs.

At the same time, in a stylish, Edwardian, red-brick house in Donnybrook, Clodagh downed her fourth gin and braced herself. It had been twenty-nine days.

CHAPTER 7

Ashling woke at twelve on Sunday, feeling rested and only mildly hungover. She lay on the couch and smoked cigarettes until *The Dukes of Hazzard* finished. Then she went out and bought bread, orange juice, cigarettes and newspapers – one scurrilous rag and one broadsheet to cancel out the rag.

After gorging herself to the point of mild disgust on overblown stories of infidelity, she decided to tidy her flat. This mostly consisted of carrying about twenty crumb-strewn plates and half-empty glasses of water from the bedroom to the kitchen sink, picking up an empty tub of Haagen Daz from where it had rolled under the couch and opening the windows. She drew the line at polishing, but she sprayed Mr Sheen around the room and the smell instantly made her feel virtuous. Cautiously she sniffed her bed-linen. Grand, it'd do for another week.

Then, even though she knew it couldn't have gone anywhere, she checked that the suit she'd had dry-cleaned hadn't been stolen. It was still hanging in her wardrobe, beside a clean top. Big day tomorrow. Very big day tomorrow. It wasn't every Monday she started a new job. In fact it had been over eight years and she was horribly nervous. But excited too, she insisted, trying to ignore her fluttery stomach.

What now? Vacuuming, she decided, because if you did it right it was great exercise for the waist. Out came her magenta and lime-green Dyson. Even now she couldn't believe she'd spent so much money on a household appliance. Money that she could just as easily have spent on handbags or bottles of wine. The only conclusion she could draw was that she was finally grown-up. Which was funny because in her head she was still sixteen and trying to decide what to do when she left school.

She flicked the switch and, energetically bending and twisting from the waist, worked her way across the hall floor. Much to the relief of her very hungover neighbour in the flat below (Joy) it didn't take long – Ashling's flat was ludicrously small.

But how she *loved* it. The biggest fear about losing her job was that she wouldn't be able to meet her mortgage payments. She'd bought the flat three years previously, when she'd finally understood that Phelim and she wouldn't be applying together to purchase a cottage with roses round the door. There had been an element of brinkmanship to it – naturally she'd hoped that Phelim would hurtle in as the credits were rolling and breathlessly agree to sign up for the regulatory three-bedroom semi in a distant suburb. But to her heavy-hearted disappointment he didn't and the purchase went ahead. At the time it had seemed like an admission of failure. But not now. This flat was her haven, her nest and her first real home. She'd lived in rented hovels since she was seventeen, sleeping in other people's beds, sitting on lumpy sofas that landlords had bought for cheapness, not comfort.

She hadn't had a stick of furniture when she'd moved in. Apart from the essentials like an iron and a pile of threadbare towels, mismatched sheets and pillowcases, everything had to be bought from scratch. Which caused Ashling to throw a rare tantrum. She fumed with seething resentment at the thought of diverting month after month of clothes money to buy all sorts of stupid things. Like chairs.

'But we can't sit on the floor,' Phelim had yelled.

'I *know*,' Ashling admitted. 'I just didn't realize it would be like this . . .'

'But you're mind-blowingly organized.' He was baffled. 'I thought you'd be great at this sort of thing. Whatjacallit? *Home-making*.'

She looked so lost and bleak that Phelim said softly, 'Oh baby, let me help. I'll buy you some furniture.'

'A bed, I bet,' Ashling said scornfully.

'Well, now that you mention it . . .' Phelim was fond of having sex with Ashling. Buying a bed for her was no hardship. 'Can I afford it?'

Ashling considered. Now that she'd reorganized

61

Phelim's finances, he was a lot better off. 'I suppose,' she said sulkily. 'If you do it on your credit card.'

Bitterly, irritably she applied for a bank loan, then bought herself a couch, a table, a wardrobe and a couple of chairs. And that, she resolved, would be that. For over a year she refused to buy blinds. 'I'll just not wash the windows,' she said. 'That way no one can see in.' And she only got herself a shower curtain when the daily puddles on her bathroom floor began to leak through to Joy's. But somewhere along the line her priorities had changed. Though she wasn't anything like the Ninja-decorator that Clodagh was, she certainly *cared*. To the point where she owned not just one but a grand total of *two* sets of bed linen (a funky denim-look set and a crisp white Zen ensemble with a waffle throw). Recently she'd shelled out forty quid on a mirror that she didn't even need, just because she thought it was pretty. Granted she'd been premenstrual and not in her right mind, but still. And the sea change was obviously complete the day she'd handed over two hundred quid for a dust-sucker.

There was a knock at the door. Joy, white as a ghost, sidled in.

'Sorry, I got a bit carried away with the cleaning,' Ashling realized. 'Did I wake you?'

'It's OK. I've to go out to Howth to see my mammy.' Joy made an anguished face. 'I can't cancel again, I've done it for the past four Sundays.

62

But how will I cope? She'll have made a huge roast dinner which she'll try to force-feed me and she'll spend all afternoon quizzing me, trying to establish if I'm happy. You know what mothers are like.'

Well, yes and no, Ashling thought. She was familiar with the 'Are you happy?' questions. Only thing was, it was Ashling who used to monitor her mother's happiness levels, not the other way round.

'If only she'd have Sunday lunch at a more civilized time,' Joy complained.

'Like Tuesday evening,' Ashling grinned. 'Now, I suppose you haven't seen Ted so far today?'

'Not yet. I presume he got lucky last night and is refusing to leave the poor girl's bedroom.'

'He really was surprisingly excellent last night. So, are you going to tell me what happened with Half-man-half-badger or do I have to beat it out of you?'

Joy instantly lightened. 'He spent the night with me. We didn't actually have sex but I gave him a b-j and he said he'll call. I wonder if he will.'

'One swallow doesn't make a relationship,' Ashling warned, with the wisdom of experience.

'Who are you telling? Give me them –' Joy leant over to the pack of tarot cards, '– till I see what they say. The Empress? What does that mean?'

'Fertility. Mind you keep taking your pill.'

'Cripes. How did *you* get on last night? Meet anyone nice?'

'No.'

'You'll just have to try harder. You're thirty-one, all the good men will be gone soon.'

I don't *need* a mother, Ashling realized. Not with Joy around.

'*You're* twenty-eight,' Ashling retorted.

'Yeah, and I sleep with *tons* of men.' More gently, Joy enquired, 'Don't you get lonely?'

'I'm just out of a five-year relationship – it takes a while to get over something like that.'

Phelim hadn't been a cruel person, but his inability to commit had had the effect of a scorched-earth policy on Ashling's attitude to love. Since he'd gone, loneliness had whistled through her like a bleak wind, but she was in no way equipped to get involved with a new man. Not that she'd been exactly inundated with offers, mind.

'It's nearly a *year*, you're well over Phelim now. New job, new beginnings. I read somewhere that a hundred and fifty per cent of people meet their partners at work. Did you see any sexy men when you had your interview?'

Immediately Ashling thought of Jack Devine. A handful. A skilled nerve-shredder.

'No.'

'Pick a card,' Joy urged.

Ashling split the deck and held a card up.

'The Eight of Swords, what does that mean?' Joy asked.

'Change,' Ashling reluctantly admitted. 'Disturbance.'

'Good, it's long overdue. Right, I'd better go. I'm just going to rub the lucky Buddha to make sure I don't puke on the bus . . . Actually, feck the Buddha. Loan us money for a taxi?'

Ashling handed Joy a tenner and two big plastic bags of rubbish, which seemed to do an embarrassing amount of clinking. 'Stick them down the chute for me, thanks.'

Quarter of a mile away in Malone's Aparthotel, Sunday was hanging heavy on Lisa's hands. She'd read the Irish papers – well, the social pages anyway. And they were pants! They seemed to consist of nothing but pictures of fat, broken-veined politicians, oozing bonhomie and backhanders. Well, they wouldn't be getting into *her* magazine.

She lit yet another cigarette and scuffed moodily about the room. What did people *do* when they weren't working? They saw their mates, they went to the pub, or the gym, or shopping, or decorating, or they hung out with their blokes. She remembered that much.

She longed for a sympathetic ear and thought about ringing Fifi, the closest thing she had to a best friend. They'd been juniors together on *Sweet Sixteen* many years ago. When Lisa moved to Features on *Girl*, she wangled Fifi the job of assistant beauty editor. When Fifi got the job of Senior Features writer on *Chic*, she tipped Lisa off when they were looking for an assistant editor. When

Lisa had left to become assistant editor of *Femme*, Fifi took over Lisa's position of assistant editor of *Chic*. Ten months after Lisa became editor of *Femme*, Fifi became editor of *Chic*. Lisa had always been able to moan to Fifi – she understood the perils and plights of their so-called glamorous jobs, when everyone else was ugly with envy.

But something was stopping Lisa from picking up the phone. She was embarrassed, she realized. And something like resentful. Though their careers had run almost parallel, Lisa had always been further down the track. Fifi's career had been a struggle but Lisa had risen without trace through the ranks. She'd been made an editor nearly a year before Fifi was, and though *Chic* and *Femme* were in almost direct competition, *Femme*'s circulation was well over a hundred thousand more. Lisa had blithely assumed that the promotion to *Manhattan* would propel her so far in front she'd be beyond catching altogether. But instead she was shunted to Dublin and Fifi was suddenly, by default, top-dog.

Oliver, Lisa gasped, happiness suddenly slotting into place. *I'll ring him.* But the warm honey-tide of good feeling immediately turned to acid. She'd forgotten for a moment. *I don't miss him*, she tutored herself. *I'm just bored and fed up.*

In the end, she rang her mum – probably because it was a Sunday and therefore traditional – but she felt like shit afterwards. Especially because Pauline Edwards was desperate to know why Oliver had rung her looking for Lisa's number in Dublin.

'We've split up.' Lisa's stomach snarled into a tight walnut of emotion. She didn't want to talk about this – and why hadn't her mum phoned her if she was that concerned? Why did she always have to ring her?

'But why have you split up, love?'

Lisa still wasn't exactly sure. 'It happens,' she said snippily, desperate to get this dealt with.

'Have you tried that counselling thingummy?' Pauline asked tentatively, reluctant to bring the ire of Lisa down on her head.

''Course.' Said with terse impatience. Well, they'd gone for one session, but Lisa had been too busy to go to any more.

'Will you be getting divorced?'

'I should think so.' In fact, Lisa didn't know. Apart from what they'd yelled at each other in the heat of anger – 'I'm divorcing you!' 'No, you can't because I'm divorcing *you*!' – nothing specific had been discussed. In fact, she and Oliver had barely spoken since the split but, inexplicably, she wanted to hurt her mother by saying it.

Pauline sighed unhappily. Lisa's big brother Nigel had got divorced five years previously. She'd had her children late in life, and she didn't understand the ways of their world.

'They say that two in three marriages end in divorce,' Pauline acknowledged, and abruptly Lisa wanted to yell that she wouldn't be getting divorced and that her mum was a horrible old trout to even suggest it.

Pauline's worry for her daughter wrestled with fear of her. 'Was it because you were . . . different?'

'Different, Mum?' Lisa was tart.

'Well, with him being . . . coloured?'

'Coloured!'

'That's the wrong word,' Pauline amended hastily, then tentatively tried, 'Black?'

Lisa clicked her tongue and sighed hard.

'African-American?'

'For crying out loud, Mum, he's English!' Lisa knew she was being cruel, but it was hard to change the habits of a lifetime.

'English African-American, then?' Pauline said desperately. 'Whatever he is, he's very nice-looking.'

Pauline said this often to show she wasn't prejudiced. Though her heart had nearly stopped with fright the first time she'd met Oliver. If only she'd been *warned* that her daughter's boyfriend was a hard, gleaming, six-foot-tall black man. Coloured man, African-American man, whatever the correct phrase was. She had nothing against them, it was just the unexpectedness of it.

And once she'd got used to him, she was able to get beyond his colour and see that he really *was* a nice-looking boy. To put it mildly.

A huge ebony prince, with smooth, lustrous skin pulled tight over slanting cheekbones, almond-shaped eyes and thin, swingy dreadlocks that ended at his jaw-line. He walked as if he was dancing and he smelt of sunshine. Pauline also suspected – though she would never have been able to consciously formulate it – that he was hung like a donkey.

'Did he meet someone else?'

'No.'

'But he might, Lisa love. A nice-looking boy like him.'

'Fine by me.' If she said it often enough, it would eventually become true.

'Won't you be lonely, love?'

'I won't have time to be lonely,' Lisa snapped. 'I have a career to think of.'

'I don't know why you need a career. I didn't have one and it didn't do me any harm.'

'Oh yeah?' Lisa said fiercely. 'You could have done with one after Dad hurt his back and we had to live on his disability.'

'But money isn't everything. We were ever so happy.'

'I wasn't.'

Pauline lapsed into silence. Lisa could hear her breathing over the phone.

'I'd best go,' Pauline eventually said. 'This must be costing you.'

'Sorry, Mum,' Lisa sighed. 'I didn't mean it. Did you get that parcel I sent you?'

'Oh yes,' Pauline said nervously. 'The face creams and lipsticks. Very nice, thanks.'

'Have you used them?'

'Weeeell –' Pauline began.

'You haven't,' Lisa accused.

Lisa showered Pauline with expensive perfumes and cosmetics that she got in the course of her job. Desperate for her to have a bit of luxury. But Pauline refused to relinquish her Pond's and Rimmel products. Once she'd even said, 'Oh, your things are too good for me, love.'

'They're not too good for you,' Lisa had exploded.

Pauline couldn't understand Lisa's rage. All she knew was that she dreaded the days when the postman knocked on her door and said cheerfully, 'Another parcel from your girl up in London.' Sooner or later Pauline was always called upon to deliver a progress report.

Unless it was a parcel of books. Lisa used to send her mum review copies of Catherine Cookson and Josephine Cox, in the mistaken belief that she'd love all that rags-to-riches romantic stuff. Until the day Pauline said, 'That was a terrific book you sent me, love, about that East End villain who used to nail his victims to a pool table.' It transpired that Lisa's assistant had mistakenly parcelled up the wrong book, and it marked a new departure in Pauline Edwards' reading. Now she thrived on gangster biographies and hard-boiled American thrillers, the more torture scenes the better, and someone else's mum got sent the Catherine Cooksons.

'I wish you'd come and see us, love. It's been ages.'

'Um, yeah,' Lisa said vaguely. 'I'll come soon.'

No fear! With every visit the house she'd grown

up in seemed smaller and more shockingly dreary. In the poky little rooms crammed with dirt-cheap furniture, she felt shiny and foreign, with her false nails and glossy leather shoes, uncomfortably aware that her handbag probably cost more than the Dralon couch she was sitting on. But though her mum and dad oohed and aawed respectfully over her fabulousness, they were fluttery-nervous around her.

She should have dressed down on her visits, to try to narrow the gap. But she needed as much stuff as possible, to wear like a suit of armour, so that she couldn't be sucked back in, subsumed by her past.

She hated it all, then hated herself.

'Why don't you come and see me?' Lisa asked. If they wouldn't make the half-hour train journey from Hemel Hempstead to London they were hardly likely to fly to Dublin.

'But with your Dad not being well and . . .'

When Clodagh woke on Sunday morning she was mildly hung-over, but in great form. Briefly at liberty to snuggle up to Dylan and ignore his erection with a clean conscience.

When Molly and Craig appeared, Dylan urged them sleepily, 'Go downstairs and break things, and let Mummy and me have a snooze.'

Amazingly they left, and Clodagh and Dylan drifted in and out of sleep.

'You smell lovely,' Dylan mumbled into

Clodagh's hair. 'Like biscuits. All sweet and . . . sweet . . .'

Some time later she whispered to him, 'I'll give you a million pounds if you get me some breakfast.'

'What would you like?'

'Coffee and fruit.'

Dylan left and Clodagh stretched like a contented starfish across the bed until he reappeared with a mug in one hand and a banana in the other. He placed the banana on his groin facing downwards, then when Clodagh looked, he faked a gasp and swung the banana upwards, like a quivering erection. 'Why Mrs Kelly,' he exclaimed. 'You're beautiful!'

Clodagh laughed, but felt the familiar guilt begin its relentless creep.

Later they went out for lunch, to one of those places that didn't make you feel like outcasts for bringing along two young children. Dylan went to procure a cushion for Molly to sit on, and as Clodagh wrestled a knife out of Molly's hand she caught a glimpse of Dylan chatting persuasively with a waitress – a Bambi-limbed teenager – who flushed at her proximity to such a good-looking man.

That good-looking man was her husband, Clodagh realized, and suddenly, oddly, she barely recognized him. Assailed by that weird see-saw feeling of knowing someone so well that out of nowhere she didn't know him at all. Familiarity generally dulled the impact of his sunny blond hair, the smile that rippled his skin into layers of parentheses around his mouth, the hazel eyes which were nearly always full of fun. She was surprised and unsettled by his beauty.

What was it Ashling had said yesterday? *Recapture the magic.*

Her mind produced an image: she was panting with desire, her groin swollen with want, being laid back in the sand . . . *Sand?* No, hold on a minute, that wasn't Dylan, that was Jean-Pierre, the knee-tremblingly seductive Frenchman whom she'd lost her virginity to. God, she sighed, that had been brilliant. Eighteen, hostelling along the French Riviera, he'd been the sexiest man she'd ever clapped eyes on. And she had very high standards, she'd never so much as kissed any of the boys she hung around with at home. But the minute she'd seen Jean-Pierre's intense moody stare, beautiful sulky mouth and loose Gallic body-language she'd decided that he was the one who'd receive the highly prized gift of her virginity.

Back to Dylan, the early magic. Ah yes. She remembered almost being in tears as she begged him to do her. 'I can't wait, oh please put it in now!' Sliding along the back seat of his car, letting her knees fall apart . . . No, *wait*, that hadn't been Dylan either. That had been Greg, the American football player who'd been on a year's scholarship to Trinity. Too bad she'd met him only three months before he went back. He'd been a handsome, sure-of-himself jock, bulky with muscle, and for some reason she'd found him completely irresistible.

Of course she'd felt like that about Dylan too. She rummaged in her past for specific memories and dusted off her favourite. The first time she'd ever seen him. Their eyes had – literally – met across a crowded room and before she'd learnt the first thing about him, she'd known everything she needed to know.

Five years older than Clodagh, he made all the other boys look like spotty, wet-behind-the-ears youths. There was a sureness and an urbane confidence about him that rendered him utterly charismatic. He smiled, he charmed, his very presence was warming, uplifting – and reassuring: even though his business was only starting up she had cast-iron faith that Dylan would always make everything all right. And he was so yummy!

She was twenty years of age, dazzled by his blond good looks and giddy with her good fortune. He was so right for her that there was no doubt but that he was the one she was going to marry. Even when her parents had insisted that she was too young to know her own mind, she'd scorned their advice. Dylan was the one for her, she was the one for Dylan.

'There you go, Molly!' He was back with the cushion that three teenage girls had fought over giving to him. It was only then that Clodagh noticed that Molly had poured half the salt into the sugar bowl.

After lunch they drove to the beach. It was a bright, blustery day, just warm enough to take off their shoes and paddle in the waves. Dylan got a man walking his dog to take a photo of the four of them clustered together against the clean, empty sand, smiling as the wind whipped their flaxen hair across their faces, Clodagh clasping one side of her skirt to keep it from sticking to her wet legs.

CHAPTER 8

Lisa showed up for work at eight o'clock on Monday morning. Start as you mean to go on. But to her disgust the building was locked. She hung around in the damp air for a while and eventually went to get a cup of coffee. Even that took some doing. It wasn't like London where coffee emporia had their doors open at the break of day.

At nine o'clock, when she left the coffee shop, it had started to rain. Her arm over her hair, she hurried along, her four-inch heels skidding on the slick pavement. Suddenly she halted and heard herself screeching at a passing young man in an anorak, 'Does it *always* rain in this naffing country?'

'I don't know,' he said, nervously. 'I'm only twenty-six.'

At the front-door Lisa was greeted by a girl called Trix. She was a rash of goosepimples in a little see-through slip-dress and was jigging from high clumpy foot to high clumpy foot to keep warm. When she saw Lisa, her face lit with admiration and she hastily ground her cigarette out.

'Howya,' she growled, exhaling her last plume of smoke. 'Killer shoes! I'm Trix, your PA. Before you ask, my name is Patricia, but there's no point calling me that because I won't answer to it. I was Trixie until the people two doors up got a poodle by the same name, so now I'm Trix. I used to be the receptionist and general dogsbody but I've been promoted, thanks to you. Mind you, they haven't replaced me . . . Over here, the lift is this way.

'I'd be the first to admit my typing isn't the best,' Trix confided, as they went up. 'But my lying is fantastic, easily sixty words a minute. I can say you're in a meeting to anyone you don't want to talk to and they'll never suspect. Unless you *want* them to suspect. I can do intimidation too, see?'

Lisa believed her.

Though she was twenty-one and peachy-pretty, Trix had a toughness that Lisa recognized. From her *own* younger days.

The first shock of the day was that Randolph Media Ireland only took up one floor – the London offices filled an entire twelve-storey tower.

'I've to bring you to see Jack Devine,' Trix said.

'He's the Irish MD, isn't he?' Lisa said.

'Is he?' Trix sounded surprised. 'I suppose he is. He's the boss anyway, or so he thinks. I take no nonsense from him.

'You'd want to have seen him last week.' She lowered her voice dramatically. 'Like a bear with a sore arse. But he's in good humour today, this means he's back with his girl. The carry-on of the

77

pair of them – they make Pamela and Tommy look like the Waltons of Waltons' Mountain.'

Further shocks were in store for Lisa – Trix led Lisa into an open-plan office with about fifteen desks. Fifteen! How could a magazine empire be run from fifteen desks, a boardroom and a small kitchen?

A horrible thought struck her. 'But . . . where's the fashion department?'

'There.' Trix nodded at a rail shunted into a corner on which was hanging a dreadful peach jumper that obviously had something to do with *Gaelic Knitting*, a bridesmaid's dress, a wedding meringue and some men's clothing.

Jesus Christ! The fashion department at *Femme* had taken up an entire room. Crammed with samples from all the high-street shops, it meant that Lisa hadn't had to buy new clothes for several years. Something would have to be done! Already her head was buzzing with plans to get on to her contacts in fashion-land – but Trix was introducing her to the two members of staff who were already in. 'This is Dervla and Kelvin, they work on other magazines, so they're not your staff. Not like me,' she said proudly.

'Dervla O'Donnell, pleased to meet you.' A large, forty-something woman in an elegant smock shook Lisa's hand and smiled. 'I'm *Hibernian Bride, Celtic Health* and *Gaelic Interiors*.' Lisa could tell at a glance that this woman was an ex-hippy.

'And I'm Kelvin Creedon.' A painfully fashionable,

peroxide-haired man in black-framed Joe Ninety spectacles grabbed Lisa's hand. She knew immediately that the specs were only for show and the glass in them was clear. Early-twenties, she reckoned he was. He radiated cool, youthful energy. 'I'm *The Hip Hib, Celtic Car, DIY Irish-style* and *Keol*, our music magazine.' His many silver rings hurt Lisa's hand.

'What do you mean?' Lisa asked in confusion. 'You edit all of these magazines?'

'And research and write them.'

'All by *yourself*?' Lisa couldn't stop herself. She looked from Kelvin to Dervla.

'With the help of the odd freelance,' Dervla said. 'Sure all we have to do is regurgitate press releases.

'It hasn't been so bad since *The Catholic Judger* went to the wall.' Dervla misjudged Lisa's shock for concern. 'That gives me Thursday afternoons to work on something else.'

'Are they weekly or monthly publications?'

Dervla and Kelvin turned to each other, their mouths open but silent in a synchronization of uncontrollable laughter to come. They'd never heard anything so funny in their lives.

'Monthly!' Dervla heaved, in disbelief.

'Weekly!' Kelvin went one better.

Then Dervla noticed Lisa's frown and hurriedly calmed down. 'No. Twice a year, mostly. *The Catholic Judger* was weekly, but everything else comes out in Spring and Autumn. Unless there's some sort of disaster.

'Remember Autumn 1999?' She turned to Kelvin.

79

Kelvin obviously did because the laughter started anew.

'Computer virus,' Kelvin explained. 'Wiped everything.'

'It wasn't funny at the time . . .'

But, clearly, it was now.

'Look.' Dervla steered Lisa towards a rack on which various glossies were displayed. She handed her a slender volume that declared itself to be *Hibernian Bride*, Spring 2000.

That's not a magazine, Lisa thought. *That's a pamphlet. A leaflet, in fact. Nothing more than a memo. Hell, it's barely a Post-it.*

'And this is *Spud*, our food magazine.' Dervla handed another pamphlet to Lisa. 'Shauna Griffin edits that as well as *Gaelic Knitting* and *Irish Gardening*.'

Another member of staff had just arrived. Too boring to qualify as even nondescript, Lisa thought in disgust – medium height, balding and wearing a wedding ring. Human wallpaper. She could hardly be bothered to say hello to him.

'This is Gerry Godson, the art director. He doesn't talk much,' Trix said loudly. 'Sure you don't, Gerry? Blink once for yes, twice for fuck off and leave me alone.'

Gerry blinked twice, and maintained a stony face. Then he smiled widely, shook Lisa's hand and said, 'Welcome to *Colleen*. I've been working on the other magazines here, but now I'm going to be working exclusively for you.'

'And me,' Trix reminded him. 'I'm her PA, you know, I'll be giving the orders.'

'Jayzus,' Gerry muttered good-naturedly.

Lisa tried hard to smile.

Trix rapped lightly on Jack's door, then opened it. Jack looked up. In repose, his face was slightly mournful and hang-dog and his sloe-black eyes held secrets. Then he saw Lisa and smiled in recognition, even though they'd never met. Everything lifted.

'Lisa?' The way her name sounded when uttered by him stirred something warm in her. 'Come in, sit down.' He skirted around his desk and came to shake her hand.

Lisa's lead-heavy foreboding gave her some breathing space. She liked the look of this Jack. Tall? Tick! Dark? Tick! Well-paid? Tick! He was a managing director, even if it was only of an Irish company.

And there was something slightly unorthodox about him that excited her. Though he wore a suit, she sensed it was under duress, and his hair was longer than would have been considered acceptable in London.

So what if he had a girlfriend? When had that ever been an impediment?

'We're all very excited about *Colleen*,' Jack insisted. But Lisa heard a nugget of weariness at the heart of his statement. His smile had disappeared and he was once more serious and broody.

Then he proceeded to tell Lisa about her 'team'.

'There's Trix, your PA, then your assistant editor, a woman called Ashling. She seems very efficient.'

'So I've heard,' Lisa said drily. Calvin Carter's exact words had been, 'You'll provide the vision, she'll do the donkey work.'

'Then there's Mercedes, who will primarily be the fashion and beauty editor, but will also contribute to general editorial. She's come from *Ireland on Sunday* –'

'What's that?'

'A Sunday newspaper. There's Gerry, your art director, who's been working on the other publications. As has Bernard, who'll be handling all the admin, billing, etc. on *Colleen*.'

Then Jack stopped. Lisa waited for him to tell her about another eight or so staff. He didn't.

'Is that it? Five members of staff? Five?' She was giddy with disbelief. At *Femme* her secretary had had a secretary!

'You also have a generous freelance budget,' Jack promised. 'You'll be able to commission stuff and use consultants, both regulars and one-offs.'

Hysteria lunged at Lisa. How had she ended up here, in this awful situation. *How?* She'd had a plan for her life. She'd always known where she was going and she'd always got there. Until now, when she'd been diverted so unexpectedly into this backwater.

'Who . . . who do the other desks belong to, then?'

'Dervla, Kelvin and Shauna, who edit all our

other magazines. Then there's my PA, Mrs Morley, Margie in advertising – she's great, an absolute Rottweiler! – Lorna and Emily in sales and the two Eugenes in accounts.'

Lisa was finding it hard to catch her breath, but she had to resist the urge to run to the ladies' and scream into her hands because Ashling, the assistant editor, was being ushered into the office.

'Hello again.' Ashling smiled warily at Jack Devine.

'Hello.' He nodded, with nothing like the warmth he'd greeted Lisa with. 'I don't believe you've met each other. Lisa Edwards – Ashling Kennedy.'

Ashling looked momentarily startled, then beamed at Lisa, openly admiring her flawless skin, her nipped-waist power suit, her shimmering ten-denier legs. 'I'm delighted to meet you,' she declared with nervous animation. 'I'm very excited about this magazine.'

Lisa, on the other hand, wasn't one bit impressed with Ashling. She'd made ordinariness into an art-form. We could all let our hair hang there, being neither curly nor straight, if we were so inclined, Lisa thought scornfully. None of us are born with smooth, processed hair, it's something you have to work at. With Trix, although her make-up was a little less than subtle, at least she showed willing.

Then Mercedes arrived and Lisa wasn't sure about her either. She was sleek and silent, dark and sinuous as liquorice.

The only one Lisa hadn't met yet was Bernard, and he turned out to be the worst of the lot. The red sleeveless tank-top he wore over his shirt and tie was obviously from when it was in fashion the first time round, and frankly that was all she needed to know about him.

At ten o'clock, the *Colleen* team, Jack and his PA Mrs Morley gathered in the boardroom for a get-to-know-each-other session. Lisa was surprised that Mrs Morley wasn't a fragrant, efficient, Miss Moneypenny type, but a sixtyish, pug-faced dragon. Jack had inherited her, Lisa subsequently discovered, when he took over from the previous Managing Director. He could have hired a new person, but for whatever reason decided not to, and consequently Mrs Morley was highly devoted. *Too* devoted, popular opinion had it.

As Mrs Morley took the minutes, Jack reiterated the brief – *Colleen* was to be a sexy, sassy read for Irish women aged eighteen to thirty. It should be open-minded, sexually overt and fun. Everyone was to have a good, hard think about features.

'How about a regular piece on meeting men in Ireland?' Ashling piped up nervously. 'Perhaps one month do a girl going to a dating agency, another month get her to surf the net, another month get her to go horse-riding . . . ?'

'Not a bad idea,' Jack said reluctantly.

Ashling gave a wobbly smile. She wasn't sure

how long she could keep this sort of thing up – ideas weren't really her strength. The feature had been Joy's suggestion – only because Joy hoped to be the guinea-pig. 'I'm always trying to meet men, anyway,' she'd said. 'I might as well get bankrolled while I'm doing it.'

'Any other thoughts?' Jack prompted.

'How about a celebrity letter?' Lisa put forward. 'Find some Irish celebrity. Like . . .' Then she was completely stumped, because she didn't know any Irish celebrities. 'Like . . . like . . .'

'Bono,' Ashling suggested, kindly. 'Or one of the girls from the Corrs.'

'Exactly,' Lisa said. 'A thousand words, about flying first-class, going to parties with Kate Moss and Anna Friel. Risqué and glam.'

'Very good.' Jack was pleased. But Lisa was back in the horrors. She'd been hit anew by the size of the task ahead of her. To set up a completely new magazine in an unfamiliar country!

'And how about an *un*celebrity letter?' Trix suggested in her hoarse voice. 'You know the sort of thing – I'm an ordinary girl, I got really pissed last night, I'm two-timing my boyfriend, I hate my job, I wish I had more money, I lifted a bottle of nail varnish from Boot's . . .'

Everyone had been nodding enthusiastically until she got to the bit about stealing the nail varnish, then the nodding slowed down and stopped. Everyone had done it but no one was going to admit to it.

Trix noticed immediately and recovered with aplomb. '. . . My ma hates my boyfriend – both of them – I bleached my hair and burnt my scalp, that kind of thing.'

'Good idea,' Jack said. 'Mercedes, any thoughts?'

Mercedes had been doodling, her dark eyes distant and opaque. 'I'm going to showcase as many Irish designers as possible. Attend the degree shows of the fashion colleges –'

'How parochial is *that*?' Lisa interrupted, caustically. 'We've got to feature international designers to be taken seriously.'

No way was she going to wear amateurish, home-made garments run up by Mercedes' mates in their bedrooms! Proper magazines like *Femme* did photo shoots of exquisite garments sent from the press offices of international fashion houses. The clothes were only on loan but more than once they'd got 'lost' after a shoot. Naturally, the models had got the blame – let's face it, didn't they all have heroin habits to support? And if the missing threads turned up in Lisa's wardrobe, then no one was any the wiser. Well, actually, everyone was very much the wiser, but there was nothing they could do about it. And it was a perk that Lisa had no intention of relinquishing.

Mercedes flicked Lisa a knowing, contemptuous look. To Lisa's surprise, she was unsettled.

'Is that it?' Jack asked.

'What about . . . ?' Ashling said slowly, barely trusting herself to speak. She suspected she was having an original thought, but couldn't be sure. 'How about a regular piece by a man? I know it's a women's magazine, but could we have a kind of A-Z of how a man's head works? What he *really* means when he says, "I'll call you." In fact,' she squeaked with excitement, 'how about showing the woman's side too? A his'n'hers piece?'

Jack gave Lisa a questioning eyebrow.

'That's so five minutes ago,' Lisa said shortly.

'Is it?' Ashling said humbly. 'OK.'

'It's the twelfth of May today,' Jack concluded the meeting. 'The board want the first issue on the stands for the end of August. That sounds like a long time for those of you who've come from weekly publications, but it's actually not. It's going to be a lot of hard work.

'But fun too,' he added, because he knew he should. Whoever he was hoping to convince, it certainly wasn't himself. 'And any problems, my door is always open.'

'Which isn't much use if you're not in your office,' Trix said cheekily. 'I mean,' she said hastily, as his face darkened, 'that you're often over at the telly studio, keeping the peace.'

'Unfortunately,' Jack directed this at Lisa, 'our television and radio operations are at different premises, half a mile away. Demands of space mean that my office is here, but I still have to spend a fair amount of time over there. But if you need me and I'm not here, you can always ring me.'

'OK,' Lisa nodded. 'And what circulation are we aiming for with *Colleen*?'

'Thirty thousand. We may not get that initially, but over six months that's what we hope to work up to.'

Thirty thousand. Lisa was appalled – if the circulation of *Femme* dropped below three hundred and fifty thousand, heads rolled.

Then Jack showed Lisa her freelance budget, but something was wrong with it – it seemed to be missing a nought. At least one.

That was it. She found herself politely excusing herself from the room and, as though in a dream, gliding to the ladies', where she locked herself in a cubicle. To her surprise she found that she was heaving and sobbing. Weeping from disappointment, humiliation, loneliness, for all that she'd lost. It didn't last long, she wasn't really a cryer, but when she finally emerged from the cubicle her heart banged hard when she saw someone standing by the basins. Plain and simple Ashling, her hands behind her back. Interfering bitch!

'Which hand?' Ashling asked.

Lisa didn't understand.

'Pick a hand,' Ashling said.

Lisa felt like smacking her. They were all mad here.

'Right or left?' Ashling urged.

'Left.'

Ashling revealed the contents of her left hand

to Lisa. A packet of tissues. Then her right hand. A bottle of rescue remedy.

'Stick out your tongue.' Ashling plopped a couple of drops on to Lisa's nonplussed tongue. 'It's for shock and trauma. Cigarette?'

Lisa angrily shook her head, then wavered and passively let Ashling stick a cigarette in her mouth and light it for her.

'If you want to fix your make-up,' Ashling offered, 'I've got moisturizer and mascara, it's probably not as good as your usual stuff, but it'll do.' Already she was rummaging.

'Did someone send you in here?' Lisa was thinking of Jack Devine.

Ashling shook her head. 'No one guessed but me.'

Lisa didn't know whether or not to be disappointed. She didn't want Jack to think she was wet, but it would be nice to know he cared . . .

'I'm not usually like this.' Lisa's face was hard. 'I don't want it mentioned again.'

'It's forgotten.'

CHAPTER 9

At the end of the first day Ashling was fit to collapse. Giddy with relief that she didn't have to struggle on to a bus or a Dart, she staggered straight home. She was lucky. At least she had a home to go to, she realized – Lisa had to go out and hunt one down.

Ashling flung herself gratefully into her flat, kicked off her shoes and checked her answering machine. The red light winked lasciviously and joyously Ashling hit 'play'. She was wild keen for company and connection, to help her process her strange, challenging day. But to her disappointment, all it was was a strange message from someone called Cormac, who would be delivering a ton of mulch on Friday morning. Wrong fecking number.

Bodysurfing the couch, she grabbed the phone and rang Clodagh. But as soon as she'd said hello, Clodagh launched into 'I'm having the day from hell!'

Against a cacophony of yelling, she raised her voice and complained. 'Craig has a pain in his tum-tums and all he had for breakfast was half a slice of toast and peanut butter. Then at lunch-time he wouldn't eat a thing and I wondered if I should try him with a chocolate biscuit, even though he goes hyper every time he has sugar, so in the end I gave him a custard cream because I thought that would be slightly better than one with chocolate –'

'Uh-huh,' Ashling nodded sympathetically, as the howling all but drowned out Clodagh.

'– which he ate, so I tried him with another but he just licked off the icing and though he doesn't have a temperature he's pale and SHUT UP! LET ME HAVE FIVE SECONDS ON THE PHONE, PLEASE. Oh, bloody hell, I can't take much more of this!'

Clodagh's plea was ragged and the screeching simply intensified.

'Is that Craig?' Ashling asked. It must be quite a stomach-ache. He sounded like he was being disembowelled.

'No, it's Molly.'

'What's up with *her*?'

Ashling was able to make out some words in all Molly's bawling. Apparently, Mummy was mean. In fact, it seemed that Mummy was horrible. And Molly didn't like Mummy. A particularly hyster-ical bout notified Ashling that Molly HATED Mummy.

'I'm washing her security blanket,' Clodagh said defensively. 'It's in the machine.'

'Oh my good God.'

Molly went bananas whenever she was separated from her security blanket. It had once been a teatowel, before Molly's incessant sucking had rotted it away to a smelly, brown-edged shapeless rag.

'It was filthy,' Clodagh said desperately. She turned away from the phone. 'Molly,' she beseeched. 'It was dirty. Ugh, nasty, pah!' Ashling listened patiently as Clodagh made spitting-yuck noises. 'It was a health hazard, it would have made you sick.'

The wailing increased a couple of pegs and Clodagh came back on the line. 'The old bitch at playgroup said Molly wouldn't be allowed to bring it any more if it wasn't washed regularly. What could I do? Anyway, I don't think it's appendicitis –'

It took Ashling a second to realize they were back to Craig.

'– because he hasn't puked and the family medical encyclopaedia says that's a sure sign. But you think of everything, don't you?'

'I suppose,' Ashling said doubtfully.

'Measles, chicken-pox, meningitis, polio, e-coli,' Clodagh reeled off miserably. 'Hold on, Molly wants to sit on my knee. You can sit on Mummy's knee if you promise to be quiet. Are you going to be quiet? Are you?'

But Molly was making no promises and a series of bangs and shifts indicated that she was being allowed to clamber on to Clodagh's knee, anyway.

Mercifully, her shrieking quietened down to ostentatious sniffs and gasps.

'And as if I wasn't at the end of my rope, fucking Dylan rings to say that not only is he going to be home late *again*, but that next week he's got to go to yet another overnight conference.'

'Fucking Dylan,' Ashling heard Molly sing-song, with perfect diction. 'Fucking Dylan, fucking Dylan.'

'. . . *Plus* he's away this Friday at some dinner in Belfast!'

More crying started up in the background. Male crying. Fucking Dylan – home early and upset at being sworn at by his wife and daughter? – Ashling wondered wryly. No, from the whingy, whiny complaints about a tummy-ache, it had to be Craig.

'I'll come over on Friday night,' Ashling offered.

'Great, that's – LEAVE IT! WOULD YOU BLOODY LEAVE IT! Ashling, I have to go,' Clodagh said, and the line went dead. That was how phone conversations with Clodagh usually ended. Deflated, Ashling sat looking at the phone. She needed to speak to *someone*. Luckily, Ted was due any minute, she could usually set her watch by his arrival. Six fifty-three.

But at ten past seven, when she was halfway through a bag of Kettle chips and Ted hadn't appeared, Ashling began to worry. She hoped he hadn't had an accident. He was a demon on his bike and wouldn't wear a helmet. At half past she rang him. To her surprise he was home!

'Why didn't you call in?'

'Do you want me to?'

'Well . . . yes, I suppose. It was my first day at my new job today.'

'Oh shite, I forgot. I'll be right down.'

Seconds later, Ted appeared – and he looked different. Unquantifiably, but undeniably. Ashling hadn't seen him since Saturday night – remarkable in itself, but she'd been too antsy about the new job to notice until now. Somehow he looked less delicate, more twinklingly robust. Usually he invaded the space of others like an unstoppable force, but there was a straight-backed jauntiness about his posture that was new.

'Congratulations on Saturday night,' Ashling said.

'I think I have a new girlfriend,' he admitted, with a bashful ear-to-ear grin. 'At least one, in fact.' At Ashling's agog face he elaborated, 'I spent yesterday with Emma, but I'm meeting Kelly tomorrow night.'

Just then Joy arrived. 'A watched pot never boils. Half-man-half-badger will never ring if I wait by the phone. Right then! Bill Gates, Rupert Murdoch or Donald Trump – I thought I'd pick captains of industry in honour of your new job.'

'But that's easy.' Ashling couldn't believe how lightly she'd been let off. 'Donald Trump, of course.'

'Oh, really?' Joy was moody. 'I thought he was a bit bouffant and blow-dried. I find it hard to

94

respect a man who spends more time on his hair than I do. Well, each to their own.'

Then she reached in her bag and waved around a bottle of Asti Spumante. 'For you. Congrats on the new job.'

'Asti *Spew*-mante,' Ashling exclaimed. 'Thank you.'

'*Spew*-mante?' Ted admired.

'*Spew*-mante,' Joy confirmed. 'Nothing but the best.'

When they'd got all the sniggery mileage they could out of saying '*Spew*-mante', Joy gasped, wide-eyed with anticipated good news, 'So? How was your first day as a glamorous magazine person?'

'I have a nice desk, a nice Apple Mac –'

'A nice boss?' Joy asked, meaningfully.

Ashling tried to formulate her thoughts. She was fascinated by Lisa's glowing, well-turned-out attractiveness and curious about the unhappiness that throbbed from her. She'd recognized her as the woman in the supermarket with the seven of everything, and she was interested in that too. But it had been a mistake to follow her to the ladies'. She'd been desperate to help, but she'd ended up being just pushy and insensitive.

'She's very beautiful.' Ashling didn't want to elaborate on her regret. 'And thin and clever and has fantastic clothes.'

Ted, the freshly minted womanizer, perked up, but Joy said scornfully, 'Not *that* boss. The good-looking man whose girlfriend bit his finger.'

Ashling felt no better thinking about Jack Devine. She'd only just started her new job and neither of her superiors seemed keen on her.

'How do you know he's good-looking?' she asked.

'He just sounds it. Geeky men don't get their fingers bitten.'

''s true,' Ted chipped in. 'It's never happened to me.'

But all that might be about to change, Ashling suspected.

Joy jogged her. 'Your boss?'

'He's – um – very serious,' Ashling settled for. Then in a splurge she admitted, 'He doesn't seem to like me.' She felt both better and worse for saying it.

'Why not?' Joy enquired.

'Yeah, why?' Ted wanted to know. How could someone not like Ashling?

'I think it's because I gave him the Band-Aid that day.'

'What's wrong with that? You were only trying to help.'

'I wish I hadn't,' Ashling realized. 'Let's get some food.'

They rang the local Thai delivery and, as was customary, ordered way too much. Even after they'd eaten till their stomachs were painfully stretched, there was loads left over.

'We just always have to go that Pad Thai too far,' Ashling said regretfully. 'OK, whose fridge do we want to leave the leftovers in for two days before we throw them out?'

Joy and Ted shrugged at each other and looked back at Ashling. 'Might as well be yours.'

'I'm worried,' Joy announced. 'My fortune cookie says I'll suffer a disappointment. Let's read our horoscopes.'

Then they got out the I-Ching and messed around with that for a while, taking several goes until they got the solution they wanted. After they'd tried and failed to find something they all wanted to watch on telly, Joy looked out the window in the direction of Snow, the club across the road. The door whores let them in free because they were local.

'Anyone fancy going over the road for a dance?' she suggested, casually. *Too* casually.

'NO!' Ashling said, fear making her emphatic. 'I have to be on top form for work in the morning.'

'I have a job too,' Joy said. 'The fastest insurance-claim processor in the west. Come on, just one drink.'

'You have no understanding of that concept. I'm surprised you can even say it. If I go out with you for "just the one" I end up at five in the morning, wrecked out of my head, dancing to Abba, watching the sun come up in a strange apartment with a group of even stranger men who I've never met before and that I never want to see again.'

'I've never heard you complain before.'

'Sorry, Joy. I'm probably just a bit anxious about the job.'

'I'll come with you,' Ted offered Joy. 'If you're not afraid I'll scare the boys away.'

'You!' Joy laughed scornfully. 'I don't think so.'

It was after nine before Dylan got home. Clodagh had managed to get both Molly and Craig to bed, which was nothing short of miraculous.

'Hiya,' Dylan said wearily, flinging his briefcase against the wall in the hall and pulling at his tie. Swallowing anger as the briefcase buckles scratched the paintwork *again*, she braced herself for his kiss. She'd have preferred it if he didn't bother. It wasn't like it meant anything, it was just an irritating habit.

She opened her mouth to launch into her horrible day, but he beat her to it. 'Christ, the day I've had! Where are they?'

'In bed.'

'Both of them?'

'Yes.'

'Should we ring the Vatican to report a miracle? I'll just go and see them, then I'll be back down.' He'd changed out of his suit and into sweatpants and a T-shirt when he came back.

'Any news?' she asked, eager for information and excitement from the outside world.

'No. Any dinner?'

Ah, dinner.

'Between Craig's stomach-ache and Molly's tantrums . . .' She opened the fridge looking for inspiration. Nothing doing. The freezer didn't help either. 'Alphabetti Spaghetti on toast do you?'

'Alphabetti Spaghetti on toast. Good job I didn't marry you for your cooking skills.' He shot her a smile. Was she imagining a certain tightness to it?

'Good job indeed,' she agreed, fetching a can from the cupboard. She couldn't be sure whether he was angry or not. He always acted sunny even when he was raging. Not that she minded, it made life easier.

'So how was work?' She tried again. 'What has you so late?'

He sighed wearily. 'You know that big American sale? The one that's been dragging on for ever?'

'Yes,' she lied, sticking bread in the toaster.

'I can't remember what the state of play was the last time I talked to you about it. Had they actually made any decisions?'

'They might have been just about to,' Clodagh attempted.

'OK, so after deliberating for ever, they finally narrow it down to three packages. Then they say they want to test them. Which, as you know, is a huge waste of fucking time so I offer them the reports from the trial sites. First they say OK, they'll accept that. Then they change their minds and send over two techies from their Ohio office to run the tests . . .'

Clodagh stirred the saucepan and tuned out. She was disappointed. This was extremely fucking boring.

Slumped at the table, Dylan let it all pour out. '. . . Then I get a phone call this afternoon, they've only gone and bought a package from Digiware, and they're not even going to test ours!'

This was the point where Clodagh tuned back in. 'But that's brilliant! If they're not even going to test yours!'

CHAPTER 10

In her cold lonely bed in the bleak room in Harcourt Street, Lisa tried to sleep, but she felt she was already in the land of nod. And in the middle of a terrible nightmare.

After the shocking day at the amateur office, she'd been quietly confident that things couldn't get any worse. That was before she'd tried to find a home to rent.

She'd thought she'd be able to use a relocation agency, but the registration fee was extortionate. And a tactfully worded offer over the phone that she'd give them a nice mention in the magazine if they waived the fee was stonewalled.

'We don't need any publicity,' the young man told her. 'More business than we can handle due to the Celtic Tiger.'

'Celtic *what*?'

'Tiger.' The young man had registered that Lisa's accent wasn't an Irish one, so he explained. 'Remember when the economies of countries like Japan and Korea were booming they called it the Asian Tiger?'

Of course Lisa didn't. Words like 'economy' just bounced right off her.

The young man continued, 'And now that Ireland's economy is going through the roof, we call it the Celtic Tiger. Which means,' he said as tactfully as he could, which wasn't very, 'we don't need any free publicity.'

'Right,' Lisa said dully, hanging up the phone. 'Thanks for the lecture on economics.'

On Ashling's advice, she bought the evening paper, scanned the letting columns for apartments and mews houses in fashionable Dublin 4, and made appointments to see a few places after work. Then she rang a taxi on the Randolph Media account to take her around them.

'Sorry love,' the taxi controller said. 'I don't know your name.'

'Don't worry,' Lisa said silkily. 'You will.' It had been years since she'd used public transport – or paid for a taxi out of her own pocket for that matter. And she didn't intend to start now.

The first property was a maisonette in Ballsbridge. It had sounded lovely in the paper – right price, right postcode, right facilities. Sure enough, the area seemed nice with plenty of restaurants and cafés, the quiet tree-lined street was attractive, all the little houses kempt and spruce. As the taxi inched along, looking for number forty-eight, Lisa's spirits lifted for the first time since she'd clapped eyes on Jack. Already she could imagine herself living here.

Then she saw it. The only house in the road that looked like it was inhabited by squatters; torn curtains at the window, the grass several feet high, a rusting car on concrete blocks in the drive. She counted along the house numbers from where she was now, wondering which one was forty-eight. Forty-two, forty-four, forty-six, forty-ei . . . ght. Sure enough, number forty-eight was the house that looked like it had had a demolition order slapped on it.

'Oh fuck,' she exhaled.

She'd forgotten. It was so long since she'd had to look for somewhere to live that it had slipped her mind what a living hell it was. That it was a series of disappointments, each one more crushing than the previous.

'Drive on,' she ordered.

'Right you are,' the taxi-driver said. 'Where are we off to now?'

The second place was slightly better. Until a little brown mouse ran along the kitchen floor and disappeared in a wiggle of oily tail beneath the fridge. Lisa's scalp buckled with revulsion.

And the third place had described itself as 'bijou' when the correct phrase was 'unbelievably tiny'. It was a one-roomed studio, with the bathroom in a cupboard and no kitchen at all.

'Tell me now, what would you want with a kitchen? You career women don't have time for cooking,' the seal-plump landlord had flattered. 'Too busy running the world.'

'Nice try, fat-boy,' Lisa muttered to herself.

Hopelessly, she trailed back to the taxi, and on the drive home to Harcourt Street had to converse with the driver, who had by now decided that they were firm friends.

'. . . and my eldest fella is great with his hands. The nicest poor divil in the whole world, he'd do anything for anyone. Changing light-bulbs, assembling tables, cutting grass, all the oul' wans on our road love him . . .'

She was certain the driver was irritating the life out of her, but when she got out of the car, she found she missed him. And now she'd never find out what had happened when he challenged the gang of girls who'd been bullying his fourteen-year-old.

Back in her joyless room, her soul gaped in a howl of misery. Everything was made even more hellish by tiredness and lack of food. She was twisted by *déjà vu*, from when she was eighteen, working on a shitty magazine and having no luck trying to rent a half-decent home. Somehow, in the board-game of life, she'd slithered down a snake and had arrived once more at the beginning. Though back then it had seemed to be a lot more fun.

She'd been desperate to escape the mean narrow confines of her home. From the age of thirteen she'd been bunking off school and taking herself up to London to shoplift. Returning home bearing eye-liners, earrings, scarves and bags and watched with anxious suspicion by her mother, who didn't dare challenge her.

At sixteen, as soon as she'd got the business of failing her O-levels out of the way, she left home and went to London for good. She and her friend Sandra – who achieved instant street-cred by changing her name to Zandra – met up with three gay boys called Charlie, Geraint and Kevin and moved into their squat in a tower block in Hackney. Where a life of wild fun began. Taking speed, going to the Astoria on a Monday night, Heaven on Wednesday nights, The Clink on Thursday nights. Doctoring their out-of-date bus passes, getting the night bus home, listening to the Cocteau Twins and Art of Noise, meeting people from all over.

Clothes were central to their lives and first up was best dressed. Advised by the boys, who had an encyclopaedic knowledge of fabulousness at their fingertips, Lisa quickly learnt how to look amazing.

In Camden market, Geraint made her buy a red, stretchy-tight Body-Map dress with a cut-out on the thigh, which she wore with red and white candy-striped tights. Her handbag was a little hard white case with a red cross on it. To complete the outfit, Kevin insisted on nicking her a pair of Palladiums from Joseph – little canvas trainers with a truck-tyre sole. Which he got to her only just in time, because he was sacked the following day. On her head Lisa wore a knitted pirate-style hat covered with safety-pins – a home-made pastiche of a John Galliano, knocked together by Kevin, who wanted to be a fashion designer. And Charlie was in charge of her hair. Hair attachments were hot news, so he bleached Lisa's hair white-blonde and affixed a waist-length blonde plait to the crown of her head. One night at Taboo, *I-D* magazine took her photo. (Though they bought it religiously for the following six months, the picture never appeared, but *still*.)

The squat had almost no furniture so there was great excitement when they found an armchair in a skip. All five of them ferried it home joyously and took turns to sit in it. Likewise, cups of tea had to be had on a rota basis, because they owned only two mugs between them. But it never occurred to anyone to buy extra ones – a terrible waste of money. The small amounts of cash they had were earmarked for buying clothes, paying into clubs (if there was no way of avoiding it) and buying drinks.

All of them eventually got jobs – Charlie as a hairdresser, Zandra in a restaurant, Kevin on the shop floor at Comme des Garçons, Geraint on the door in a cutting-edge club, and Lisa in a high-street clothes shop, where she lifted more of the stock than she actually sold. A wonderful barter system got going. Charlie would do Lisa's hair, she'd steal a shirt for Geraint, Geraint would let them into Taboo for nothing, Zandra would give them free tequila sunrises at the restaurant where she worked. (A mini-barter system was in operation there, because the barman wouldn't insist on dockets from Zandra in exchange for low-grade sexual favours.) The only person who wasn't in the loop was Kevin because the shop he worked at was so expensive yet so minimal that, if he nicked one single thing, the entire stock would diminish by twenty-five per cent. But he added general, free-floating kudos to the whole group in these frenzied days of mid-to-late-eighties label worship.

None of them would spend money on food – like cups and furniture, that too was a waste. If ever they were hungry they'd descend on the restaurant where Zandra worked and demand to be fed. Or else go on a shoplifting spree at their local Safeway. Strolling around the aisles, eating as they went, then shoving the wrapper or the banana skin at the back of the shelves. Sometimes Lisa insisted on actually taking stuff out with her, she liked the thrill it gave her.

Life continued like this for eighteen months, until the wonderful intimacy began to disintegrate into squabbles and rows. The novelty of having a rota for cup use had begun to wear thin. Then Lisa's magazine-executive boyfriend decided to take a risk and swing her a job on *Sweet Sixteen*. Though she had no qualifications and barely an education, she was scarily smart. She knew what was in, what was on its way out, who was worth knowing, and she always looked spectacularly, astonishingly, just-this-minute fashionable. Seconds after something had appeared in *Vogue*, Lisa was arrayed in a cut-price version of it, and, most importantly of all, dressed with *conviction*. Many people wore puff-ball skirts because they knew they should, but most of them couldn't shake the accompanying air of confusion and shame. Lisa sported hers with aplomb.

Then, as now, the magazine she was working on was low-budget crap and it was hard to find a flat that she could afford to rent. But the difference was that back then having a shit job on a magazine was thought to be fantastic – being employed by a magazine *at all* was what was important. And trying to find a half-decent place to live was a huge step forward – after living in the squat. Those were circumstances to be savoured. A source of pride, not embarrassment. Even though she was at the bottom of the heap, she was still the success story of Five Live in a Squat in Hackney.

And now look at them. Charlie worked in a salon in Bond Street and had lots of private clients, all of them horribly rich women. Zandra reverted to Sandra, went home to Hemel Hempstead, got married and had three children in speedy succession. Kevin was also married – to Sandra. It turned out he'd only said he was gay because he thought it was fashionable. Geraint was dead, he'd tested HIV positive in 1992 and his lungs gave out three years later. And Lisa, look at Lisa now. All those years of hard work, just to end up like this, back at the start. *How had it happened?*

Back in the nightmarish present, Lisa climbed into her hotel-room bed and smoked cigarette after cigarette, waiting for the Rohypnol to deliver four hours of merciful oblivion. But round and round the same ugly thoughts went. She was appalled at the huge task ahead of her on *Colleen* and hated being here. But there was no way out. She couldn't return to London. Even if there was an editor's job going – which there wasn't at the moment – you're only as good as your last ABC audit. She'd have to make *Colleen* a sure-fire success before anyone else would employ her. Trapped.

She picked up the foil card of Rohypnol and suddenly suicide seemed gloriously tempting. Would sixteen tablets be enough to kill herself? Probably, she decided. She could just close her eyes and eddy away from everything. Go out on a blaze of glory, while her name was still a byword for successful, high-circulation magazines. Preserve her reputation for all eternity.

She'd always been a survivor, and had never before contemplated suicide – and she was only doing so now because dying seemed the most appropriate way to survive. But the more she thought about it, the more killing herself wasn't an option: everyone would simply think she'd cracked under the pressure and they'd gloat like mad.

She squirmed, thinking of every magazine

person in Britain showing up at her funeral, bringing their murmury soundtrack of *She couldn't hack it, you know. Poor girl, couldn't stay the pace.* Turning to each other in their sleek black suits – they wouldn't even have to change out of their work clothes for the funeral – and congratulating themselves that they were still, by virtue of being alive, players. No burn-out here, no sir!

Not being able to stay the pace was the worst crime in magazine publishing. Worse than hitting the burgers hard and becoming a size twelve, or telling the world that short hair was in when everyone else's money was riding on shoulder-length locks. Working on the principle that there was only so much endurance knocking around, magazine folk joyously embraced the news that a colleague was 'taking a long, well-deserved rest' or 'spending more time with their family'.

A tragic accident was the only way out, Lisa decided. A *glamorous* tragic accident, she amended. Forget falling under a low-rent Irish bus, that would be even more embarrassing than topping herself. She'd have to fall out of a speedboat, at the very least. Or crash in an orange ball of flame while helicoptering to some fuck-off location.

. . . She was on her way to Manoir aux Quatre Saisons, I believe.

Actually, I heard it was Balmoral Castle. At the personal request of you-know-who.

But what a fitting way to go. Fabulous in death as in life.

Burnt to a crisp, I'm told, like an overdone steak.
The superbitchy tones of Lily Headly-Smythe, editor of *Panache*, interrupted Lisa's sleepy reverie.

. . . Rumour has it that Vivienne Westwood's going to base her next collection on it, all the models will be done up like burn victims.

Fantasy back on track, Lisa eventually fell asleep, comforted by thoughts of her society-pages death.

CHAPTER 11

The week carried on. Lisa moved through her grey-bordered life like a sleepwalker. Albeit, a well-dressed, bossy one.

On Friday, the rain stopped and the sun came out, which caused great excitement amongst the staff – they were like children on Christmas morning. As they arrived into work, there was a stream of comments.

'Glorious day.'

'Aren't we blessed with the weather?'

'Fabulous morning.'

Just because it had stopped flaming raining, Lisa thought, with contempt.

'Remember last summer?' Kelvin shouted across the office to Ashling, his eyes sparkling gleefully behind his black-framed fake glasses.

'Indeed I do,' Ashling replied. 'It was on a Wednesday, wasn't it?'

Everyone roared laughing. Everyone except Lisa.

Mid-morning, Mai tripped gracefully into the office, flashed a sly, sweet smile around and asked, 'Is Jack in?'

Lisa experienced a small thrill. This was obviously

Jack's girl and what a surprise. Lisa had expected some pale, freckly Irish girl, not this coffee-coloured little piece of exotica.

Ashling, standing at the photocopier, copying several million press releases for distribution to every clothes designer and cosmetic manufacturer in the universe, paid attention also. It was the finger-biter, looking as though butter wouldn't melt in her cherry-plump mouth.

'Have you an appointment?' Mrs Morley drew herself up to her full four foot eleven, intimidatingly extending her enormous bosom.

'Tell him it's Mai.'

After a long, hard glare, Mrs Morley trundled away. While she waited, Mai absently twirled a slender finger in her heavy hair, looking every inch a wet dream. Then Mrs Morley was back. 'You can go in,' she said, her disappointment obvious.

Mai passed through the office in lemon-scented silence, and the second Jack's door closed behind her there was a collective release of breath and a clamour of talk.

'That's Jack's girlfriend,' Kelvin informed Ashling, Lisa and Mercedes.

'More trouble than she's worth, if you ask me,' Mrs Morley said grimly.

'I'm not so sure about that, Mrs Morley,' Kelvin said lasciviously. Mrs Morley turned away with a disgusted sniff.

'She's half-Irish, half-Vietnamese,' Silent Gerry piped up.

'They fight like cats and dogs,' Trix thrilled. 'She's really violent.'

'Well, that's not her Vietnamese side,' Dervla O'Donnell said firmly, delighted to abandon *Hibernian Bride* for a moment. 'The Vietnamese are a very gentle hospitable people. When I was travelling there –'

'Ah, here,' Trix moaned. 'The ex-hippy's having another 'Nam flashback. I feel rigor mortis kicking in.'

Ashling continued with her press releases, but the photocopier groaned slowly, made a few clicks that it shouldn't have, then ground into unwelcome silence. The display panel flashed a yellow message. 'PQ03?' Ashling questioned. 'What does that mean?'

'PQ03?' The older office members looked at each other. 'Haven't a clue!'

'That's a new one.'

'But be grateful for small mercies. It usually breaks down after two copies.'

'What should I do?' Ashling asked. 'These press releases have to go out in the post tonight.'

She glanced at Lisa, hoping she'd let her off the hook. But Lisa's expression remained smooth and closed. At the end of the first week it was clear to Ashling that Lisa was a slave-driver with huge vision for the magazine. Great in many ways, but not if you're the person landed with the responsibility of single-handedly implementing every one of Lisa's ideas.

'No point asking any of these eejits to fix it.' Trix nodded scornfully at Gerry, Bernard and Kelvin.

'They'd only make things worse. Jack's fairly handy with machinery – though I wouldn't disturb him at the moment,' she added meaningfully.

'I'll do something else.' Ashling returned to her desk, momentarily paralysed by the volume of work on it. She decided to press on with her list of the hundred most sexy, interesting, talented Irish people. Everyone from DJs to hairdressers to actors to journalists. And as quick as Ashling was coming up with names, Trix was arranging for Lisa to have breakfast, lunch, afternoon tea or dinner with them – Lisa was on a crash-course to infiltrate the movers and shakers of Irish society.

'After all those meals you'll be the size of a house,' Trix laughed.

Lisa smiled scornfully. Just because you ordered food didn't mean you had to eat it.

The office hummed with work until Jack's office door opened and Mai exited at high speed. Instantly, everyone jerked their heads up in antic-ipation, and they weren't disappointed. Mai made a violent attempt to slam the exit door behind her, but it was wedged permanently open, so she had to satisfy herself with giving it an angry kick.

Seconds later, Jack came out, also going at high speed. His eyes were dark, his face was like thunder and his long legs were gaining fast on Mai. But halfway through the office he seemed to come to his senses and slowed down. 'Ah, fuck it,' he muttered, and banged his fist down on the photocopier. There was a whirring noise, then a click, then page after page began to flop out of the machine. The photocopier was working again!

'We have the technology! Jack Devine saves the day,' Ashling declared and started to clap. The others followed suit. Jack glared around at them as the entire office applauded, and then, to everyone's surprise, he began to laugh. Instantly, he looked like a different person – younger and nicer.

'This is madness,' he muttered.

Ashling quite agreed.

Jack hovered uncertainly. Should he follow Mai or . . . Then, on Ashling's desk, he saw a pack of Marlboro, a cigarette extended from the box. The office was technically non-smoking but, by general consensus, everyone smoked. Except for Boring Bernard who surrounded himself with Thank You For Not Smoking signs. He'd even got himself a little fan.

With a raise of his eyebrows, Jack indicated a silent 'Can I?' and extracted the cigarette with his lips. Striking a match, he lit up, extinguished the match with a firm flick of his hand, then inhaled deeply.

Ashling followed all of his movements, repulsed yet unable to look away.

'Looks like I picked the wrong girl to quit smoking.' Jack trailed back to his office.

'I need your help, girls,' Dervla O'Donnell boomed, distracting everyone. She leapt up from *Hibernian Bride*'s Autumn fashion spread, her large-is-lovely silk-knit three-piece swishing, as she began pacing. 'What will the well-dressed wedding guest be wearing in Autumn 2000? What's hot, what's happening, what's now?'

'Well, I see *chins* are definitely in, dear,' Lisa twinkled, and with a tilt of her head, indicated Dervla's plenitude of chinnage.

A gasp of shock from the office segued seamlessly into laughter, uplifting Lisa. She was proud of her clever, bitchy tongue and the power it gave her.

Dervla stood stock-still in astonishment, as all around her, colleagues laughed, then she too attempted a good-sport's smile.

'Isn't this what it's all about?' With fake heartiness, Jack raised his pint to Kelvin and Gerry. 'No women here to annoy us?'

Kelvin flicked a glance around the pub. The Friday night clientele included a fair few women.

'But none of them are sitting here with *us*, wrecking our heads,' Jack elaborated.

'I wouldn't mind if that Lisa was sitting here,' Kelvin said. 'Jayzus, she's beautiful.'

'Gorgeous,' Gerry agreed, moved to speaking.

'And have you noticed the way that though her eyes stay still, her nipples follow you around the room?' Kelvin remarked.

Both Gerry and Jack looked slightly taken aback by this.

'Mercedes is pretty tasty too,' Kelvin enthused.

'She hasn't got much to say for herself, though,' Gerry said, in an open-and-shut case of the kettle calling the pot black.

Kelvin grinned at Gerry. 'It's not her conversational skills I'm interested in.'

They sniggered and nudged in dirty approval.

'Pass us the ashtray, Kelvin,' Jack interrupted. As Kelvin obliged, Jack chortled miserably, 'The last time I said that to someone they turned around and said, "You've ruined my life, you bastard."'

Gerry and Kelvin shifted uncomfortably. Jack was destroying the Friday-night feel-good factor.

'Leave it alone,' Kelvin advised, then made a valiant attempt to steer things in the right direction. 'Isn't Ashling a dote?'

'Lovely. Like a nice kid sister,' Gerry agreed.

'And a good-looking girl, too,' Kelvin added generously. 'Just not a stunner like Lisa or Mercedes.'

A small eel of discomfort squirmed in Jack – Ashling made him feel funny. Something like shame, or perhaps it was irritation.

'I'm only *saying*,' Jack returned to more pleasant things, 'isn't it nice not having any women here? So if I remark that it's a lovely sunny evening, no one will turn around and say "Get out you loser, I'm sorry I ever met you."'

With an exaggerated sigh, Kelvin gave in. 'So it's all off with Mai again?'

Jack nodded.

'Would you not just give up on it?'

'You're always fighting,' Gerry threw in his tuppenny's worth.

'She drives me wild,' Jack insisted, in frustration. 'You don't know what it's like!'

''Course I do, I'm married,' Gerry said.

'No! I don't mean like that –'

'Love 'em and leave 'em,' Kelvin interrupted with a laddish leer. 'That's my motto. Or rather, *Not* love 'em and leave 'em.'

And that was quite enough about emotions, Kelvin decided.

To think how glad they'd all been when Jack had first started squiring Mai! It had been over a year since Dee, his long-term girlfriend, had abruptly left him, and it was good to see him back in the game. Or so they'd thought. But after the honeymoon period had worn off – which took about four days – Jack seemed almost as unhappy with Mai as he had been in the aftermath of Dee's departure.

To keep Jack off the subject of women, Kelvin asked, 'How's the latest ruckus with the unions at the television station?'

'Sorted,' Jack growled. 'Until the next time.'

'Jayzus, rather you than me.' Kelvin knew that Jack was constantly walking a tightrope between the demands of management, the demands of the

119

unions and the demands of the advertisers. No wonder he was always stressed.

'And viewing figures are up,' Gerry said.

'Are they?' Kelvin exclaimed, not terribly interested. 'Fair fucks to you, Jack.' He turned to Gerry. 'It's your round. Buy our glorious leader a drink.'

Cars, Kelvin decided. *That's* what they'd talk about next.

Lisa was the last one out of the office on Friday evening. The streets were thronged and the setting sun was dazzling. Picking her way through the good-humoured revellers spilling out of pubs on to the streets of Temple Bar, she headed determinedly for Christchurch. But memories tugged faintly at her. Of other sunny Friday evenings. Sitting with Oliver by the river in Hammersmith, sipping cider, peaceful and free after a hard week.

Had that really been her?

She pushed Oliver away and tried to think of something else, then sticking out from under a pub table she saw a pair of white shins, crisscrossed with red lines. Trix!

At lunchtime, in honour of the blue sky and above-freezing temperature, Trix had shaved her legs in the ladies' and bared them, bloodied but unbowed, to the world. She'd nearly cleared Ashling out of plasters.

Lisa hurried on, pretending she hadn't seen Ashling waving to her to come and join them.

The good weather had obviously put Ashling in

mind of defoliating her legs too, because Lisa had overheard her booking a lunchtime leg-wax. Oddly enough, though, she hadn't tried to swing a freebie. It seemed she was just going to go in as a civilian and pay the going rate. But if Ashling didn't have the nous to use – OK *abuse* – her position as assistant editor of a women's magazine, it wasn't Lisa's job to wise her up.

There had never been much chance that Lisa would be friendly to someone as ordinary as Ashling. But because Ashling had caught her crying and treated her as though she needed tenderness, Lisa disliked her immensely.

She disliked Mercedes too, for totally different reasons. Mercedes, silent and self-possessed, rattled her.

When Ashling had hung up from booking her leg-wax, Lisa had made the whole office laugh by saying, 'Now your turn to book one, Mercedes. Unless, of course, gorilla legs are in this summer.'

Mercedes shot Lisa a black look, so dark that Lisa held back what she'd been about to say next, which was that with her colouring, Mercedes was an ideal candidate for sideburns and a moustache.

'Hey, it's a joke.' Lisa smiled bitchily at Mercedes, compounding the damage by making her seem like a bad sport as well as hairy.

To piss off both Ashling and Mercedes, Lisa was extra-sweet to Trix. It was a power-generating technique she'd used in the past – divide and conquer. Select a pet, shower them with intimacy, then suddenly abandon them in favour of another. Rotating the position engendered love and fear. Except for Jack, she was going to be nice to him all the time. He was the only thing in her life that was giving her hope. She'd discreetly studied how he responded to her and it was different to the way he treated the other female staff. He was amused by Trix, polite to Mercedes and seemed to positively dislike Ashling. But to Lisa he was respectful and solicitous. Admiring, even. And so he should be. She'd been getting up even earlier than usual this week, taking extra care with her already pampered appearance, expertly applying gossamer-thin layer after gossamer-thin layer of fake tan to give her a golden glow.

Lisa was clear-eyed about her looks. In her natural state – not that she'd been in that for a very long time – she was a pretty enough girl. But with huge amounts of effort she knew she'd upgraded herself from attractive to fabulous. As well as the usual attention to hair, nails, skin, make-up and clothes, she popped huge amounts of vitamins, drank sixteen glasses of water a day, only snorted cocaine on special occasions and every six months had a botulism injection in her forehead – it paralysed the muscles and gave a lovely wrinkle-free appearance. For the past ten years she'd been constantly hungry. So hungry that she barely noticed it now. Sometimes she dreamt about eating a three-course meal, but people do the oddest things in dreams!

Despite her confidence in her looks, Lisa had to admit that Jack's girlfriend had come as a bit of a shock. Lisa had blithely assumed that she was being pitted against an Irish girl, which would be a cake-walk. But she wasn't too discouraged. Tearing Jack away from his passionate, exotic girlfriend was currently one of the least taxing aspects of her life.

Finding somewhere to live was much more of a challenge. All week, after work, she'd been viewing places, and nothing remotely suitable had come along yet. Tonight she was viewing an apartment in Christchurch, which didn't look too bad. Though the rent was expensive, it was in a modern complex and it was walking distance from work. The downside was that it would mean sharing with someone, and it was a while since Lisa had shared with anyone, especially a woman. The owner of the flat was called Joanne.

'It's great living here because you can walk to work,' Joanne enthused. 'Which means you'll save £1.10 each way on the bus-fare.'

Lisa nodded.

'Which is £2.20 a day.'

Lisa nodded again.

'Which is eleven pounds a week.'

Lisa's nod was slightly reluctant this time.

'Which adds up to forty-four pounds a month. Over five hundred pounds a year. Now, the rent. I need a month's deposit, two months paid in advance, and a two-hundred-pound deposit in case you disappear leaving a large phone bill.'

'But –'

'And what usually happens is that you'd give me thirty pounds a week towards groceries. Milk, bread, butter, that kind of thing.'

'I don't drink milk –'

'But for your tea!'

'I don't drink tea. Or eat bread. I never touch butter.' Lisa put a hand on her slender hip and looked at Joanne's rather larger one. 'Besides, how many pints of milk can you buy for thirty pounds? You must take me for an idiot.'

Back on the street, Lisa felt wretched. She missed London so badly. She hated being here and having to go through this. She had a perfectly good flat of her own in Ladbroke Grove. She'd give anything to be there.

Yet another shock-wave of exhaustion and displacement hit. In London she was inextricably woven into the fabric of fashionable life, but she knew nobody here. And she didn't want to. She found them all so irritating. No one turned up on time for anything in this lousy country and one person even had the cheek to say, 'The man who made time made plenty of it.' As a magazine person it was *her* prerogative to be late.

Desolately, she trailed back to her horrid little hotel, wishing Trix had been able to fix up a dinner with someone semi-famous for this evening.

She hated having free time, her ability to process it had atrophied. Though it hadn't been that way for ever – she'd always grafted hard and been

124

ambitious, but once upon a time there had been something *more*. Before the constant looking over her shoulder at the hordes of younger, smarter, tougher, more ambitious girls swarming up behind her had distilled her life to a focused treadmill.

She had a few more flats and houses to look at this weekend – the time would pass fast enough. And tomorrow she was show-casing a couple of hairdressers, getting her colour done in one and having her hair cut in another. The trick was to have a few that were cravenly obligated to you, so that if one couldn't squeeze you in for an emergency blow-dry, another could.

She'd made a bargain with herself. She'd give herself a year to make a rip-roaring success of this joke of a magazine, then surely the powers that be in Randolph Media would recognize her contribution and reward it. Maybe . . .

After three speedy post-work drinks, Ashling got up to leave, but Trix implored her to stay out.

'C'mon, let's get twisted and bond by trashing everyone we work with!'

'I can't.'

'You *can*,' Trix urged earnestly. 'All you have to do is try.'

'That's not what I mean.' But Trix had a point. While Ashling certainly had bitchy *thoughts*, she rarely gave vent to them because she had an edgy suspicion that what goes around comes around. No point trying to explain that to Trix, though, she'd laugh her head off. 'I mean I'm going to see my friend Clodagh.'

'Get her to come here.'

'She can't. She's got two kids and her husband's in Belfast.'

Only then would Trix relinquish her.

Ashling jostled through the Friday-night throng and hailed a taxi. Fifteen minutes later she arrived at Clodagh's, for pizza, wine and a bitching session about Dylan.

'I hate when he goes away to these bloody dinners and conferences,' Clodagh exclaimed. 'And he goes to far too many for my liking.'

This hung in the air until Ashling said anxiously, 'You don't think he's . . . *up* to something?'

'No!' Clodagh chuckled. 'I didn't mean that. I just mean I envy his, his . . . freedom. I'm stuck here with the pair of them while he's in some fancy hotel getting an uninterrupted night's sleep and a bit of privacy. What wouldn't I give . . .' She trailed off wistfully.

Later on in bed, after she'd nervously locked doors and windows, Clodagh found herself thinking about what Ashling had said about Dylan being *up* to something. He wouldn't, would he? Have an affair? Or the occasional anonymous, away-from-home shag? Fast, furious and faceless? No, she knew he wouldn't. Apart from anything else, she'd kill him.

But in a strange little way, the thought of Dylan

having sex with someone else turned her on. She thought about it some more, shuffling through a few familiar fantasies. Would they do it like she and Dylan did? Or would it be more inventive? Wilder? Faster? More passionate? As she visualized the porn-movie scenarios, her breathing quickened, and when she was ready she gave herself a couple of quick, intense orgasms. Then fell into a deeply contented sleep until she was woken by Molly needing to do a wee-wee.

CHAPTER 12

Ashling spent all Saturday afternoon traipsing around the shops, looking for a smart, sexy suit for work. What she actually wanted, though she was only dimly aware of it, was to look like Lisa. Perhaps then she'd feel deserving of her new job and the anxiety that dogged her might lift. But no matter what she tried on, Lisa's lacquered *élan* eluded her. As closing time loomed, she made a couple of desperation purchases and staggered home, exhausted and dissatisfied.

The boy wasn't actually in her doorway, he was crouched beside it on his orange blanket. It was the first time Ashling had seen him awake. Some passers-by threw him a coin, some more threw him a look that was a mix of disgust and fear, but most people genuinely didn't see him. They had airbrushed him out of their reality.

She had to pass within inches of him to get to her front-door and was uncomfortably unsure of what the correct etiquette was, but felt she should say something. After all, they were neighbours.

'Um, hi,' she grunted, her eyes sliding quickly over his.

'Hiya,' he grinned up at her. He was missing a front tooth.

As she hurtled away from him, he nodded at her glossy shopping bag. 'Did you get anything nice?'

She froze, halfway between him and her door, desperate to escape. 'Ah, not really. Just a couple of things for work, you know.'

She wanted to cut her tongue out – how *would* he know?

'What's that they say?' He squinted his eyes in thought. 'Don't dress for the job you have, dress for the job you want. Is that right?'

Ashling was too mired in embarrassment to focus. 'Would you . . . ?' She shrugged her rucksack off her shoulder, her progress to her purse impeded by the large, glossy bag strewn across her. 'Would you like . . . ?'

She gave him a pound, which he accepted with a gracious inclination of his head. Flushed with shame at the disparity between what she'd given him and what she'd just spent on a shirt and a handbag she didn't even need, she thumped angrily up the stairs. I work hard for my money, she fumed. Extremely hard, she amended, thinking of the week she'd just had. And I haven't bought anything in ages. And it's all on credit anyway. And it's not *my* fault he's an alcoholic or a heroin addict. Although, in fairness, she hadn't smelt alcohol from him and he hadn't seemed out of it on anything.

Safe in her flat, with the door slammed protectively behind her, she exhaled. There but for the grace of God go I, she thought. I could have ended up on the streets. And then she scolded herself for such melodrama. Things had never been that bad.

She flung her bags on the table and her shoes on the floor, wrecked after her day. And now she was expected to put on her party clothes and go out with Joy. She'd love not to. Being a thirty-something was like experiencing adolescence in reverse. Her body was changing and often she was struck by strange, sometimes shameful urges. Like wanting to stay in on her own on a Saturday night, with only a video and a tub of Ben and Jerry's for company.

'But you'll never meet a man if you don't go out,' Joy regularly complained.

'I do go out. Anyway, I've got Ben and Jerry. They're the only men I need.'

But tonight she *had* to go out. For the first issue of *Colleen*, she and Joy were going to a salsa club to report on the chances of meeting men there. She'd never had to do anything of the sort for *Woman's Place* and there were times, like right now, when she dearly missed her old job. Not just because she'd never had to give up a Saturday night for her old job. But because she could have done her stuff in *Woman's Place* in her sleep while her duties in *Colleen* still weren't entirely clear. She feared she could be told to do *anything* and her stomach was twisted into a knot as she waited to be told to do something that she wasn't able to. Ashling liked certainty and the only thing certain about working at *Colleen* was that she hadn't a clue what was coming next.

Nerve-wracking!

Exciting, she corrected. *And* glamorous. And it was a great laugh working with so many new people – in her old job there had only been three other full-time staff. But then again, they'd all been sweethearts. No awkward types like Lisa or Jack Devine. But none as good fun as Trix or Kelvin either, she reminded herself firmly. Now was not the time to go all nostalgic and pathetic.

She stuck a bag of popcorn in the microwave, then flung herself on the couch, watched *Blind Date* and prayed for Joy not to come. She'd been up till six in the morning playing with Half-man-half-badger, perhaps she'd be too unwell to go out.

No chance.

Though she was more fragile than usual.

'I'd like a cup of tea,' she said, when she arrived. 'Plenty of sugar.'

'That bad?'

'I've the shakes. Worth it, though. I'm mad about Half-man-half-badger, Ashling. But he was supposed to ring me today and – oh no, this milk tastes sour. Fuck! I bet I'm pregnant. In nine months' time I'll give birth to a half-baby-half-badger.'

'No,' Ashling said, looking into her cup in which little white flecks were floating. 'I just think the milk is sour.'

Joy flung open the fridge and examined the four cartons of milk within, all of them past their use-by date. 'What are you doing?' she demanded. 'Playing Russian Roulette with the milk? Running a yoghurt factory? And have you eaten?'

Ashling indicated the almost-empty bowl of popcorn.

'You're funny,' Joy said. 'In some ways you're so organized, but in others . . .'

'You can't be good at everything. I'm well balanced.'

'You should take better care of yourself.'

'That's like the dog calling the cat's arse hairy!'

'But you'll get scurvy.'

'I take vitamins. I'm fine. Where's Ted?'

Ashling had barely seen Ted all week. Not only did they work in opposite directions now, so that he no longer gave her a backer to work, but since the owl triumph he'd been sampling his way through the girls who'd expressed interest in him. Though he'd annoyed the shite out of her when he'd been a constant fixture in her flat whining about not having a girlfriend, Ashling missed him and resented his new-found independence.

'You'll see Ted later. We're invited to a party. Architecture students. One of them does a bit of stand-up so some of the comedians should be there. And where there are comedians, Half-man-half-badger is usually to be found!'

'I'm not so sure about the party,' Ashling said cautiously. 'Especially if it's students.'

'We'll see,' Joy said easily – *too* easily. Ashling flicked her a nervous glance. 'I can't believe I'm putting make-up on again. It seems only like minutes since I took it off,' Joy said, curving on lipstick without the aid of a mirror, then turning her lips inwards, blotting them against each other with a panache that Ashling envied. 'Don't forget the camera.'

As they hit the streets, Ashling looked for the homeless boy, but he and his orange blanket were nowhere to be seen.

'Single women and homosexuals.' Joy summed up the fifty-strong crowd in one hawk-eyed sweep. 'A dead loss but as we're here we might as well get drunk. How much expenses have we?'

'Expenses?'

Joy shook her head and sighed.

There was an hour's class before the club began. The instructor, who introduced himself as 'Alberto, from Cuba,' was a fairly nondescript-looking man. Until he started to dance. Sinuous and lithe, graceful and sure, he was suddenly beautiful. Strutting, pointing, swivelling on the ball of his foot, he demonstrated the steps they'd be attempting.

'The state of your man,' Joy complained crossly.

'Ssshhh!'

Ashling loved to dance. Despite her lack of waist she had a great sense of rhythm, so when the joyous, sunshiny trumpet music started again and Alberto instructed, 'Everyone, join me,' she needed no second bidding.

The steps were basic enough. It was the panache with which you did them that mattered, Ashling realized, mesmerized by Alberto's lubricated hips.

Most of the class were lumpish and clumsy – Joy in particular from lack of sleep and a hangover – and Alberto seemed genuinely distressed by how atrocious everyone was. Ashling, however, picked up the moves smoothly.

'Wasn't this a fantastic idea?' she declared to Joy, her eyes shining.

'Feck off.'

'Smile for the camera! And look as if you're dancing.'

Joy did a couple of club-footed steps while Ashling snapped, then Joy took over the camera.

'Try and photo some men for the article,' Ashling hissed at her.

After the class, the club began properly. Experienced salsa and merengue dancers began to flood in, the women in short, flared skirts and high T-bar shoes, the faces of the men impassive as casually, expertly they twirled and manoeuvred women to the loud upbeat rhythms.

'I can't believe this is Ireland,' Ashling said to Joy. 'Irish men! Dancing! And not just the twelve-pints-of-Guinness shuffle, either.'

'Real men don't dance,' Joy was keen to leave.

'These ones do.'

Salsa was very much a contact sport. Ashling homed in on one couple. They danced right up close, as if their bodies had been velcroed together.

Below the waist their limbs were a blur, but above the waist they barely moved. Groin to groin, chest to chest, his left hand held her right one above their heads, the soft skin of their inner arms joined along the full length. His right hand was firmly on the small of her back. All the while their feet perfectly performed the complicated steps, the man gazed into the woman's eyes. Their heads remained still.

Ashling had never seen anything so erotic in all her life. A bud of yearning yawned open within her and it felt like pain. Stirred by a nameless need, she watched the dancers, her mouth bitter-sweet with longing. But for what? The hard, sweet heat of a man's body?

Perhaps . . .

Jolting her from her introspection, a man asked Ashling to dance. He was short and going bald.

'I've only had one lesson,' she offered, hoping to get out of it.

But he assured her he wouldn't do anything too complicated – and then they were off! It was like driving a car, Ashling decided. One minute you're static, the next you're moving smoothly, all because of what you're doing with your feet. Forward and back, they stepped and swayed, he twirled her away from him, she returned smoothly and without missing a beat recommenced the dance, forward and back, dipping and flowing. It gave her some inkling of what it must be like to be able to do it well.

'Well done,' he told her at the end.

'Can we go?' Joy said tersely, when Ashling returned to her seat. 'What a waste of time this was. Not a man in sight. Just one dance with a short-arse slaphead to show for our trouble.'

'Oh go on, please, just for five minutes,' Joy begged. 'I don't know where I stand with Half-man-half-badger and he's bound to be there. Please.'

'Five minutes, I mean it, Joy, that's all I'm staying.'

The party – like most student parties in Dublin – was held in Rathmines, in a four-storey, red-brick Georgian house that had been converted into thirteen tiny oddly shaped flats. It had the obligatory high ceilings, original features, peeling paint and overpowering smell of damp.

The first person Ashling saw when she walked in was the enthusiastic bloke who'd given her the note saying 'Bellez-moi'.

'Shite,' she exhaled.

'What?' Joy hissed, terrified that Ashling had spotted Half-man-half-badger snogging someone else.

'Nothing.'

'There he is!' Joy noticed. Leaning against a wall – a risky business in these gerry-converted flats – was her quarry. She slipped her moorings and was gone. Suddenly alone, Ashling gave Bellez-moi a cheesy, sweaty-apologetic grin. To her great alarm, instead of repelling him, it sent him hurtling towards her.

136

'You never called me,' he declared.

'Mmmm.' She tried another smile, while inching away.

'Why not?'

She opened her mouth to launch into a long list of lies. I lost the piece of paper, I'm deaf and dumb, there was a typhoon in Stephen's Street and the phone lines were down . . .

Unexpectedly, she had it. 'I can't speak French,' she said triumphantly. How about that for a watertight excuse?

He smiled the wistful smile of one who knows when he's not wanted.

'I'm sure you're very nice and everything,' she added hastily, keen not to cause any hurt. 'But I didn't know you and –'

'Well you're never likely to if you don't ring me,' he pointed out, pleasantly.

'Yes, but . . .' Then she hit on something. 'Isn't it more traditional for the man to ask for the woman's number, and for him to phone her?'

'I was trying to be liberated, but right you are then, can I have your number?'

He has freckles, she thought, wondering how to get out of this. She didn't want to give her number to an enthusiastic man with freckles. But he had his pen out and his eyes were keen and warm. She swallowed away the rage of being put in such a spot. Pushed it down, buried it. 'Six, seven, seven, four, three, two –'

She wavered over the final digit. Should she say

'Two' when it was actually 'Three'? The moment took for ever.

'Three,' she said, in a sigh.

'And your name?' His smile flashed bright in the darkened room.

'Ashling.'

What was his name? Something silly. Cupid, or something.

'. . . Valentine,' he said. 'Marcus Valentine. I'll call you.'

This was one instance, Ashling thought angrily, when 'I'll call you' meant just that. Why did the awful ones always ring and the good-looking ones never?

Through the crowds she spotted Joy conversing energetically with Half-man-half-badger. Good, now she could go home. 'See ya,' she said to Marcus.

She was too old for this studenty-type shite. On the way out she tripped over Ted, talking to a gamine redhead. He was smiling a smile Ashling didn't recognize: no longer a panting, please-love-me rictus, but something more contained. Even his body language had altered. Instead of bending forward, he tilted away slightly, so the girl had to lean towards him.

'Howya.' Ashling greeted him with a punch to his upper arm.

'Ashling!' Excitedly he tried to trip her up.

Greetings having been exchanged, he turned to the little redhead. 'Suzie, this is my friend, Ashling.'

Suzie gave a suspicious nod.

'Have you a drink?' Ted asked Ashling.

'No, I'm not staying. I'm knackered.'

Indecision zigzagged across Ted's thin face before he surprised everyone by saying, 'Hold on, I'll come with you.'

Outside, in the cool night air, Ashling exclaimed, 'What are you at? She was into you.'

'No point being too eager.'

Ashling felt a pang. She and Ted used to take it in turns to be the walking wounded. His new-found confidence had altered things between them.

'Anyway, she's a comedy groupie,' he said. 'I'll see her again.'

You couldn't get a taxi in Dublin for love nor money on a Saturday night. Those who lived in distant suburbs tried to beat the four-hour queues by walking out of town in the hope of flagging a taxi on its way back in. Which meant that on Ted and Ashling's walk home into town, there was a constant stream of Night-of-the-Living-Dead-style drunken zombies lurching in their dozens towards them.

'So how's the job going?' Ted asked, side-stepping another zigzagging reveller.

Ashling hesitated. 'Great in lots of ways. It's glamorous. Sometimes. When I'm not cross-eyed from photocopying press releases, that is.'

'Have you found out why the Mercedes girlie is called after a car?'

'Her mother is Spanish. Actually, she's very nice,

once you talk to her,' Ashling elaborated. 'She's just quiet and extremely posh. Married to a rich fella, hangs around with a horsey crowd and I get the impression her job is only a hobby. But she's nice.'

'And how are you getting on with the boss-man who doesn't like you?'

Ashling's stomach tightened. 'He still doesn't like me. Yesterday he called me Little Miss Fix-it just because I offered him two Anadins for his headache.'

'The bollocks. Maybe you were enemies in a former life and that's why you don't get on in this one.'

'Do you think so?' Ashling exclaimed. Then took one look at Ted's grinning face. 'Oh, you don't, I see. Oh, ye of little faith. The next time you want your future foretold, don't come to me.'

'Sorry, Ashling.' He flung his arm confidently around her neck. 'Well, this will cheer you up – I'm doing a gig at the River Club next Saturday night. Will you come?'

'Didn't I just say that I'm not foretelling your future? You'll have to wait and see.'

CHAPTER 13

On Monday morning Craig followed his mother around the room, whining, 'Why are you tidying?' Clodagh snatched up a snarl of tights and flung them in the linen basket, then launched herself on the mountain of clothes on the bedroom chair, her arms a blur as she tossed jumpers into drawers, dressing gowns on to pegs and – after a short hesitation where everything became just too much – everything else under the bed.

'Is Grandma Kelly coming?' Craig pestered.

He fully expected the answer to be in the affirmative – this sort of frenzy was usually followed a short time afterwards by a visit from Dylan's mother.

'Nope.'

Craig ran behind Clodagh, as she Tasmanian-devilled into the *en suite* bathroom, and noisily jostled a toilet-brush around the bowl.

'Why?' he demanded.

'Because,' she hissed, irritated at the stupidity of the question, 'because the cleaning lady is coming.

'Molly, hurry,' Clodagh roared in the direction

of Molly's elephant-friezed room. 'Flor will be here any minute.'

The thought of staying in the house while Flor did her stuff was beyond the pale. Not just because all Flor wanted to talk about was her womb, but because Flor's very presence made Clodagh feel horribly middle-class and exploitative. She was young and able-bodied – having her house cleaned by a fifty-eight-year-old woman with problems up the frock was indefensible.

She'd tried staying in for a couple of Flor's visits, but ended up feeling like an outlaw in her own home. It seemed that every room she went into, Flor arrived seconds later, girt about with vacuum cleaners and varicose veins, and Clodagh never quite knew what to say.

'Ah . . .' followed by an uneasy smile. 'I'll just, er, move, ah, out of your way.'

'Not at all,' Flor would insist. 'Stay right where you are.'

Only once had Clodagh taken Flor at her word, and sat flicking through an interiors magazine, pulsing with shame, while Flor huffed and puffed with the Hoover around her feet.

Flor charged five pounds an hour. Guilt compelled Clodagh to pay her six. So uncomfortable did she feel that Clodagh couldn't bear to even see Flor, always making it her business to be well gone before she arrived.

'Molly,' she bellowed, thundering down the stairs. 'Hurry!'

In the kitchen, one eye on the clock, she grabbed her pile of wallpaper samples and scribbled a note to Flor on the back of one. In a couple of strokes she drew a Hoover – an upstanding rectangle with a twirly lead snaking from it. Then she sketched a few squares and drew rainfall coming down on top of them. Next she drew two arrows – one pointing to the pile of shirts on the table, the other pointing to the duster and Mr Sheen next to them.

Now Flor would know that Clodagh wanted her to hoover, to wash the kitchen floor, to iron clothes and to dust and polish.

Anything else? Clodagh did a quick zoom around her head. Next door's cat, that's what. She didn't want Flor letting him in like she did last week. Tiddles Brady had made himself so comfortable he was practically watching telly with the remote control in his paw when she'd got home. And the minute Molly and Craig saw him they fell in love and roared crying when the cat was promptly escorted off the premises. So, speedily drawing a circle for his face, on top of a bigger circle for his body, Clodagh finished the quick portrait of Tiddles by doing his ears and whiskers.

'Get me a red crayon,' she ordered Molly.

Molly duly returned, offering a blunt, yellow pencil and a Banana-in-pyjamas.

'Oh, *I'll* get it. If you want anything done properly, you have to do it yourself.'

Talking angrily to the air, Clodagh rummaged madly through the painting box and found the crayon, then – with no little satisfaction – gouged a big, red X through the cat. Surely Flor would understand that?

Her last drawing done, Clodagh sighed heavily. She'd love a cleaning woman who could read. It had taken her weeks to find out that Flor was illiterate. In the beginning, she used to leave her all kinds of complicated notes, requesting Flor to do specific things like take the washing out of the washing machine when it finished its cycle, or defrost the freezer.

Flor never complied and although Clodagh used to lie awake at night fuming, she was too mortified to take her to task. Despite the problems, she didn't want to lose her. Cleaning women were like gold-dust. Even the crap ones.

Not to mention that Clodagh had no faith in her own ability to command respect in this situation. She had visions of herself trying to berate Flor in a voice that quavered with lack of conviction, 'Now look here, my good woman, this simply won't do.'

In the end she forced Dylan to be late for work one morning so he could have it out with Flor. And, of course, she 'fessed up to Dylan, who was sympathy itself. Dylan had what they called Good People Skills. And, on Dylan's suggestion, they came to their current arrangement where Clodagh drew her instructions to Flor.

Between the guilt and the drawings, it almost seemed easier to do the housework herself.

Almost, but not quite. Despite everything, Clodagh savoured the one morning a week when the pressure was off her. Taking care of the house was like painting the Forth Bridge, only worse. She was never on top of things, and the minute something was done it needed to be done again. No sooner was the kitchen floor mopped – no, wait! *Even while she was mopping it* – they were skidding across it in their shoes, etching stripes of mud through her good work. And her linen basket seemed to be like the refillable pint of mythology. Even after she'd done three loads of washing and to her knowledge laundered every item of clothing in the house, her warm glow of achievement disappeared the instant she went into her bedroom – for the linen basket which had been empty mere minutes previously would be mysteriously once more full to overflowing.

At least she didn't have to worry about the garden. Not because it was nice. On the contrary, it was a muddy shambles, the grass flattened and sparse due to being overrun by children, and there was a great bald patch beneath the swing. But she was absolved from having to do anything about it until Molly and Craig were grown up. Just as well. She'd heard terrible horror stories about gardeners from hell.

After several false starts – Molly wanted to wear her hat, Craig had to go back in and get his Buzz Lightyear – Clodagh hurriedly piled them both into the Nissan Micra. As soon as she put the key in the ignition, Molly screeched, 'I have to go wee-wee.'

'But you've just gone.' Clodagh's exasperation was heightened by the fear of running into Flor.

'But I have to go again.'

Molly was only recently toilet-trained, and the novelty of her new-found skill hadn't worn off yet.

'Come on, then.' Roughly, Clodagh bundled Molly from her car-seat and hustled her back into the house, turning off the alarm she'd only just set. As predicted, despite much contorting of her face and promises that 'It's coming,' Molly couldn't summon any wee-wee. Back to the car again and away they went.

After she'd dropped Craig at school, Clodagh wasn't sure where to go. Usually on Mondays, she dumped Molly in playgroup and took herself off to the gym for a couple of hours. But not today. Molly had been suspended for a week from playgroup for biting another child, and the gym had no crèche. Clodagh decided to go into town and go around the shops until it was safe to go home. The day was sunny and mother and daughter traipsed slowly up Grafton Street, stopping – at Molly's urging – to stroke a homeless boy's dog, admire a flower stall and dance to a fiddle player. Passers-by smiled indulgently at the beautiful Molly, cute and ludicrous in her pink, furry, deer-stalker hat, attempting to do Riverdance.

As they made their way up the street Clodagh was in a pocket of besottedness, her heart swollen and sore with love. Molly was so funny, with her little sergeant major's strut, marching along with her chest puffed out, wanting to befriend every child she encountered. It wasn't always easy being a mother, Clodagh admitted dreamily. But at times like this she wouldn't change her life for anything.

The paper seller openly admired the short, shapely woman trailing a small girl in her wake.

'*Herald*?' he offered hopefully.

Clodagh looked at it with regret. 'But what would be the point?' She elaborated. 'I haven't had time to read a paper since 1996.'

'Not much profit in buying one so,' the paperman agreed, appreciating the back view of Clodagh as she walked away from him.

She knew he was watching her and it felt surprisingly good. His bold, roguish stare stirred memories of when men used to look at her like that all the time. It felt like a very long time ago, almost as if it had happened to someone else.

But what was she doing? Getting excited because a newspaper seller had given her the glad eye?

You're married, she scolded herself.

Yeah, she answered wryly, *married alive*.

It took a contented hour and a half to reach the Stephen's Green Centre and by then, according to the law of averages, Molly and Clodagh were due a bust-up. Sure enough, when Clodagh wouldn't buy Molly a second ice-cream, Molly promptly threw the mother of all tantrums. She behaved as though she was having an epileptic fit, thrashing about on the floor, banging her head on the tiles, screeching abuse. Clodagh tried to pull her up but Molly wriggled like an octopus. 'I hate you!' she screamed and though Clodagh was ashrivel with embarrassment, she forced herself to speak in a steady voice, assuring Molly that a second ice-cream would give her a stomach-ache and promising that if she didn't get up and behave herself *immediately*, she'd be going to bed early every night for the next week.

Scores of hard-faced mothers passed, laden with children, whom they cuffed and hit on an automatic rota. 'Hey, Jason,' *Ddush!* 'leave Tamara alone.' *Smackkk!* 'Zoe,' *Thump!* 'if I catch you at Brooklyn again I'll fucking kill you.' *Clouttt!* With their scornful looks, the women derided Clodagh's liberal principles. *Give that brat a good belt*, their school-of-hard-knocks' faces sneered. *Going to bed early, my foot. Bate a bit of sense into her, it's the only language they understand.*

Clodagh and Dylan had made a decision never to hit their children. But when Molly started kicking her, while continuing to screech, Clodagh found herself yanking the child off the floor and administering a smart smack to her bare leg. It seemed as if the whole of Dublin gasped. Suddenly all the slab-faced child beaters had melted away, and instead Clodagh was assailed by pair after pair of accusing eyes. Everyone around her looked like they worked for ChildLine.

A wave of crimson shame slapped her in the

148

face. What was she doing, assaulting a defence-less little girl? What was wrong with her?

'Come on.' Hastily she tugged the roaring Molly away, appalled by the mark of her hand on Molly's tender leg. To atone for her guilt, Clodagh immediately bought Molly the ice-cream that had prompted the ructions in the first place, and expected peace for precisely the length of time it took Molly to eat it.

Except the ice-cream started to melt and Clodagh was asked to leave a fabric shop after Molly rubbed her cone carefully along a bolt of curtain muslin, patterning it with a thick white trail. The morning had soured and, wiping a Father Christmas beard of ice-cream from Molly's chin, Clodagh couldn't help feeling that life seemed to have had more of a sparkle to it once, a kind of yellow glow. She'd always rushed forward to greet her future, blithely confident that what it delivered would be good. And it hadn't ever let her down.

Her requests of life had never been overly ambitious and she'd always got what she wanted. On paper everything was perfect – she had two healthy children, a good husband, no money worries. But lately everything felt like unrelenting drudgery. Had done for quite a while, actually. She tried to remember when it had started, and when she couldn't, fear squeezed perspiration through her pores. The thought of this mind-set crystallizing into anything like permanence was terrifying.

By nature she was a happy, uncomplicated person –
this she could see by comparing herself with
poor Ashling who tied herself in knots about
almost everything.

But something had changed. Not so long ago
she was fuelled by anticipation and optimism.
What was different, what had gone wrong?

CHAPTER 14

'Diet Lilt or Purdeys?' Ashling mused. 'I don't know.'

'Well, make your mind up,' Trix urged, her pen poised over her spiral-bound notebook. 'The shop'll be closed if you don't hurry.'

Though the *Colleen* team had been working together less than two weeks, already they had a routine. A shop run was done twice a day, morning and afternoon. This was separate from the lunch run and the hangover-cure run.

'Uh-oh,' Trix observed. 'Here's Heathcliff.'

Jack Devine strode into the office, all tumbled hair and troubled face.

'I just can't make my mind up,' Ashling lamented, agonizing between drinks.

'Of course you can't,' Jack said nastily, without breaking stride. 'After all, you're a *woman!*'

His office door slammed behind him and heads were shaken in sympathy.

'The reunion lunch with Mai obviously wasn't,' Kelvin observed, wagging a beringed finger.

'What a tormented man.' Shauna Griffin looked up from proof-reading this Summer's *Gaelic*

Knitting, her voice trembling. 'So handsome, yet so unreachable, so unhappy.'

Shauna Griffin was a large, fair woman who bore an uncanny resemblance to the Honey Monster. She regularly exceeded the recommended dosage of Mills & Boons.

'Unhappy?' Ashling asked scornfully. 'JD? He's just bad-tempered.'

'That's the first bitchy thing I've ever heard you say about anyone,' Trix exclaimed hoarsely. 'Congratulations. I knew you had it in you! You see what you can achieve when you put your mind to it.'

'Diet Lilt,' Ashling replied drolly. 'And a bag of buttons.'

'White or brown?'

'White.'

'Money.'

Ashling handed over a pound, Trix wrote it all down on her list and moved on to the next person.

'Lisa?' Trix asked, adoringly. 'Anything?'

'Hmmm?' Lisa jumped. She'd been far away. Jack had discovered that she hadn't found anywhere to live yet, so after work he was taking her to see a house that a friend of his wanted to let. She'd been worried that he would get back with Mai over their lunch, but it looked as if her path was clear . . .

'Cigs?' Trix urged. 'Sugar-free gum?'

'Yeah. Cigs.'

The door opened again and Jack emerged,

looking faintly distraught. Trix hopped nimbly back to her desk, and with a practised flick of the wrist opened her drawer, threw her cigarettes in and slammed it shut. Jack roamed amongst the desks and no one would meet his look. Those that could inched and hid their cigarettes behind something. Lisa had a box of Silk Cut open beside her mouse-pad, but though Jack wavered and seemed like he might stop, he sped up again and passed by. Everyone flinched. Then he got to Ashling and halted and the office exhaled silently. Safe, for a while.

Against her will, Ashling's face was pulled up to look at him. Silently he tilted his head at her box of Marlboro. She nodded warily, hating her compliance. He was so unpleasant to her, but she seemed to be the only one he cadged cigarettes from. She obviously had Gobshite stamped on her forehead.

His eyes coolly watching her, he fastened his lips around the filter and, as usual, slowly, smoothly slid the cigarette from its box. Jerkily, she passed him her box of matches, taking care not to touch him. Without moving his eyes from hers, he struck a match, held the flame against the tip, then shook it out. Inclining the cigarette upwards, he pulled deep. 'Thanks,' he murmured.

'When are you going to start buying smokes again?' Trix demanded, now that her own were briefly safe. 'You obviously can't give them up. And it's not fair, you must earn millions more than Ashling but you've been bumming loads of cigarettes off her.'

'Have I?' He looked startled.

'Have I?' He turned his gaze on to Ashling and she seemed to wither away from him in her seat. 'Sorry, I hadn't noticed.'

''s OK,' she mumbled.

Jack disappeared back into his office and Kelvin observed drily, 'Betcha he's inside there *kicking* himself for exploiting the workers by nicking their smokes. Jack Devine, Working-Class Hero.'

'*Wannabe* Working-Class Hero, more like,' Trix scorned.

'How so?' Ashling couldn't hide her curiosity.

'He'd love to be a humble craftsman, and do an honest day's work for an honest day's pay.' Trix's contempt for such modest aspirations was almost tangible.

'Problem was,' Kelvin expounded, 'he was born middle-class and burdened with all kinds of advantages. Like an education. Then he gets an MA in communications. Next,' he lowered his voice ominously, 'he begins to display excellent managerial skills.'

'Fair broke his heart,' Trix sighed. 'I reckon he's riddled with middle-class guilt. That's why he's always offering to fix things. And why he has all those macho hobbies.'

'Which macho hobbies?'

'Well, he goes sailing, that's macho,' Trix offered.

'Not very working-class though, is it? Drinking

pints, now *that's* macho,' said Kelvin. 'And riding sexy half-Vietnamese women,' he added, 'that's very macho too.'

Ashling sidled tentatively up to Lisa. 'Can I ask you something?'

'No, thank you,' Lisa sang, not even looking up from her desk. 'I don't want to come for a drink with you and Trix or your friend Joy or anyone else this evening. Or any evening.'

Everyone sniggered, to Lisa's gratification.

'I wasn't going to ask you that.' An embarrassed liver-coloured patch crawled up Ashling's neck. She'd only been trying to be nice to a stranger in Dublin, but Lisa made it sound like she *fancied* her. 'It's a work-related question. Why don't we have a problem page with a difference?'

'What's the difference, Einstein?'

'We get a psychic to do the anwers, instead of a counsellor.'

Lisa was thoughtful. Not a bad idea. Very zeitgeisty, what with everyone on the hunt for a spiritual element to fix their lives. She believed none of it herself – taking the line that her happiness was very much in her own hands – but that was no reason not to peddle it to the masses. 'Maybe.'

Relief soothed the sting of Lisa's innuendo. In the short time Ashling had been working at *Colleen*, constant anxiety about her lack of ideas had gnawed at her. Then Ted suggested that she think about what *she'd* like from a magazine and suddenly avenues opened up. Anything to do with tarot, reiki, feng shui, affirmations, angels, white witches and spells piqued her interest.

Jack's door opened again and everyone flung themselves protectively on their cigarettes.

'Lisa?' Jack called. 'Can I have a word?'

'Certainly.' Elegantly she got up from her desk, wondering what he wanted to talk to her about. Could it be that he was going to ask her out?

When he instructed her to shut the door her excitement mounted. And instantly disappeared when he said apologetically, 'There's no easy way of saying this.'

He paused, his handsome face shuttered by discomfort.

Lisa said coolly, 'Go on.'

'We're not making the advertising,' he said, baldly. 'Nobody's biting. We're only up to –' He checked the memo on his desk, '– twelve per cent of what we'd projected.'

Lisa twitched with fear. This had never happened before. Though they'd always negotiated off rate-card, designers and cosmetic companies had been falling over themselves to take out full-page ads when she'd been editor of *Femme*. And as everyone in magazines knows, the income generated from selling ads is far in excess of that garnered from cover-price sales. At least it should be. If companies can't be persuaded that a particular publication is the right vehicle in which to adver-tise their product, it goes under. Panic swept up

Lisa in a prickly wave. How would she ever live down the failure of a stillborn magazine?

'It's early days,' she tried.

Reluctantly he had to shake his head. It wasn't, they both knew that. Before *Colleen*'s editorial staff had arrived, Margie had been doing pre-production work for over a month: interested advertisers had had plenty of time to bite. Lisa burned with humiliation. She wanted this man to respect and desire her and instead he was bound to think she was a failure.

'But don't they know . . . ?' she couldn't stop herself from blurting.

'Know what?'

She tried to reformulate and couldn't. 'Know that I'm the editor?'

'Your name carries a lot of weight,' Jack said, tactfully, and when she saw how unpleasant he too was finding this, it soothed the sting. 'But new marketplace, new audience, no track record . . .'

'I thought you said that Margie was a Rottweiler. That she could persuade *God* to place an ad.' When in doubt, blame someone else. A motto that had served Lisa well thus far in her career.

'Margie's great at getting ads from Irish companies,' Jack explained. 'But the London office is handling the international cosmetic and fashion houses.

'Where are we at?' he asked. 'What kind of definite features have we? We need to throw a couple of bones to the London office, for them to show the potential ad-placers.'

Lisa's face was a white mask as she searched around in her head. Definite features! She'd been in this fucking job less than two weeks, thrown in at the deep end, in a strange country. She'd been knocking herself out trying to get a handle on things, and already they wanted to know definite features!

'Just a rough idea,' Jack said, with heartbreaking gentleness. 'Sorry to do this to you.'

'Why don't we all go to the boardroom for a progress meeting?' Lisa suggested, an unresponsive wobbliness about her knees. And to think that everyone thought editing a magazine was glamorous. It was the most terrifying, sleepless-night-inducing job, with no certainty, no respite. Just trying to make the figures every month. And as soon as you'd strained and sweated yourself to the limit to do so, you had to turn around and start all over again. All you were was a glorified salesman. In an attempt at dynamism she swept from Jack's office, but her leg muscles were pulpy and she had a sheen of perspiration above her lip. 'Boardroom, everyone, now!'

All the people who didn't work on *Colleen* sniggered, delighted that they weren't being bollocked.

'Right then.' Lisa played for time by giving a terrifying smile around the boardroom table. 'Perhaps you'd all like to tell Jack and me what you've been doing for the past two weeks. Ashling?'

158

'I've sent out press releases to all the fashion houses and –'

'Press releases?' Lisa asked, sarcastically. 'Is there no *beginning* to your talents?'

Dutiful sniggers issued from Trix, Gerry and Bernard.

'So punters are going to pay £2.50 to read *Colleen*'s press releases? Features, Ashling, I'm talking features! What have you?'

Bewildered by her aggression, Ashling gave her salsa report. As she described the lesson, the teacher and the other pupils Lisa relaxed slightly. This was good. Encouraged by Lisa's nodding, Ashling enthused about the club that had been on after the lesson. 'It was great. Proper old-fashioned dancing with lots of body contact. It was actually very –' For some reason she hesitated over using the word with Jack Devine in the room. He made her so uncomfortable. 'Very *sexy*.'

'And the romance factor?' Lisa asked, cutting to the chase. 'Did you meet any blokes?'

Ashling squirmed. 'I, um, had a dance with a man,' she admitted.

As everyone squealed and fell over themselves to get details, Jack Devine watched her through half-closed eyes.

'It was only a dance,' Ashling protested. 'He didn't even ask me my name.'

'You got photos of the club,' Lisa said. It wasn't a question. At Ashling's nod, she went on,

'We'll do a four-page spread on it. Two thousand words, asap. Make it entertaining.'

Clammy dread flushed down Ashling and she would have given anything to still be working at *Woman's Place*. She couldn't write. Toiling hard at the boring stuff was her forte, she was really, really marvellous at it, and that had been the basis *Colleen* had hired her on. Couldn't Mercedes write it, or one of the freelancers?

'Problem?' Lisa twisted her mouth sarcastically.

'No,' Ashling whispered. But her guts seized in fear as she realized she was in over her head. Joy would have to help her. Or perhaps Ted – he had to draft lots of reports for his job in the Department of Agriculture.

Next on the agenda was Trix's column on an ordinary girl's life. The first one was on the perils of two-timing. On what a pain it was to be in bed with one boyfriend and for another to call to the house and for your mother to let him in. It was funny, outrageous and entirely true.

'Good Lord, Patricia Quinn,' Jack shook his head in amusement. 'I've been living a very sheltered life.'

'I wouldn't recommend it,' Trix exclaimed. 'Him and me Ma in the lounge watching *Heartbeat*, and me trapped in the bedroom with the other one, making excuses not to leave. I aged ten years.'

'And that'd make you what? Twenty-five?' Jack's eyes crinkled with laughter.

Ashling looked at him in a type of sour wonder.

Why is he always so horrible to me? Why isn't he ever amused by me? Just as she concluded that perhaps she simply wasn't amusing, she caught sight of Lisa's face. A lambent determination and hard admiration. She fancies him, Ashling realized, and her stomach flip-flopped. If anyone could lure Jack Devine away from the exotic Mai, Lisa could. What must it be like to have that kind of power?

Then Lisa outlined a 'fun' feature that she'd thought of that very minute. A review of the sexiest hotel beds in Ireland. Graded according to crispness of bed linen, firmness of mattress, size of bonking space, and 'the handcuff factor' – wrought iron bedheads or the limbs of four-poster canopies were ideal.

'God, whatever they're paying you, you're worth it!' Trix overflowed with admiration.

'Mercedes?' Lisa challenged.

'We're going to Donegal on Friday to shoot an exclusive of Frieda Kiely's Winter collection,' Mercedes said smugly. 'We should get a twelve-page spread from it.'

Frieda Kiely was an Irish designer who sold very well abroad. She made wild, gorgeous confections; rough Irish tweed matched with feather-light chiffon; sheeny Ulster linen married with squares of crocheted silk; knitted sleeves that reached the floor. The whole effect was romantic and untamed. A bit *too* untamed for Lisa, actually. If you were paying those kind of prices – not that she ever would, of course – she'd prefer the sleek tailoring of Mr Gucci.

'How about an interview with her?' Lisa suggested.

Mercedes laughed. 'Oh no, she's bonkers. You wouldn't get a word of sense from her.'

'Exactly,' Lisa barked. 'It would make for interesting reading.'

'You don't know what she's like . . .'

'We're showcasing her Winter collection, the least she can do is tell us what she has for breakfast.'

'But –'

'Impress me,' Lisa glinted, in a parody of Calvin Carter. Which might have amused Mercedes had she known what Lisa was doing. But she didn't, so her only option was to flash Lisa a nasty glare.

Jack turned his attention to Gerry. 'How are we getting on with the cover?'

Lisa watched anxiously. Gerry was so quiet that she paid him no attention and consequently she hadn't a clue if he was any good at his job. But Gerry whipped out several cover prototypes – three different girls overlaid with a selection of typefaces and text. The mood he'd created was remarkably sexy and fun.

'Excellent,' Jack enthused.

Then he turned to Lisa. 'And how are we getting on with the celebrity column?'

'Working on it,' Lisa smiled smoothly. Bono and the Corrs were refusing to return her calls.

'But more interestingly, even though we're a women's magazine and our audience will be ninety-five per cent women, I think there's a real case for having a column by a man in *Colleen*.'

Just a minute, Ashling thought, her brain bruising with shock, *that was my idea . . .*

Her mouth worked, making silent 'Oh's and 'Ah's, as Lisa continued blithely, 'There's a stand-up comedian and my sources tell me he's about to go stellar. Thing is he won't do anything for a women's magazine, but I'm going to convince him otherwise.'

You bitch, Ashling thought. *You fucking, fucking bitch.* And didn't anyone else remember? Hadn't anyone else noticed . . . ?

'I . . .' Ashling managed.

'What?' Lisa shot, her golden face terrifying, her grey eyes as hard and cold as marbles.

Ashling, never the best at standing up for herself, mumbled, 'Nothing.'

'It'll be a great coup,' Lisa smiled at Jack.

'Who is he?'

'Marcus Valentine.'

'Are you serious!' Jack was genuinely animated.

'Wh – who?' Ashling asked, shock heaped upon shock.

'Marcus Valentine,' Lisa said impatiently. 'Have you heard of him?'

Ashling nodded mutely. That freckly bloke hadn't looked like a man 'about to go stellar'. Lisa *must* be mistaken. But she seemed so sure of her facts . . .

'He's on on Saturday night in a place called the River Club,' Lisa said. 'You and I will go, Ashling.'

'The River Club?' Ashling had gone nearly as hoarse as Trix. 'Saturday night?'

'Yesss.' Lisa writhed in impatience.

'My friend Ted is on too,' Ashling heard herself say.

Lisa narrowed her eyes appraisingly. 'Oh yeah? Great. We can get a backstage introduction.'

'Good job I haven't any plans for Saturday night,' Ashling heard spilling from her normally meek mouth.

'That's right,' Lisa agreed, coolly. 'Good job.'

As everyone filed out of the boardroom, Lisa turned to Jack. 'Happy?' she challenged.

'You're amazing,' he said, with simple sincerity. 'Quite amazing. Thank you. I'll talk to them in London.'

'How soon will we know?'

'Probably not until next week. Don't worry, you've come up with some great ideas, I suspect it'll be fine. Six o'clock OK with you to go and see the house?'

Raw and raging with injustice, Ashling returned to her desk. She was never going to be nice to that bitch again. To think she'd felt sorry for her, friendless in an unfamiliar country. She'd tried to forgive Lisa her constant bitchy put-downs on the basis that she must be unhappy and frightened. Sometimes to Ashling's shame she'd even half-laughed when Lisa had implied that Dervla was fat, Mercedes hairy, Shauna Griffin in-bred, herself pathetically clingy. But now, Lisa Edwards could die of loneliness for all she, Ashling Kennedy, cared.

Slapped on her George Clooney screen-saver was a yellow Post-it, saying that 'Dillon' had rung. She peeled it off, the screen crackling with static. Surely it wasn't October already? Dylan rang Ashling twice a year. In October and December. To ask what he should get Clodagh for her birthday and for Christmas.

She rang him back.

'Hi Ashling. Time for a quick drink tomorrow after work?'

'Can't. I've got a horrible article to write – maybe later in the week, OK? Why, what's up?'

'Nothing. Maybe. I'll be away at a conference. I'll give you a shout when I get back.'

CHAPTER 15

'Ready, Lisa?' Jack asked, appearing at her desk at ten past six.

Watched silently by their gossip-hungry colleagues, they left the office and got the lift down to the car-park.

The second they were in the car, Jack ripped his tie from his neck and flung it into the back seat, then tore open the first two buttons on his shirt.

'That's better,' he sighed. 'And go for it yourself,' he invited. 'Take off whatever you want –' He broke off the end of the sentence abruptly and a mortified hiatus followed. The heat of his discomfort reached Lisa. 'Sorry,' he muttered grimly. 'That came out wrong.'

Agitatedly he ran his hand through his messy hair, so that the front stood up in silky peaks before flopping back down on to his forehead.

'No problem.' Lisa smiled politely, but the tiny downy hairs on the nape on her neck rose sharply. Shocked and excited at the image of undressing for Jack in his car, feeling those dark eyes on her naked body, the cool of the leather seats against the heat of her skin. Nipping her lip in determination, she vowed to make it happen.

After a suitable recovery period Jack spoke again. 'Let me tell you about the house.' He steered into the Dublin evening traffic. 'The deal is, Brendan is going to work in the States. He's got an eighteen-month contract, which might be extended, but it would mean that you'd have the place for a year and a half, anyway. After that we'd have to see.'

Lisa shifted noncommitally. It didn't matter because she didn't intend to be here in a year and a half's time.

'It's off the South Circular Road, which is very central,' Jack promised. 'It's an area of Dublin that still has a lot of character. It hasn't been yuppified to fuck.'

Lisa's spirits started a slow slither. She was *desperate* to live in a place that had been yuppified to fuck.

'There's a strong sense of community. Lots of families live here.'

Lisa wanted nothing to do with families. She wanted to be surrounded by other singles and to bump into attractive men at her local Tesco Metro buying Kettle Chips and Chardonnay. Dully, she watched Jack's hands on the steering wheel, her churning misery calmed by the confidence with which they glanced off and guided the leather.

He swung the car off the main road on to a smaller road, then on to an even smaller one. 'There it is.' He pointed through the windscreen.

Crouching on the pavement was a little red-brick artisan's cottage. Lisa took one look at it and hated it. She liked modern and fresh, airy and spacious. This house promised cramped, dark rooms, ancient plumbing and an unhygienic free-standing kitchen with a horrid Belfast sink.

Reluctantly she got out of the car.

Jack approached the house, put the key in the lock, pushed the door and stood back to let Lisa pass. He had to duck his head to fit through the doorway.

'Wooden floors,' she remarked, looking around.

'Brendan had them done a couple of months ago,' Jack said proudly.

She forbore from enlightening him that those in the know were completely over wooden floors and that carpets were very much in the driving seat.

'Sitting-room.' Jack led her into a small, ash-floored room containing a red couch, a telly and a cast-iron fireplace. 'That's an original,' Jack nodded at it.

'Mmmmm.' Lisa loathed cast-iron fireplaces – they were so *busy*.

'Kitchen.' Jack trailed her through to the next room. 'Fridge, microwave, washing machine.'

Lisa looked around. At least the cupboards were fitted and the sink was an ordinary aluminium one – she'd rather run the risk of Alzheimer's than live with a Belfast sink. But her satisfaction ebbed when she noticed a scrubbed-pine kitchen table, with four sturdy, rustic chairs! Heartsore, she thought of the wheely turquoise Formica table and four woven-wire chairs in her kitchen in Ladbroke Grove.

'He said something about the boiler playing up. I'll just take a quick look.' Half-disappearing into a cupboard, Jack rolled up his sleeves, displaying brown forearms, with planes of muscles which shifted with the movements of his hands.

'Pass me the spanner from that drawer there, will you?' Jack indicated with his head. Lisa wondered if he was putting on a special macho display in her honour, then she remembered Trix saying he was handy with machinery, and felt her sap rising. She'd always had a weakness for men who were good with their hands, who got smeared in oil and came home at the end of a hard day's fixing things, slowly unzipped their overalls and said meaningfully, 'I bin thinkin' 'bout ya all day, baby.' She also had a weakness for men with six-figure salaries and the power to promote her when she didn't really deserve it. How nice would it be to combine the two?

Jack banged and twiddled with things for a short time longer before saying. 'It looks like the timer is gone. You can get hot water, but you can't pre-set it. I'll sort it out for you. Let's see the bathroom.'

To her surprise the bathroom passed the test. Washing herself needn't necessarily be a lightning raid, with a loofah in one hand and a stopwatch in the other.

'Nice bath,' she admitted.

'Handy little shelf there beside it,' Jack agreed.

'Just big enough for two glasses of wine and a scented candle.' Lisa's swift glance was meaningful. And wasted. To her frustration Jack had marched onwards to the next room.

'Bedroom,' he announced.

It was bigger and brighter than the other rooms, though it was still afflicted with a country-cottage feel. Sprigging on the white curtains, echoed by sprigging on the duvet cover and *way* too much pine. Pine headboard, big pine wardrobe, pine chest of drawers.

Even the mattress is probably made of pine, Lisa thought scornfully.

'It overlooks the garden.' Jack pointed out the window at a smallish square of grass, bordered by shrubs and blooms. Lisa's heart sank. She'd never had a garden before and she didn't want one. She liked flowers as much as the next woman, but only when they came in a big, cellophane bouquet, with an enormous satin ribbon and a card of congratulation. She'd rather die than take up gardening, the accessories were gruesome – elastic-waisted trousers, ridiculous floppy hats, silly baskets and mad Michael Jackson gloves. It was Not A Good Look.

And though she'd told *Femme* readers last July that gardening was the new sex, she hadn't meant a word of it. Sex was sex. Perennially. She missed it.

'He said something about having a herb garden,' Jack said. 'Will we check it out?'

He shot the bolt on the back door, and again had to duck his head on the way out. She followed his straight-backed progress across the little lawn, wryly amused by her own admiration. The birds chattered in the benign evening light, the air was pungent with grass and earth and for a second she didn't hate everything.

'Over here.' He waved her towards a bed and folded his long legs into a crouch. To show willing, Lisa half-heartedly hunkered beside him.

'Mind your suit.' He extended his arm protectively. 'Don't get muck on it.'

'What about yours?'

'I couldn't give a feck about mine.' He turned and gave her an unexpectedly mischievous smile.

Up close she saw he had a tiny chip from one of his front teeth. It added to his maverick air. 'If I get enough grass-stains on it, it'll have to go to the cleaner's and I won't be able to wear it tomorrow . . . And wouldn't that be terrible?' he asked drily.

Lisa laughed and, just for the hell of it, moved her head closer to his. She watched his pupils narrow and dilate through several expressions – confusion to interest to *extreme* interest back to confusion and then blankness. It took far less than a second. Then he turned away and asked, 'Is that coriander or parsley?'

One of his locks of hair was winding around

itself into a curl. Lisa wanted to put her finger in and spring it.

'What do you think?' he asked her again.

Feeling as if they were speaking in code, she looked at the leaf in his hand. 'I don't know.'

Between his thumb and forefinger, he crumbled the leaf, then held it to her face. Intimately close. 'Smell,' he instructed.

Her eyes closed, she inhaled, trying to breathe in his skin.

'Coriander,' she said in triumph. She was rewarded with another smile from him. His mouth went kind of curly at the corners . . .

'And there's basil, chives and thyme,' he indicated. 'You can use them for cooking.'

'Yeah,' she smiled. 'I can sprinkle them on my takeaways.'

There was no point pretending to him. The days of being bonkers-besotted and wanting to cook for her beloved were long gone.

'You don't cook?'

She shook her head. 'I don't have time.'

'That's what I keep hearing,' he said.

'Does, er, Mai cook?'

Big mistake. Jack's face went back to being closed and broody. 'No,' he said shortly. '– At least not for me,' he added. 'Come on, let's go.

'So what do you think of the house?' he asked, once they were back inside.

'I like it,' Lisa lied. It was the best place she'd seen but that wasn't saying much.

'It's got a lot of things going for it,' Jack agreed. 'The rent is decent, the area is nice and you can walk to work.'

'That's right,' Lisa said, with a darkness that puzzled him. 'And I could save myself £1.10 each way.'

'Is that how much? I wouldn't know because I'm usually in the car myself . . .'

'Which is £2.20 a day.'

'I suppose it must be . . .'

'£11 a week. Taken over the course of a lifetime, it comes to quite a lot.' At Jack struggling to maintain an expression of polite interest, Lisa broke through to lightness. Laughing, she told him about her experience with stingy Joanne. Then she told him about the other terrible places she'd viewed. About the man in Lansdown Park who had given his pet snake the freedom of the living-room, the house in Ballsbridge so untidy it looked as if it had just been burgled.

'Well, you can move in here straight away,' Jack offered.

He stood up and began the awkward jingling of change in his pockets that Lisa recognized of old. It was what men did as they tried to pluck up the courage to ask her out for a drink. She could see the struggle in his eyes and his body was coiled as if he was about to launch into something.

Get on with it, she urged silently.

Then his eyes cleared and all tension seemed to

fall away. 'I'll drop you back to your hotel now,' he said.

Lisa understood. She sensed that he was attracted to her and she also sensed his reservations. Not only did they work together, but he was involved with someone else. No matter. She'd work her mojo on him and overcome his objections. She'd enjoy it – making Jack fall for her would take her mind off all her grief.

'Thank you for finding me somewhere to live.' She smiled sweetly at Jack.

'It's a pleasure,' Jack replied. 'And don't hesitate to ask for whatever you need. I'll do everything I can to make your move to Ireland easier.'

'Thanks.' She flicked him another flirty little smile.

'You're far too busy and too important to *Colleen* to waste your time viewing flats.'

Oh.

Curled on a chair, Lisa lit a fag and stared out of the hotel window on to Harcourt Street. She was bothered by mild guilt. So mild it was barely there, but the fact that it existed at all was worthy of comment. It was that bloody Ashling. She'd been so pathetically surprised when Lisa had nicked her idea.

Well, tough, that's the way it goes. That's why Lisa was an editor and Ashling a dogsbody. And Lisa had been terrified, absolutely craven when Jack had told her the advertising situation. Fear always made her treacherous and ruthless.

At the moment the initial bowel-clenching terror had somewhat abated. Her brand of pushy optimism meant she was encapsulated in a bubble of hope where it seemed reasonably possible to generate all the advertising that was needed. Nevertheless, the fact was that Lisa's ass was the one on the line. If the magazine bombed, Ashling's life wasn't over and Lisa's was, simple as that. OK, everyone thought she was a bitch, but they had no conception of the pressure she was under.

With a long sigh, Lisa exhaled a plume of smoke – the memory of Ashling's shocked face needled her, made her feel mildly shitty.

She'd always been able to control her emotions before. It had been easy to subjugate them to the greater good, that of the job. She'd better regain her grip.

CHAPTER 16

Daily, invitations to press launches arrived in the post – everything from new lines in eye-shadow to openings of shops – and Lisa and Mercedes ruthlessly shared them out between them. Lisa, as editor, got first refusal. But Mercedes, as fashion and beauty editor, had to be allowed to go to a good few too. Ashling, Cinderella-like, stayed behind to mind the shop and Trix was way too far down the feeding chain ever to stand a chance of going.

'What happens at a publicity do?' Trix asked Lisa.

'You stand around with a bunch of other journalists and a few celebrities,' Lisa said. 'You talk to anyone important, you listen to the presentation.'

'Tell me about this one you're going to today.'

A shop called Morocco was opening its first Irish branch. Lisa couldn't have cared less, it had been open for years in London, but the Irish franchise holder was treating it as a big deal. Tara Palmer Tompkinson was flying over from London for the launch, which was being held in the Royalton-inspired splendour of the Fitzwilliam hotel.

'Will they have food?' Trix asked.

'There's usually something. Canapés. Champagne.'

In fact, Lisa dearly hoped there would be food because she'd started a new eating plan – instead of the Seven Dwarves diet she'd moved on to the Publicity diet. She could eat and drink what she liked, *but only at publicity events*. Lisa knew the importance of being thin, but she refused to be a traditional diet slave. Instead she incorporated unusual limitations and rewards into her relationship with food, always keeping the challenge fresh and interesting.

'Champagne!' Excitement made Trix Don-Corleone-hoarse.

'That's if they're not a low-rent outfit, and if they are they don't get a plug in the mag. Then you get your goody bag and leave.'

'A *goody* bag!' Trix lit up at the mention of something free. Something that she didn't have to go to the trouble of stealing. 'What kind of goody bag?'

'Depends.' Lisa pouted jadedly. 'With a cosmetic company you usually get a selection of the new season's make-up.'

Trix squeaked with delight.

'With a shop like this, perhaps a bag –'

'A bag!' She hadn't had a free bag in *years*, not since they'd started electronically tagging them.

'Or a top.'

'Oh my God!' Trix jigged in excitement. 'You're so lucky!'

177

After a long, thoughtful pause, Trix suggested over-innocently, 'You know, you should really take Ashling along with you.' The pecking order was such that there was no chance Trix would ever be allowed to go until Ashling was. 'She's your deputy editor. She should know what the drill is if you ever get sick.'

'But . . .' Mercedes' smooth olive face was anxious at the suggestion of someone else muscling in on such sacred ground. There were only so many free lipsticks to go round.

Mercedes' palpable alarm coupled with the residue of guilt around Ashling made Lisa's decision easy. 'Good idea, Trix. OK, Ashling, you can ride shotgun with me this afternoon. That is,' she added disingenuously, 'if you'd like to come.'

Ashling had always been bad at holding a grudge. Especially when there was free stuff involved. 'Would I like to come?' She disappointed herself by exclaiming, 'I'd *love* to come.'

Lisa had lunch at the Clarence with a bestselling author whom she was trying to persuade to write a regular column. It was a success. Not only did the woman agree to do the column for a knockdown fee in exchange for regular plugs for her books, but Lisa escaped the lunch almost unscathed. Despite swirling her food energetically around her plate, all she ate was half a cherry tomato and a forkful of corn-fed chicken.

She returned to work triumphant and was

trawling through her mail when Ashling showed up beside her desk, with her bag and jacket.

'Lisa,' Ashling said anxiously. 'It's two-thirty and the invite is for three. Should we go?'

Lisa laughed in sardonic surprise. 'Rule number one – never be on time. Everyone knows that! You're too important.'

'Am I?'

'Pretend.' Lisa returned to her pile of press releases. But after a while she found herself looking up and saw that Ashling's avid eyes were fastened on her.

'For crying out loud!' Lisa exclaimed, bitterly regretting ever inviting Ashling.

'Sorry. I'm just afraid everything will be gone.'

'What everything?'

'The canapés, the goody bags.'

'I'm not leaving until three, and don't ask me again.'

At three-fifteen, Lisa reached under her desk for her Miu Miu tote, and said to a quivering Ashling, 'Come on, then!'

The taxi journey through the traffic-thronged streets took so long that even Lisa began to worry that all the canapés and goody bags would be gone.

'What now?' she demanded irritably, as a policeman thrust his meaty paw at them, indicating that they should stop.

'Ducks,' the driver said shortly.

As Lisa wondered if 'ducks' was a Dublin

swearword along the lines of 'feck', Ashling exclaimed, 'Oh, look, ducks!'

You what! Lisa wondered, then before her startled eyes a mother duck strutted across the road, trailing six ducklings in a line behind her. Two policemen were holding up both directions of traffic to guarantee a safe passage to the duck family. She could hardly believe it!

'Happens every year.' Ashling's eyes were alight. 'The ducks hatch on the canal, then when they're big enough, they come down to the lake on Stephen's Green.'

'Hundreds of them. Shags up the traffic entirely. Annoy the shite outta you,' the taxi-driver said fondly.

This fucking city . . . Lisa sighed.

As Lisa and Ashling alighted outside the Fitzwilliam hotel, the day was chilly and blustery, the mini-heatwave of the previous week but a distant memory.

'One leg-wax doesn't make a summer,' Ashling thought sadly, back to wearing trousers again after a long summer skirt had enjoyed a too-brief airing the day before. Then she forgot the weather and ecstatically elbowed Lisa. 'Look! It's your woman, what's-her-name? Tara Palmtree Yokiemedoodle.'

And indeed it *was* Tara Palmtree Yokiemedoodle, parading up and down on the pavement outside the hotel, surrounded by a throng of frantically clicking photographers.

'Givvus a bit of leg there, good girl, Tara,' they urged.

Ashling headed for the road, to walk around the ring of photographers, but Lisa marched determinedly into the thick of them.

'Oi, who's she?' Ashling heard.

Then Lisa gushed, 'Taaaaraaaaa, darling, long time no see,' wrestled Tara into a reluctant air-snog, then swivelled them both to face the cameras. The photographers froze from their incessant clicking, then took in the golden, caramel-haired woman, cheek-to-cheek with Tara, and commenced their clicking with renewed fervour.

'Lisa Edwards, editor-in-chief, *Colleen* magazine,' Lisa moved amongst the photographers, informing them. 'Lisa Edwards. Lisa Edwards. I'm an old friend of Tara's.'

'How do you know Tara Palmtree?' Ashling asked, in awe, when Lisa returned to her on the sidelines, where she'd been completely ignored by the photographers.

'I don't.' Lisa surprised her with a grin. 'But rule number two – never let the truth stand in the way of a good story.'

Lisa swept into the hotel, Ashling trotting behind her. Two handsome young men came forward, greeted them and relieved Ashling of her jacket. But Lisa airily refused to relinquish hers.

'May I remind you of rule number three,' Lisa muttered tetchily, *en route* to the reception room. 'We *never* leave our jacket. You want to give the

181

impression that you're very busy, just popping in for a few minutes, that you've a far more interesting life going on out there.'

'Sorry,' Ashling said humbly. 'I didn't realize.'

Into the party room where a see-through-skinny woman dressed head-to-toe in Morocco's Summer collection established who they were and made them sign a visitors' book.

Lisa scribbled a perfunctory few words, then handed the pen to Ashling who beamed with delight.

'Me too?' she squeaked.

Lisa pursed her lips and shook her head in warning. *Calm down!*

'Sorry,' Ashling whispered, but couldn't help taking great care as she wrote neatly, 'Ashling Kennedy, Assistant Editor, *Colleen* magazine.'

Lisa ran a French-manicured nail down the list of names. 'Rule number four, as you know,' she advised, 'look at the book. See who's here.'

'So we know who to meet.' Ashling understood.

Lisa looked at her as if she was mad. 'No! So we know who to avoid!'

'And who should we avoid?'

With contempt, Lisa surveyed the room, full of liggers from rival magazines. 'Just about everyone.'

But Ashling should know all this – and it had just become clear to Lisa that she hadn't even a grasp of the basics. In high alarm, she whispered, 'Don't tell me you've never been to a publicity bash before? What about when you were with *Woman's Place*?'

'We didn't get many invites,' Ashling apologized. 'Certainly nothing as glamorous as this. I suppose our readership was too old. And when we *did* get invited to the launch of a new colostomy bag or sheltered-housing project or whatever, Sally Healy was nearly always the one who got to go.'

What Ashling didn't add was that Sally Healy was a round, mumsy type, who was friendly to everyone. She had none of Lisa's hard, lacquered rivalry or strange, aggressive rules.

'See him over there –' Awestruck, Ashling indicated a tall, Ken-doll-type man. 'He's Marty Hunter, a television presenter.'

'*Déjà vu*,' Lisa snorted. 'He was at the Bailey's bash yesterday and the MaxMara one on Monday.'

This plunged Ashling into a distressed silence. She'd had high hopes for this do. She'd wanted to shepherd and mind Lisa and prove to her that she needed her. And she'd anticipated that she'd win some much-coveted respect from Lisa by her indispensable insider knowledge on famous Irish people – knowledge that Lisa, as an English woman, couldn't possibly hope to possess. But Lisa was miles ahead of her, already had a handle on the celebrity situation and seemed irritated by Ashling's amateurish attempts to help.

A roaming waitress stopped and thrust a tray at them. The food was Moroccan-themed: couscous, Merguez sausages, lamb canapés. The drink, surprisingly, was vodka. Not very Moroccan, but Lisa didn't care. She ate what she could, but couldn't go berserk, because she was constantly talking to people, Ashling trailing in her wake. Energetically, charmingly, Lisa worked the room like a pro – although it delivered few surprises.

'Same old, same old,' she sighed to Ashling. 'The Irish Liggerati – most of these sad losers would show up at the opening of a can of beans. Which brings me smoothly to rule five: use the fact that you still have your jacket as an excuse to escape. When someone becomes that soupçon *too* boring, you can say you have to go to the cloakroom.'

Wandering around the room were a few doe-eyed models, their unformed, unripe bodies dressed by Morocco. Now and again a PR girl shunted one of them in front of Ashling and Lisa, who were expected to ooh and aah about the clothes. Ashling, hot with embarrassment, did her best, but Lisa barely looked.

'It could be worse,' she confided, after another adolescent jerked and twisted in front of them, then departed. 'At least it's not swimwear. That happened at a sit-down dinner in London – trying to eat my meal while six girls stuck their bums and boobs into my plate. Ugh.'

Then she told Ashling what Ashling was beginning to realize anyway. 'Rule number – what are we up to now? six? – there's no such thing as a free anything. Come to something like this and you have to endure the hard sell. Oh no, there's that creepy bloke from the *Sunday Times*, let's move over here.'

Ashling became more and more diminished by Lisa's encyclopaedic knowledge of almost everyone in the room. She'd been living in Ireland less than two weeks and already it seemed she'd bonded with – and dismissed – most of *Who's Who*.

With her stapled-on smile securely in place, Lisa swivelled discreetly on her Jimmy Choo heel. Had she missed anyone? Then she spotted a pretty young man, squirming uncomfortably in a too-new-looking suit.

'Who's he?' she asked, but Ashling had no idea. 'Let's find out, shall we?'

'How?'

'By asking him.' Lisa seemed amused at Ashling's shock.

Assuming a wide smile and twinkling eyes, Lisa descended on the boy, Ashling tagging behind. Up close he had spots on his youthful chin.

'Lisa Edwards, *Colleen* magazine.' She extended her smooth, tanned hand.

'Shane Dockery.' He ran a miserable finger under his tight shirt collar.

'From Laddz,' Lisa finished for him.

'Have you heard of us?' he exclaimed. No one else at this bash had a clue who he was.

''Course.' Lisa had seen a tiny mention of them in one of the Sunday papers and had jotted down their names, along with any other names that she thought she should know. 'You're the new boy-band. Going to be bigger than Take That ever were.'

'Thanks,' he gulped, with the enthusiasm of the as-yet-unestablished. Perhaps it had been worth getting togged out in these terrible clothes after all.

As they moved away, Lisa murmured, 'See? Just remember, they're more frightened of you than you are of them.'

Ashling nodded thoughtfully and Lisa commended herself on her kind patronage. Helped, probably, by the copious quantities of vodka she was sipping. Speaking of which . . . ? Instantly a waitress appeared at her side.

'Vodka is the new water.' Lisa raised her glass to Ashling.

When Lisa had eaten and drunk her fill, it was time to leave.

'Bye.' Lisa wafted past the stick-insect on the door.

'Thank you,' Ashling smiled. 'The clothes were lovely and I'm sure *Colleen* readers will love them –!' Ashling's sentence ended in a gasp as someone pinched her arm very, very hard. Lisa.

'Thank you for coming.' Stick-insect pressed a plastic-wrapped parcel into Lisa's hands. 'And please accept this little goodwill gesture.'

'Oh, thanks,' Lisa said vaguely, trailing away.

Then one was pressed into Ashling's eager hands. Her face aglow, she dug her nail into the plastic to tear it open. Then gasped anew as someone pinched her arm again.

'Oh, er, yeah, like, thanks.' She tried and failed to sound casual.

'Don't touch it,' Lisa muttered, as they strolled across the lobby to collect Ashling's jacket. 'Don't even look at it. And never, *ever* tell a PR girl that you'll give them coverage. Play hard to get!'

'Rule number seven, I suppose,' Ashling said sulkily.

'That's right.'

After they'd left the hotel, Ashling flicked Lisa an enquiring look, then glanced at her present.

'Not yet!' Lisa insisted.

'When, then?'

'When we get around the corner. But no hurrying!' Lisa upbraided, as Ashling almost started to run.

The minute they were round the corner, Lisa said, 'Now!' And they both tore the plastic off their parcels. It was a T-shirt, with Morocco emblazoned across the front.

'A T-shirt!' Lisa spat in disgust.

'I think it's beautiful,' Ashling said. 'What will you do with yours?'

'Bring it back to the shop. Change it for something decent.'

The following day both the *Irish Times* and the *Evening Herald* ran a front-page picture of the Tara and Lisa clinch.

CHAPTER 17

At quarter to seven on Saturday morning, Clodagh was woken by Molly. Headbutting her.

'Wake up, wake up, wake up,' Molly invited, fractiously. 'Craig is making a cake.'

There were some benefits to having children, Clodagh thought wearily, dragging herself from the bed – for instance, she hadn't had to set an alarm clock for five years.

She was meeting Ashling in town. They were going shopping.

'And I think we should start early,' Ashling had said. 'To miss the crowds.'

'How early?'

'About ten.'

'Ten!'

'Or eleven, if that's too early.'

'Too early? I'll have been awake for several hours by then.'

After she'd cleaned up the cake mess, Clodagh gave Craig a bowl of Rice Krispies, but he wouldn't eat them because she'd poured too much milk into the bowl. So she made him another bowl, this

188

time getting the milk – cereal ratio just right. Then she gave Molly a bowl of Sugar-Puffs. As soon as Craig saw Molly's breakfast, he took violently against his Rice Krispies, declaring that they were poisonous. With much spoon-banging and milk-splashing, he loudly demanded Sugar-Puffs instead. Clodagh wiped a splatter of milk from her cheek, opened her mouth to begin a speech about how he'd made his choice and that he had to learn to live with it, then couldn't be bothered. Instead she picked up his bowl, tipped the contents into the bin and grimly banged the box of Sugar-Puffs down in front of him.

Craig's delight dimmed. He didn't really want them now. Getting them had been too easy, yet not quite right.

As Clodagh tried to get ready for her trip into town, the children obviously sensed she was trying to make good her escape. They were more clingy and demanding than usual and when she got into the shower, they both insisted on accompanying her.

'Remember the days when I was the one who used to get into the shower with you,' Dylan observed wryly when she emerged, trying to dry herself, children hanging on to her.

'Yeees,' she said, nervously. She didn't want him remembering how raunchy their sex-life once used to be. In case he asked for his money back. Or worse still, tried to reactivate things.

'Here, dry her.' She pushed Molly towards him. 'I'm in a hurry.'

As Clodagh reversed her Nissan Micra out of the drive, Molly stood at the front door and bawled, 'I want to go!' with such agony that several of the neighbours rushed to their windows to see who was being murdered.

'So do I!' Craig screeched in harmony. 'Come back, oh Mummy, come back.'

Contrary little bastards, Clodagh thought, as she sped down the road. They spent most of the week telling her that they hated her, that they wanted their daddy, then the minute she tried to have a couple of hours for herself, she suddenly became flavour of the month and immersed in guilt.

At quarter past ten both Ashling and Clodagh turned up outside the Stephen's Green centre. Neither of them apologized for being late. Because they weren't. Not by Irish standards.

'What's wrong with your eye?' Ashling asked. 'You're like your man out of *Clockwork Orange*.'

In alarm, Clodagh scrambled to get a mirror from her bag. One of Molly's Petit Filous fell out.

'Here.' Ashling had beaten her to it with the mirror.

'It's my make-up,' Clodagh realized, surveying herself. 'I've only done one eye. When Craig saw me putting on my slap, he made me do his and I must have just forgotten to finish mine . . . You'd think Dylan would have told me! Does he ever look at me any more?'

At the mention of Dylan, Ashling felt awkward.

190

She was due to meet him on Monday night for the quick drink he'd requested, and for some reason she felt funny about mentioning it to Clodagh. And funny about keeping it from her too. But until she knew what it was about she sensed it was better to keep her mouth shut. Maybe Dylan was planning a surprise holiday for Clodagh – it wouldn't be the first time.

'I have some stuff.' Ashling fished a mascara and eyeliner from her bag.

'Your tardis,' Clodagh laughed. 'Hey! Chanel mascara? I mean, *Chanel*?'

Ashling beamed with embarrassed pride. 'It's my new job, you see. I got it free.'

Just for a moment Clodagh couldn't move. She swallowed and it sounded very loud to her. 'Free? How?'

As Ashling launched into a garbled story of how someone called Mercedes was off in Donegal and how someone else called Lisa had gone to a charity lunch to bond with posh Dublin people and how someone else called Trix looked too like a Spice Girl to be allowed out, so Ashling had to represent *Colleen* at the Chanel Face of Autumn. 'And they gave me a goody bag when I left.'

'That's brilliant,' Clodagh said hollowly. And she looked at Ashling's happy delighted smile and of course it *was* brilliant. But where had all the promise of her own life leaked away to?

'Come on, let's burn plastic,' Ashling urged.

'Where'll we start?'

191

'Jigsaw. My magic lose-half-a-stone-in-an-instant trousers have gone a bit bobbly on me and I'm hoping to replace them . . . Although I don't give much for my chances,' she admitted gloomily.

'Why? Horoscope not good today?' Clodagh teased.

'Actually, smarty-pants, it wasn't bad, but that makes no difference. The minute I find something I like, they rush around and take them off all the hangers. Next thing you know the line is discontinued!'

In shop after shop, as Ashling tried on pair after pair of very disappointing trousers, Clodagh wandered through a parallel universe of clothes. She couldn't imagine wearing any of them.

'Look at how short these dresses are!' she exclaimed, then clutched herself. *Did I just say that?*

'That's good, coming from the woman who once wore a pillowcase as a skirt.'

'*Did* I?'

'Oh, they're not dresses anyway.' Ashling had just noticed what Clodagh had been looking at. 'They're tunics. To wear over trousers.'

'I'm completely out of touch,' Clodagh said forlornly. 'But it happens without you noticing and suddenly what you look for in a garment is how well it hides puke stains . . . Look at the cut of me,' she sighed, indicating her black flares and denim jacket.

Ashling twisted her mouth wryly. Clodagh

mightn't be a fashion queen but she'd still give anything to look like her – her legs short and shapely, her small waist emphasized by her fitted jacket, her long thick hair wound casually on top of her head.

'See that colour green?' Clodagh pounced on a pale-mint top. 'Well, can you imagine that in a blue?'

'Um, yeh,' Ashling lied. She suspected this had something to do with decorating.

'That's the exact colour we're getting the front-room papered in,' Clodagh glowed. 'They're coming on Monday and I can't *wait*.'

'Already? That was quick. It's only a couple of weeks since you first started talking about it.'

'I decided to just go for it, that awful terracotta's been bugging the life out of me, so I told the decorators it was an emergency.'

'I thought the terracotta was beautiful,' Ashling opined. So had Clodagh not so long ago.

'Well, it's not,' Clodagh said firmly, and turned her attention back to clothes, determined to get a handle on them. Eventually she bought a tiny slip-dress from Oasis, so short and see-through that Ashling thought even Trix might baulk at it – and you don't get too many of them to the pound!

'When will you wear it?' Ashling enquired curiously.

'Dunno. Bringing Molly to playgroup, collecting Craig from painting. Look, I just want it, OK?'

Defiantly she paid with a credit card that

declared her to be Mrs Clodagh Kelly. Ashling experienced a pang – and she could only presume she was jealous. Clodagh earned no money of her own, yet she always had plenty. Wouldn't it be lovely to live her life?

Off they set again.

'Oh look at those little dungarees!' Clodagh declared, diving in off the street to a chi-chi children's shop. 'They'd be dotie on Molly. And wouldn't this baseball cap be gorgeous on Craig?'

Only when Clodagh had spent more on each of her children than she had on herself did her guilt abate.

'Will we go for coffee?' Ashling suggested, when the spending frenzy ended.

Clodagh hesitated. 'I'd rather go for a drink.'

'It's only half twelve.'

'I'm sure some places open at ten.'

That hadn't actually been what Ashling had meant, but however.

So while Dubliners basked in unexpected weekend sunshine, drinking double skinny mocha lattés and pretending to be in Los Angeles, Ashling and Clodagh sat in a gloomy, old men's pub, where the rest of the clientele looked like a government health warning against the dangers of the demon drink. Not an unbroken vein between them.

Ashling chattered excitedly about her new job, about the famous people she'd nearly met, about the free T-shirt she got from Morocco, and Clodagh's spirits slid into the bottom of her gin-and-tonic.

'Maybe I should get a job,' she suddenly interrupted. 'I always *meant* to go back to work after Craig.'

'That's right, you did.' Ashling knew Clodagh was vaguely defensive that she wasn't one of those super-women who did a full-time job as well as rearing children.

'But the exhaustion was beyond belief,' Clodagh insisted. 'Whatever you hear about the agony of labour, nothing prepares you for the hell of sleepless nights. I was forever shattered and waking up was like coming round from an anaesthetic. I *couldn't* have held down a job.'

And luckily Dylan's computer business was doing well enough that she didn't have to.

'Do you have time now for a job?' Ashling asked.

'I *am* very busy,' Clodagh acknowledged. 'Apart from a couple of hours when I go to the gym, I never have a moment to myself. Mind you, it's all inconsequential stuff; changing clothes that've been puked on or having to watch Barney video after Barney video . . . Although,' she said, with a glint in her eye, 'I've put an end to Barney.'

'How?'

'I've told Molly that he's dead.'

Ashling roared laughing.

'Told her he'd been knocked down by a lorry,' Clodagh continued grimly.

Ashling's smile faded. 'You didn't . . . really?'

'I did, really,' Clodagh said smartly. 'I'd had quite enough of that big purple fucker and all those awful irritating brats, delivering morals and telling me how to live my life.'

'And was Molly upset?'

'She'll get over it. Shit happens. Am I right?'

'But . . . but . . . she's two and a half.'

'I'm a person too,' Clodagh said defensively. 'I have rights too. And I was going mad from it, I swear I was.'

Ashling considered in confusion. But maybe Clodagh was right. Everyone just expects mothers to sublimate all of their own wants and needs for the good of their children. Perhaps that wasn't very fair.

'Sometimes,' Clodagh sighed, heavily, 'I just wonder, what's the point? My day is filled with ferrying Craig to school, Molly to playgroup, Molly home from playgroup, Craig to his origami lessons . . . I'm a slave.'

'But bringing up kids is the most important job anyone can do,' Ashling protested.

'But I never have any adult conversation. Except with other mothers, and then it's all so competitive. You know the sort of thing – "My Andrew is much more violent than your Craig." Craig never hits anyone, while Andrew bloody Higgins is a junior Rambo. It's so humiliating!' She fixed Ashling with a bleak look. 'I see magazine articles about the competitiveness of the workplace, but it's nothing compared to what takes place in the mother-and-toddler group.'

'If it's any consolation, I've been worried sick all this week because I've to write an article on a salsa class,' Ashling provided. 'It's literally kept me awake at night. You don't have to deal with that kind of worry.' To finally bring her round, Ashling finished softly, 'And above all, you have Dylan.'

'Ah now, marriage isn't all it's cracked up to be.'

Ashling wasn't convinced. 'I know you have to say that. It's the rule, I've seen it in action. Married women simply aren't allowed to say that they're mad about their husbands, unless they're *just* married. Get a group of married women together and they compete to see who can diss their husband the most. "My one leaves his dirty socks on the floor," "Well my one never noticed that I got my hair cut." I think you're all just embarrassed by your good fortune!'

Back out on the sunlit street, Ashling heard a familiar voice shout, 'Salman Rushdie, Jeffrey Archer or James Joyce?'

It was Joy.

'What are you doing up so early?'

'Haven't been to bed yet. Hiya.' Joy nodded warily at Clodagh. Clodagh and Joy didn't really like each other. Joy thought Clodagh was too spoilt and Clodagh resented Joy for her closeness with Ashling.

'Go on, then,' Joy urged. 'Salman Rushdie, Jeffrey Archer or James Joyce?'

'James Joyce alive or decomposing?'

'Decomposing.'

Ashling considered her gruesome choice and Clodagh's face was a picture of leftoutness. 'James Joyce,' Ashling finally decided. 'Right, you cow. Gerry Adams, Tony Blair or Prince Charles?'

Joy winced. 'Ooooh! Well obviously *not* Tony Blair. And not Prince Charles. It's going to have to be number one.'

Ashling turned to Clodagh. 'Your turn.'

'What do I do?'

'You pick three horrible men and we have to choose which one we sleep with.'

Clodagh hesitated. 'Why?'

Ashling and Joy glanced at each other. Why indeed?

'Because it's . . . um . . . fun.'

'I have to go.' Joy rescued the situation. 'I'm afraid I'm going to die. See you later. What time are we going to the River Club?'

'I said I'd meet Lisa there at nine.'

'You have all these friends that I don't know.' Clodagh stared resentfully after her. 'Her, and that Ted. I'm buried alive.'

'Well, why don't you come out with us? I keep inviting you.'

'I could, couldn't I? Dylan can bloody well babysit for a change.'

'Or Dylan could come too.'

CHAPTER 18

Ashling had been wrong – Marcus Valentine didn't ring her. She could hardly believe her luck. All week her answering machine had crouched in her flat with the menace of an unexploded bomb. If she came in from work and the light was flashing red, her heart leapt into her mouth. But, though there was a message from Cormac saying that a skip for the dead branches would be delivered on Tuesday and another to say that the skip would be collected on Friday, there was not a word from Marcus Valentine. By Saturday evening, when she got home from her day's shopping with Clodagh, she knew there wouldn't be.

But as she painted her fingernails (and a fair portion of her surrounding fingers also) light-blue in honour of the gig at the River Club, she realized there was a small chance Marcus would notice her in the audience. She hoped he wouldn't, she *really* hoped he wouldn't. The spoils from her day's shopping were spread out on her bed – light-blue Capri pants, killer sandals, white waist-tied shirt. Maybe she shouldn't wear them tonight – after

199

such a lucky escape wouldn't it be foolhardy to look nice?

But she'd only be cutting off her nose to spite her face. There'd be other people there – she had to think about them.

Around nine o'clock, Ted and Joy showed up. Joy complimented Ashling on her funky pastel glamour, but Ted was agitatedly whispering, 'My owl has got no wife. Shit, that's wrong! My wife has got no nose. No! Shit, shit, shit! . . . We might as well stay at home,' he said tearfully. 'I'm going to be atrocious. People have expectations of me now. It was different when I didn't have a following. My owl has got no nose . . .'

Already Ashling was plopping a drop of rescue remedy on his tongue, rubbing lavender oil on his temples and shoving the Serenity Prayer under his nose. 'Read that, and if it doesn't do the trick, we'll move on to the Desiderata.'

'Bring me the lucky Buddha,' he hyperventilated from the couch.

'How's Half-man-half-badger?' Ashling asked Joy, as they hefted the statue to Ted.

'*Mick* is fine.'

Things must be serious, if Joy was now calling Half-man-half-badger by his real name. Next they'd be visiting garden centres together.

Ted perked up after he'd polished the lucky Buddha, located a comforting tarot card and had his horoscope read to him. (Ashling read out Aries even though Ted was a Scorpio, because Scorpio wasn't looking so hot.)

'Now, the pair of you are to be on your best behaviour tonight,' Ashling warned. 'You're to be very nice to Lisa.'

'She needn't think she'll be getting any special treatment from me,' Joy said defensively.

'Is she a total bitch?' asked Ted.

'Not as such.' *Not always, in any case.* 'But she's tricky. The trickiest of tricky biscuits. Let's go.'

Looking their very best, the three of them clattered and chattered down the stairs. Buoyed up by that bright Saturday-night sensation of standing right on the very fringe of their future. The exhilarating anticipation that the rest of their life was ripe to reveal itself.

The homeless boy was sitting on the pavement outside, with his ever-present orange blanket, which wasn't very orange any more. Ashling ducked her head – every time she saw him she felt obliged to give him a pound and she was beginning to resent it. Then she snuck a glance at him and he wasn't even looking, he was reading a book.

'Hold it, lads, I just want to . . .' She trotted back to him.

'Howya!' He looked up, pleasantly surprised, as if they were old friends who hadn't met for ages. 'You're looking well. Off out?'

'Er, yes.' She held out a pound which he didn't take.

'Where to?'

'Comedy gig.'

'Nice,' he nodded, as if he was at comedy gigs all the time. 'Who?'

'Someone called Marcus Valentine.'

'I've heard he's very funny.' He finally made eye contact with the coin in her hand. 'Would you put that away, Ashling. I don't want you tipping me every time you see me. You'll be afraid to come out of your flat.'

Ashling neighed with nervous laughter. Most times as she came down the stairs lately, she was praying fervently that he wouldn't be there. 'How do you know my name?' she asked, almost flattered.

'Don't know. I must have heard your pals saying it.'

Ashling plunged into silence as something bizarre occurred to her. She finally voiced it. 'What's your name?'

'My friends call me Boo,' he grinned up at her.

'Pleased to meet you, Boo,' she said automatically, and before she knew what was happening, he'd stuck up his grubby hand and she was shaking it.

The book face-downwards on his lap was *An Encyclopaedia of Mushrooms*.

'Why are you reading *that*?' Ashling was astonished.

'I've nothing else.'

She had to run to catch up with Joy and Ted.

'Another of Ashling's waifs,' Ted observed archly, the neediness he'd displayed not ten minutes earlier completely forgotten.

'Ah, shut up.'

Imagine having to spend Saturday night begging on a cold street, reading a book about mushrooms.

CHAPTER 19

Lisa had hoped to make some progress with Jack by getting him along to the comedy gig. It would have been a great chance to socialize with him, under the pretext of work. But she never got an opportunity to casually suggest it because a crisis had erupted at the television station – a regular occurrence, apparently – and he'd been out of the office trouble-shooting, all day Thursday and Friday. This also meant that she missed out on being praised by him for getting her picture in the paper and generating a little advance publicity for *Colleen*. It pissed her off.

On Saturday, she'd managed to fill her day buying things for her 'new' house. She'd moved in the previous night and was keen to dilute the effect of all that pine. Besides, there was nothing like being busy to keep one step ahead of herself. Though, like everything else in this horrible country, the interiors shops were pitifully, depressingly bad.

No one had heard of Japanese rice-paper blinds, pocketed shower curtains or cupboard handles in the shape of glass flowers. She'd managed to track down decent ecru bed-linen, but not in the size she needed and it would take for ever to order because they had to import it from England.

Then she got 'home' and had to wait half an hour for the water to heat up for her shower. So much for Jack saying he'd sort out the timer for her. Men, they were all alike, all mouth and trousers. And sometimes not even trousers.

Sour and resentful after her alarmingly disappointing day, she was nevertheless pleased to be going out on the trail of Marcus Valentine. At least she was doing something constructive. Since the bad news about the advertising situation, the need to get brilliant columns for *Colleen* had greatly intensified.

Shortly after nine, she arrived at the River Club. Like everything else in Ireland, it was a disappointment – smaller and scruffier than she'd expected. K-Bar, it wasn't.

She hadn't been sure if she'd get a chance to buttonhole Marcus Valentine, but just in case, she'd worn her I'm-a-regular-girl-and-not-a-scary-magazine-bitch-at-all outfit. Frayed, embroidered jeans, slip-on trainers, slashed-neck T-shirt. Though her make-up was plentiful, it was subtle to the point of invisibility. She looked young, pretty and approachable, as if she'd just thrown on the first things that came to hand, and not as though she'd spent an hour staring into her (pine) mirror, carefully calculating the effect she would have.

She scouted around the milling room for

Ashling and her mates, but no sign, so she went to the bar and ordered a cosmopolitan. That was the ultra-fashionable martini quaffed at K-bar and Chinawhite and all the other red-hot watering holes she used to frequent in London.

'A what?' asked the round, red-faced barman, bursting out of his nylon shirt.

'A cosmopolitan.'

'If it's magazines you require, there's a place a few doors down,' he apologized. 'All we sell here is drink.'

Lisa wondered if she should give him instructions on how to make it, then realized she didn't know. 'A glass of white wine,' she snapped irritably. Perhaps they wouldn't even have that. She'd have to drink that disgusting Guinness.

'Chablis or Chardonnay?'

'Oh – ah, Chardonnay.'

She lit a cigarette and scanned the throng. By the time she'd finished the cigarette and glass of wine, Ashling still hadn't appeared.

Perhaps her watch was wrong. Lisa saw a group of lads standing nearby, selected the best-looking one and asked, 'What time is it?'

'Twenty past nine.'

'*Twenty* past?' It was worse than she'd thought. 'Been stood up?'

'No! But the arrangement was for nine.'

The boy heard her accent. 'You're English?'

She nodded.

'They'll be here soon enough. Definitely before ten.

But you see, round here, nine o'clock is only a figure of speech.'

Lisa felt her black demon stir. This fucking country. She fucking hated it.

'But we'll talk to you until they come,' he offered with a gallant smile. He stuck his fingers in his mouth, gave a piercing wolf-whistle and beckoned back the friends who'd drifted away.

'No need . . .' Lisa attempted.

'No bother,' he assured her. 'Lads,' he told his five pals, 'this is –' He flourished his hand at Lisa, waiting for her name.

'Lisa,' she said sulkily.

'She's from England. Her friends are late and she feels like a thick standing on her own.'

'Well, stick with us,' a small, ferrety boy urged. 'Get her a drink there, Declan.'

'Irish hospitality,' Lisa muttered contemptuously.

The six boys nodded with enthusiasm. Though if they were honest, it had nothing to do with legendary Irish hospitality and everything to do with Lisa's caramel hair, slender hips and long, smooth brown shins sticking out of the end of her artfully ragged jeans. If Lisa had been a man, she'd be staring into her pint, completely ignored.

'Deal's off, here she is.' In relief, Lisa saw Ashling coming through the door.

As soon as Ashling saw Lisa, the glory of her new clothes disappeared and she felt lumpish and diminished. Nervously she introduced Joy and Ted, then to Ashling's horror, Joy turned to Lisa and said, her chin tilted challengingly, 'Jim Davidson, Bernard Manning or Jimmy Tarbuck – and you *must* sleep with one of them.'

'*Jo-oy!*' Ashling shoved her. 'Lisa's my *boss*.'

But Lisa got it immediately. She went into thoughtful mode and after detailed consideration, said, 'Jim Davidson. Now, let me see. Des O'Connor . . .'

This took Joy aback no end.

'. . . Frank Carson or . . . or . . . Chubby Brown.' Lisa's eyes were narrowed with glee and malice as Joy flinched.

After some thought, Joy sighed heavily, 'Des O'Connor, then.'

'She's not so bad,' Joy muttered to Ashling, as they bagged some seats.

Ted was on first, and although it was only his third public appearance, there was a crowd of people already firmly on his bandwagon. His earlier emotional episode in Ashling's flat had been quite unnecessary. When he opened his act by shouting into the audience, 'My owl has gone to the West Indies,' a hard-core of about six studenty types yelled back, 'Jamaica?'

'No,' Ted replied, and several people chorused along with the rest of the gag, 'She went of her own accord.'

Ted had added loads of new owl stuff, all of which went down a bomb.

'What do you call a funny owl? – a hoot! . . .

What do you call a stupid owl – a te-wit! . . . What do you call a stupid owl who's coming on to a girl who isn't into him – a te-wit to woo! . . . Now for some political stuff. That Charlie Haughey – I mean, where did he get all them owls from?'

Though most of the room was in kinks of laughter, Lisa saw straight through Ted. 'I know he's your friend, but this is a clear case of the Emperor's New Hugo Boss suit,' she said scathingly.

'He's only doing it to get a girlfriend,' Ashling explained humbly.

'Perhaps that's all right then.' Lisa knew about the end justifying the means.

There were two other comedians on after Ted, then it was Marcus Valentine's turn. The chemical make-up of the air seemed to alter, becoming charged with piquant anticipation. When he finally took the stage the audience went hysterical. Ashling and Lisa both sat up and paid attention, but each for very different reasons.

For a male stand-up Marcus Valentine was a strange sort of beast. His act contained no references to masturbating, hangovers or Ulrike Johnson. Most irregular. Instead his skill was being A Man Perplexed by Modern Life. The kind of person who pops into a supermarket because he's run out of butter and goes into a tailspin because he can't decide between spreadable butter, unsaturated butter, polyunsaturated butter, salted butter, unsalted butter, reduced-fat butter, low-fat butter and stuff that wasn't butter at all and was only pretending to be. He was charming and likeable, in a freckly kind of way. Baffled and vulnerable. And he had a very nice body. Ashling catalogued all this in alarm.

Hastily she enumerated the reasons she'd rejected Marcus Valentine. One – his enthusiasm. There was nothing sexy about bright eyes and lack of cynicism. Sad, but true. Two – his freckles. Three – his keenness on her. Four – his stupid name.

But as she stared up at him, long-legged and broad-chested, she realized she was in mortal danger of falling foul of the man-on-a-stage rule. Coupled with the fact that he'd said he'd ring her and hadn't. It was a fatal combination. *I'm not going to do this*, she told herself, *I'm just not going to do this* . . . The mental equivalent of sticking her fingers in her ears and going, 'LALALALA I can't hear you, I can't hear you . . .'

'Snowflakes!' Marcus declared, his eyes wide and guileless as he scanned the room. 'They say that no two are alike.'

He let a pause build, then bellowed, 'But how do they *know*?'

As people writhed with hilarity, he asked in bewilderment, 'Have they compared each of them? Have they *checked*?'

Then he moved on to his next piece.

'There was a young lady I wanted to ask out,' Marcus told his besotted audience.

Maybe that's me? Ashling found herself wondering.

He strolled across the stage, as if deep in thought. The overhead lights hit the hard planes of his thighs.

'But the last time I asked a young lady for her phone number, she said "It's in the book." The problem was I didn't know her name and when I asked her, she said –' He paused and with impeccable timing went on, '"Oh, that's in the book too."'

The venue erupted, but the laughter was sympathetic and of the at-least-it's-not-just-me type.

'So I decided I'd act a bit cool.' He gave a klutzy grin and everyone melted. 'Thought I'd model myself on Austin Powers and ask the young lady to call *me*. So I wrote my name and number on a bit of paper and then I asked myself what would Austin Powers say.' He closed his eyes and held his fingertips to his temples, to show that he was communing with Austin Powers. 'And suddenly I knew. Bellez-moi!' Marcus declared. 'Suave, slick, sophisticated. What woman could resist? Bellez-moi!'

I'm famous. Ashling had an hysterical urge to stand up and tell everyone.

'And guess what?' Marcus scanned the audience with a cute, goofy expression. His connection with each person was taut. They strained towards him, full of love, as he stretched the anticipatory silence to its furthest reach, holding his public in the palm of his freckly hand. 'She never rang!'

No doubt about it, Marcus Valentine had loser star-quality.

Lisa was out of her seat the minute he left the stage. He'd already refused to have lunch with her when Trix had rung his agent but she hoped that extreme flattery and herself in person would change his mind. Ashling watched her block him off at the edge of the stage and wondered if she should follow. She didn't want to get too near to Marcus, in case he saw her. In case he thought . . . But Ted was besieged by fans and Joy had just seen Half-man-ha – . . . *Mick* talking to another woman and had gone to investigate. After sitting alone for a while longer, Ashling got up.

With curiosity, she watched Marcus watching Lisa as she did her pitch. His head was to one side and he had a perplexed quirky way of turning down his mouth that was delightful. Then Lisa stopped talking and he began. He was in the middle of something that looked very like a refusal, when his eye snagged Ashling's and he stopped abruptly.

'Hi,' he mouthed, and gave her a huge smile, holding her eyes, projecting warmth. As if we have some understanding, Ashling thought uncomfortably. He thinks I came here specially to see him.

He continued talking for a short time longer, but kept sneaking looks, then touched Lisa's arm in valediction and came over.

'Hello again.'

'Hello.'

'What are you doing here?'

She paused, looked up from under her lashes

and smiled. 'I thought Macy Gray was playing.'
Fuck! she realized. *I'm flirting with him.*

His laugh was appreciative. 'Did you enjoy the show?'

'Uh-huh.' She nodded and did that eyelash look again.

'Will you let me take you out for a drink sometime?'

Now *that* would teach her. She was like a rabbit caught in headlights, who'd bitten off more than she could chew. As it were.

I can't fancy him just because he's famous and admired. That would make me very shallow.

'OK.' Her voice had decided to go on ahead without her. 'Call me.'

'Your number . . . ?'

'You have it.'

'Give it to me again to be on the safe side.'

Marcus began an elaborate pantomime of patting himself, vaguely seeking a pen and paper.

Luckily, Ashling had the equivalent of a small stationery cupboard in her bag. She scribbled her name and phone number on a page torn from a notebook.

'I'll treasure this,' he said, folding it small and shoving it deep into the front pocket of his jeans. 'Next to my heart,' he promised, in a tone dense with innuendo. 'I'm leaving now, but I'll be in touch.'

Confused with herself, Ashling watched him leave. Then, aware that Lisa was looking at her with amusement, she escaped to the ladies'. Where her path to the wash-basin was partially blocked by a small girl with tragic eyes who was standing in front of the mirror, renewing her eye-liner and making herself look even more tragic. As Ashling turned the tap on, the tragic girl turned to her taller friend, who was idly doing circle after circle of jammy pink lip-gloss on her mouth, and said, 'Frances, you'll never believe it, but that was me, you know.'

'What was?'

'The girl who Marcus Valentine gave that Bellez-moi note to.'

Ashling jerked violently, hooshing water down her front. No one noticed.

Frances did a slow, incredulous body-turn, her lip-gloss applicator frozen against her mouth. Her tragic friend elaborated, 'It was last Christmas, we stood next to each other for two hours in a taxi-queue.'

'But why *didn't* you bellez him?' Frances levered her lip-gloss wand away from her mouth and vigorously shook the tragic girl by the shoulders. 'He's yummy. Yummy!'

'I just thought he was some freckly eejit.'

Frances surveyed the shorter girl for a long, thoughtful time before delivering judgement. 'Do you know something, Linda O'Neill? You deserve your unhappiness, you really do. I'll never feel sorry for you again.'

Ashling, still washing her hands like someone in the terminal stages of obsessive compulsive disorder, was mesmerized. She spent her entire life looking for Signs, and if this wasn't a Sign, then she didn't know what was. Give it a lash with Marcus Valentine, the celestial oracle was urging her. Even if he *was* handing out Bellez-moi notes like they were flyers, she had a good feeling about this. A very good feeling.

When Ashling re-emerged, Lisa was about to leave. Now that she'd got what she wanted, she saw no reason to hang around this low-rent club any longer.

'Bye then, see you at work on Monday,' Ashling said, awkwardly, not sure how chummy she should be.

Lisa wriggled through the crowds, her face satisfied. Not a bad night's work. Seeing Marcus Valentine had convinced her that he was certainly worth pursuing. Though it wouldn't be easy. He wasn't half as guileless in real life. In fact, he was smart – and slippery. Lisa suspected he had no objection to writing a column *per se*, but that he was holding out for a quality newspaper. To combat which she could feed him some bollocks about possibly syndicating his column to Randolph Media publications worldwide.

And there was that surprise twist – he seemed to fancy Ashling. Between both women, they could launch a pincer approach. The column was as good as in the bag.

But best to move fast and get it all sewn up before he dumped Ashling. Because he *would* dump

Ashling. Lisa knew his type of old. Catapult a nondescript man to a form of stardom and he can't help availing himself of the extra-curricular girls.

It could get messy – Ashling seemed like one of those pathetic women who took heartbreak hard and the last thing Lisa needed at this busy time was an assistant editor going off the rails. She couldn't understand weak people who cracked up. It was the sort of thing she'd *never* do. Of course, this was all based on the assumption that Ashling would go out with Marcus. Perhaps she wouldn't, and who could blame her? In Lisa's opinion, he was gross. Those freckles! And making a roomful of pissed people laugh did *not* cancel them out.

'Lisaaa, see yaaa. Bye Lisaaa.' The lads who'd 'minded' Lisa at the beginning were waving to her. 'Bye.' To her surprise, she smiled.

At the door, she passed Joy, deep in argument with a man with a grey streak through the front of his long, black hair. On a wild whim Lisa whispered as she passed, 'Russ Abbott, Hale or Pace, and you *must* sleep with one of them.'

Joy whirled around, but Lisa was headed for home. As she strode through the streets, she was aware that there had been something about tonight. She had felt . . . it had been . . . Suddenly she knew. Fun! It had been fun.

CHAPTER 20

And then Lisa woke up the next morning and felt that she couldn't go on. Just like that. She'd never felt so hopeless. Even in the terrible ugly dying days with Oliver she hadn't felt so full of despair – back then she'd flung herself into her work, taking bitter comfort that one area of her life was still working.

The thing was that Lisa didn't really hold with depression as a concept. Depression was a feeling other people got when their lives were insufficiently fabulous. Same as loneliness. Or sadness. But if you had enough nice shoes and ate in enough amazing restaurants and had been promoted over someone who deserved it more than you, there was no need to feel bad.

That was the theory, in any case. But as she lay in bed she was shocked by the extent of her depression. She blamed the curtains and the plethora of pine – it was enough to send any style-conscious person over the edge. She hated the stillness beyond the gauzy light of the room. *Fucking garden*, she thought savagely. What she wanted was the purr of taxis, the slamming of car doors, the sounds of well-dressed people coming and going. She wanted *life* outside her window. She had a hangover from the night before – she'd lost count of the number of white wines she'd had and ensuring that every second drink is a mineral water tends to lose its benefit when you're on your twentieth round. She blamed that Joy.

But the real hangover was emotional. She'd enjoyed herself, had fun, and something had been triggered by the high-spiritedness of the night before, because she just couldn't stop thinking about Oliver. She'd been doing so well until now. Always managing to block out thoughts of him in the last – she let herself count back – nearly five months. In fact, once she wasn't resisting thinking about it, she actually knew how many days it had been. One hundred and forty-five. It's easy to keep track when someone chooses New Year's Day to leave you.

Not that she'd done much to persuade him to stay. Too proud. *And* too pragmatic – she'd decided that their differences were irreconcilable. There were some things that she wouldn't – couldn't – back down on.

But on this terrible morning, all she could remember were the nice bits, the early days, bubbling with hope and love-to-be.

She'd been working at *Chic*, and Oliver was a fashion photographer. On the Way Up. He'd bounce gracefully into the office, his little dreads flying, usually carrying an enormous kit-bag, his bulging shoulder dwarfing it. Even when he was late for an appointment with the editor – in fact, especially when – he'd always stop for a chat with Lisa.

'How was New York?' she asked, in one conversation.

'Rubbish. I hate it.'

'Oh, really?' Everyone else seemed to love it, but Oliver never bought into the received wisdom.

'And did you photo any supermodels while you were there?'

'Oh, yes. Lots.'

'Yeah? Dish the dirt then, what's Naomi like?'

'Great sense of humour.'

'And Kate?'

'Oh, Kate is very special.'

Though Lisa was disappointed that he didn't share insider stories of tantrums and heroin taking, the fact that he was impressed by no one impressed her very much.

Even before you saw him, you always knew when he was in the office. He was perpetually surrounded by commotion – complaining that they'd screwed up his expenses, protesting that they'd printed his beloved shots on too-cheap paper, arguing and laughing energetically. His voice was deep and would have been chocolatey-seductive, except he was too vibrant. When he laughed in public, people always turned to look. If they weren't already looking, that is. The beauty of his big hard body coupled so incongruously with his rippling grace was bamboozling. When he used to come into the office, Lisa would study him discreetly. 'Black' was the wrong word, she used to think. It was far more complex and subtle than that. Everything *gleamed* – his skin, his teeth, his hair. Not to mention sweat on the editor's brow. What sort of fuss was he going to kick up today?

Though he was still making a name for himself, he was honest, opinionated and difficult. He never crawled to anyone and when people pissed him off he let them know. It was this confidence, as much as his beauty, that made Lisa decide she wanted him. That his star was very much in the ascendant didn't hurt either, of course.

Since she'd first started going out with boys, Lisa had always dated strategically. She just wasn't the type of girl who went out with an insurance clerk. Not that it ever felt quite that cold-blooded. She never made herself go out with a well-connected man *whom she didn't like*. Hardly ever, anyway. But she had to admit there were men whom she'd fancied that she knew she'd never take seriously: a charmingly grave court clerk by the name of Frederick; Dave, the *sweetest* plumber; and – the most unsuitable of all – a sparky petty criminal called Baz. (At least that was the name he told Lisa, but there was no guarantee it was his real one.)

Occasionally she allowed herself a little treat, and had a quick fling with one of these gorgeous no-hopers, but never made the mistake of thinking there was any future in them. They were human Milky Ways – the man you can eat between meals without ruining your appetite.

Her *real* relationships were with a different calibre of men. A dynamic magazine executive – it was this romance which led to her getting her first job on *Sweet Sixteen*. An Angry Young Man novelist, who ditched her rather nastily, and whose novels she subsequently ensured got vitriolic reviews (which made him even angrier than he already was). A controversial music journalist, whom she was mad about until he discovered acid jazz and grew a goatee.

Oliver straddled the two categories of men. He was beautiful enough to belong in the first, but talented and stylish enough to hold his own in the second.

With every visit that Oliver made to *Chic*, the connection with Lisa intensified. She knew he liked and respected her, that their attraction was much, much more than physical. In those far-off days, not everyone she worked with hated her, but the more she became Oliver's favourite, the more she became Most Loathed Colleague.

Especially after she began doing special favours for him. When she tracked down four missing transparencies, Oliver had good-humouredly blasted the rest of *Chic*. 'Listen up, you lot of useless tossers, this lady here is a genius. Why can't the rest of you be like her?'

At that, a disgusted glance shot around the office

like an electric current. Lisa may well have found the missing transparencies, but she'd done bugger all else for the previous two days.

Lisa had been vaguely aware that Oliver had had a girlfriend, but it came as no surprise when the news broke that he was once again single. She knew she was next in line. Though they flirted like mad with each other, they were never coy. Their solidarity was so obvious, it would have been disingenuous to deny it.

So obvious was it that Flicka Dupont (assistant features editor), Edwina Harris (fashion junior) and Marina Booth (health and beauty editor) hatched a plot to cut her out of her share of a basket of free John Frieda shampoos, on the basis that she was getting enough perks.

The expected day finally dawned when Oliver showed up at *Chic*, made straight for Lisa and said, 'Babes, can I take you for a drink on Friday night?'

She hesitated, about to play hard to get, then thought better of it. With a shaky laugh she exhaled, 'OK.'

'You were going to make me suffer, weren't you?' he exclaimed.

'Uh-huh,' she nodded solemnly.

They both screamed with laughter so loud that, three desks away, Flicka Dupont muttered, 'Please!' and had to twiddle her finger in her ear to dislodge the ringing.

Flicka later sniffed to Edwina, 'I don't envy her.'

'Gosh, neither do I!'

'He's a loose cannon.'

'A pain in the bum,' Edwina agreed.

They plunged into silence.

'I'd quite like to have sex with him though,' Flicka eventually admitted.

'*Would you really?*' Edwina had never been the sharpest knife in the drawer.

On the appointed Friday night, Oliver and Lisa went for a drink. Then he took her for dinner, where they had such fun that afterwards they went to a club and danced for hours. At three a.m. they went to his flat and had breathless, long-awaited sex, before snatching a few hours' sleep. The following morning they awoke in each other's arms. They spent the rest of the day in bed, talking, dozing and intermittently savaging each other with passion.

That evening, sated, they voluptuously rose from their lovers' nest and Oliver took Lisa to a fairly crappy French restaurant, its only virtue that it was walking distance. Lit by red candles stuck in wine bottles, they fed each other tasteless mussels and tough coq au vin.

'It's the most delicious food I've ever tasted.' Lisa licked her fingers and gazed across the table at him.

On the way home, they got swept up into an Armenian wedding that was being held in the local church hall. 'Come, come,' an expansive man invited, as they drifted past. 'Celebrate my son's happiness.'

'But . . .' Lisa protested. This was no way for a style warrior such as herself to spend Saturday night! What if someone she knew saw her?

But Oliver said easily, 'Why not? Come on, Lees, might be fun.'

Drinks were pressed into their hands, and they sat in a bubble of dream-like ease as all around, young and old in embroidered, flouncy peasant clothes, danced strange polka-like jigs to shrill, speedy bazouki-style music. An old woman with a headscarf and a thick accent pinched Lisa's cheek affectionately, smiled from Oliver to her and said, 'In laff. So in laff.'

'Does she mean I am or you are?' Lisa asked anxiously, belatedly realizing that she might be wearing her heart on her sleeve too much.

'You, lady.' The old woman gave a gappy smile.

'Naff off,' Lisa muttered.

Instantly Oliver exploded into laughter, his beautiful lips stretched around his rows of strong, white teeth. 'Touchy!' he teased. 'Must be because you *do* love me.'

'Or maybe you love me,' she replied huffily.

'I never said I didn't,' he replied.

And though it wasn't the kind of thing she normally went around feeling, there, in the unexpectedness of that surreal, beautiful wedding party, Lisa felt as though they'd been touched by the hand of God.

On Sunday morning, they'd awoken coiled around each other. Oliver bundled her into his car and belted up the motorway to Alton Towers, where they spent the day daring each other to go on ever more dangerous roller coasters. Even though she was terrified, she went on the Nemesis ride because she didn't want to show fear with him. And when she went a bit green and staggery he laughed and said, 'Too much for you, babes?' To which she replied that she had an inner-ear disorder. Oliver challenged and interested her more than any man had ever done. He was like herself, only more so.

Then they went home for pizza and bed. Their first date lasted sixty hours and ended when he dropped her off at work on the Monday morning.

By their third excursion they were officially in love.

On their fourth, Oliver decided to take her down to Purley to meet his mum and dad. Lisa thought it was a fantastically good sign, but, as it happened, it was almost the undoing of them. The unravelling began when they'd been in the car about half an hour and Oliver remarked, 'I'm not sure Dad will be home from work yet.'

'What does he do?' Lisa had never thought to ask before, it hadn't seemed important.

'He's a doctor.'

A doctor! 'What kind of doctor?' *A doctor of road-hygiene – in other words, a street sweeper?*

'Just a GP.'

The shock rendered her speechless. Here, she'd

been affectionately thinking of Oliver as a bit of rough, and it turned out that he'd been middle-class all along and *she'd* been the bit of rough. There was no way now that she could take him to meet her parents.

For the rest of the drive, she hoped and prayed that, despite the dad being a doctor, they might be poor. But when Oliver drove up to a big, square house, the fake-Tudor lead-paned windows, the Laura Ashley Austrian blinds and the plethora of knick-knacks on the visible window-sills declared that they weren't exactly strapped for cash.

Before they'd set off, she'd expected Oliver's mum to be a big-thighed, good-natured woman in Minnie Mouse shoes who drank Red Stripe at breakfast and laughed in a high-pitched, 'Heee! Heee! Heee!' Instead, as she answered the door, she looked like the queen. A few shades darker, but with the helmet curls and Marks & Spencer's prim duds, all present and correct.

'Pleased to meet you, dear.' The accent was pure Home Counties and Lisa felt her self-esteem wither even further.

'Hello, Mrs Livingstone.'

'Call me Rita. Do come through. Daddy's late at the surgery, but he should be here soon.'

They were led into the well-appointed sitting-room and when Lisa saw that the soft furnishings had had their plastic covering removed, it was the final blow.

'Tea?' Rita suggested brightly, stroking the

golden labrador which had laid his head in her lap. 'Lapsang Suchong or Earl Grey?'

'Don't mind,' Lisa muttered. What was wrong with PG Tips?

'This wasn't what I'd expected,' Lisa couldn't stop herself from whispering when she and Oliver were alone.

'What *did* you expect? Dat we be eatin' rice'n'-peas, drinkin' rum,' Oliver slipped into a perfect Caribbean accent, 'an' dancin' to steel drums on de porch?'

Exactly! It's the only reason I came.

'I don't think so, my dear.' He changed swiftly to BBC wartime speak. 'For we are Brrrritish!'

'The correct name for us, so I'm told,' Rita had reappeared with a tray containing a plate of unsweet, no-fun, handmade biscuits, 'is "Bounties". Or "Choc-ices".'

'Wh – why?' Lisa was confused.

'Brown on the outside, white on the inside.' She flashed a sudden, melon grin. 'That's what my family call us. And you can't win because the white neighbours hate us too! Next-door told me that the value of their house went down by ten grand when we moved in.'

Unexpectedly, totally at odds with her M&S appearance, she gave a high-pitched laugh. 'Heee! Heee! Heee!' And Lisa felt the chip on her shoulder dissolve like the sugar she didn't take in her tea. Well, so long as the neighbours hated them, that was all right then, wasn't it? They weren't half as scary now.

227

On their fifth date Oliver and Lisa talked about moving in together. They explored the notion further on the sixth. Their seventh date consisted of driving a van from Battersea to West Hampstead and back again, as they ferried Lisa's considerable wardrobe from her flat to his. 'You're going to have to lose some of this kit, babes,' he said in alarm. 'Or else we're going to have to buy a bigger place.'

Perhaps, Lisa subsequently realized, even then there were signs that all was not as it should have been. But, at the time, she was blind to them. Nothing had ever felt so right. She felt that he truly saw and accepted her, with all her ambition, energy, vision and fear. She reckoned they were two of a kind. Young, keen, ambitious, succeeding against the odds.

Around then, the concept of a soul-mate was a very fashionable one, recently imported from LA. Lisa was now the proud possessor of one.

Shortly after they got together, Lisa moved to *Femme* as deputy editor. This coincided with Oliver becoming a red-hot property. Even though he wasn't always popular on a personal level – some people found him just that little bit *too* difficult – all the glossies were suddenly scrambling and competing against each other to use him. Oliver shared himself out equally between them all, until Lily Headly-Smythe promised to use one of his photos for the Christmas cover of *Panache*, then changed her mind.

'She broke her word. I'll never work for *Panache* or Lily Headly-Smythe again,' Oliver declared.

'Until next time,' Lisa laughed.

'No.' His face was serious. 'Never.'

And he didn't, not even when Lily sent him an Irish Wolf-hound pup by way of an apology. Lisa was full of admiration. He was so strong-willed, so idealistic.

But that was before his intractability was turned on her. She didn't like it so much then.

CHAPTER 21

Ashling wasn't having such a fantastic Sunday either.

She'd woken up bubbling with anticipation concerning Marcus Valentine. Curious and expectant, she felt gloriously ready – for a date, a bout of flirting, a dose of flattery. Very definitely *something* . . .

The morning was spent mooning around, encapsulated in warmth, her positive faculties on full alert. But as the day faded without a phone call, her inner smile curdled into irritability. To pass the time and expend excess energy she did a bit of cleaning.

Not that Marcus had said *when* he'd ring. Her disenchantment wasn't so much rejection as the feeling of missing a good opportunity. Because even though she couldn't say for sure that she fancied him, she suspected that she might. Certainly, she was willing to give it her best shot. Emotionally, she was all dressed up with nowhere to go and it wasn't nice.

Look at me, she thought, scrubbing the bath with frustrated force. *I've been here before. Waiting for a man to ring.* Too late, she realized how much she'd enjoyed that brief pocket where she was no longer cut-up about one man and before she'd become hung-up on another. *Serves me right for being shallow enough to fall for a man-on-a-stage.*

How she regretted not having bellez'ed him when she'd had her chance. And it was too late now because she couldn't find the note. She had no memory of actually throwing it out – she'd have remembered because she would have thought she was being cruel. But a rummage through pockets and bedside drawers yielded nothing, except guilt-triggering receipts and a flyer for a computer sale.

Back to the cleaning. But after wiping out the inside of the microwave, she needed a boost, so decided to try to get a sneak preview of her future. Her angel divination cards didn't promise anything, so to hurry along Marcus's call, Ashling – rather sheepishly – unearthed her Wish Kit. Which hadn't seen the light of day since the last days of Phelim. She was aware that this did not bode well.

The kit consisted of six candles, each emblazoned with a word – Love, Friendship, Luck, Money, Peace and Success – and six corresponding boxes of matches. The Friendship, Money and Success candles hadn't even had their wicks lit, the Peace and Luck candles were burnt down slightly, but it was the Love candle that had seen the most action. It was the black fruit-gum of the packet. Reverentially, with the last Love match,

Ashling lit the candle, which burned away merrily for about ten minutes until it ran out of wax, then flickered and died.

Ah, shite, Ashling thought, *that better not be a Sign.*

Early evening Ted showed up, suffering from the trough that comes after a great high. Despite having met lots of girls, he wasn't taken with any of them.

'What about that fantastic one you were talking to when I left? Did you sleep with her?'

'No.'

'Ted! You can't say that. Even if you didn't ride her, you have to say you did to protect her honour.'

But Ted wasn't amused. 'She said I smelt funny. Like her granny.'

'Can't people be very mad?'

'No, actually.' Ted was annoyed. 'She was right. I *did* smell like her granny.'

As Ashling wondered aloud how Ted knew what the girl's granny smelt like, Ted overrode her accusingly. 'And do you know what I reckon it was?'

'What?'

'That fecking gear you rubbed on me before we went out.'

'Oh, the lavender oil.' Sometimes Ashling felt horribly unappreciated.

'That's a granny smell, isn't it?' Ted wouldn't let it go.

'I thought stale urine was more customary.'
Feeling hard-done-by made Ashling uncharacteristically sharp.

'Ah, she wasn't right for me anyway,' Ted
conceded grumpily. 'They're all too young and
silly, and they like me for the wrong reasons . . .
Your friend Clodagh,' he asked, suddenly. 'Still
married, is she?'

'Of course she is.'

'Is something wrong with you?' Ted had realized that he wasn't the only one down in the
mouth.

Ashling considered, and decided not to moan
about Marcus not ringing. He hadn't broken any
promises and could ring at any stage. So instead
she said lightly, 'Sunday-evening blues.' She'd
often discussed with Ted, Joy, Dylan – anyone who
had a job, in fact – the thunderclap of dread that
clangs inside at around five o'clock on a Sunday
afternoon. When it hits like a ton of bricks that
you've to go to work on Monday morning. Even
though there's still some hours of the weekend
left to run, it's to all intents and purposes over as
soon as you get that deathknell despair.

Ted looked at his watch and seemed happy with
that explanation. 'Ten past five. Right on the
button.'

'I've got cabin fever. Let's go out.' Ashling had
just remembered one of the basic rules of male-
female engagement. Of course Marcus hadn't
rung – she'd been waiting by the phone! All she

had to do was leave her flat and he'd be burning up the phone lines.

Before they left she grabbed a couple of books for Boo. She'd been caught humiliatingly on the hop the previous night when she hadn't a novel in her handbag to give to him in place of the mushroom encyclopaedia. But as she shoved *Trainspotting* into her bag, she went into a loop. Would he be offended if she gave him a book about heroin addiction? Would he think she was implying something?

Best to be on the safe side. Back it came out of the bag. Instead she brought *Fever Pitch* and some science-fiction crap that Phelim had given her two birthdays ago and that she'd never read. A boy's book. But, on the street, there was no sign of Boo.

Ted and Ashling went to the Long Hall for a couple of rather subdued drinks, followed by a low-key pizza at Milano's, then home again. As Ashling let herself back in, the first thing she did was look for the red flashing light on her answering machine. And there it was! She'd been so poised for disappointment that she thought she was conjuring it up. She stood and watched, as the light blinked on and off. Little red circle, no little red circle, little red circle, no little red circle . . . It was a message, all right. As she pressed the 'play' button, an awful thought afflicted her. *If this is from Cormac saying that he'll be delivering a lorry-load of shrubs on Wednesday, I'll scream.*

But the message was from neither the mystery

gardening supplier nor from Marcus Valentine. It was from Ashling's father.

Oh God, what's happened?

His voice was preceded by silence overlain with crackles, static scrapes and adenoidal breathing. Then he said to someone in the room with him, 'Will I talk now?'

The other person – Ashling's mother, presumably – said something that Ashling couldn't hear, then Mike Kennedy said, 'There were a few short ones, and a long one. God, I hate these yokes . . . Ashling, Dad here. I feel like a terrible eejit talking to a machine. We were just thinking we hadn't heard from you in a while. Are you all right? We're grand here. Janet rang us last week, she had to get rid of the cat, he kept head-butting her while she was asleep. And we'd a letter from Owen, he thinks he's discovered a new tribe. Not *brand* new, of course. Just new to him. I suppose you're busy with your new job, but don't forget us, will you? Hahaha. Ah, bye so.'

More crackles and breathing. Then, 'What'll I do now? Just hang up? I don't have to press a button or anything?'

Abruptly the connection was severed.

Ashling stewed in guilt and resentment, Marcus Valentine completely forgotten. She could feel the pressure for a visit to Cork coming on. At the very least she'd have to call them. Especially if her younger sister Janet managed to circumvent the eight-hour time difference to ring from California, and her brother Owen could get a letter to them from the Amazon Basin.

She flicked a glance at the photo she kept on top of her telly. It had been there so long that she was usually blind to it. But the emotions stirred up by the phone call made her take it and stare at it, as if looking for clues.

It hit home, as it always did, that Mike Kennedy had been a good-looking man. Bold and tall, he laughed out at the camera, all early-seventies sideburns and hair curling on his patterned shirt collar. It was funny because on the one hand he was her dad. But on the other, he looked like the kind of bad man you'd see at a party and be drawn to, but whom your self-preservation would warn you well away from.

Mike had his arm around Janet, aged four. She was bent at the waist and had her fist shoved between her legs – she'd wanted to go to the toilet, the camera had always had that effect on her. Leaning against Mike, holding the three-year-old Owen in her pucci-swirled polyestered arms, was Monica. She was smiling happily, looking unfeasibly young, her hair smooth and set, her mascara Priscilla Presley glam. And stage centre, wedged between the two adults, her six-year-old's eyes crossed comically, was Ashling.

Lucifer, Before the Fall, she always thought when she inspected this picture. They looked like such a perfect little family. But she often wondered if, even then, the rot had already set in.

Replacing the photo, she came back to the present. It had been about three weeks since the last time she'd rung her mum and dad. It wasn't that she'd forgotten to since – she thought about it a lot, but could nearly always think of excuses not to.

However, she was never really at peace with her lack of communication. She was aware that Clodagh rang her own mother daily. Although Brian and Maureen Nugent were very different from Mike and Monica Kennedy. Maybe if Brian and Maureen had been her parents she'd be better at keeping in touch.

CHAPTER 22

Monday morning. Traditionally, the bleakest of all mornings. (Except following a bank holiday, when Tuesday morning gets a go.) Nevertheless, it perked Lisa up no end. The thought of going into the office made her feel in control – at least she'd be doing something to help herself. Then she tried to have a shower and the water was stone cold.

But she temporarily shelved the notion of collaring Jack about the timer on her boiler when Mrs Morley let slip that he'd been working over the weekend, sorting out irate electricians and hard-done-by cameramen. He looked exhausted and black of mood.

Ashling, grey and late, was also finding the day hard. Even more so when Jack Devine stuck his head out of his office and said, curtly, 'Miss Fix-it?'

'Mr Devine?'

'A word?'

Alarmed, she stood up far too quickly and had to wait for her blood supply to catch up and restore her sight.

'Either you're in big trouble or else you're riding him,' Trix whispered gleefully. 'What's going on?'

Ashling was in no mood for Trix and her antics. She hadn't a clue why Jack Devine wanted to speak to her in private. With a presentiment of doom, she crossed to his office.

'Close the door,' he ordered.

I'm going to be sacked. She was in the horrors.

The door clicked behind her and instantly the room shrank – and darkened. Jack, with his dark hair, dark eyes, dark-blue suit and dark mood, tended to do that. To make matters worse, he wasn't behind his desk, he was balanced on the front and there was very little space between the two of them. He made her so *uncomfortable*.

'I wanted to give you this, without the rest of them seeing.'

She found herself leaning away from him, although there was nowhere to go. He thrust a plastic bag at her, which she accepted dumbly. Hazily, she noticed that it was a bit big for a letter of notice.

She just held it in her hands, and with an impatient laugh Jack said, 'Look inside.'

Crumpling plastic, Ashling peered into the pearly light of the bag. To her surprise it contained a carton of two hundred Marlboro, with a red rosette stuck crookedly on the cellophane.

'Because I kept bumming your cigarettes,' Jack dead-eyed her. 'I'm, er, sorry,' he added. He didn't sound it.

'It's beautiful,' she mumbled, stunned by the reprieve – and the rosette.

For the first time since she'd met him, Jack Devine laughed properly. An honest-to-God, head-thrown-back, belly laugh. 'Beautiful?' he exclaimed, alight with mirth. 'Sailing boats are beautiful, eight-foot waves are beautiful. But cigarettes beautiful? Actually, maybe you're right.'

'I thought you were going to sack me,' Ashling blurted.

His face twisted with surprise. 'Sack you? . . . But Little Miss Fix-it,' he said, his voice suddenly soft, his eyes playful, 'who else would keep us in plasters, Anadins, umbrellas, safety pins, what's the thing for shock – remedy something . . . ?'

'Rescue remedy.' She could do with some right now. She needed to get out. Just so she could breathe again.

'What are you so scared of?' he asked, even more softly. It seemed to her that his bulk moved closer.

'Nothing!' she squealed like a bus's brakes.

With his arms folded, he considered her. Something in the way his mouth kinked up at the corners made her feel girlish and silly, like he was mocking her. Then, in an instant, he seemed to lose interest. 'Go on,' he sighed, moving back behind his desk. 'Off you go . . . But don't tell any of the others,' he nodded at the bag. 'Else they'll all be wanting one.'

Ashling went back to her desk, her legs belonging to someone else. Hold the front page.

Jack Devine in Not-Such-a-Miserable-Bastard-As-He'd-Originally-Seemed shock. But the oddest thing of all was that Ashling kind of thought that she preferred him the other way. Though later that day, it was business as usual.

Mercedes lurched into the office, and everyone nearly fell off their chairs when they saw that she was uncharacteristically displaying emotion. A lot of it. As per Lisa's instructions she'd gone to try and interview mad Frieda Kiely. And even though Mercedes had spent the weekend in Donegal shooting a twelve-page spread of Frieda's clothes, Frieda kept her waiting an hour and a half, then professed to have never heard of her or *Colleen*.

'Who are you?' she'd demanded. '*Colleen*? What the hell's that? What is that?'

'She's a maniac. A mad bitch,' Mercedes hissed, then fell into another fit of humiliated convulsions. 'A mad fucking BITCH!'

'A premenstrual psycho hoor from hell.' Kelvin was very keen to get on the right side of Mercedes.

'A schizoid slapper,' Trix threw in.

'And a right skinnymalinks,' said Boring Bernard, who had no idea what she looked like but who liked a good bitch as much as the next mummy's boy. 'There'd be more meat on a tinker's stick after a good row.'

Trix looked at him scornfully. 'That's a compliment, you gobshite. You haven't a clue!'

Insult after insult was heaped upon Frieda Kiely, except from Ashling who had heard somewhere that she really was mad. Apparently she was mildly schizophrenic and disinclined to take her medication.

'But,' Ashling interrupted, feeling someone should defend her, 'don't you think before we give out about her, we should walk a mile in her shoes?'

'That's right,' said Jack, who'd emerged to see what all the commotion was. 'Then we'd be a mile away from her and we'd have her shoes. Sounds good to me.' He shot Ashling a jeering smile, then barked, 'For God's sake, Ashling, act your age, not the speed limit.'

Lisa was amused. 'What *is* the speed limit in this country?'

'Seventy,' Jack said, slamming back into his office.

Ashling hated Jack again. Things were back to normal.

Even though Marcus Valentine didn't have her work number, Ashling's whole being gulped when, at ten to four, Trix handed her the phone and said, 'A man for you.'

Ashling took the receiver, waited a moment to compose herself, then cooed, 'Heeeyyy.'

'Ashling?' It was Dylan and he sounded puzzled. 'Have you a cold?'

'No.' In disappointment she reverted to her normal voice. 'I thought you were someone else.'

'How about that drink this evening? I can come into town at whatever time suits you.'

'Sure.' It would keep her from her phone vigil at home. 'Call into the office around six.'

Then, very quickly, she rang home to see if there were any messages. It was only fifteen minutes since the last time she'd checked, but you never know.

Or maybe you do, because no one had phoned.

At quarter past six, Dylan caused a mild stir when, blond hair flopping into his eyes, he showed up in a well-cut linen suit and an immaculate white shirt. As he stood at Ashling's desk, there seemed to be something wrong with him, a lopsidedness as if his shoulder was dislocated.

'Are you OK?' Ashling got up, walked around him and found that the reason his whole body was twisted was that he was trying to conceal an HMV bag behind his back.

'Dylan, I won't tell that you've been buying CDs.'

'Sorry,' he shrugged sheepishly. 'This is what comes of working in the wilds of Sandyford. Whenever I come into town, I go berserk in music shops. The guilt kinda gets to me.'

'Your secret is safe with me.'

'New jacket?' Dylan asked, as Ashling switched off things.

'Actually, yes.'

'Let me see.'

Insisting that she stood still, he ran a glance along her shoulders, nodded and said, 'Yeah.' Ashling tried, in vain, to suck in her waist, as he skimmed a look down the side-seams, nodded and said, 'Yeah' again, even more approvingly, then looked up. 'Suits you,' he finished with a smile. 'Really suits you.'

'You're nothing but a rogue.' Ashling's pleasure had mounted while the examination continued. Dylan was always outrageously lavish with compliments. Yet despite knowing that he flung them around like snuff at a wake, it was hard not to half-believe him, harder still not to glow with delight. 'You're *dangerous*,' she radiated.

'Come on.' She turned to go and saw that Jack Devine was nearby, moodily flicking through a file on Bernard's desk. She smiled a nervous goodbye and for an alarming second thought he was going to ignore her. Then he exhaled heavily and said, 'Goodnight, Ashling.'

Lisa had been in the ladies' refreshing her make-up in honour of that evening's outing with a famous Irish chef whom she hoped to convince to do regular cookery features. As she hurried back into the office to get her jacket, she rounded the door too quickly and smacked into a blond man she hadn't seen before. She bumped her shoulder against his chest, and felt, briefly, the heat coming through his thin shirt.

'Sorry.' He placed his big hands on her shoulders. 'Are you all right?'

'I think so.' As she straightened herself up, they took a long, keen look at each other. Then she saw Ashling at his side. Was he her boyfriend? No, surely not.

'Who was *that*?' Dylan asked, when the lift doors had closed behind them.

'You're a happily married man,' Ashling reminded him.

'I only asked.'

'Her name is Lisa Edwards, she's my boss.' But Ashling was reminded of the conversation she'd had with Clodagh about all the conferences Dylan attended. *Is he faithful to her*? Quickly she asked, 'Where'll we go for this drink?'

He took her to the Shelbourne, which was thronged with post-work revellers.

'We'll have to stand,' said Ashling. 'We'll never get a seat.'

'Never say never,' Dylan twinkled. 'Hold on.'

Next thing he'd swooped down on a tableful of people, had a quick, smiley chat, then returned to Ashling. 'Come on, they're leaving.'

'Since when? What did you *say* to them?'

'Nothing! I just noticed they were nearly finished.'

'Hmmm.' Dylan was so charmingly persuasive, he could sell salt to Siberia.

'Hop in there, Ashling – bye, thanks very much.' All smiles, he bid farewell to the table donators. Then, with suspicious speed, he tussled through the masses at the bar and returned with drinks. Good things had a habit of just happening to Dylan, and as he placed her gin-and-tonic in front of her, Ashling wondered, as she occasionally did, what it must be like to be married to him. Utter bliss, she suspected.

'Tell me everything, *everything*, about this great new job,' Dylan ordered, energetically. 'I want to know all about it.'

Ashling was swept along on his contagious enthusiasm. Thoroughly enjoying herself, she outlined all the different personalities at *Colleen* and how they interacted – or didn't, as the case may be – with each other.

Dylan laughed a lot, seemingly genuinely entertained, and Ashling half-fell into the trap of thinking she was a great raconteur. This was all part of the same carry-on as when Dylan had admired her new jacket – his great gift was making people feel good about themselves. He couldn't help it. Not that it was insincere, Ashling knew. Just a little over-the-top. She shouldn't make the mistake of telling the same lame-brain stories to other people and expecting similar gales of laughter.

'Christ, you're funny.' He clinked his glass against hers in a toast of praise. His flirtatious manner always implied more than he was prepared to deliver. Not that Ashling took it seriously. At least, not any more.

'So how's the computer business?' she eventually asked.

'Christ! Insanely busy! We can't fill orders fast enough.'

'Wow!' Ashling shook her head in wonder. 'When I first met you you weren't sure if the company would survive the first year. Look at you now!'

The mood hiccupped slightly, almost inpalpably, over the mention of the time they'd first met. But, as luck would have it, they had nearly finished their drinks, so Ashling jumped up. 'Same again?'

'Sit down, I'll get them.'

'Not at all, I'll –'

'Sit down, Ashling, I insist.'

That was another thing about Dylan. He was effortlessly, stylishly generous.

When he returned with the drinks, Ashling asked curiously, 'So was there a special reason you wanted to meet me . . . ?'

'Yeeaaahhh,' Dylan drawled, fiddling with a beermat. 'Yeah, there was.' Suddenly he wasn't at all comfortable, and this in itself was cause for alarm. 'You haven't noticed . . . anything . . . ?' He stopped and didn't go on.

'Anything?'

'About Clodagh.'

'How d'you mean?'

'I'm . . .' Big, long pause. '. . . kind of worried about her. She never seems happy, she's often snappy with the children and sometimes even . . . slightly irrational. Molly accused Clodagh of slapping her and we've never slapped the kids.'

Another uncomfortable gap, before Dylan continued. 'This is probably going to sound stupid, but she's always doing the house up. No sooner are we finished one room than she's talking about redoing another. And trying to talk to her about any of this is getting me nowhere. I was wondering . . . I thought that maybe she might be depressed.'

Ashling considered. Now that she thought about it, Clodagh had seemed dissatisfied and quite difficult lately. She did seem to be doing an excess of decorating. And telling Molly that Barney was dead had struck Ashling as weird. Shocking, even. Although Clodagh's defence that she had feelings too had seemed reasonable. But now, in the context of Dylan's concern, it instantly flipped over into being ominous again.

'I don't know. Maybe,' Ashling said, deep in thought. 'But it's tough with kids. Very demanding. And if you're having to work long hours . . .'

Dylan leant forward, listening intently to Ashling as though her words could be held or collected. But when she trailed away into abject silence, he said, 'I hope you don't mind me saying this – but I thought that you might know some of the signs. Because of your mother . . .

'Your mother?' he prompted, when Ashling remained mute. 'She had depression, didn't she?'

Dylan's gentleness wasn't enough to cajole Ashling to speak.

'And I thought Clodagh might be the same . . . ?'

Suddenly Ashling was back there, mired in the craziness, the bewilderment, the ever-present terror. Her ears rang with long-ago yelling and screaming and her mouth muscles were unresponsive with the desire not to talk about it. Firmly, almost aggressively, she said, 'Clodagh is nothing like my mother was.'

'No?' Dylan's hope was laced with prurient curiosity.

'Decorating the front-room isn't depression. Well, at least it's not depression as I know it. She's not refusing to get out of bed? Or wishing she was dead, is she?'

'No.' He shook his head. 'Not at all. Nothing like that.'

Although her mother hadn't started off that way. It had been gradual, hadn't it? Against her will, Ashling lapsed into the past and she became nine years old again, the age she'd been when she'd first realized that something wasn't quite right. They'd been on their holidays in Kerry when her dad commented on a glorious sunset. 'A beautiful end to a beautiful day. Isn't it, Monica?'

Staring straight ahead, Monica had said heavily, 'Thank God the sun is setting. I want today to be over.'

'But today was glorious,' Mike challenged. 'The sun shone, we played on the beach . . .'

All Monica said was, 'I'm ready for today to be over.'

Ashling had paused from fighting with Janet and Owen, feeling excluded and unsettled. Parents weren't supposed to have feelings, not those sort,

249

anyway. They could complain when you didn't do your homework or eat your dinner, but they weren't allowed to have their own private unhappinesses.

At the end of their two weeks away, they came home, and it seemed like one minute her mum was young, pretty and happy, the next she was silent, sunken and had stopped colouring her hair. And she cried. Constantly, silently, just letting tears pour down her face.

'What's wrong?' Mike asked, again and again. 'What's *wrong?*'

'What's wrong, Mum?' Ashling asked. 'Have you a pain in your tummy?'

'I've a pain in my soul,' she whispered.

'Take two Junior Disprins.' Ashling parroted what her mother said to her when she had a pain somewhere.

Other people's disasters set Monica off. Three solid days were spent crying about a famine in Africa. But when Ashling came home with the joyous news, gleaned from Clodagh's mother, that 'they're sending in food', Monica had moved on and was now weeping for a baby boy who'd been found in a cardboard box. 'That poor child,' she convulsed. 'That poor, defenceless child.'

While her mother cried, her dad smiled enough for the two of them. Smiled hard. Smiled always. He had a busy and important job. That's what everyone said to Ashling – 'Your daddy has a very busy and important job.' He was a salesman and he made his journeys, from Limerick to Cork, from Cavan to Donegal, sound like the adventures of the Fianna. So busy and important was he that he was often away from Monday to Friday. Ashling was proud of this. Everyone else's dad came home at half past five every evening, and she couldn't help scornfully feeling that their jobs mustn't count for much.

Then her dad came home at the weekends and smiled and smiled and smiled.

'What'll we do today?' He'd clap his hands together and beam around at his family.

'What do I care?' Monica mumbled. 'I'm dying inside.'

'Sure, what would you want to do a stupid thing like that for?' he joshed.

Turning to Ashling, he smiled and said, as if sharing a secret, 'Your mother's artistic.'

Her mother had always written poetry. She'd even had a poem published in an anthology when Ashling was a baby, and since the crying and strangeness had begun, she'd written a lot more. Ashling knew about poems. They were pretty rhyming words about sunsets and flowers, usually daffodils. But when, at Clodagh's giggling instigation, they sneaked a look at some of Monica's poems, Ashling was shocked raw by them. Through the haze of distress there was one thing she was violently grateful for – that Clodagh couldn't really read.

The poems didn't rhyme, the verse lengths were

251

all wrong, but it was the individual words that were the greatest cause for concern. There were no flowers in Monica Kennedy's poems. Instead there were strange, brutal terms that Ashling spent a long time deciphering.

Stitched into silence,
my blood is black.
I am broken glass,
I am rusting blades,
I am the punishment and the crime.

Back in the present, Ashling found Dylan watching her with anxious interest. 'Are you OK?' he asked.

She nodded assent.

'For a minute I thought we'd lost you there.'

'I'm fine,' Ashling insisted. 'Clodagh hasn't started writing poetry, has she?' She made herself smile as she asked.

'Clodagh! The very thought.' Dylan quietly chuckled, as if realizing how silly he'd been. 'So if she starts writing poems, then I should be worried?'

'But until then, don't bother. She's probably just tired and needs a break. Can't you do something nice? Cheer her up by going on a holiday or something?' *Another one,* she thought bitchily. She felt a vague resentment that Dylan was asking *her* for advice on how to make Clodagh's life even nicer.

'I can't take any time off at the moment,' Dylan said.

'Well, go out for a fancy-shmancy dinner then.'

'Clodagh's worried about the babysitters.'

'Why, what's wrong with them?'

Dylan laughed, slightly embarrassed. 'She's afraid that they might be child-abusers. Or that they might hit the kids. To be honest I sometimes worry too.'

'Jesus, they keep inventing new things for everyone to worry about. So get someone you can trust. How about your mother?'

'Oh no!' Dylan quirked his mouth down ruefully. 'That would be *so* not a good idea.'

Ashling nodded. True enough. The only time that young Mrs Kelly and not-so-young Mrs Kelly saw eye-to-eye was when they were nose-to-nose in an argument – usually over the best way to take care of Dylan and Dylan's children.

'And Clodagh's mother is crippled with arthritis,' Dylan said. 'She wouldn't be able to manage the kids.'

'I can babysit if you want,' Ashling offered.

'On a weekend night? A wild young thing like yourself?'

After a hesitation, she said, 'Yes . . . Yes,' she said again, more firmly and with slight defiance, 'why not?'

If she was genuinely unavailable, it would increase the chances of Marcus Valentine ringing.

'That's spectacular.' Dylan perked up. 'Thanks Ashling, you're a pet. I'll book a table for Saturday night. I'll see if I can get one at L'Oeuf.'

But of course, Ashling thought, amused despite herself. *Where else?* L'Oeuf was the elder statesman of Dublin restaurants. It had the unique distinction of always being in fashion – *despite* not serving Asian fusion or Modern Irish. Perennially glamorous, the food would bring a tear to your eye. So would the prices.

'Your mammy, she's better now, isn't she?' Dylan tried to make up for forcing the issue in the first place.

'Better' was a relative concept and anyway, that wasn't always the point, but to please him, Ashling nodded and said, 'Yes, she's better now.'

'You're a great girl, Ashling.' Dylan bade her farewell.

I am, Ashling thought drily, *Aren't I?*

CHAPTER 23

Ten minutes away from Dylan and Ashling, Lisa and Jasper Ffrench, the celebrity chef, were dining at the Clarence. Jasper had specifically requested that he be taken there, just so he could scorn the food as not being a quarter as good as what he produced in his eponymous restaurant. He was good-looking, unpleasant, manifestly thought he was a genius and had nothing but jealousy for everyone else in his field. 'Amateurs,' he declared, waving his sixth glass of wine, 'they're nothing but amateurs and dilettantes. Marco Pierre White – amateur! Alasdair Little – amateur!'

Jesus Christ, you're a pain. Lisa nodded and smiled. Good thing that difficult men were her speciality. 'That's why you're the one we've chosen to be part of *Colleen's* success, Jasper.'

Not exactly true. Jasper was the one who was chosen because Conrad Gallagher had already turned her down, pleading pressure of work.

As Jasper made great inroads into the second bottle of wine, Lisa dazzled him with talk of synergy. Without actually promising it, she implied that a column in *Colleen* could easily lead to his own programme on Channel 9, Randolph Media's television station.

'I'll do it!' Jasper decided. 'Bike me over a contract in the morning.'

'I actually have one here,' Lisa said smoothly, striking while the iron was hot.

Jasper scribbled his signature, and only just in time, because there was a tricky moment when the waiter came to take her plate away. As usual, Lisa had moved her food around, but had eaten almost nothing.

'Was there anything wrong with your dinner?' the waiter asked.

'No. It was delicious but –' Lisa became aware of Jasper glaring across the table at her and quickly amended her verdict to a more neutral, 'It was fine.'

'If it was anything like as insultingly bad as mine I'm not surprised she couldn't force it down,' Jasper challenged. 'Black-pudding blinis? That's beyond a cliché. That's a joke!'

'I'm sorry to hear that, sir.' The waiter flat-eyed Jasper and his cleared plate. He used to work for him, the mad bastard. 'Would you care to order dessert?'

'No, we would not care!' Jasper said hotly – to Lisa's chagrin, because this week she was on a pudding diet. The lighter end of the scale, of course: fresh fruit, sorbets, fruit mousses. It had been well over a decade since the dizzying punch of Death by Chocolate had passed her lips.

Oh well, no matter. She paid the bill, and they both got up to leave, one of them less steadily than the other. By the door they shook hands, then Jasper attempted a drunken lunge at Lisa, which she tactfully deflected. Just as well she'd already got the contract signed.

Jasper tottered balefully up the street and the moment Lisa was by herself, the bleakness rushed in again. Why? Why was everything so much harder here? She'd been OK in London. Even after Oliver had walked out, she'd kept going. Pressing on, fulfilling her vision, making things happen, always certain there would be a prize of sorts for her. But the prize went to someone else and she was in Ireland and her coping mechanisms didn't seem to work so well here.

She hadn't rung her mum yesterday, even though it was Sunday. She'd been too depressed. She had only got dressed to go to the foul corner-shop for a tub of ice-cream and five newspapers, and as soon as she returned to the house, she got back into her wrap and spent the day moping in a fug of cigarette smoke. Her only contact with humanity had been the local eight-year-olds kicking their football repeatedly up against her front door.

Before she flagged a taxi she popped into a newsagent's to buy cigarettes and her heart lifted when she saw that the new *Irish Tatler* was out. *Irish Tatler* was one of *Colleen's* competitors and deconstructing it would give her something to do for the rest of the evening. All at once home didn't seem so repellent.

'Hiya Leeesa.' A gaggle of little girls playing on the road yelled at her when she got out of her cab. 'Your dress is sexy.'

'Thank you.'

'What size are your shoes?'

'Six.'

A huddled conference followed that. How big was a six? Too big for them, they reluctantly decided.

Letting herself in, she flung her bag on the floor, flicked on the kettle and checked her answering machine. No messages, which wasn't really surprising because almost no one knew her number. It didn't stop her feeling like a failure, though.

She kicked off her lovely shoes, flung her dress on a chair and was changing into drawstring pants and a shortie T-shirt when the doorbell rang. Probably one of the little girls to ask if they could have her handbag when she didn't want it any more.

With a sigh she flung open the door, and there, standing on her step, bending his tall bulk to fit the doorway, was Jack.

'Oh,' she said, stupid with surprise.

It was the first time she'd seen him out of his suit. His long, collarless shirt was open to mid-chest. Not by design, but because the buttons were missing. His khakis looked as if they'd done service in two world wars, and had a flap torn across the right knee, exposing a smooth kneecap and a three-inch square area of hairy shin. His hair looked even messier than usual, as did his face – Jack was a man who needed to shave twice a day.

Leaning against the doorframe, he displayed a device in the palm of his hand, like a policeman flashing ID. 'I have a timer for your boiler.'

It sounded vaguely suggestive.

'Sorry it wasn't sooner.' Then he hesitated. 'Is now a good time?'

'Come in,' Lisa invited. 'Come in.'

She was taken aback because in London, no one ever just called around to her flat. She'd never made an arrangement to see anyone without first opening her Psion or Filofax and playing the I'm-busier-and-more-important-than-you game. It was an elaborate ritual, governed by strict rules. At least five different dates must be offered and rejected before an actual one can be agreed on.

'Next Tuesday? Can't, I'll be in Milan.'

Which is the cue for the other party to respond, 'And I can never do Wednesdays because that's my reiki night.'

An acceptable reply to that is, 'And Thursdays are out for me because my Alexander Technique tutor comes.'

The ante is upped by the second party coming back with, 'The weekend after that is out of the question. Cottage in the Lake District with friends.'

To which the smart money responds, 'The whole

259

of the following week is gone for me. LA, on business.'

Once a date has been finally fixed, it is still acceptable – indeed expected – for you to cancel on the day, pleading jet-lag, a client dinner or having to go to Geneva to make seventy people redundant.

Like Gucci sunglasses and Prada handbags, Time Poverty was a status symbol. The less time you had the more important you were. Jack obviously didn't know.

He looked around in admiration. 'You've been here – how many? – three, four days and already the place looks nicer. Look at that –' He pointed to a glass bowl overloaded with white tulips. 'And that.' A vase of dried flowers had caught his attention.

Good job he couldn't see the cups under her bed that were in the early stages of growing mould, Lisa thought. Her homes were always a triumph of style over hygiene. She must try and sort out a cleaner . . .

'Can I get you a drink?' she offered.

'Any beer?'

'Um, no, but I've some white wine.'

She experienced ridiculous pleasure when he accepted a glass.

'I'll just get my stuff from the car,' he said, ducking out and returning shortly afterwards carrying a blue metallic container.

Oh God, he had a toolbox! She had to sit on

her hands to keep herself from touching him, from ripping off the last few buttons on his shirt, exposing his broad chest, which was *just* the correct degree of hairiness, sweeping her hands up the smooth skin of his back . . .

'D'you mind if I open the back door?' He interrupted the clinch that was taking place in her head.

'Um, no, go ahead.' She watched him cross the room and shoot the bolt that hadn't been touched since the last time he'd been here. A fragrant breeze crept into the kitchen, bringing the dense, evening-time scent of foliage and the whistles and cheeps of birds winding down after the day. Nice. If you liked that kind of thing.

'Have you sat in your garden yet?' Jack asked.

No. 'Yes.'

'It's so peaceful out there, you'd hardly know you were in a city,' he nodded through the doorway.

'I know.' *Tell me about it!*

'Here goes.' He eyed the boiler. 'This looks like a straightforward enough job, but you never know.'

Then he rolled up his sleeves, revealing the sinews of his lovely wrists, and set to work. Lisa sat in the kitchen, hugging one knee, enjoying, too much, the presence of an attractive man in her home. No matter what, she decided, they were *not* going to talk about the advertising situation. There would be no downers, this was a tailor-made opportunity to flirt.

'So tell me all about you,' she ordered with confident coquetry, to his back.

'What do you want to know?' He was none too civil as he banged and bashed metal against metal. Then he swung around, and exclaimed in mild outrage, 'Lisa, come on! That kind of question would wipe anyone's mind blank.'

'Well, tell me how you've ended up being Managing Director of a commercial television station, a radio station and several successful magazines at the age of thirty-two.' OK, so she was talking it up a bit, but she was in the business of flattery.

'It's a job,' Jack said shortly, as if he suspected she was taking the piss. 'I was sacked from my previous job, I had a living to earn.'

Sacked? She didn't like the sound of that. 'Why were you sacked?'

'I proposed a radical notion, which involved paying staff what they were worth and giving them a voice in management. In return they were going to make concessions on demarcation and overtime, but the board decided that I was too much of a leftie and out I went.'

'A *leftie*?' Lefties weren't much fun, were they? They made you go on marches and they had awful cars. Trabants. Ladas. That's if they had a car at all. But Jack had a Beemer.

'In my younger, more idealistic days,' he hit the pipe an almighty belt with a spanner, 'I might have been called a socialist.'

'But you're not one now?' Lisa said, in alarm.

'No,' he chuckled grimly. 'Don't sound so worried. I threw in the towel when I saw that most workers are happy doing the lotto or buying shares in privatized state bodies, and their economic well-being is something they're happy to take care of themselves.'

'Too right. All you have to do is work hard enough,' Lisa soothed. That, after all, was what she had done. She was working-class – well, she would have been if her dad had actually *worked* – and it hadn't been to her disadvantage.

Jack turned and gave her a complex smile. Wry and sad.

'Give me a quick career history,' Lisa asked.

Jack turned back to the boiler and reeled off with no obvious enthusiasm, 'Left college with an MA in communications, did the obligatory Irish stint abroad – two years in a New York media group, four in San Francisco at a cable network – returned to Ireland just in time for the economic miracle, worked for a newspaper group, got the boot like I said. Then two years ago old Calvin Carter gives me the gig here.'

'And how do you unwind?' Lisa enjoyed the sight of Jack's shirt stretched tight across his back muscles as he toiled. 'Like,' she gave a mischievous smile, which was unfortunately wasted on him, 'do you play golf?'

'That's the last time I come to fix your boiler,' he muttered.

'I didn't think you were a golf man, somehow,' she giggled. 'So what *do* you do?'

'Lisa, don't *ask* me these questions. I know –' Over his shoulder he flashed a fleeting half-smile, 'I fix boilers. I call around to random houses un-announced and insist on fixing people's boilers. Sometimes when they're not even broken.' He fell silent to concentrate on methodically winding a screw, then said, 'What else? I hang out with my girlfriend. I go sailing.'

'In a yacht?' Lisa asked eagerly, ignoring the mention of Mai.

'No, not really. Not at all, actually. It's a one-man craft, not much bigger than a surfboard. Ah, let's see. I play Sim City half the night, does that count?'

'What's that – a computer game? 'Course it counts. Anything else?'

'I d'know. We go to the pub, or out to eat, and we talk a lot about going to the movies but – and I really don't understand this – we never end up going.'

Lisa wasn't pleased with the 'we' in that sentence. She presumed it referred to Jack and Mai and she didn't know what they did instead of going to the movies, but she could take a guess.

'I see some friends from my college days, I watch a fair bit of telly but hey, just doing my job!'

'Oh yeah,' Lisa scorned playfully. Then she real-ized something. 'That's what you enjoy most, isn't it? Working on the television station?'

264

'Ye—' Then she watched Jack's back tense up as he remembered who he was talking to. 'Er, I enjoy the magazines too. You wouldn't believe the amount of work Channel 9 generates for me . . .'

'So you could have done without *Colleen* and all that extra work?' Lisa teased.

Jack tactfully deflected her question. 'Thing is, Channel 9 is currently very gratifying. After two years of real graft and struggle, finally the staff are well paid, corporate sponsors are pleased and consumers are getting intelligent programming. And we're nearly on the point of attracting investment so we can commission even more quality programming.'

'Top,' Lisa said vaguely. She'd heard enough about Channel 9 for now. 'What else do you do?'

'Aahhhhh,' Jack thought out loud. 'I see my parents most weekends. Just pop in for an hour here and there. They're not as young as they used to be so time with them seems that much more precious. You know what I mean?'

With desperate haste Lisa changed the subject. 'Do you ever go to restaurant openings? Or first nights? That kind of thing?'

'Nope,' Jack said shortly. 'I hate them. I was born without the shmooze gene, although I'm sure you don't need me to tell you that.'

'How so?' Lisa dissembled.

'Ah, come on, I'm a narky bollocks.'

'You've never been to me,' Lisa said, which wasn't to say that she hadn't noticed his tantrums.

'I don't mean to be,' he said with vague wistfulness. 'It just . . . sort of . . . happens, and I'm always sorry afterwards.'

'So your bark is worse than your bite?'

He swung around. 'Done!' he said, putting down his spanner. Then he added softly, 'Not always. Sometimes my bite is very bad.'

Before she could take him up on that provocative statement, he was clattering spanners and screwdrivers back into his toolbox. 'It's on a twenty-four-hour clock, should be no bother to set, hot water any time you like. See you tomorrow and sorry for arriving unannounced.'

'No proble –'

Suddenly he was gone, the house seemed too empty, and Lisa was alone – very alone – with her thoughts.

Oliver had cared about clothes, about parties, about art and music and clubs and knowing the right people. Jack was a badly dressed closet-socialist who sailed on a surfboard and who had no social life to speak of. But he was also big and sexy and dangerous and smelt nice, and hey, you can't have everything.

CHAPTER 24

You're a great girl, Ashling, you're a great girl, Ashling. Dylan's farewell to Ashling carouselled in her head, as she walked home from the Shelbourne. And only stopped when she popped into Café Moka for something to eat.

When she finally reached home, Boo was sitting outside.

'Where've you been?' Ashling asked. 'I haven't seen you in a couple of days.'

He threw his look heavenwards. 'Women!' he exclaimed, good-naturedly. 'Always trying to keep tabs on you.' His eyes were bright in his unshaven face. 'I felt like a change of scene.' He waved a grubby hand in a playfully louche gesture. 'A beautiful shop doorway in Henry Street beckoned, so I laid my hat there for a couple of nights.'

'So you sleep around,' Ashling said. 'Typical man.'

'It meant nothing,' Boo said earnestly. 'It was just a physical thing.'

'Last night I had books for you.' Ashling was annoyed at being caught, once more, on the hop.

Until she remembered that she had a review copy of a Patricia Cornwell in her bag. No one at the office had wanted it so Ashling had taken it for Joy.

'Would you be into this?' Awkwardly she tugged it from her bag. Boo's eyes blazed with so much interest that she felt slightly sick. She had so much, he had nothing except an orange blanket.

'Deadly,' he breathed. 'I'll mind it, make sure nothing happens to it.'

'You can keep it.'

'How come?'

'I got it, er, free. At work.'

'Cool job,' he congratulated. 'Thanks, Ashling, I appreciate this.'

'It's nothing,' she said, stiffly. Upset by the unfairness of the world, angry with herself for having so much power, guilty because she did so little.

As she stuck her key in the door, he called, 'What did you think of Marcus Valentine?'

'I don't know.' For a moment she was about to launch into a long explanation of how she hadn't fancied him, then she'd seen him on the stage and couldn't help changing her mind, how she was dying for him to ring her and hoped that there might be a message waiting for her and . . . hold on a minute.

'Funny,' she smiled weakly at Boo. 'He was really funny.'

Funny is fecking well right. Saying he'd ring, then

not bothering his arse. She ran up the stairs in her haste to see if there was a message.

At the sight of the red light flashing, her head went giddy. She hit 'play', and as the tape rewound to the start, she did a quick lap where she rubbed the lucky Buddha, touched her lucky pebble, stroked her lucky crystal and pulled on her lucky red bobble hat. 'Please, Benign Force in the Universe that I choose to call God,' she prayed, 'let him have rung.'

There was obviously some confusion in the space–time continuum, because her prayers were answered. But they were the *wrong* prayers. Out-of-date prayers – the message was from Phelim. So many times in the past Ashling had prayed for Phelim to ring her, and now that he had, it was too late.

'G'day, Ashling,' he crackled from Sydney. 'How're you going?' He sounded sunny and Australian, then he lapsed back into a Dublin accent. 'Listen, I'm after forgetting to buy my ma a birthday present and it's more than my life's worth. Would you get her an ornament or something, you know better than me what she likes, and I'll see you right. Thanks, you're a gem.'

'Bloody eejit,' she muttered, pulling off her lucky red bobble hat. If she hadn't sorted him out with tickets, visas, passports and Australian dollars, Phelim would still be trying to figure out how to leave the country. She'd almost had to physically put him on the plane with a note around his neck.

Then she noted her reactions – a complete absence of nausea, nostalgia or yearning. Contact with Phelim usually upset her, but it looked like she'd started to believe her own publicity. She really *was* over him.

She picked up the phone and rang Ted. 'If only Civil Servant-Boy could be here,' she said, by way of greeting.

'I'm on my way.'

'Get Joy as well.'

Moments later Ashling greeted Ted and Joy by saying, 'I'm having man trouble.'

'Me too,' Joy said, almost boastfully.

'Half-man-half-badger?'

'Half-*prick*-half-badger,' Joy corrected. 'Giving me the runaround. But what man, Ashling, is giving you trouble? Mr Sexy Delicious at work? I think I predicted this, didn't I?'

'Who? Oh, Jack Devine?' The memory of the two hundred cigarettes made her uncomfortable, so she moved swiftly along to the 'act your age, not the speed limit' accusation, and once again knew where she stood. 'That bastard?'

Joy gave Ted a smug, I-told-you-so smile. 'Feelings *are* running high,' she observed indulgently.

'It's not Jack Devine,' Ashling insisted. 'It's that stand-up comedian, Marcus Valentine.'

'*What*,' Joy asked testily, 'are you on about?'

So Ashling told the whole story, about meeting Marcus at the party on the quays, the Bellez-moi note –

270

'But he said that in his act!' Ted said excitedly. 'The girl he was talking about was you. This is outstanding!'

Ashling held up her hand for silence. 'Then I met him again the weekend before last at the party in Rathmines and I still didn't fancy him. But I saw him on Saturday night and I think I started to like him. And he said he'd ring me and he hasn't.'

'But of course he hasn't!' Joy exclaimed. 'It's only Monday.'

With her words, sanity returned to Ashling. 'You're absolutely right! I'm tying myself up in knots as usual and I'm not even sure I fancy him. And to think I spent all day yesterday on edge. Will I ever learn . . . ?'

'If he's going to call you, it'll be on Tuesday or Wednesday,' Joy said, with confidence.

'How do you know?'

'It's in the boys' rulebook. Ted, take note. You meet a girl on Saturday night and you never ring before Tuesday because you might seem too keen. If the call doesn't happen on Tuesday or Wednesday it doesn't happen at all.'

'What about Thursday?' Ashling asked, in alarm.

'Too close to the weekend,' Joy shook her head knowingly. 'They reckon your plans are already made and they don't want to risk rejection.'

'Actually, Saturday night's already booked.' Ashling was briefly distracted. 'I said I'd babysit for Dylan and Clodagh.'

Ted gasped, 'Can I come?'

Joy said in contempt, 'Don't tell me he fancies the princess.'

'She's beautiful,' Ted said.

'She's totally spoilt and –'

'Can I come?' Ted ignored Joy and implored Ashling.

'Ted, if someone is babysitting for Clodagh, the idea is that Clodagh *isn't there*.' Ashling was annoyed at Ted as good as asking her to broker a flirtation between himself and her very married friend.

'All the same . . . Look, will you ask her if I can come? You'll never be able to manage two kids by yourself.'

Ashling was caught between irritation and the realization that Ted was right. On her own she was no match for the combined might of Molly and Craig. 'OK, I'll ask.' But if Clodagh was as neurotic about the care of her children as Dylan had said, there was no way she'd let Ted into the house.

'I'd say Marcus Valentine will call tomorrow night or Wednesday.' Joy was tired of talking about Clodagh.

'I won't be here tomorrow night.'

'Where are you going?'

'Salsa lesson.'

'What!?'

'I liked it,' Ashling defended herself. 'It's only for ten weeks. And I'm disgustingly unfit.'

'You're going to get really skinny,' Joy wailed.

'I am not,' Ashling blustered. 'I've been a member of the gym for years and I'm not one centimetre smaller.'

'It might make a difference if you were to go once in a while,' Joy said, drily. 'Paying the monthly membership isn't enough.'

'I used to go,' Ashling said, in sulky defence. And indeed she did, doing hundreds of variations of sit-ups and waist-exercises. Crunchies and obliques and waist-twists. Repeatedly touching her knee with her opposite elbow until her face filled with blood and little veins burst in her eyes. But when it became clear that even if she crunchied herself into a coma, her waist was stubbornly going to refuse to get any smaller, she gave up. The rest of her wasn't so bad, she decided, so there was nothing to be gained by exercising.

Salsa was different. She wasn't going for her waist. She wanted to have fun.

'You've got a hobby,' Joy accused, in a fresh bout of worry. 'You're going to be one of those funny people who have hobbies.'

'It's not a *hobby*,' Ashling said in alarm. 'It's just something I want to do.'

'And what do you think a hobby is?'

'Speaking of salsa,' Ted said, 'I've looked over your article and it's outstanding. I've made a couple of suggestions, but it's fine as it is.'

'Really?' Ashling said, hardly daring to believe it. She'd sweated hard over it for three whole nights last week and reckoned she'd even managed to make it slightly funny, but she wasn't sure if she'd been imagining it.

'I enjoyed it. It made a nice change to work on something like that, instead of doing a report on the eradication of brucellosis amongst dairy herds. How sexy is that?' Ted said, not without bitterness. 'No wonder Clodagh isn't interested in me. The sooner I get my transfer to the Department of Defence the better.'

He lapsed into a reverie of machine guns, armoured cars, dirty faces, complicated penknives and other macho paraphernalia.

'And look what I've done for you.' Joy whipped out a sheet of paper. It contained several drawings of shoe soles, illustrating the sequence of steps for a salsa routine. Joy had sketched them in funny, cartoonish fashion, with arrows and dotted lines to indicate what happened.

'What a smart idea!' Ashling exclaimed. 'You're both fantastic.' The dreaded article was shaping up to being something decent. Apart from the photos of herself and Joy, she'd had Gerry the Art Director do a search for a picture of two dancers. He'd found a great one, the woman bent backwards from the waist, her black hair brushing the floor, the man leaning meaningfully over her. Very sexy. Ashling experienced a brief respite from the nagging suspicion that she wasn't really able for her job.

The phone rang, and as the answering machine

was still on, they listened intently to see who it was. Could it be Marcus Valentine?

'It won't be. I keep telling you,' Joy sighed with annoyance, 'it's only Monday.'

It was Clodagh.

'Be still your beating heart,' Joy said sarcastically to Ted.

Brief though the message was, in the context of Dylan's anxiety it made Ashling edgy.

'Ashling,' Clodagh spoke to the room, 'can you call me? I want to talk to you about . . . something.'

CHAPTER 25

On Tuesday morning when a glittery-faced Trix clattered into the office in her plastic platforms, she was accompanied by a faint but unmistakable smell of fish. Ashling noticed it the moment she arrived, then every subsequent arrival began sniffing in alarm as soon as they came through the door. Pointing it out to Trix was, however, a little awkward, and the matter remained unaddressed until the arrival of Kelvin. After all, he was a twenty-something lad and vulgarity was his currency.

'Trix, you smell of what I can only hope is fish.'

'It *is* fish.'

'Might we ask why?'

'I wanted a man with wheels,' Trix said sulkily.

Kelvin slapped himself around the face a couple of times. 'No!' he said cheerfully. 'I'm awake now and it still doesn't make sense.'

'I wanted a man with wheels,' Trix said angrily. 'So I met Paul and he delivers fish, and he's let use the van after work.'

Not surprisingly, the thought of Trix sitting in all her shiny, happy finery alongside a shoal of fish reduced the office to convulsions.

'I sit up front with the driver,' she protested, to no avail. 'Not in the back with all the fish.'

'What about your other boyfriends?' Kelvin asked.

'Kicked them to the kerb.'

Oh, to be as tough as her, Ashling thought, keying furiously. She was inputting her salsa article. As soon as it was all typed, she gave it to Gerry, who scanned in Joy's sketches and the photos.

'I'm going to play around with different typefaces and colour,' he said. 'Give me some time, then we'll show it to Lisa. Have faith, I'll make it purty.'

'I trust you,' Ashling promised. Gerry was an oasis of calm, quiet reassurance, who never seemed to panic, no matter how seemingly obscure or difficult the request.

While she waited, she rang Clodagh. 'You said you wanted to talk to me about something,' she said anxiously.

'I do.' There was the usual background cacophany. 'Craig's off sick, and Molly's banned again from playgroup.'

'What's she done now?'

'Apparently, she tried to set fire to the place. But she's only a little girl, exploring the world, finding out what matches do. What do they expect?' Another wave of bawling issued forth. 'At least she has a spark of curiosity. But I'm losing my fucking reason here, Ashling.'

That's what I'm afraid of.

'Which is what I want to talk to you about . . .

MOLLY, PUT THAT KNIFE DOWN. DOWN!!!
NOW!!! Craig, if Molly hits you, will you for God's
sake HIT HER BACK!!! . . . You big Jessie,'
Clodagh breathed, in quiet contempt. 'Got to go,
Ashling, I'll ring later.'

And Clodagh was gone. So Dylan was right,
something *was* up. Ashling swallowed. Feck it,
anyway.

Trying to distract herself, she pressed a few
buttons on the computer, her fingers eager when
she saw she'd been e-mailed. It was a joke sent
by Joy. What's the difference between a hedgehog
and a BMW?

'I've a joke for you,' Ashling called out to the
office in general. Instantly all work was abandoned. It didn't take much. 'What's the difference
between –'

'Heard it,' Jack Devine barked, striding towards
his office.

'You don't even know what I'm going to say,'
Ashling protested.

'With a hedgehog the pricks are on the *outside*.'
Jack slammed his door.

Ashling was astonished. 'How did he know?'

'This is the BMW/hedgehog joke?' Kelvin asked.

When Ashling nodded, Kelvin explained kindly,
'It's been doing the rounds the past couple of
days. And as Jack drives a Beemer, he's been told
it quite a lot.'

'Aahhh. I just thought he'd had another scrap
with his girlfriend.'

'Have you any idea the kind of pressure poor Mr Devine is under?' Behind her desk, Mrs Morley had risen to her feet (although she looked no taller). Her voice was high with protective anger. 'He was in negotiations with the technicians' union until ten o'clock on Saturday night. And this morning he has three executives coming from London, including the group accountant, to discuss very serious matters with him, and none of you care. Although you should,' she finished ominously.

Even though she was generally viewed as a doom-mongering old boot, her words had a sobering effect on everyone. Especially on Lisa. Still no word on the advertising revenue. Her nerves were cast-iron, but even she was finding this wearing.

Jack came out of his office.

'They've just rung,' Mrs Morley said. 'They'll be here in ten minutes.'

'Thanks,' Jack sighed, running his hands distractedly through his tumbled hair. He looked tired and worried and Ashling suddenly felt sorry for him.

'Would you like a cup of coffee before your meeting?' she offered, sympathetically.

He turned his dark eyes on to her. 'No,' he said, narkily. 'It might keep me awake.'

Well, get lost in that case, Ashling thought, all sympathy gone.

'Ashling, take a look,' Gerry invited. Ashling rushed to his screen and was full of admiration for how he'd laid out the article. A four-page spread, which looked colourful, funny, engaging and interesting. The text was broken up into strips and sidebars, and the entire piece was dominated by the erotic photo of the dancing couple, the woman's long hair sweeping the floor.

He printed it all off and Ashling took it to Lisa, as though it was a sacred offering. Without speaking, Lisa surveyed the pages. Even the expression on her face gave nothing away. The silence endured for so long that Ashling's excitement started to dampen and turn into worry. Had she got it all wrong? Perhaps this wasn't what Lisa had wanted at all.

'Spelling mistake here.' Lisa's voice was toneless. 'Typo here. And another one. And another one.' When she got to the end she shoved the sheets away and said, 'Fine.'

'Fine?' Ashling asked, still waiting for an acknowledgement of how much work and worry had gone into it.

'Yes, fine,' Lisa said, impatiently. 'Tidy it up, then run it.'

Ashling glared. She was so disappointed she couldn't help it. She wasn't to know that this constituted very high praise from Lisa. When employees of *Femme* were subjected to her screaming 'Get this piece of shit off my desk and completely rewrite it,' they used to take it as a tribute.

Then Lisa changed the subject totally when she remembered something. Over-casually, she asked, 'Hey, who was that man you were with last night?'

'What man?' Ashling knew exactly who she was talking about, but was exacting a tiny, petty revenge.

'Blond bloke, you left with him.'

'Oh, Dylan.' Then Ashling said nothing more. She was enjoying this.

'And who is he?' Lisa eventually had to ask.

'An old friend.'

'Single?'

'He's married to my best friend. So you like my article?' Ashling said stubbornly.

'I said it's fine.' Lisa was irritable. Then her next words rubbed salt into the wound. 'I think we'll make it a regular feature. Knock together another piece about meeting men for the October issue. What did you suggest at the first meeting we had? Going to a dating agency? Horse-riding? Surfing the net?'

She remembered *everything*, Ashling thought, impossibly burdened by the thought of having to make this monumental effort next month and every month. And never getting fecking well praised for it!

'Or you could do something on the chances of meeting men at a comedy gig,' Lisa said, with an artful smile.

Ashling shrugged uncomfortably.

'Has he called you yet?' Lisa asked suddenly.

Ashling shook her head, embarrassed at what

a loser she was. Had he rung Lisa? Probably, the gloaty cow. After some seconds without speech the curiosity got too much. 'Has he called you?'

To her surprise, Lisa also shook her head.

'Prick!' Ashling said energetically, cruising on relief.

'Prick!' Lisa agreed, with an unexpected giggle.

All at once it seemed very funny that he'd rung neither of them.

'Men!' The burdensome anticipation Ashling had carried since Saturday dissolved into giddy laughter.

'Men!' Lisa agreed, frothy with merriment.

At that moment, both of them were drawn to look at Kelvin, who was standing mid-floor, idly scratching his balls and staring into space. He looked so like a *man* that when their eyes swivelled back to each other, they jack-knifed into convulsions.

Spasms of mirth issued from Lisa's core. Which so uplifted and liberated her that she realized it was a long time since she'd really laughed. A proper belly-laugh where nothing else mattered.

'What?' Kelvin demanded edgily. 'What's so funny?'

That was enough to start them again. Their mutual suspicion was washed clean by the high tide of hilarity, and they were – for the moment, at least – warm with unity.

Her mouth still dolphin-wide with the remnants of glee, Lisa on impulse said to Ashling, 'I've got an invite to a make-up demo this afternoon. D'you want to come?'

'Why not?' Ashling said lightly. Grateful, but no longer pitifully so.

The make-up presentation was by Source, who were the current big thing, favoured by super-models and It girls. Reassuringly expensive, all their products were organic, the packaging was bio-degradable, recyclable or reusable, and they made a big song and dance because they ploughed some of their profits back into replanting trees, patching up the ozone layer *et cetera*. (The actual amount was 0.003 per cent of the post-tax profit, after the shareholders had received their dividend. In practice the sum amounted to a couple of hundred quid, but even if people knew, they wouldn't care. They'd bought wholesale into the notion of 'Source – responsible beauty'.)

The Morrison hotel was the site of the demon-stration, just far enough away from the office for Lisa to insist on getting a taxi. It would have been quicker if they'd walked because the traffic was so bad, but she didn't care. In London she'd never walked anywhere and she considered it a slur on her status to be expected to here.

One of the function rooms of the hotel had been converted into an old-fashioned pharmacy for the day. The Source girls wore white doctors' coats and were positioned behind miniature apothecary desks (made of MDF, tampered with to look like aged teak). All around were glass-stoppered bottles, medicine droppers and prescription jars.

'Pretentious nonsense,' Lisa laughed scornfully into Ashling's ear. 'And when they speak about the new season's products, they behave as if they've just discovered a cure for cancer. But first a drink! . . . Wheatgrass juice!' Lisa exclaimed, when the waiter deconstructed the contents of his tray for her. 'Pants! What else have you?'

She beckoned another waiter, whose tray was covered with silver canisters, each with a tube like a bendy opaque straw. 'Oxygen?' Lisa said, in disgust. 'Don't be daft. Bring me a glass of champagne.'

'Make it two,' Ashling said nervously. The mere sight of the green, lumpy wheatgrass juice was making her feel sick, and to the best of her knowledge, she could get oxygen any time she liked. They had three glasses of champagne each, much to the envy of the other liggers, who were timidly sipping their free wheatgrass juice and trying not to barf. Only Dan 'I'll try anything once' Heigel from the *Sunday Independent* had sampled the oxygen and became so lightheaded that he had to lie down in the lobby, where tourists were stepping over him and smiling indulgently, thinking he was the quintessential example of a mouldy drunk Irishman.

'Come on,' Lisa eventually said to Ashling. 'We ought to go for our lecture, then we can claim our free gift.'

Lisa was right, Ashling noted. Caro, who

demonstrated the cosmetics for them, was remarkably earnest and humour-free about the products.

'This season's look is shimmery,' she said, lovingly stroking some eye-shadow on to the back of her hand.

'That was last season's look too,' Lisa challenged.

'Oh no. Last season's was shimmer*ing*.' This was said without a trace of irony.

Lisa poked a sharp elbow into Ashling and they shared a shudder of silent mirth. It was nice to have someone to have a laugh with at these things, Lisa realized.

'We've broken new ground this season by producing a lip-gloss for the browbone, we're very excited about it . . . any inconsistency in texture is because, unlike other cosmetic houses, we refuse to corrupt our products with animal fats. A small price to pay . . .'

Finally, the worthy demonstration came to an end, and Caro clinked together a selection of the new season's cosmetics. All the products were in thick brown glass containers, like old-fashioned medicine bottles, and were packaged into a replica of a doctor's case.

She handed it to Lisa, who was obviously in charge. But when Ashling and Lisa didn't move off, Caro said anxiously, 'Only one gift per publication. Our philosophy at Source is to discourage excess.'

Lisa and Ashling exchanged a moment's aghast rivalry.

'I knew that,' Lisa said lightly, gliding carelessly from the room, her grip claw-tight around the goody bag. Possession was nine-tenths of the law, leastways it was last time she'd checked. Out into the hall she went, and across the lobby, not breaking stride as she stepped over the still prone Dan Heigel.

'Nice knickers,' he murmured.

'Why d'ya have to wear trousers?' he asked as, a second later, Ashling hopped over him.

When Lisa judged that they were far enough away from the hotel, she slowed down. Ashling caught up and gave the freebie an anxious look.

'It depends on what's in it,' Lisa said, tight-lipped. She'd just remembered why she liked to work alone. When you don't, you might have to share – make-up, praise, stuff. Opening the doctor's case, she said, 'You can have the eye-shadow. Hey, it's shimmery!'

But it was also a funny sludge colour that neither of them would wear.

'And you can have the lip-gloss for the browbone too. I'll keep the neck-cream and the eye-liner.'

'And the lipstick?' Ashling asked, a knot of longing in her stomach. The lipstick was the real prize, a wonderful muted brown, with a perfect matt finish.

'I get the lipstick,' Lisa said. 'After all, I'm the boss.'

Don't we know it? Ashling thought, resentfully.

CHAPTER 26

On Tuesday night Ashling went to her salsa class. As before, the women outnumbered the men by about ten to one. Ashling had to dance with another woman, who asked her if she came here often.

'It's the first class,' Ashling pointed out.

'Oh right, I forgot. Anyway, isn't it nice to have a hobby?'

After the class, pink-cheeked and glowing, Ashling belted home to check her answering machine, but the moment she opened the door, she saw the long, unblinking baleful stare of the red light. Ah well, there was still Wednesday night. All wasn't lost.

As she rooted in the kitchen cupboards, looking for something to eat, she fretted, wondering if perhaps Marcus had lost her phone number. But no. He'd shoved it deep in his pocket and said he'd keep it close to his heart. Besides, it was the second time she'd given it to him, which lessened the chances of him mislaying it.

She surveyed the spoils: half a bag of tortilla chips, slightly soft; a carton of black olives; four

287

Hobnobs, also slightly soft; a dented can of pineapple; eight slices of stale bread. A poor turnout, she'd have to go to the supermarket tomorrow.

She was dying for something hot, so she shoved two slices of stale bread into the toaster. As she waited she experienced a burst of impotent frustration with Marcus. For knocking a hole in her life and opening the way to let anticipation come creeping in. She'd been fine before he'd started pestering her.

Why was he pestering her, anyway? Now that she'd seen him on stage her entire opinion had changed. Instead of being a man that she wouldn't go near, Marcus Valentine was a desirable commodity and she wasn't sure if she was worthy of him.

Halfway through a slice of toast, the phone rang, rocketing her adrenalin levels. Brushing buttery crumbs from her face, she crossed the room and snatched it up. 'Hello?' All breathless expectation. Which instantly died away. 'Oh Clodagh, hi.'

'Are you at home?' Clodagh asked.

'Um, what do you think?'

'Sorry. What I mean is, can I come over?'

Oh no. Ashling's mood bottomed out. Bad stuff ahead. Immediately she wrote off her plans to ring her parents – she had only so much endurance. 'Come on round,' she assured Clodagh. 'I'm in for the evening.'

★   ★   ★

288

'I'm just popping over to Ashling's for an hour,' Clodagh called to Dylan, who was watching telly in the half-papered front-room.

'Are you?' he asked, in surprise. This was a break from the norm, Clodagh rarely went out in the evenings. And never without him. But before he could question her further, she was already slamming the door and reversing the Nissan Micra out into the road.

'I need to talk to you,' Clodagh announced, as Ashling let her into the flat.

'So I gather,' Ashling said, dismally.

'And I need you to do me a favour.'

'I'll do my best.'

'Hey, do you know there's a homeless man sitting in your doorway?' Clodagh abruptly changed tack. 'He said *hello* to me.'

'That's probably Boo,' Ashling said, idly. 'Young, brown hair, smiley?'

'Yes, but . . .' Clodagh faltered. 'Do you *know* him?'

'Not intimately, but . . . well, we have the odd chat in passing.'

'But he's probably a drug addict! He might mug you with a syringe – that's what they do, you know. Or break into your flat.'

'He's not a drug addict.'

'How do you know?'

'He told me.'

'And you believed him?'

'You can tell.' Ashling was suddenly irritable.

289

'If someone is drunk or stoned you can tell just by talking to them.'

'So how come he's homeless then?'

'I wouldn't know,' Ashling admitted. It had seemed rude to ask. 'But he's very nice. Normal, actually. And I wouldn't blame him if he did drink or take drugs – being homeless looks horrible.'

Clodagh pushed her lower lip out mutinously. 'I don't know where you get these people from. But just be careful, will you? Anyway, I need to talk to you. I've made a decision.'

'What is it?' *Going on anti-depressants? Leaving Dylan?*

'The time has come,' Clodagh lowered herself down on to the couch. Getting herself comfortable she repeated, 'The time has come . . .'

'For *what*?' Nerves made Ashling snap.

'. . . for me to go back to work,' Clodagh finished.

This wasn't what Ashling had been expecting. She'd been braced for something a lot uglier. 'What? You? Go back to work?'

'Why not?' Clodagh was defensive.

'Er, exactly. Why not? But what triggered this?'

'Ah, I've been thinking about it for a while. It probably isn't healthy to pour all my energies into my children.' Privately Clodagh reckoned that that was where the terrible, itchy-uncomfortable feelings of dissatisfaction were coming from. 'I need to get out of the house more. Have adult conversations.'

'And that's all you wanted to talk to me about?' Ashling needed to check.

'What else would there be?' Clodagh sounded surprised.

'Nothing.' Ashling could have smacked Dylan, getting her worked up into a state of high anxiety, when it was clear that all that was wrong with Clodagh was boredom. 'So what kind of job were you thinking of?'

'Don't know yet,' Clodagh admitted. 'Don't really mind. Anything . . . Although,' she added ruefully, 'whatever it is, it'll be hard to go back to taking orders from other people. People who aren't my children, that is.'

As Ashling rearranged her mood to fit in with this unexpected turn of events, Clodagh fell into a reverie. She was always reading books where housewives started their own business. Where they turned their great baking skills into a cake industry. Or set up a health club for women. Or channelled their pottery hobby into a thriving enterprise, employing, oh, at least seven or eight people. They made it sound so easy. Banks lent them money, sisters-in-law minded children, neighbours converted the garage into an HQ, everyone rallied round. When the café flooded, the world and its granny mucked in to clear up: customers, postmen, innocent passers-by and someone the heroine had had a bad argument with. (This usually signalled the end of the disagreement.)

And these fictional enterprising women invariably bagged a man into the bargain.

But you have a man, Clodagh reminded herself.

Yes, but . . .

So could she set up her own business? What could she do?

Nothing, if she was honest. She sincerely doubted that anyone would pay to eat something she'd cooked. In fact, with Craig and Molly she almost had to pay *them* to eat their meals. She couldn't see people shelling out good money to come to her restaurant and eat Petit Filous and microwaved Pot Noodles – even if she did offer a free food-cooling service by blowing on everything before she served it. *And* allowed the customers to rub their leftovers into their hair.

As for handicrafts – she'd rather give birth than do pottery. Nor had she any idea how to go about setting up a health club.

No, it seemed as if a more conventional route to earning a living was on the cards for Clodagh. Which is where Ashling came in.

'So I wondered if you'd type my CV for me?' Clodagh asked. 'And listen, I don't want Dylan to know about this. Not yet, anyway, his pride might be hurt. If he wasn't the sole bread-winner, do you know what I mean?'

Ashling wasn't entirely convinced, but she decided to let it go. 'OK. What hobbies will I put you down for? Hang-gliding? S&M?'

'White-water rafting,' Clodagh giggled. 'And human sacrifices.'

'And you're sure you feel OK?' Ashling still needed to have it underlined.

'I do now. But to be honest, I'd been very down for a while, it was really starting to get to me.'

Maybe Dylan wasn't being a total drama queen, after all, Ashling decided. Perhaps he'd had some reason to worry.

'But now I know what to do,' Clodagh said cheerfully, 'everything's going to be all right . . . Hey.' She suddenly remembered something. 'Dylan tells me you're babysitting for us on Saturday night.'

So Operation Cheer-Up-Clodagh was still going ahead?

'We're going to L'Oeuf,' Clodagh shivered in delight. 'It's ages since I've been out.'

'Listen, what if Ted babysat with me?' Hopefully Clodagh would blow that idea out of the water.

'Ted? The small dark one?' Clodagh considered. 'OK, why not? He looks harmless.'

CHAPTER 27

Ashling got in early to type up Clodagh's CV, then got Gerry to arrange it, all fancy. As she waited for him to print it out, she was shocked to find herself doodling 'Ashling Valentine'. *Grow up!* Better do some work. Instead she did something even more unpleasant. She rang her parents. Her father answered.

'Dad, it's Ashling.'

'Ah, hello!' He sounded overjoyed to hear from her. 'How are things?'

'Oh, good, good. And you're all well?'

'Never better. So when are we going to see you? Any chance of you coming down for a weekend?'

'Not just yet.' She shrivelled with guilt. 'You see, I sometimes work weekends at the moment.'

'That's a pity, mind you don't overdo it. But the job's going well, is it?'

'Very well.'

'Hold on, your mother wants a quick word.'

'Listen, Dad, I can't really talk, I'm at work. I'll ring some evening. I'm glad you're all good.'

Then she hung up, feeling a little bit better, a little bit worse. Relieved that she'd rung and wouldn't have to do it again for a couple of weeks, guilty because she couldn't give them what they really wanted. She lit a cigarette and inhaled deeply.

Lisa was late.

'Where were you?' Trix asked. 'Everyone's been looking for you.'

'You're my PA,' Lisa said, impatiently. 'You're supposed to know. Look in my appointment book.'

'Oh, your *appointment* book,' Trix said. '*Of course.*' She turned to the appropriate page and read out, '"Interviewing mad Frieda Kiely." That's where she was, lads.'

'That's right,' Lisa announced, loud enough for everyone – particularly Mercedes – to hear. 'I visited Frieda Kiely at her *atelier* this morning. She's a sweetie. An absolute sweetie.'

Actually, she'd been a nightmare. A grotesque nightmare. Unpleasant, crazily hyper and so far up her own bum there was a chance she might never reappear. Which would be no bad thing, Lisa thought.

When Lisa had arrived, Frieda had been stretched on a chaise longue, dressed in one of her own over-the-top frocks, her long grey hair tumbling to her waist. She was half-lying on bundles of fabric and tucking into a McDonald's breakfast. Though Lisa had confirmed the interview with Frieda's assistant that very morning, Frieda insisted there was no such arrangement.

'But your assistant . . .'

'My assistant,' Frieda overrode her in bellowing tones, 'is a useless moron. I shall sack her. Julie, Elaine, whatever your name is – YOU'RE FIRED! . . . But as you're here,' Frieda conceded. She was in the mood for a little fun.

'Can you tell me about yourself?' Lisa tried to grasp the reins of the interview. 'Where were you born?'

'Planet Zog, darling,' Frieda drawled.

Lisa eyed her. She was inclined to believe her. 'If you'd prefer to talk about the clothes –'

'Clothes!' Frieda spat. 'They're not clothes!'

Weren't they? But if they weren't clothes, then what were they? Lisa wondered.

'Works of art, you moron!'

Lisa did not respond well to being called a moron. She was finding this very, very hard. But she had to think of the good of *Colleen*.

'Perhaps –' She swallowed away rage. 'Perhaps you can tell me why you're so successful.'

'Why? Why?' Frieda's eyes popped with disgust. 'Because I'm a bloody genius, that's why. I hear voices in my head.'

'Perhaps you should see a doctor.' Lisa couldn't stop herself.

'I'm talking about my spirit guides, you idiot! They tell me what to create.'

A ratty Yorkshire terrier wearing a miniature stovepipe hat scampered into the room, yapping with horribly shrill barks.

'Ooooh, come to Mommy.' Frieda gathered the dog to her enormous bosom, dragging him across squares of tweed and an egg McMuffin. 'This is Schiaperelli. My muse. Without him, my genius would simply disappear.'

Lisa began to hope that a horrible accident would befall the dog. This sentiment increased when Schiaperelli effected introductions by clamping his sharp teeth around Lisa's hand.

Frieda Kiely was appalled. 'Ooooh, did the nasty journalist put her dirty hand in your mouth?' She glared at Lisa. 'If Schiaperelli becomes ill, I shall sue you. You and that rag of a newspaper you represent.'

'It's not a newspaper. It's *Colleen* magazine. We did a shoot in Donegal of your –'

But Frieda wasn't listening. Instead she heaved herself up on to her elbow and roared through the door at her assistant. 'Girl! Someone in this building smells of turnip! Find out who it is and get rid of them. I've told you before I won't stand for it.'

The assistant appeared from the outer office and said calmly, 'You're imagining things, no one smells of turnip.'

'I can smell it. You're fired!' Frieda shrieked.

Lisa stared at her hand. The little bastard had left his teethmarks on her skin. She'd had enough. There was no way they could run a piece on this madwoman.

In the outer office, the assistant – who was

actually called Flora – rubbed Lisa's wound with arnica ointment that was obviously there for that very purpose.

'How many times a day does she sack you?' Lisa asked.

'Countless. She can be difficult,' Flora soothed. 'But that's because she's a genius.'

'She's an insane bitch.'

Flora cocked her head to one side and considered. 'Yes,' she mused, 'that too.'

Lisa caught a taxi to the office. Under no circumstances would she give Mercedes the satisfaction of knowing she was right, that Frieda Kiely *was* a maniac.

'Frieda was a charming woman,' Lisa told the staff of *Colleen*. 'We really bonded.'

She watched Mercedes for her reaction, but her dark eyes gave nothing away.

Half an hour later, Jack came out of his office, marched straight over to Lisa and said, 'London rang.'

She turned her expertly made-up grey eyes on him, her throat too full of anxiety to permit speech. Jesus Christ, what a morning!

Jack stalled for impact, before slowly saying, with dramatic effect, 'L'Oréal . . . have placed . . . a four-page ad . . . every issue . . . for the first . . . six . . . months!'

He took a moment to let the news hit home. And then he smiled, happiness flooding across his generally troubled face. His curly mouth kinked upwards, displaying his cheeky chipped tooth, and his eyes were bright and delighted.

'What kind of discount?' Lisa's numb lips mumbled.

'No discount. They're paying full ratecard. Because we're worth it, ha ha.'

Lisa remained still, watching his face with a kind of wonder. It was only now that they were back on track that she let herself feel the full extent of the terror that had been present for the past week. Jack didn't need to tell her that L'Oréal's vote of confidence would probably be enough to convince other cosmetic houses to buy space.

'Good,' she managed.

Why did he have to tell her in front of everyone? If they'd been closeted in his office she could have flung herself into his arms and given him a hug.

'Good?' He widened his eyes playfully.

'We should celebrate.' Lisa began to gather herself and let the relief in. 'Have lunch.'

Her happiness levels continued to rise when Jack agreed, 'We should.'

They locked eyes and exchanged a moment of dizzy euphoria.

'I'll book a table. Trix,' Lisa called, joyously, 'cancel my lunch-time hair appointment!'

It was nearly like the old days.

'While you're here, Jack, take a look at this.' Lisa waved something at him.

From three desks away, Ashling – who'd been

299

following everything with interest *anyway* – saw that Lisa was showing Jack her salsa article.

'Told you I'd knock this magazine into something fabulous,' Lisa laughed up at him.

'You certainly did,' he agreed, skimming over the piece, nodding with approval. 'This is excellent stuff.'

Impotently, Ashling watched. Somehow Lisa had appropriated all the credit for *her* work. It wasn't fair. But what was she going to do about it? Nothing. Too scared of confrontation. All at once she heard herself call, 'Glad you like it!' Her voice was shaking. She was trying to come across as casual, but she knew she sounded stilted and strange.

Surprised, Jack jerked his head towards Ashling.

'I wrote the piece,' she said, apologetically. 'I'm glad you like it,' she added, without conviction.

'And Gerry typeset it,' Lisa scolded. 'And I came up with the concept. You're going to have to learn about team-work, Ashling.' Lisa directed her rebuke to Ashling directly at Jack.

But Jack was studying the sexy photo, then he began flicking from the woman to Ashling, his dark eyes bold and suggestive. Ashling was hot and uncomfortable from his scrutiny.

'Well, well.' His lips curled up at the corners, as though he was stuffing back a huge grin. 'So, Ashling, this is what you get up to in your spare time? Dirty dancing?'

'It's not . . .' She wanted to hit him.

'Seriously, it's a superb piece. You've done very well,' Jack said, dropping all innuendo. 'Hasn't she, Lisa?'

Lisa's mouth attempted many different shapes, but there was no escape. 'Yes,' she was forced to say. 'She has.'

Lisa booked a table at Halo for herself and Jack. Best to assume control because she had a feeling if she left it to him they'd end up at Pizza Hut.

Half an hour before the off she took herself to the ladies' to ensure she looked her very, very best. What a stroke of luck she'd worn her lavender Press and Bastyan suit today. Although if it hadn't been that suit it would have been something equally glam. As a magazine editor, you never knew when you might be called upon to be fabulous. Always Prepared, that was her motto.

There was no way her flimsy grosgrain-ribbon sandals would survive the short walk along the quays – they barely held it together as she strolled around the office. Not that Lisa resented their being so impractical – some shoes exist just to display a fierce, short-lived burst of beauty. Why else did God invent taxis?

Assessing herself in the mirror, she was grudgingly pleased. Her eyes were bright and wide (thanks to white eye-liner on her inner rim), her complexion dewy (courtesy of Aveda Masque) and her forehead smooth and wrinkle-free (all down to the Botox injection she'd had just before she'd left London). She brushed her hair until it gleamed – this took no time at all. It *always* gleamed, thanks to leave-in conditioner, anti-frizz hairspray and being blow-dried by a professional.

At ten to one their taxi arrived and she and Jack left together, watched beadily by the entire office. Lisa was thrilled to get him all to herself, in such close proximity, and planned to use the confined space in the car to 'accidently' jostle her slim, bare legs against his. But as soon as they got in, Jack's mobile rang and he spent the journey arguing with the radio station's legal advisor about an injunction that had been slapped on them, regarding a controversial interview with a bishop who'd had an affair. The opportunity to jostle simply didn't arise.

'I can't see what the problem is,' Jack complained into the mouthpiece. 'It's a novelty these days to find a bishop who *hasn't* had an affair. In fact, why do we even want to interview the guy?'

'How are you, Lisa?' the taxi-driver asked. 'Have you found a flat yet?'

Lisa leant forward. Who was this strange man who had such intimate knowledge of her life? Then she saw that he was the same taxi-driver who'd taken her around to view flats during her first week in Dublin.

'Oh yes, I've got a little house off the South Circular,' she said politely.

'The South Circular?' He nodded approvingly.

'One of the few remaining parts of Dublin that hasn't been yuppified out of all existence.'

'Oh, but it's still very nice,' Lisa defended it.

Then she remembered something she'd wanted the answer to. 'So what happened after you confronted the gang of girls who were bullying your fourteen-year-old daughter? You didn't have time to finish telling me the last time.'

'They haven't touched her since,' he smiled. 'She's a changed girl.'

When Lisa got out of the car he said, 'The name's Liam. You can ask for me in future if you want.'

Jack was still on the phone when they were shown to their centre-floor table in the beautiful, bustling restaurant. This pleased Lisa. Jack might look like he'd found his suit in a skip, but he was speaking authoritatively on a mobile. It went a long way to redress the balance. Some nearby diners anxiously reached for their phones when they saw Jack on his, and made a couple of entirely unnecessary calls.

After promising that he'd come up with a solution by five o'clock. Jack snapped his phone away. 'Sorry about that, Lisa.'

'No problem,' she smiled prettily, demonstrating her new Source lipstick to its best advantage.

But the phone call had put paid to Jack's earlier rush of levity. He was once again turbulent and serious and couldn't be persuaded to flirt. Though there was nothing to say that she couldn't.

'To us,' Lisa smiled meaningfully, touching her wine glass against Jack's. Then she added, just to confuse him and keep him on his toes, 'Long may *Colleen* prosper.'

'I'll drink to that.' He raised his glass and managed a smile, but was clearly preoccupied. All he wanted to talk about was work. Readership profiles, printing costs, the value of having a book page. Nor did he seem very at home in the cutting-edge chic of Halo. Laboriously he wrestled with his starter of unwieldy frisée lettuce, trying to persuade the curls of it on to a fork and then to stay in his mouth. 'Christ,' he suddenly exclaimed, when another mouthful made a springy bid for freedom, 'I feel like a giraffe!'

Lisa went with the mood. She saw no point in trying to re-create the relaxed banter of the night in her kitchen, he just wasn't interested. He was too busy, too stressed, and she was flattered that he'd agreed to come for lunch at all. And if he wanted to talk work, she could talk work. With her admirable ability to turn most things to her advantage, she decided that now was as good a time as any to ask Jack about the possibility of syndicating a possible column from Marcus Valentine to some of their other publications.

'Has he actually said he'll do a column for us?' Jack asked, almost enthusiastically.

'Not exactly . . . not yet.' She smiled confidently across the table. 'But he will.'

'I'll make enquiries about syndication. You're full of bright ideas,' he acknowledged.

It wasn't until they were leaving the restaurant that Jack became human again. 'So how's the boiler timer working out for you?' he asked, with an agreeable sparkle in his eyes.

'Top,' Lisa twinkled. 'I can have long, hot showers any time I like.' She said 'long' and 'hot' in a long, hot way. Slow, languid, sensuous.

'Good,' he said, his pupils dilating in a gratifying flicker of interest. 'Good.'

Lisa was almost home from work when she bumped into a wrecked-looking, mustardy-blonde woman wearing a bobbly track-suit and – very incongruously – carrying a DKNY tote. *Lisa's* DKNY tote. At least it had been until she'd given it to Francine, one of the little girls on the road. She had a feeling the fried-looking woman – Kathy? – was Francine's mother.

'Hello Lisa,' she beamed. 'Are you well?'

'Yes, thank you,' Lisa said coolly. How did everyone round here know her name?

'I'm just off to work. Silver-service gig at the Harbison. Thirty quid into your hand and your taxi home.' Kathy appeared to be talking about waitressing. She waved two hundred pounds' worth of handbag at Lisa. 'I'll be late. See ya.'

Lisa was suddenly visited with inspiration. 'Um, Kathy – it *is* Kathy, isn't it? Would you be interested in a cleaning job?'

'I thought you'd never ask!'

'Oh? Why's that?'

'Er, you're a busy woman, when would you get time for cleaning?' What Kathy really meant was that Francine had inveigled an invitation into Lisa's house and had reported back that it was a right pigsty. 'Miles worse than ours!'

Ashling, meanwhile, had spent Wednesday evening ferrying a gift-wrapped Portmeirion bowl to Phelim's mother, thus completing her set.

'My work here is done,' she teased.

Then she had to sit for way too long in Mrs Egan's kitchen, listening to the familiar lament.

'Phelim didn't know what side his bread was buttered on. He should have married you, Ashling.'

She waited for Ashling to agree but, for the first time ever, she didn't.

When Ashling got home, there was no message on her machine. Damn Joy and her boys' rule-book.

'It's only nine o'clock, you pessimist,' Joy berated, when she arrived to accompany Ashling on her vigil. 'Still plenty of time. Open a bottle of wine and I'll tell you all the nice things Mick said to me last night.'

Ashling could hardly keep up with the roller-coaster twists and turns of Joy and Mick's relationship. They were almost as bad as Jack Devine and his little finger-biting friend. She located the corkscrew, poured two glasses of wine and settled in to analyse, syllable by syllable, everything Mick had ever said to Joy.

'. . . So then he said that I was the kind of woman who liked late nights. What do you think he meant by that? He means I'm the kind of woman you party with but don't marry, doesn't he?'

'Maybe he just means that you like late nights.'

Joy shook her head energetically. 'No, there's always a subtext . . .'

'Ted says there isn't. That when a man says something he means just what he says.'

'What would he know?'

Reading meaning into everything was so involving that when the call came at seven minutes past ten, Ashling had nearly forgotten she was waiting for it.

'Answer it.' Joy nodded at the ringing phone. But Ashling was almost afraid to, in case it wasn't him.

'Hello,' she said tentatively.

'Hello, is that Ashling, patron saint of comedians? It's Marcus here. Marcus Valentine.'

'Hi,' Ashling said. '*It's him,*' she mouthed silently at Joy, then dabbed her fingertip about her face to indicate freckles. 'What did you call me?' she giggled.

'Patron saint of comedians. At Ted Mullins's first gig, you helped him out, remember? And I thought to myself, that girl is a comedian's friend.'

She considered – yes, she liked the idea of being patron saint of comedians.

'So, how are you?' he asked. She decided she liked his voice. You'd never know it belonged to a freckly man. 'Been to any good comedy gigs lately?'

She giggled again. 'I was at one on Saturday night.'

'You'll have to tell me all about it,' he laughed, in his freckle-free voice.

'I will,' she heard herself giggle in reply. From far away she wondered what was with all the giggling. She sounded like a half-wit.

'Any chance that you'd come out to play this Saturday night?' he invited.

'Oh, I can't.' There was genuine regret in her voice. She thought about explaining about having to babysit for Clodagh and somehow managed to stop herself. It wouldn't do any harm if he thought she had a life.

'Going away for the bank-holiday weekend?' He sounded disappointed.

'No, just busy on Saturday night.'

'And I'm busy on Sunday.'

Conversation stalled, then erupted simultaneously on both sides.

'Doing anything on Monday?' he asked, at the same time as she suggested, 'How about Monday?'

She giggled. Again.

'Sounds to me like we have a plan,' he said. 'How about I call you on Monday morning – not too early – and we take it from there?'

'I'll see you then!'

'You will,' he said, his pitch warm and full of promise.

Ashling put down the phone. 'Oh my God, I'm going out with freckly Marcus Valentine on Monday.' She was frothy with excitement and shock. 'I haven't been on a date for years. Not since Phelim.'

'Happy now?' Joy asked.

Ashling nodded cautiously. Now that he had rung, there was always the fear that she'd go off him again.

'Right then,' Joy ordered. 'Let's get you into training. Repeat after me, "Oh Marcus! Marcus!"'

The following morning when Ashling arrived at work, Lisa called her over. 'Hey, guess who rang me last night?'

Ashling looked at her combative, competitive expression, at the triumph that lit her grey eyes.

'Marcus Valentine?' Who else could it be?

'Too right,' Lisa agreed. 'Marcus Valentine.'

'Oh yeh?' Ashling put her hand on her hip with bold attitude. ''Cos he rang me too.'

Lisa's mouth half-opened at this unexpected news. She'd thought she was the winner.

'When are you meeting him?' Ashling asked.

'Next week some time.'

'Is that so? Well, I'm going out with him on Monday night . . . That's sooner,' she added, just in case Lisa hadn't noticed.

She and Lisa locked into a tense, truculent scowl.

'So I win!' Ashling didn't know what had come over her.

Startled, Lisa glowered at Ashling, at her meek face doing its best to be confrontational. She'd been bested. And to her surprise, she thought it was funny. She began to laugh. 'Good for you,' she chortled.

It took Ashling a moment to swing with the change of mood, then she too started laughing. They were both being ridiculous!

'God, Lisa, it's not even as if we want the same thing from him,' Ashling was briefly brave enough to say. 'Why are you bothered?'

'Dunno.' Lisa indicated ignorance with a downward moue. 'I suppose a girl's got to have a hobby.'

CHAPTER 28

The offices of Randolph Media buzzed with an end-of-term mood. It was the Friday of the June bank-holiday weekend (which had thrown Lisa entirely because in England the bank holiday had been the previous weekend), coupled with the news about the L'Oréal ads, coupled with the fact that Jack Devine was elsewhere, coupled with the arrival of a crate of champagne which was meant to be a reader-competition prize. ('What area of France does champagne come from? Answers on a postcard to . . . First one out of the hat wins twelve of the best . . .')

Lisa looked at the champagne, looked at her watch – quarter to four – and looked at her staff. They'd worked so hard over the past three weeks and *Colleen* was actually shaping up to be not a total disaster. She'd just remembered how important it was to keep morale up amongst the workers. Well actually, if she was honest, she had to admit that she was in the mood for a drink and suspected she might have a mutiny on her hands if she poured one just for herself.

Theatrically, she cleared her throat. 'Ahem,' she

said gaily, 'would anyone care for a glass of champagne?' Meaningfully, she inclined her glossy head at the crate, and it was the work of a moment for everyone to realize what she was getting at.

'But what about the reader competition?' Ashling asked anxiously.

'Shut the fuck up,' Trix hissed, then turned to Lisa. 'That would be the business, Lisa,' she toadied, loudly. 'We can celebrate you getting that loads-a-money ad from L'Oréal.'

No second bidding was needed. The words, *'Lisa says we can drink the reader-competition champagne, Lisa says we can drink the reader-competition champagne,'* blew like a whispering breeze across the office. Tools were downed and demeanours relaxed. Even Mercedes looked cheerful.

'But we don't have any glasses.' Lisa was suddenly anxious.

'No problem.' Before Lisa changed her mind, Trix was already ferrying a trayful of dirty coffee-cups to the ladies'. The first time in six months that she'd done the washing-up. She was back in double-quick time and it didn't matter a damn that she hadn't rinsed the mugs properly because any excess of foaming could be attributed to the champagne.

'It's not terribly chilled, I'm afraid,' Lisa said graciously, putting a chipped 'Windsurfers do it standing up' mug full of frothing champers into Kelvin's beringed hands.

'Who gives a fiddler's!' Kelvin enthused, delighted to be included, despite not working on *Colleen*.

The small clump of clerical staff waited anxiously in their corner to see if they were getting any. Huge sighs of relief all round when Lisa popped the cork on a second bottle and arrived bearing mugs emblazoned with the respective legends 'I can't believe it's not butter', 'Kia-Ora, I'll be your dawg' and two 'Does exactly what it says on the tin's.

'Your good health, Mrs Morley.' Lisa gave 'I can't believe it's not butter' to Jack's over-protective PA.

'Cheers,' Mrs Morley muttered suspiciously.

When everyone had a mug, Lisa raised hers and said, 'To all of you. Well done for all your hard work over the past three weeks.'

Ashling and Mercedes exchanged a moment's incredulity. You'd swear Lisa was drunk already. Everyone then drank deeply, except for Trix. But only because she'd already finished hers. And it didn't take the others long to catch her up. Silence stretched, as everyone's eyes flickered between the foam at the bottom of their empty mugs (which continued to crackle and fizz in a strange radioactive fashion) and the ten remaining bottles.

Lisa shattered the silence. 'Shall we open another?' she asked innocently, as if it had just occurred to her.

'We could, I s'pose.' Trix did a good imitation of not caring either way.

'Sure, why wouldn't we?' One mugful had considerably softened Mrs Morley.

But as Lisa was unwinding the wire helmet, the office door opened and everyone tensed. Fuck!

There was a good chance that Jack would go mental if he caught them slugging reader-competition champagne during office hours.

But it wasn't Jack, it was Mai. Her heels were enormous and her hips were tiny. But not as small as her waist. Ashling was queasy with envy and admiration.

Mai seemed rather taken aback by the complete silence in the office and the way everyone was staring guiltily at her. 'Is Jack in?'

The silence endured.

'No,' Mrs Morley mumbled, wiping her mouth in case she had a champagne moustache. 'He's gone to put manners on the people at the television studio.' Then she triumphantly folded her arms, her demeanour implying that, really, it was Mai who Jack should be putting the manners on.

'Oh.' Mai's plump mouth was pouty with disappointment. She twirled to go, her wall of silken hair swishing with voluptuous weight.

'You can wait if you like,' Ashling found herself saying.

Mai swung back. 'Would that be allowed?'

'Sure! In fact, why don't you have a drink?' As soon as she'd said it, Ashling braced herself for the wrath of Lisa. Bad move to invite their boss's girlfriend to join in with their lead-swinging. Ashling suspected she was perhaps a little tipsy.

But instead of being furious, Lisa agreed, 'Yeah, have a drink.'

The thing was, Lisa was as curious as everyone else about Mai. More, probably, all things considered.

'Cheers.' As Mai accepted a mug from Lisa, Ashling said hospitably. 'Come over to my desk and pull up a chair.'

Trix and Lisa also gravitated immediately to Ashling's desk, reeled in by avid interest in the exotic Mai.

'I like your bag,' Lisa said to Mai. 'Lulu Guinness?'

Mai gave a surprisingly raucous bark of laughter. 'Dunnes.'

'Dunnes?'

'A chain store,' Ashling explained, with red-cheeked earnestness. 'Like Marks & Spencer.'

'Only cheaper,' Mai added, with another snigger. Despite her lotus-blossom face she suddenly seemed very ordinary.

As Lisa circulated, topping up mugs, Mai said, with sly humour, 'This is a great place to work, do you do this every day?'

There followed a burst of slightly hysterical laughter. 'Every day? Not at all! Not at all! Special occasions, bank holidays, that kind of thing.'

'You won't tell Jack on us, will you?' Trix asked.

Mai flickered her eyes in caustic scorn. 'As if!'

'Where do you work? What, um, what do you do?' Trix dared to ask.

Mai tossed her heavy hair, her tilted eyes were

all-knowing and instantly she'd become an inscrutable, mysterious babe again. 'I'm an exotic dancer.'

This plunged the office into a short, nonplussed silence, before everyone rallied in ultra-blasé fashion. 'Isn't that lovely?' they chorused stoutly. 'Good girl yourself.'

'Aren't we having great weather for it?' Boring Bernard got it wrong, as usual.

'Good for you,' Lisa managed. She bet that Jack and Mai had great sex and she flared with bilious jealousy.

'What's an exotic dancer?' Mrs Morley muttered to Kelvin.

'I believe it involves some, er, nudiness,' he whispered tactfully, mindful of her elderly sensibilities.

'Oh, so she's a lap-dancer. She must be minting it.' Mrs Morley studied Mai with something suddenly akin to respect.

'No, I'm fecking not an exotic dancer,' Mai said scornfully, flipping back to being ordinary. 'I'm joking. I work flogging mobile phones but because of the way I look people expect me to be some sort of sex kitten.'

'Isn't that desperate altogether?' another enthusiastic chorus kicked off. 'Fierce! Aren't people awful eejits?'

'Have I got this right, she's *not* a lap dancer?' Mrs Morley discreetly enquired of Kelvin, who shook his peroxide head. It was hard to tell who was more disappointed.

'It's dreadful tereostyping,' Ashling complained. *I'm twisted*, she realized.

'It is,' Mai complained, fuelled by her second mug of washing-up liquid and champagne. 'I was born and brought up in Dublin, my father is Irish, but because my mother is Asian, men treat me like I'll know all these special Oriental tricks in the scratcher. Ping-pong balls and the like. Or else they're shouting, "Egg-flied lice" after me in the street.' She sighed heavily. 'Either way, it gets me down.'

She flicked a look around at Kelvin and Gerry who were watching her lasciviously, then huddled nearer to Ashling, Lisa and Trix and said candidly, 'That's not to say that I'd *never* try the ping-pong balls. Of *course* I'd lay on something special if I really fancied the guy.'

Like Jack, do you mean? Everyone wanted to ask. But no one had the nerve. Not even Trix. But as the number of full bottles continued to diminish and the empties mounted up, tongues loosened.

'What age are you?' Trix asked.

'Twenty-nine.'

'And how long have you been going with Jack?'

'Nearly six months.'

'He's terrible cranky sometimes,' Trix admitted.

'Who are you telling! Since the business of *Colleen* started, he's been in a fouler. He works too hard and worries too much, then he goes sailing to unwind and I never get to see him. I blame you lot for his bad mood!'

'That's funny!' Trix exclaimed. 'Because we blame *you*.'

At that, Mai began shifting and wriggling in her seat.

'Sorry, are we embarrassing you? We'll shut up,' Ashling interjected. But with disappointment. She was finding this fascinating.

'No, it's OK,' Mai grinned, still wriggling. 'Knickers up my bum, drives me mad.'

She was so pretty and fresh and brazen that Lisa swallowed. She was sure she hadn't imagined Jack's interest in her, but she could see how he'd find Mai alluring.

By the time Jack returned, everyone had kicked back to such an extent that they didn't even bother to hide it.

'Having fun?' he half-smiled.

''sabankoliday,' glared Mrs Morley, an infrequent tippler, who in the last hour and a half had passed through suspicion, mellowness, marvellous well-being, maudlin regret, and had now arrived, as expected, at aggression.

'Certainly is,' he agreed.

'Hello, Jack.' Mai gave a shark's smile. 'I was passing and I thought I'd come in to say hello.'

Jack looked embarrassed.

Mai followed him into his office and closed the door very firmly.

When Trix put her mug up against the door, then put her ear to it, everyone laughed. But no mug was needed. Mai's voice, high-pitched and

318

berating, carried to the furthest desks. 'How dare you ignore me when I visit you . . . If you think I'm going to put up with . . .'

Nothing at all could be heard from Jack, but he must have been saying something because there were pauses between Mai's accusatory bursts.

'Keep all the exits clear,' Kelvin said, like an air-hostess.

And sooner rather than later, Jack's door opened, Mai emerged, blazed a furious trail to the door and then she was gone, leaving the air humming with her absence. She hadn't said goodbye to anyone.

'Now that the floorshow is over, I'm going,' Kelvin announced, swinging his inflatable orange rucksack on to his back. 'I've seventy-two hours of Class As ahead of me.'

'Me too,' Trix said.

'Me three,' Boring Bernard agreed, once more grasping the wrong end of the stick.

Everyone packed up and sloped off, until the only people left were Jack and Ashling. Jack because he was waiting for a call from New York, and Ashling because she was meeting Joy at half six and didn't think there was any point going home. While she waited, she kept working because she was in the process of setting up a database for Lisa, and had fallen very behind because of the earlier impromptu drinking session.

'Leave it, Miss Fix-it,' Jack groused. 'It's a bank holiday. Anyway you're jarred, you'll just have to do it all again on Tuesday.'

'You're right.' Ashling was just sober enough to know that she was drunk. 'I'm making a pig's mickey of it.'

'Go home,' he ordered.

It was nearly half six anyway. Fuzzily she picked up her bag, then asked tentatively, 'Doing anything nice for the long weekend, JD?' Only because she had a drop taken.

'JD?' Jack enquired, curiously.

'I mean, Jack, Mr Devine, whatever.' Ashling was embarrassed to have let slip her own private nickname for him. 'Doing anything nice?'

Jack was surly. 'Don't know. I'll visit my parents on Sunday. The rest depends on the weather. If I can't go sailing, I'll just bunker down and watch Star Trek videos.'

'Star Trek? Well, er, "Live long and prosper,"' Ashling encouraged, trying to do the Vulcan split-finger salute.

Jack stared at her narkily. 'Illogical, Captain Fix-it. I won't be doing any prospering this weekend.'

'Why not?'

With sudden embarrassment, he admitted, 'It can't have escaped your notice that my girlfriend is in a strop.'

Ashling couldn't help it. The words were out before she knew it. The drink talking. 'Why do you always fight with her? She's lovely. Can't you make a bit more of an effort? She says she never sees you because you're always out sailing. Perhaps if you went less often . . . ?'

She realized she'd way overstepped the mark and waited for the wrath of Jack, but instead he laughed, albeit unpleasantly.

Too late Ashling remembered that there were two sides to every story. 'Isn't it true?'

Jack paused. 'Far be it for me to bitch about someone who isn't here to defend themselves.'

'So you don't go sailing?'

'I do.'

'But . . .' Then Ashling thought that perhaps she understood. 'Does she say it's OK for you to go, then get cross afterwards?'

After a hiatus, Jack admitted reluctantly, 'Something like that.'

'But you see,' Ashling explained, 'even though she says it's OK to go, she doesn't mean it. Go on, talk to her, be nice.' Her eyes lit up. Problem solved.

'Little Miss Fix-it,' Jack shook his head indulgently, 'why do you have to make everything all right for everyone?'

'But I'm only . . .'

'Little Miss Fix-it,' he repeated, amused. 'I'll think about it. And how about you – are you going away for the weekend?'

'No.' Ashling was shy as soon as the spotlight was trained on her. 'I'll just see my friends and stuff . . . ' Go out with Marcus Valentine, hopefully, but she wasn't telling Jack that.

'Have a good one,' he said.

As Ashling headed for the door, Jack, suddenly

321

curious, called after her, 'Hey! Miss Fix-it! Do you ever watch Star Trek videos?'

Ashling looked over her shoulder and shook her head. 'No.'

'I suppose not,' he said.

'I've nothing against them.'

'That's what they all say,' Jack muttered.

'But I'm more of a Doctor Who girl, myself.'

CHAPTER 29

On Saturday evening, at a quarter to seven, Ashling and Ted arrived on Ted's bike for babysitting duties *chez* Dylan and Clodagh.

'They *own* this?' Ted took in the double-fronted red-brick house.

'Fantastic, isn't it?' Ashling stood on the doorstep and rang the bell.

'We won't have to change nappies, will we?' Ted asked, suddenly stricken.

'No, they're too old for that. We'll just have to play with them, amuse them.'

'Well, that should be easy enough.' Ted cleared his throat and self-consciously smoothed back a lock of his hair. 'Ted Mullins, funniest man in Dublin, reporting for duty, sir!'

'They might be a bit young for post-modern, ironic stand-up.' Ashling's heart sank. 'I'd say the Three Little Pigs would be more their cup of Ribena.'

'We'll see about that,' Ted corrected. 'People underestimate children's intelligence. Will I ring the bell again?'

It took a while before the door was answered. Dylan arrived, his arms soapy, his T-shirt wet and sticking to his chest.

'How's it going?' He seemed distracted. Then Ashling and Ted noticed the echoey howls and bawls coming from upstairs.

'I'm bathing Craig,' Dylan explained.

'He doesn't seem happy.'

'The worst is yet to come. I still have to rinse his hair.' Dylan winced. 'It'll sound like he's being burnt alive, but don't be alarmed . . . I'd better get back.' He was halfway up the stairs. 'Clodagh's in the kitchen.'

Clodagh was at the table desperately trying to persuade Molly to eat something. Anything that wasn't a biscuit, crisp or sweet. In the last couple of weeks, Molly had gone on hunger-strike, just for the hell of it.

Ashling passed Clodagh a folder containing ten copies of her CV.

'What's thi –? Oh right, thanks.' In a fluid motion, Clodagh stuffed the folder beneath a pile of children's books strewn on the table.

'Aren't you going to get ready?' Ashling took in Clodagh's jeans and T-shirt. 'Your taxi will be here soon.'

'I just want to make sure she eats something . . .'

'Why don't I try?' Ted offered gallantly.

But Molly stuck her bottom lip out and let it tremble theatrically at the suggestion.

'Thanks, but . . .' Clodagh wearily continued

battering a spoon against Molly's sparse but clenched teeth. Nothing doing. Now that Molly had an audience, there was no chance that she'd eat a thing.

'Have some scrambled egg, love,' Clodagh urged.

'Why?'

'Because it's good for you.'

'Why?'

'Because there's protein in it.'

'Why?'

As well as refusing to eat proper food, Molly had recently started on the 'Why?' game. Earlier that day she'd asked twenty-nine 'Why?'s in a row. Clodagh had gone along with it in a fatalistic curiosity to see how far it would go, but she'd cracked before Molly had.

'Your hair's gorgeous.' Ashling admired, stroking Clodagh's thick honey-gold tresses.

'Thanks. I got it blow-dried for tonight.'

Then Ashling remembered the newly papered front-room and ran in for a look.

'It's fantastic!' she enthused eagerly on her return. 'It totally changes the mood of the room. You've a real eye for colour.'

'I suppose.' Clodagh was no longer terribly interested. She'd been very excited about her new wallpaper. But now that it was done, satisfaction and fulfilment evaded her.

Suddenly everyone looked ceilingwards as an eruption of bloodcurdling shrieks broke out in the room above them. The rinsing of Craig's hair.

'It really does sound like he's being burnt alive,' Ashling giggled. 'Poor little thing.'

After a while the shrill screams died down into hysterical whimpers. Back to the force-feeding.

'Everyone has to eat their dinner if they want to grow up to be big strong girls.' Clodagh approached once more with her spoonful of scrambled egg.

'Why?'

'Because they just do.'

'Why?'

'Because.'

'Why?'

'Because.'

'Why?'

'Just FUCKING because.' Clodagh clattered down the spoon, bouncing yellow particles around the table. 'This is a waste of time. I'm going to get ready.'

As Clodagh swept from the room, Ted passed Ashling a shocked, wide-eyed, 'Jayzus!' look. 'Bad idea to let children see your weakness,' he observed, knowingly.

Clodagh stuck her head back in. 'I used to think that too. You wait until you have children yourself,' she accused. 'You'll have loads of rules and none of them will work.'

Ted hadn't meant to *criticize* Clodagh. It was just that he'd thought his tough-love approach to child-rearing might help her. He felt misunderstood and acutely embarrassed. Even more so when Molly pointed her spoon at him and crowed maliciously, 'Mummy hates you.'

Clodagh belted up the stairs. No chance of having the long, relaxing aromatherapy bath she'd planned. Barely time to have a quick shower before scribbling on some make-up. Then, reverentially, she put on the pink and white little slip-dress that she'd bought the day she'd gone shopping with Ashling. It had hung in the wardrobe ever since, its pristine newness a reminder that her social life was non-existent.

She watched herself anxiously in the mirror. Bloody hell, it was short. Shorter than she remembered. And see-through. But when she put on a black half-slip to cover her modesty, she just looked stupid, so she took it off again. Underwear on display was fine, she told herself. Better than fine. *Compulsory*, actually, if you wanted to call yourself well-dressed. Her problem was that she'd been in jeans and T-shirts for too long. So she stuck her feet into high sandals, told herself she looked brilliant and appeared at the top of the stairs like a movie star making an entrance.

'How do I look?'

Everyone gathered below, gazing up. There was a kind of nonplussed pause.

'Fabulous,' Ashling enthused, a split-second too late.

Ted was open-mouthed with admiration as he watched Clodagh's treadmilled legs making their way down the stairs.

'Dylan?' Clodagh enquired.

'Fabulous,' he echoed.

She wasn't convinced. She was sure she'd seen a caveat in his eyes, but he was smart enough not to voice it. Craig, however, was unencumbered by such reticence. 'Mummy, your dress is too short and I can see your wonderpants.'

'No, you can't.'

'Yes, I can!' he insisted.

'No, you can't,' Clodagh corrected. 'You can see my knickers. Boys wear wonderpants and girls wear knickers . . . Unless they're Ashling's friend, Joy,' she muttered to herself, astringent bitchiness erupting from nowhere.

Molly, engaged in the act of washing her hands with blackberry jam, was the only person who seemed not to care what Clodagh wore or didn't.

'You look very well too,' Ashling said to Dylan. And indeed he did, in his unstructured, navy suit and biscuit-coloured shirt.

'You sweetheart,' he grinned.

'Ponce,' floated into Ashling's ear, so small and contemptuous that she almost thought she'd imagined it. It seemed to emanate from Ted's direction.

'Are we right?' Dylan looked at his watch.

'Just a minute.' Clodagh was in a flurry of leaving phone numbers. 'Here's Dylan's mobile,' she scribbled. 'And here's the number of the restaurant just in case the mobile's out of coverage . . .'

'It's not likely to be a problem in the middle of Dublin,' Dylan interjected.

' . . . and this is the address of the restaurant, if you can't get us on the phone. We won't be late.'

'*Be* late,' Ashling urged.

Clodagh grabbed Molly and Craig, hugged them fiercely and said – without much conviction – 'Be good for Ashling.'

'And Ted,' Ted added, bunching his mouth in what he thought was a suave manner at Clodagh.

'And Ted,' Clodagh muttered.

Just before they left, to wish them God-speed, Molly firmly placed a blackberry-jam-covered hand on Clodagh's bottom. Unfortunately – or maybe it was fortunately – she didn't notice.

CHAPTER 30

As soon as Clodagh closed the front door, pitiful wailing from Molly and Craig began on the other side. With a helpless look at Dylan, Clodagh turned to go back in again.

'No!' he commanded.

'But . . .'

'They'll stop in a while.'

Feeling as if she was being ripped in two, she got into the taxi and submitted to being driven into town. Fucking unconditional love, she thought bitterly. What a terrible burden it was.

Their table at L'Oeuf was booked for seven-thirty – they'd been given a choice of seven-thirty or nine, and Clodagh felt that nine was far too late. She was often in bed by then. She liked to get a few hours' kip in before having to rise at four a.m. to sit and sing songs in the dark for an hour. Dylan and Clodagh were the first diners to arrive. They proceeded in hushed, reverential silence into the empty, white, Grecian-columned room and Clodagh became ever more anxious about her dress. It seemed to draw astonished looks from the po-faced staff. Trying to tug it down to make it longer, she hurried to the safety of the table. She'd been out of the loop too long and no longer knew what was the right or wrong thing to wear. Sinking into her chair and shoving her thighs under the forgiving cover of the table, where the error of her on-display knickers was hidden away out of sight, she gratefully ordered a gin-and-tonic.

As she perused her broadsheet-sized menu, twelve or fourteen black-and-white-attired staff stood to attention in various parts of the silent room. When she looked up from her menu, they'd all exchanged places, but neither she nor Dylan had seen them move.

'It's like something out of a science-fiction film,' she whispered.

Dylan laughed, the sound loud in the empty room, and Clodagh's head abruptly tightened as she experienced that peculiar feeling again – that she didn't know him. But this was the man she'd once thought she'd die if she didn't possess. Stirred by an echo of that intense love, she was suddenly struck dumb. Perplexed because she couldn't think of a single thing to say to him.

Only for a second. Then, *of course*, she had oodles of stuff. *I mean*, she thought, loose with relief, *this is Dylan*.

'Do you think I should take Molly to the doctor?'

Dylan didn't answer.

'If she doesn't knock off the hunger-strike soon,' Clodagh chattered, 'I'll really have to. She's getting no nourishment from all the chocolate and –'

'What are you having to start?' Dylan interrupted, brusquely.

'Oh! Oh, I don't know.'

'The menu's spectacular,' Dylan said, a little too pointedly.

'Oh right.'

'Can't you forget about the kids just for a couple of hours?'

'Sorry. Am I driving you mad?'

'Round the bend,' he agreed, in exasperation.

She began to settle down. After all, she was in a lovely restaurant with her lovely husband. They were drinking gin-and-tonics and eating tomato bread. Delicious food and several bottles of wine would soon be on their way, and her children were safe at home with two people who weren't paedophiles or child-batterers. What could be nicer?

'Sorry,' she repeated, and this time really did study the menu. 'I see what you mean,' she acknowledged. 'Oh, they've mussels. And goat's cheese soufflé. Bloody hell! *What'll I have?*'

'Starter or soup,' Dylan said thoughtfully, 'that is the question.'

'"*Or?*"' Clodagh challenged. 'What's this "or" word? I think what you mean is "and".'

With the desperation of one who rarely gets out, Clodagh over-ordered wildly, mad-keen to wring as much enjoyment as possible from this infrequent treat. Starters and sorbets and soups and side-orders. Main-courses and red wine and white wine and water.

'Sparkling or still?' The waiter asked, his hand hurting. Now he knew how Tolstoy felt, having to write *War and Peace*.

Puzzled, Clodagh looked at him – surely it was obvious? – 'Both!'

'Very good.'

'Is there anything else we can order?' Clodagh shivered gleefully, when he'd gone.

'Not for the moment,' Dylan laughed, swept up in her enthusiasm. 'But wait till we've got this consignment out of the way.'

'Will we have dessert *and* cheese?'

''Course. Irish coffees?'

'And dessert wine. And petit fours.'

'French coffees?'

'Mais oui! I might even have a cigar.'

'That's my girl.'

By the time they were a couple of courses in, Clodagh was dreamy from food and drink, but still bothered by an inability to relax. Then she realized what the problem was.

'It's such a long time since I've had an uninterrupted dinner that I can't break the habit,' she said. 'I keep getting the urge to jump up and cut up other people's dinners for them . . . See your man over there?' – she indicated a New-York-loft-boy type who was playing with his food – 'I want to stick a bit of his *filet mignon* on a fork and say, "Open wide for the birdy." In fact, I think I will.'

Dylan was half-appalled and amused as Clodagh

pretended to stand up. Then she stopped and twisted and turned anxiously.

'Why . . . ? Why am I sticking to the chair?' She put a hand down to investigate. 'I've a patch of black sticky stuff on my bum. Tar, maybe. Damn, on my lovely new dress. How did I manage that?' Tentatively she brought her fingertips to her nose, sniffed, then started to laugh. 'It's blackberry jam. Bet it was Molly, the little brat. She's a scream, isn't she?'

'She's brilliant.' Dylan wasn't entirely undreamy himself.

'Would you say they're all right?' Clodagh asked, suddenly anxious.

'Of course! And Ashling and Ted have the mobile number. They'll ring if anything goes wrong.'

'Like what? What could go wrong?'

'Nothing.'

'Give me your mobile and I'll make a quick call.'

Dylan's eyes pleaded with her. 'Can't you just leave it for one night? We've only been gone an hour.'

'You're right,' Clodagh agreed. 'I'm being ridiculous.'

She turned her attention back to her chowder.

'No, I can't bear it,' she burst out. 'Give me the mobile.'

With a sigh Dylan handed it over.

'Hello, Ted, it's Clodagh, just checking that everything's OK.'

'We're having a blast,' Ted lied, as Ashling

held her hands over Craig's and Molly's agape mouths.

'So, can I have a word with them?'

'They're, um, busy. Playing. Yes, that's right, playing with Ashling.'

'Oh. Well, then, see you later.

'It's very annoying,' Clodagh said mournfully, as she snapped the phone closed. 'They drive me mad all week, I can't wait for even five minutes away from them, then I go out for the evening and I worry about them!'

'We can go home if you want,' Dylan said tightly. 'And have oven-chips and a non-stop string of demands.'

'When you put it like that . . . Sorry, Dylan. I am actually having a nice time. A very nice time.'

Not quite the same could be said of Ashling and Ted. It had taken ages for Craig and Molly to stop crying after their parents had left. They'd eventually quietened down – but only after they'd commandeered the telly to watch *The Little Mermaid* and Ted had to forgo watching *Stars in Their Eyes*.

'And it's celebrity night,' he complained bitterly.

To pass the time Ted went through Dylan's enormous record and CD collection with jealous admiration, exclaiming when he found an impressively rare one. 'Look at that. Bob Marley's *Catch a Fire – in its original sleeve*. How'd he manage that, the lucky bastard?'

Ashling found it hard to care. Men and their music collections. Phelim used to be the exact same.

'Fuck's sake!' Ted burst out. 'Burning Spear's first two albums on Studio One! I thought you could only get them in Jamaica.'

'Dylan and Clodagh went to Jamaica on the honeymoon,' Ashling deadpanned.

'Lucky for some.' He managed to inject a world of longing into those three words. '. . . The complete Billie Holiday on Verve,' Ted sounded like he might puke. 'Where'd he get that? I've been looking for *years* for it! . . . Tool,' he added.

'Aha!' He pounced gleefully on something. 'This is a right skeleton in the cupboard! What's Mr Cooler-than-thou doing with a Simply Red album? There goes his street-cred.'

'Sorry to disappoint you, but that's Clodagh's.'

'Clodagh likes Simply Red?' Ted's face was a picture.

'She used to, in any case.'

'"Used to" is OK.' Ted was weak with relief. He thought Clodagh was a goddess, but if she was a fan of Mick Hucknall's he might have to reconsider. Surely no goddess could have such an inexcusable lapse in taste?

As soon as *The Little Mermaid* ended, Craig and Molly clamoured loudly to be entertained. But when Ted tried his owl routine on them, Molly told him to go home *now* and Craig began to cry.

Ted took it hard, especially when Ashling hiding and reappearing from behind a paper bag had them in convulsions.

'Little bastards,' he muttered. 'Loads of people would give their right arm for this opportunity.'

'But they're only kids.'

Craig began pulling at Ashling, demanding 7-Up. When it didn't appear instantly, the tears started again.

'Spoilt brat.' Ted was scathing.

'No, he's not.'

'Yes, he is. If he lived in Bangladesh, he'd be working eighteen hours a day in a sweatshop, you know . . . Then he'd have something to cry about,' Ted added, darkly.

The evening was a very long one. Ashling and Ted had to provide a non-stop supply of laughs, stories, sweets, tickling, drinks, lorry-throwing, Barbie-football and that old favourite, Hiding Your Hand up Your Sleeve.

'Where's Molly's hand gone?' Ted asked wearily, as gleefully Molly secreted her hand up her sleeve for the millionth time. 'Oh dear,' he said flatly. 'Molly's lost her hand. Someone's stolen it.' Then as Molly triumphantly thrust her hand back into the public arena, Ted said moodily, 'Oh what a surprise! Here it is again. Where's Molly's hand gone . . . ?'

When bedtime came, getting them to go to bed *and stay there* was like trying to nail jelly to the wall.

'If you don't go to sleep, the bogeyman will come and get you,' Ted threatened.

'There's no bogeyman,' Craig said confidently. 'Mummy said.'

Ted reconsidered. Surely something must scare him? 'OK, if you don't go to sleep, Mick Hucknall will come and get you.'

'What's that?'

'I'll show you.' Ted nipped downstairs, grabbed the CD and ran back up. '*That's* Mick Hucknall.'

Ashling, downstairs savouring a moment of peace, looked up in alarm as a terrible, screaming cacophany broke out in the room above her. Seconds later Ted appeared, looking furtive and guilty.

'What's going on?' she demanded.

'Nothing.'

'I'd better go up.'

Ashling spent several fruitless minutes trying to calm Craig.

'What did you say to him?' she accused Ted, when she came back down. 'He's absolutely inconsolable.'

Dylan and Clodagh arrived home, swaddled in the kind of loving glow that makes everyone else feel excluded and lacking. They lurched into the house, Clodagh's arm around Dylan, his hand firmly on her bum (on the side that wasn't covered in blackberry jam).

As soon as Ashling and Ted had been dispatched

into the night, Clodagh winked at Dylan, nodded at upstairs and said, 'Come on.' It was exactly four weeks since the last time they'd had sex, but she was so awash with drunken magnanimity that she would have thrown in a bonus session even if he hadn't been due one.

'I'll just switch off lights and lock doors,' he said.

'Hurry,' she said coquettishly, safe in the knowledge that he wouldn't.

They'd long passed the stage of luxuriously undressing each other. Clodagh was already naked under the duvet when Dylan came to bed and a swift, thirty-second swish of lycra and cotton had him stepping out of his clothes. Clodagh lay back, closed her eyes and submitted to being kissed for a few minutes; then, as always, Dylan moved to her nipples. When he finished at that, there was a silent, unacknowledged struggle. Because this was the point at which Dylan usually liked to shimmy down her body to administer cunnilingus, but Clodagh couldn't bear it. It was so boring and simply added several wasted minutes to the whole procedure. Tonight she won, managing to head him off at the pass. She proceeded directly to fellatio, treating him to between four and five minutes of it, and its cessation was his cue to climb aboard. For a special treat – birthdays and anniversaries – Clodagh would go on top. But tonight wasn't the deluxe version, just the standard missionary one. She clasped Dylan to her in a smooth ballet of comfortable familiarity. Once she was into it, it wasn't so bad, she decided. It was the anticipation that distressed her so. As always, Dylan waited for her to pretend to come before gathering pace, pumping away as though a stopwatch was being held over him. *It's about time we did this room up again*, Clodagh thought, as he machined back and forth in a panting, whimpering blur. *The carpet could probably stay, but I'd really like to paint the walls.*

'Oh God,' Dylan begged, shoving his hands under her buttocks and banging himself into her at ever-faster speed. 'Oh God, oh God.'

Automatically, Clodagh obliged with an absentminded moan. That should hurry things along. *Purple and cream walls, perhaps.* Then Dylan was spasming in ecstasy and collapsing with a groan. The only break from the norm was that they weren't interrupted by either of their children, clamouring to join in.

Fifteen minutes from start to finish and all over for another month. Clodagh sighed with contentment. Thank God he wasn't one of those men who insisted on pleasuring you all night long. She'd have had to kill herself long ago if that had been the case.

Ted and Ashling whizzed through the darkened streets, *en route* to the Cigar Room, for 'just the ten'. When they dismounted the bike, Ted slapped his palm on his forehead in a gesture that looked vaguely rehearsed.

'Well, feck it,' he exclaimed, with ire that, oddly, lacked conviction. 'I'm after leaving my jacket at Clodagh's. I'll have to call around during the week to collect it.'

In a house in a bleak, sea-facing corner of Ringsend, Jack and Mai were just about wrapping up their reunion ride. Earlier, Mai had been stunned by Jack arriving at her flat and apologizing for not having greeted her at the office yesterday with enough warmth for her liking. Then he'd whisked her to his house, where he fed her, poured good wine into her, and took her to bed.

He was so unexpectedly sweet that while they were making love, she didn't – as she often did – pretend to look at her watch. A couple of times recently she'd even used the remote control to switch on the telly while they were on the job. It had driven him wild. 'It's a bit more interesting than what you're doing to me,' had been her explanation, although it wasn't true. But it kept him insecure and kept her in control.

Hard work, mind.

They lay in a post-coital glow. 'You're wonderful,' he said out of nowhere.

'Am I?' She sat up on her elbow and shot him a provocative, malicious smile. 'Except I've crap taste in men, right?' She braced herself for a spiky come-back from Jack, but he just busied himself winding his fingers in her long hair. 'Are you OK?' she asked, high with surprise.

'Couldn't be better. Why?'

'Nothing.'

Mai was badly confused. Why wasn't Jack giving as good as he got? He usually managed to give *better* than he got.

'Tomorrow afternoon I'm going to visit my parents,' he said.

Mai rolled her eyes. 'Nice one! And what am I? Chopped liver?'

This was one of their favourite rows – the lack of time Jack had for Mai. But Jack interrupted Mai's fledgling rant by saying, 'Would you like to come?'

'Where?' She was astonished. 'To meet them?'

When Jack nodded she wailed, 'But what will I wear? I'll have to go home and change first.'

'No bother.'

Mai snuck another confused look at him. This was very weird. Maybe . . . perhaps . . . could it be that all her game-playing and manipulation had actually worked? That she'd finally got Jack where she wanted him . . . ?

CHAPTER 31

Lisa woke up on Sunday morning, and instantly wished she hadn't. Something about the quality of the stillness beyond her bedroom window was telling her that it was very, very early. And she didn't want it to be very, very early. She'd like it to be very late. Preferably mid-afternoon. Ideally, already tomorrow.

She lay still, her ears straining for the sounds of mothers shouting, children fighting, the heads being pulled off Barbies, anything that might indicate that the world outside was in motion. But apart from a gaggle of birds camped in her garden, chirping and cheeping like they'd won the lottery, she heard nothing.

When she could no longer bear not knowing, she turned over in her rumpled bed and warily confronted the alarm clock. Seven-naffing-thirty. In the morning.

The bank-holiday weekend was taking for ever to pass. Exacerbated, no doubt, by the fact that she was entirely on her own.

For some reason she hadn't expected that she'd have to endure it solo. During the week, she'd had at the back of her mind that Ashling would ask her along for a drink, or to a party, or to meet that mad Joy or Ted or *something*. Let's face it, it seemed that Ashling was perpetually inviting her to things. But on Friday evening, giddy and giggly after the champagne orgy, it wasn't until she reached home and had sobered up considerably that she realized that no invitation had been issued by Ashling. Cheeky cow. Bombarding her with invites which she didn't want, then neglecting to issue them when she could have done with them!

Moodily she lit a cigarette, breaking her rule about not smoking in bed.

What was it about living in Dublin? In London she'd never had spare time. There had been an endless pile-up of appointments awaiting her rejection. And, in the rare cases when there had been any unexpected leisure time, she could always fill it with work.

But not here. It had been impossible to organize any appointments for the weekend. All the lazy-bastard journos and hair-dressers and DJs and designers were going away, and even if they weren't, they were in kick-back mode and disin-clined to meet her.

Worse still, she couldn't go into work on Monday because the building wouldn't be open. As soon as she'd heard on Friday morning, she'd marched straight into Jack's office and kicked up a right stink. 'Can't the porter, what's his name – Bill? – come to let me in and then go straight home again?'

'On a bank holiday?' Jack had seemed genuinely amused. 'Bill? Not a hope of it.'

Lazy, shiftless pillock, Lisa had thought, in impotent fury. In London, they'd always come to let her in.

'Why don't you take it easy?' Jack had advised. 'You've achieved so much in such a short time, you deserve a rest.'

But she didn't want a rest, she was too hyper. Three entire days, how was she going to fill them? And why didn't *he* suggest that they did something together, she'd wondered in frustration. She knew he was interested in her, she'd seen it more than once in his face.

'Go out on the town. Have a few drinks,' he'd urged.

With whom?

She'd contemplated going to London for the weekend, but was too ashamed. Where would she stay? Her flat had tenants in and she'd let her friendships lapse – most of them bit the dust during the frenzied empire-building she'd done in the past two years and the only person she'd ever given any of her precious time to was Fifi. But she'd been too mortified to contact Fifi since she'd been banished to Ireland. If she went to London she'd have to stay in a hotel like a – she shuddered – like a . . . *tourist.*

But on Friday night, when she realized that she'd be killing so much time over the weekend it would be a veritable bloodbath, she decided she could handle being a tourist in London. Which was when she discovered that all the flights out of Dublin were booked. Everyone was desperate to escape this foul little country. Who could blame them?

As it happened, Saturday wasn't too bad. She got her hair cut, her eyelashes tinted, her pores steamed and her nails done, all twenty of them. Everything for free. Then she got in her weekly shopping. For the next seven days she was only going to eat food starting with the letter 'A' – apples, avocados, artichokes, anchovies and absinthe.

Because she was feeling so fragile, she bent the rules to let an apricot Danish into her basket. Which was greatly appreciated because the unpleasantness of spending Saturday night in, alone, was quite shocking, really.

And here she was on Sunday morning, still with two full days to go.

Go back to sleep, she begged herself. *Go back to sleep and massacre a couple of hours.*

But she couldn't. Although it was no wonder, she thought bitterly, seeing as she'd been tucked up in bye-byes at ten o'clock the night before.

She got out of bed, had a shower, and even though she took an inordinate amount of time over it and almost scrubbed herself raw, she found she was dressed and ready by quarter past nine. Ready for what? Buzzing with energy that had nowhere to go, she wondered, what do people *do*?

They went to the gym, she supposed, throwing her eyes to heaven (and wishing there was someone there to see her do it). Lisa prided herself on never going to the gym, especially not in Dublin. It was wildly passé, all that stair-mastering and cross-country rowing. The Irish fitness industry was so behind the times they still thought spinning was a novel idea! No, Lisa was more interested in the less violent and more fashionable forms of body sculpting. Pilates, power-yoga, isometrics. Preferably one-on-one with a body doctor who included Elizabeth Hurley and Jemina Khan among his clients.

The only problem with something like Pilates was that, as it didn't actually raise your metabolism, best results were achieved when combined with a starvation diet. Which was where devices like the letter-'A' diet came in. Surprisingly few foods started with the letter 'A'. If it had been 'B', things would have been very different. Bacon, Bounties, Bacardi, brie, bread, biscuits . . . And if she ever really needed to streamline down to the bone, she'd spend a week doing 'Y'. Yams, that was about it. And yellow peppers, at a stretch. Oh, and Yorkies, she'd forgotten about them. Perhaps 'Z' would be safer.

After breakfasting on an apple, an apricot and a glass of Aqua Libra, she managed to make it to ten o'clock. But when she feared she might attempt to strike up a conversation with the walls, she made a decision. She was going to go shopping. And it wasn't just free-form retail therapy, either – she had a purpose. Sort of, in any case . . . She planned to organize floor-to-ceiling wooden blinds for an entire wall in her bedroom, to counteract the country-cottage feel and endow it with a more cubey, urban air. Then she'd run a piece on it in the magazine and let them pick up some of the bill.

But when she reached Grafton Street she was shocked to find that none of the shops were open yet and the only other people around were bewildered-looking tourists.

This fucking country, she thought, for the hundredth time. Where was everyone? Probably at church, she decided contemptuously.

One o'clock, the man in the newsagent's told her. The shops opened at one o'clock. So she sat in a café, her legs crossed, drinking almond lattés and reading a newspaper. Only the frenzied bouncing of her foot as she tried to chivvy along time gave any indication of her inner hysteria.

And what was with the freak meteorological conditions, she wondered. There was a total absence of torrential rain or galeforce winds – surely a first for a bank holiday? Instead there was brave, jaunty sunlight against the hopeful blue of the sky and for some reason this reminded her of other times, which in turn made her sad, and she couldn't be doing with that. Oh no!

Quickly she reminded herself of her theory – she wasn't sad, her life had just dipped below the required Fabulous level. There was no negative emotion that couldn't be cured by the application of a little fabulousness and it was very important that she remembered it during these turbulent times. She'd admit that she'd forgotten it recently – last Sunday, for example, when she'd spent the day isolated and in despair.

Eventually the blinds emporia flung wide their doors, and then Lisa felt that they needn't have bothered. None of the pathetic interiors shops could handle a request for such a large blind. They recommended that she try a department store. And even though Lisa wasn't a department-store kind of girl, she decided that beggars couldn't be choosers.

On the fourth floor, in the curtain department, she bagged a busy little man hurrying past with a tape-measure around his neck.

'I need custom-made blinds.'

'I'm your man,' he confidently assured her.

But when she gave him the dimensions, then pointed out the wooden slats she wanted, he changed colour. Becoming a much paler one.

'Nine foot long?' he hooted. 'And fourteen foot wide?'

'That's right,' Lisa agreed.

'But missus,' he protested, 'that'll cost a fortune!'

'That's all right,' Lisa said.

'But have you any idea how much it'll cost?'

'Tell me.'

He did a series of speedy calculations on some

brown wrapping paper, then shook his head in anxiety.

'How much?'

But he wouldn't tell her. Whatever it was, it was too much, he'd decided.

'Hold on, hold on, I'm thinking. How about getting it in a cheaper material?' he said, flicking his trained eye along the shelves. 'Forget about the wood altogether. We could do it in plastic, how about that? Or canvas?'

'No, thank you. I definitely want it in wood.'

'Or you can get ready-made blinds.' He changed tack. 'I know they wouldn't be quite the right size and the material wouldn't be as nice, but it'd be miles cheaper. Come over here and look.' And grabbing her by the hand, he tugged her over to inspect some hideous vertical office-window blinds.

She dashed her hand away. 'But I don't want these! I want the wooden ones and I promise I can afford them!'

'I beg your pardon,' the man said humbly. 'I just didn't want you having to shell out all that money, but if you're sure . . .'

Lisa sighed raggedly. This fucking country. 'I've been saving up,' she decided to reassure him. 'It's OK.'

'You've been saving up?' All at once he rallied. 'Well, that's different, then.'

As she gave him her details, her irritation faded. When he leant over and confided to her that he thought the prices in the shop were shocking, that he and his wife waited for the sale, she became almost touched by his concern. *I'm losing it*, she suddenly thought. It's official, I'm going round the bend. Touched by a curtain salesman who won't sell me what I want.

It was barely six when she reached home. Scraping the bottom of the barrel in the search for activities, Lisa rang her mum and gave her her new phone number. Though she wondered why she bothered because her mum never rang her. Too worried about her phone bill. Even if there was some disaster, Lisa thought sourly, like if her dad died, her mum would probably still wait until Lisa rang to tell her.

After the usual enquiries into each other's health, Pauline had some good news for Lisa. 'Your dad says that that funny wedding of yours probably isn't valid here anyway and that you probably don't need to get divorced.'

The word 'divorced' slammed into Lisa with abrupt force. It was such a heavy, final word. Quickly she recovered to snippily tell her mum, 'Well, that's where you're wrong.'

Pauline swallowed at the expected censure. Of course she was wrong. She was always wrong around Lisa.

'Oliver registered it when we got back.'

'Well, that's that, then.'

'That *is* that, then.'

In the silence that followed, Lisa found herself remembering the Friday morning in bed when she and Oliver had decided on a We're-young-and-fabulous-Londonites' whim to fly to Las Vegas for the weekend and get married.

'We'll never get flights,' Oliver had laughed, wildly taken with the whole idea.

''Course we will.' Lisa had the confidence of one who always gets what she wants. And of course they did – those were the days when the world still worked for her. That very evening, giddy with excitement and alarm at what they were doing, they flew to Vegas. Where, weirded out by jet-lag and the spooky-blue desert sky, they found that getting married was frighteningly easy.

'Should we?' Lisa giggled, about to lose her nerve.

'That's why we're here.'

'I know, but . . . it's rather extreme, isn't it?'

Oliver's exasperated eyes collided with hers. Lisa knew that look. With Oliver you didn't start things that you didn't mean to finish.

'Come on, then!' Exhilaration and terror gave her laughter a shrill edge.

They plighted their troth in the twenty-four-hour Chapel of Love, their vows witnessed by an Elvis Presley lookalike and a Starbucks server. The bride wore black.

'Yew may kiss the braaaaade.'

'We're married.' Lisa was in fits, as they were shunted out to make way for the next couple. 'This is unreal.'

'I love you, babes,' Oliver said.

'I love you too.'

And she did. But most of all she was dying to get back, to madden everyone with envy of the kitsch glamour of their marriage. Beachside ceremonies in Saint Lucia didn't hold a candle – this was a scoop! She couldn't *wait* to go to work on Monday, for someone to ask, 'Do anything nice at the weekend?' – so that she could reply casually, 'Actually, I flew to Las Vegas and got married.'

'You'd want to get a good solicitor, then.' Pauline's voice brought her back to the present. 'Make sure you get what you're entitled to.'

''Course,' Lisa said irritably.

Actually, she had no idea what getting divorced entailed. For one so pragmatic and dynamic, she'd uncharacteristically dragged her feet on the ending of her marriage. Perhaps her mum was right and she *should* get a solicitor.

But after she hung up Lisa couldn't stop thinking about Oliver. Pesky feelings popped to the surface like blisters and out of nowhere, in some sort of a mad lapse, she was on the verge of lifting the phone and ringing him. The thought of hearing his voice, of making up with him, filled her with surging hope.

She'd had compulsions to call him before, but this was the worst so far, and she was only able to talk herself down with the reminder that he was the one who had left her. Even if he had said that she'd left him with no choice.

She moved away from the phone, suffering actual physical symptoms from the effort. Her heart pounded from thwarted chances. Only moments before, reconciliation had seemed possible, and the low that followed the high made her giddy. Lighting a cigarette with a trembling hand, she urged herself to forget him. Out with the old and in with the new. Think of Jack. But Jack was probably having non-stop sex with minxy Mai.

Jesus, she yearned, she'd love some sex . . . With Jack. Or Oliver. Either of them. Both of them . . . Her head filled with an image of Oliver's hard body, looking as though it had been carved out of ebony, and the memory made her actually groan out loud.

She looked at her watch. Again. Half past seven. Why couldn't the day just hurry up and *end*?

Then her doorbell rang, and her heart leapt into her throat. It might be Jack doing one of his unscheduled house-calls! Thrusting her face into the mirror to check that she was presentable, she quickly smoothed mascara away from under her eyes. Stroking down her hair, she hurried to the door.

Standing on her step looking up at her was a small boy in a Manchester United T-shirt and with an elaborate, shaven-headed, long-fringed haircut. All the little boys on the road had similar 'dos.

'How's it GOING, Lisa?' he said, in a remarkably loud voice. Confidently he leant against the doorpost. 'What are you UP to? Will you come out to PLAY?'

'Play?'

'We need a REF.'

Other children appeared behind him. 'Yeah, Lisa,' they urged. 'Come on out.'

She knew it was absurd, but she couldn't help being flattered. It was nice to be wanted. Blocking out memories of other bank-holiday weekends when she'd variously helicoptered to Champneys, flown first-class to Nice and holed up in a five-star hotel in Cornwall, she fetched a jacket and spent the rest of Sunday sitting on her doorstep, keeping score while the children on her street played a very aggressive form of tennis.

Jack Devine had rung his mother on Sunday morning. 'I'll be out later,' he said. 'And can I bring a friend?'

His mother had nearly choked with excitement. 'A lady friend?'

'A lady friend.'

Lulu Devine tried very hard to keep her mouth shut and failed utterly. 'Is it Dee?'

'No, Ma,' Jack sighed, 'not Dee.'

'Ah well. Any sightings of her?' Lulu was torn between missing the woman who'd ditched her beloved only son and partisan hatred of her.

'Actually, yes,' Jack admitted. 'I saw her in Drury Street carpark. She sends you her regards.'

'How is she?'

'She's getting married.'

Hope sprang eternal. 'To you?' Lulu gasped.

'No.'

'The bitch!'

355

'Ah no,' Jack soothed. At the time it hadn't been the most welcome news he'd ever received, but not the worst either. 'She was right not to marry me. We'd grown apart. She just saw it sooner than I did.'

'And this girl you're bringing today?'

'Her name is Mai. She's great, but a bit nervous.'

'We'll be nice to her.'

Wearing a demure fifties-style shirtwaister that she'd bought in an Oxfam shop almost as a joke, and sandals that were only a shameful three inches high, Mai sat beside Jack for the drive to Raheny.

'Will they mind me being half-Vietnamese? Are they racist?'

Jack shook his head in alarm. 'Not at all.' He touched her hand in support. 'Mai, don't worry, they're decent people.'

'And they're both teachers, you say?'

'Retired now, but they were.'

Lulu and Geoffrey pulled out all the stops – welcoming Mai with two-handed handshakes, dashing the newspapers off the couch so she could sit on it, showing Mai photos of Jack when he was little.

'He was *gorgeous*,' Lulu sighed meltingly, flashing Mai a picture of Jack as a pretty four-year-old on his first day at school. 'And look at this one.' A colour shot of a gawky teenage Jack standing next to a little table.

'I made that table,' Jack said proudly.

'He's great with his hands,' Lulu confided.

I know, Mai agreed, and for a horror-stricken second wondered if she'd said it aloud.

Mai's nervousness continued to be lovebombed away, and things were going well until she noticed a photo on the mantelpiece. A younger, thinner, less careworn Jack with his arm around a tall, brown-haired girl who smiled with upright confidence. Lulu clocked it at the exact same moment, and she collided with Mai in a horrified eye-meet. Why hadn't she hidden it?

'Who's your friend?' Mai asked Jack, almost enjoying tormenting herself. She knew all about Dee, how she and Jack had lived together since their college days and how, when after nine years together they'd decided to get married, Dee had done a runner. She was dying to get a look at her.

The potential awkwardness was sidestepped by the arrival of Karen, Jack's older sister, with her husband and her three children. No sooner were their rowdy greetings out of the way than Jenny, Jack's younger sister, rolled in, also with her husband and children in tow.

'Come on, we'll head off,' Jack said presently, when Mai started to look overwhelmed.

Lulu and Geoffrey watched the car pull away.

'A lovely girl,' Lulu said.

'With a most unusual job,' Geoffrey remarked.

'Selling mobile phones?'

Geoffrey twisted to look at her in surprise. 'Selling mobile phones? That's not what she told me!'

CHAPTER 32

Hair. On legs. Too much of it. Ashling was in a depilatory dilemma. She'd got her legs waxed a couple of weeks before during the Phantom Summer, so the hairs were too short to be done again. But they were too long, oh yes, *way* too long, to go to bed with someone.

So was she planning to sleep with Marcus Valentine? Well, who knows, she thought. But she didn't want her hairy legs to be an impediment.

She could shave them, she supposed. Except she couldn't. Once you start getting your legs waxed, it is strictly *verboten* to undo all the good work by shaving them and turning them bristly and spiky again. Julie, the girl who waxed her legs, would kill her.

It had to be Immac and due to some terrible lapse, Ashling was out of it. Ted was dispatched to the nearest chemist with a handwritten note.

'Why can't you go?' he grumbled, embarrassed.

Ashling indicated the tin-foil wrapped around her head. 'I've hot oil in my hair. If I went out like this everyone would think the aliens had landed.'

'As if! They'd know the aliens wouldn't be able to find a parking space in this city. Ah, Ashling,' he complained. 'do I have to give the note to the girl? Can't I just pick it off the shelf?'

'No. There are too many variations and you're a man. I want plain-flavoured mousse and you'd come back with lemon-flavoured gel. Or worse, you might even get me the spatula one. Now, please go!'

Astonishingly, the mission was successful and Ashling repaired to the bathroom to stand in the bath, her legs fizzing with noxious white stuff as she waited for the hairs to burn off. She sighed. Sometimes it's hard to be a woman.

The beautifying frenzy had kicked off when Marcus phoned on Monday afternoon and suggested, 'How about it?'

'How about what?'

'Whatever. A drink? A bag of chips? Rampant sex?'

'A drink sounds great. So does a bag of chips.'

He took a moment. 'And the rampant sex?' he enquired, like a cute little boy.

Ashling swallowed and tried to sound jokey. 'We'll have to see about that.'

'If I'm good?'

'If you're good.'

Then Ashling *raced* into action, a blur of rubbing stuff on her or rubbing stuff off. Over the course of the afternoon she washed and heavily conditioned her hair, exfoliated her entire body, removed the chipped polish from her toenails and applied fresh stuff, melted away the hairs on her legs, slathered herself in Gucci Envy moisturizer which was only wheeled out on special occasions, combed quarter of a tube of smoothing creme through her hair, plastered herself in make-up – this was no time for subtlety – and drenched herself in Envy eau de parfum.

Ted arrived back to oversee the final preparations. He was keen that Marcus and Ashling hit it off so that he could advance his stand-up career through close contact with Marcus. 'Look sexy,' he urged, slouched on Ashling's bed, watching her apply her third and final layer of mascara.

'I'm TRYING!' she heard herself shout. Clearly she was more nervous than she'd realized. Look at what hope did to her! Sending all her longing for love and stability on the rampage, and turning her into a nervous wreck. Sometimes, like now, she thought perhaps she *felt* too much. Was this normal? she wondered. Probably. And if it wasn't? Well, she'd had a deprived childhood, she thought wryly.

OK, maybe not deprived *deprived*. But deprived of routine, deprived of ordinariness. After her mother's first bout of depression, normal service had never really resumed. Instead, life as they'd all known it had slipped away. For ever: though they didn't know this at the time.

The irony of it was that initially Ashling had actually been excited when regular mealtimes began to be neglected. When she got a grass-mark on her cardigan, she was glad not to be shouted at. But as the days passed, eventually even she could see that the clothes she was putting on were filthy. Relief had given way to anxiety. *This isn't right.*

'Will I wear this today?' She presented herself to her mum in a filthy summer dress. *Notice me, notice me.*

Her mum's dead eyes looked out from a face dragged down in formless grief. 'If you want.'

Janet and Owen were kitted out no better. And neither was her mum – she'd always been so pretty and nicely dressed and now didn't even notice that she was out in public wearing a shirt stained with egg.

That summer they went to the local park a lot. Monica used to exclaim, 'I can't stay in this house,' and hustle all of them out. But even in the park she rarely stopped crying, and she never had a hanky. So Ashling, thinking it inappropriate that her mother wiped her tears with her sleeve, began to fold a tissue into her cardigan pocket every time they went out.

Once at the park Ashling would try to stage-manage things so that at least Janet and Owen had fun. When they agitated for ice-cream, Ashling was very anxious that they should get it: should they become upset, she feared it would blow the lid off everything. But her mother never remembered to bring any money, so Ashling had a pink and brown plastic purse in the shape of a dog's face which she began to bring instead.

As the summer advanced, Monica developed a new and alarming habit. Sitting listlessly on a bench, she would pluck and tear at a cut on her arm, only satisfied when it started to bleed. It was around then that Ashling began to carry a small bundle of Band-Aids around with her.

Something had to give. Surely someone had to notice?

She began to pray that her mother would get better and that her father wouldn't go away every Monday morning and not come back until Friday. Then, when prayers didn't produce the desired results, she incubated a bizarre conviction that if she flushed the toilet three times whenever she used it, everything would be all right. Next she developed the notion that when she came down the stairs she had to do a twirl at the bottom. Simply *had* to, and if she forgot to do it she had to go back to the top of the stairs and do the whole ritual again.

Superstitions started to take on great import-ance. If she saw one magpie – sorrow – she anxiously scanned the sky for a second one – joy. One day she spilt salt and to avoid any more tears threw some over her left shoulder. Where it landed in the trifle. Her mother gazed gormlessly at the grains of salt dissolving into the layer of cream, then put her head on the kitchen table and wept. No change there.

Ted's bellowing tuned her back in to the present. 'Ashling, speak to me! What do the tarot cards say about tonight?'

She recovered quickly, very, very glad that it was now and not then. 'Not bad. Four of Cups.' No need to mention that she'd plucked and discarded the more ominous Ten of Swords first. 'And my horoscope in two of the Sunday papers is good,' she continued. And not so good in two others, but what harm? 'And the Angel Oracle card I picked was the Miracle of Love one.' Eventually it had been anyway, after Maturity, Health, Creativity and Wisdom.

'Is that what you're wearing?' Ted nodded at her black three-quarter-length pants and waist-tied shirt.

'Why?' Ashling asked defensively. She'd dressed very carefully, and was especially pleased with the shirt because, due to some trick of the light, it created a false-waist syndrome.

'Haven't you got a short skirt?'

'I never wear short skirts,' she muttered, wondering anxiously if she might have overdone her blusher. 'I hate my legs. Have I too much blusher on?'

'Which one's blusher? The red stuff on your cheeks? No, put on some more.'

Immediately Ashling wiped some off. Ted's motives were suspect.

'Where are you meeting him? Kehoe's? I'll walk you there.'

'No you bloody well won't,' Ashling said, firmly.

'But I only . . .'

'No!'

The last thing Ashling wanted was Ted hanging around, pestering Marcus adoringly, asking if he could be his new best friend.

'Well, good luck then,' Ted said plaintively, as Ashling flung her lucky pebble into her new embroidered handbag, thrust her feet into wedge sandals and prepared to leave. 'I hope this is a romance made in heaven.'

'So do I,' Ashling admitted, then paid hasty lip-service to God or whoever was Celestial Minister for Romance, 'if it's meant to be.'

'Bollocks to that,' Ted scorned.

A brief orgy of Buddha rubbing, and Ashling was gone.

I will like Marcus Valentine and he will like me, I will like Marcus Valentine and he will like me . . . As she affirmationed her way along Grafton Street in her mince-inducing sandals, her Louise L. Hay-type chant was interrupted by a wolf-whistle. Marcus Valentine *already*? God, that Louise L. Hay was good gear!

But it wasn't Marcus Valentine. On the other side of the road, minus his orange blanket, was Boo. He was with two other men whose unshaven faces and funny clothes – the type that you couldn't purchase were you to try – identified them as men without homes also. They were eating sandwiches.

Some impulse of politeness forced her to cross over.

'So Ashling,' Boo flashed his gappy grin, 'you didn't go away for the bank holiday?'

Ashling shook her head.

'No, neither did I,' Boo said with dignity. Then he smote his forehead at his rudeness and swung his arm to encompass the two men who were with him. One was young, straggly haired and skeletal, the waistband of his sweatpants barely clinging to his starved hips. The other was older and had his face buried in a huge beard and insane hair, as if wild cats had been Sellotaped all around the border of his face. He wore once-white plimsolls and a dinner suit that had manifestly been tailored for a much shorter man.

Boo, by comparison, looked almost normal.

'Sorry! Ashling, this is JohnJohn,' he indicated the younger of the two men. 'And this is Hairy Dave. Lads, this is Ashling, my sometimes neighbour and all-round decent human being.'

Feeling slightly embarrassed, Ashling shook hands with both of them. What if Clodagh saw her now – she'd have a fit! Chewbacca in particular looked filthy and when his crusty hand clasped Ashling's she fought back the urge to shudder.

A passer-by nearly twisted his head off as he took a good look at the unlikely quartet, Ashling so fresh and fragrant, the other three anything but.

'You look deadly,' Boo remarked, with naked admiration. 'You must be meeting a man.'

'I am,' she said. Then, provoked by sudden fondness for Boo, she admitted, 'You'll never guess who it is.'

'*Who*?' All three of them gasped and leant in closer. Ashling had to hold her breath.

'Marcus Valentine,' she said, tying it in with an exhalation.

Boo erupted into merry-eyed laughter.

'Is he the comedian?' Hairy Dave asked in a slow, thick growl.

Ashling nodded.

'The one who does the stuff about owls?' JohnJohn got all excited.

God Almighty! Had Ted's fame spread so far that even marginalized citizens knew about him? Wait until she told him!

'That's Owl Ted Mullins you're thinking of,' Boo explained to JohnJohn. 'Marcus Valentine does the stuff about butter and snowflakes.'

'Don't know him.' JohnJohn was disappointed.

'He's cool. Ashling, this is deadly news! Well, I hope you enjoy yourself.'

'Thanks. I'll leave you to have your dinner in peace.' Ashling indicated the sandwiches they'd stopped eating when she showed up.

'Marks & Spencer,' Boo said. 'They give us whatever they haven't sold. I know their clothes are gone a bit boring, but the sangers are delicious!'

Suddenly the three men stiffened as if sensing danger. Ashling looked. Two policemen at the top of the road seemed to be the problem.

'They look bored.' JohnJohn sounded worried.

'Come on!' Boo urged, and they scooted away. 'Bye Ashling.'

When she arrived at the pub, Marcus was there already, sitting in combats and a T-shirt, a pint of Guinness in front of him. Something jumped in Ashling at the sight of him. He'd turned up. This was really happening.

Ambiguity wrestled within her – how did she feel about him? Was he the enthusiastic freckled eejit whom she'd refused to bellez? Or the confident performer whose phone call she'd longed for? His appearance didn't do anything to clear up the confusion, being neither wildly attractive nor laughably geeky. There was no getting away from it – he looked ordinary. His hair was an auburny-brown buzz-cut, his eyes weren't any obvious colour, and of course there was the small matter of the freckles. But she liked ordinary. She deserved ordinary. No point flying too close to the sun.

And even though he was ordinary, his height meant that at least he was the deluxe version of it. He had a nice body.

When he saw her he stood up and beckoned. There was a space beside him on the bench and she squeezed in.

'Hello,' he said solemnly, when she was settled.

'Hello,' she replied, equally solemnly.

Then they both sort of giggled. Now *he* was at it.

'Can I get you a drink?' he asked.

'You can. A vodka-and-tonic, thanks.'

When he came back with her drink she flashed him a relaxed grin. He was so friendly-looking it was hard to take this seriously. Which trickled a dispiriting stream of disappointment through her. She didn't fancy him. All that anxiety waiting for his phone call, *wasted*. She probed a bit more, leapfrogging from his freckles to her feelings and back. No, she definitely didn't fancy him. The hairs could have stayed on her legs. Ted could have been spared the humiliating trip to the chemist. Ah, well. But maybe they could be friends. In fact, he could probably help Ted's stand-up career, after all.

Brazenly she smiled at him and demanded, 'So what have you been up to lately?'

Abruptly she remembered that this was the man who was about to, in Lisa's words, 'go stellar', and there and then her lighthearted disrespect evaporated. Only seconds before she'd have gaily told him her most embarrassing moments, but perplexingly her brain had just wiped itself clean of all topics of conversation.

'A bit of this, a bit of that,' he replied.

Her turn. What should she say? The last thing, the very *last* thing she should mention was his career as a comedian. It would be naïve, and because he was so successful he must be sick of being praised and commended.

So it came as a right surprise when into the

tongue-tied silence he said, 'So you enjoyed the gig last Saturday?'

'I did,' she said. 'Everyone was very funny.'

She sensed an anticipation from him, so she continued carefully, 'I thought you were fantastic.'

'Ah, it wasn't one of my best,' he twinkled, with a shadow of his on-stage goofy vulnerability. The air of relief from him was palpable.

Ashling's turn again. 'Do you have a job, you know, apart from, er, being funny?'

'I write software for Cablelink, to do with upgrading the network to fibre optics.'

'Er, is that so?'

'Fascinating stuff,' he smiled ruefully. 'No wonder I have to do stand-up. And what do you do?'

Oh-oh. 'I work for a women's magazine.'

'What's it called?'

'Ah, er, *Colleen.*'

'*Colleen?*' His expression changed. 'They're on at me to write a column. Lisa someone.'

'Edwards. Lisa Edwards. She's my boss,' Ashling admitted, feeling guilty even though there was no need.

Suspicion altered his face into something hard and cold. 'Is that why you came out with me? To persuade me to write a column?'

'No! Not at all.' She had a horror of being thought pushy. 'I've nothing to do with it and I don't care if you never do it.'

Not exactly true. If he agreed to do the column it'd be a feather in her cap, but she wasn't going to press it. But she was moved by his insecurity and out of nowhere a protective urge sprang to life in her.

'Honestly,' she said softly, 'I'm only here with you because I want to be. Nothing to do with anything else.'

'OK,' he nodded thoughtfully. Then he laughed, 'I believe you, you've an honest face.'

Ashling screwed up her nose. 'God, what an awful thing to have.' She indicated his empty pint glass. 'More tea, vicar?'

'Oh? No. Ashling, can I ask you,' his tone was apologetic, 'would you mind if we dropped into a comedy gig? Just for half an hour? There's someone that I'd love to have a look at.'

'Sure, why not?' This clearly wasn't going to be a soft-lighting-and-expensive-dinner kind of date. Just as well, really.

The gig was only a couple of streets away, in another pub. Marcus was greeted at the door like royalty and, to Ashling's amusement, both of them were waved through without having to pay. In the crowded room, people kept coming up to him – mostly other comedians – and Marcus introduced Ashling to all of them. I could get used to this, she thought.

The gig was similar to the others Ashling had been at. Loads of people crammed into a small dark room, with a tiny patch of stage in the corner. The comedian Marcus was interested in modelled himself on a manic depressive and called himself Lithium Man.

When he finished his ten-minute stint, Marcus touched Ashling lightly. 'We can go now.'

'But I don't mind if we stay . . .'

He shook his head. 'No. I want to talk to *you*.'

He smiled through the gloom, and Ashling suddenly noticed that though he was ordinary, he erred on the good-looking side of it.

When they were resettled in another pub, Marcus asked, 'So what did you think of Lithium Man?'

Ashling paused. 'To be honest, I didn't really like him.'

'Yeah? How so?' Marcus seemed very interested in her opinion, and she was flattered.

'I don't think it's clever to make fun of mental illness,' she admitted. 'Not unless you're really funny, and he wasn't.'

'And who do you think is funny?' he asked, intently.

'Well, you obviously.' She laughed a bit shrilly at that, but he didn't seem to mind. 'Who do you like?'

'Well, me obviously.' They giggled conspiratorially at that. 'And Samuel Beckett.'

Ashling squealed with laughter until she realized he was serious. *Shite*.

'I think he's the best comic writer of the century,' Marcus enthused.

'I once saw *Waiting for Godot*,' Ashling said tentatively. No need to mention that it was a school outing and she hadn't been able to make head nor tail of it. But apart from the Beckett hiccup, the evening passed without incident. The drinks flowed and Marcus was charming and interested in her. Because of his freckles, she was relaxed around him and told him lots of things. About her salsa classes – she had to admit she was thrilled she'd actually taken it up because she must seem like a person with 'interests' – her fondness for handbags and how, lots of the time, she loved her new job on *Colleen*. 'Although that's not a hint,' she said, suddenly anxious.

'I know. But be honest, is the pressure on you to bring them the head of Marcus Valentine?'

'N-no,' she stuttered.

'And they're not leaning on you at work about it?' he asked again.

'No way.' Ashling was adamant. 'There's been no mention of it, actually.'

'Oh.' After a spell of silence he added, 'I see . . . I see.'

Looking out from under his eyelashes, he smiled slightly at her, and with a sudden warmth burring in her solar plexus, Ashling realized that she found him attractive. He must be the kind of person who grows on you. And he wasn't really like his stage persona at all. Just as well – goofy gobshites weren't exactly bedroom fodder.

Then he shifted, tilted his head against Ashling's and said in a low, meaningful tone, 'Would you like a bag of chips?'

'No, thanks.'

'So we've had a drink, you don't want chips, all that remains on the agenda is . . .' *The rampant sex!*

Though she'd lost count of the number of drinks she'd had, the idea filled her with sudden, inexplicable paralysis. Not exactly fear, but not exactly *not* fear either. She really liked him, she found him attractive, but . . .

'Oh, would you mind . . . You see, I hadn't planned to be out late tonight. Work in the morning and all that.'

'Oh right. Sure,' he said evenly, but he wouldn't look her properly in the eye. 'We'd better get going then.'

He kissed her when he dropped her home, but somehow she wasn't convinced by it.

CHAPTER 33

Soft, pudgy hands stroking her face . . . Halfway between sleeping and waking, Clodagh dreamily savoured the heat of Molly's hands touching the sensitive, yielding skin of her face. Lying on Clodagh's chest, Molly breathed with earnest weight as she trailed her tender, sticky fingers along Clodagh's chin, her cheeks, around her nose, her forehead and . . . OW! *Ouch!* Stars went off in her brain.

'You punched me in the eye, Molly!' Clodagh yelled, in shock from the violent awakening.

'Mummy woke up,' Molly said, in fake surprise.

'Oh course Mummy woke up.' Clodagh cupped her hand over her blinded eye, which was sluicing water as though from a burst dam. 'Getting a belt in the eye usually does that to a person.'

Shrugging Molly off her, she stumbled to the mirror to check the damage. She needed to look her best today because she had an appointment at an employment agency.

One side of her face was normal, the other was collapsed into tearful, bloodshot disaster. Damn. Then she noticed the pile of clothes on her chair, and went into her usual pre-Flor frenzy of tidying and hanging.

'Get dressed, Craig,' she called. 'Molly, hurry, put your clothes on. Flor will be here.'

Thundering down the stairs, breakfast was the usual war-zone.

'Don't want the All-Bran,' Craig screeched and bawled. 'Want the Coco Pops.'

'You can't have the Coco Pops until the All-Bran is eaten,' Clodagh said, pretending for a moment that she might be obeyed.

Her weekly shop included six-pack selection boxes of cereal, of which the Sugar-Puffs and Coco Pops always got scoffed immediately, while the boring ones like All-Bran mounted up in an abandoned slush-pile. Until they'd been consumed, she tried to resist being bullied into opening a new selection. And always caved in. Particularly today because time was of the essence. Tearing cellophane from a virgin six-pack, she thumped the Coco Pops in front of Craig. Then in her nightdress she hurried out to the car, retrieving several shopping bags from their hiding place in the boot. She often did that when she bought something new to wear. Even though Dylan never complained about her spending money on clothes, it didn't stop her feeling guilty.

But this was different. While Dylan had been at work on the bank holiday, Clodagh had dumped the children with her arthritic mother and gone on a mini-spree. The bags that she hustled into the house contained young, funky party clothes, clothes that she wasn't entirely confident how to wear. She'd also bought a suit in honour of her visit to the employment agency – about which Dylan knew nothing. She didn't know why she hadn't told him but she had a vague, free-floating suspicion that he wouldn't approve.

Back in her room, she frantically snapped price tags and labels from the grey skirt and jacket and got dressed. The suit had been expensive. Sick-makingly so, but she reasoned that she'd get to wear it again and again when she got a job. Fifteen-denier tights, high black shoes and a white shirt followed. After she'd applied lipstick and arranged her hair into a neat French twist, she felt she looked good.

Apart from her bloodshot eye, that is.

She wasn't in time to escape Flor this morning. She was lumbering through the gate just as Clodagh was hustling Craig and Molly out the door.

'How are you, Flor?'

'I was over at Frawley on Friday,' Flor replied. Frawley was her doctor. Though Clodagh had never met him, she felt she knew him intimately.

'What had he to say?'

'It's got to come out.'

'What has?'

'My womb, what else?' Flor hooted in surprise.

'Bloody hell, that's awful news.' Clodagh summoned energy to administer sympathy and woman-to-woman understanding.

'It is not!'

'Aren't you upset?'

'Why would I be?'

'Aren't you worried that you'll feel . . .' Clodagh stalled. She'd been about to say, 'Less of a woman?' But that was way too tactless. Instead she settled for, 'Aren't you worried that you'll feel a loss?'

'Not a bit if it,' Flor said gaily. 'Whip it out. Sure, it's only a nuisance. No good ever came of it. What would you like me to do for you today?'

'Oh.' Clodagh was mortified. 'A little bit of ironing, if you're able. And maybe the bathroom. Whatever you're able for really . . .'

Pushing open the door of the city-centre employment agency, fear and excitement manifested themselves in Clodagh's trembling hands. She stopped before a young girl with a pale-haired chignon, whose fresh, apricot-bloom skin was smothered with heavy foundation.

'I have an appointment with Yvonne Hughes.'

The girl stood up. 'Hello,' she said coolly, with surprising confidence. 'I'm Yvonne Hughes.'

'Oh.' Clodagh had expected someone a lot older.

Then Yvonne gave her the mother of all firm handshakes, as though she was in training to be a male politician. 'Take a seat.'

Clodagh palmed over her CV, which had got slightly bent in her bag.

'Now let's have a look.' Yvonne had a delicate,

very deliberate way with her hands. She kept stroking the CV with the pads of her splayed, child-like fingers, flattening it out, straightening it up, realigning it with the edge of her desk. Then before she turned the page she took a moment to grasp the corner of it between her thumb and forefinger and did a brief frenzy of rubbing, just to make sure she hadn't picked up two pages at once. For some reason, this really irritated Clodagh.

'You've been out of the workplace for a long time?' Yvonne said. 'It's . . . how many . . . over *five* years.'

'I had a baby. I never intended to stay away so long, but then I had another child, and the time never seemed right until now.' Clodagh defended herself in a rush.

'I . . . seeeeeee . . .' Yvonne continued to toy with Clodagh's nerves as she studied her career details. 'Since you've left school, you've worked as a hotel booking clerk, receptionist at a sound studio, cashier in a restaurant, filing clerk in a solicitor's office, goods inward for a clothing company, cashier at Dublin zoo, receptionist in an architect's firm and a booking clerk at a travel agent's?' Clodagh had made Ashling put down everything she'd ever done, just to show that she was versatile. 'You stayed . . . *three days* at Dublin zoo?'

'It was the smell,' Clodagh admitted. 'No matter where I went I could smell the elephant house. I'll never forget it. Even my sandwiches tasted of it . . .'

'Your longest stint was at the travel agent's,' Yvonne interrupted. 'You were there for two years?'

'That's right,' Clodagh said, eagerly. Somehow she'd moved forward so that she was sitting on the edge of her chair.

'Were you promoted in that time?'

'Well, no.' Clodagh was taken aback. How could she explain that you could only be promoted to be a supervisor and that everyone both despised and pitied the supervisors.

'Have you done any of the travel-agency exams?'

Clodagh nearly laughed. The very thought! That's why you leave school, isn't it? So that you never have to sit another exam?

Yvonne twiddled her fingers in the air, before bringing each one down separately, to deliberately, hypnotically stroke the page flat again. 'What software did you use there?'

'Ah . . .' Clodagh couldn't remember.

'Have you typing and shorthand?'

'Yes.'

'How many words a minute?'

'Oh, I don't know. I just type with my first two fingers,' Clodagh elaborated, 'but I'm very fast. As fast as some people who've done a course.'

Yvonne's child-like eyes narrowed. She was annoyed, although not to the extent that she would have you believe. She was just playing, having fun with the power she had. 'So can I take it that you don't actually have any shorthand?'

'Well, I suppose, but I could always . . . No,' Clodagh admitted, having run out of energy.

'Have you any basic word-processing skills?'

'Ah, no.'

And even though Yvonne knew the answer, she asked, 'And you're not a graduate?'

'No,' Clodagh admitted, fixing Yvonne with one normal eye and one red-veined one.

'OK.' Yvonne exhaled long-sufferingly, licked a finger and used it to smooth down a ragged corner of the CV. 'Tell me what you read.'

'How do you mean?'

There was a pause, so tiny it barely existed, but Yvonne had created it to convey what a hopeless idiot she thought Clodagh was.

'*FT? Time?*' Yvonne prompted. She didn't exactly sigh, but she might as well have. Then she added cruelly, '*Bella? Hello!?*'

All Clodagh read were interiors magazines. And *Cat in the Hat* books. And occasional blockbusters about women who set up their own businesses and who didn't have to sit through humiliating interviews such as this one when they wanted a job.

'And I see you count tennis among your interests. Where do you play?'

'Oh, I don't *play*.' Clodagh gave a near-teenage giggle. 'I mean I like watching it.'

Wimbledon was about to start, there had been lots of pre-transmission publicity on telly.

'And you go to the gym?' Yvonne read. 'Or do you just like watching that too?'

'No, I really go,' Clodagh said, on much more solid ground.

'Although that hardly counts as a hobby, does it?' Yvonne asked. 'That's like saying sleeping is a hobby. Or eating.'

This caught Clodagh on the raw.

'And you're a regular theatre-goer?'

Clodagh wavered, then admitted, 'I'm not really. But you've to put down something, don't you?' (When Clodagh and Ashling had finally stopped inventing joke hobbies such as rally driving and devil worship, and had tried to assemble a list of *real* ones, pickings had been slim.)

'So what are your interests?' Yvonne challenged.

'Ah . . .' What *were* her interests?

'Hobbies, passions, that kind of thing,' Yvonne said impatiently.

Clodagh's mind had frozen. The only thing she could think of was that she liked playing with her split ends, peeling the broken bit along the shaft of the hair, seeing how far up it would go. She could spend hours amusing herself thus. But something stopped her from sharing this with Yvonne. 'You see, I have two children,' she said feebly. 'They take up all my time.'

Yvonne flashed her an if-you-say-so glance. 'How ambitious are you?'

Clodagh recoiled. She wasn't at all ambitious. Ambitious people were weird.

'When working at the travel agent's, what gave you the most job satisfaction?'

Making it through the day, as far as Clodagh remembered. The idea was – and it was the same for all of the girls she worked with – they went in, suspended their real lives for eight hours and poured their energies into enduring the wait.

'Dealing with people?' Yvonne prompted. 'Ironing out glitches? Closing a sale?'

'Getting paid,' Clodagh said, then realized she shouldn't have. The thing was, it had been a very long time since she'd done any kind of interview. She'd forgotten the correct platitudes. And, as far as she remembered, she'd always been interviewed by men before, and they'd been a damn sight nicer than this little cow.

'I'm not really interested in working in a travel agent's again,' Clodagh said. 'I wouldn't mind if you got me a job in a . . . magazine.'

'You'd like to work in a magazine?' Yvonne pretended she was finding it hard to stifle a smile.

Clodagh nodded cautiously.

'Wouldn't we all, dear?' Yvonne sang.

Clodagh decided she hated her, this powerful, merciless child. Calling her 'dear' when she was half her age.

'What kind of salary did you have in mind?' Yvonne asked, turning the screws.

'I don't . . . ah . . . I hadn't thought . . . What do *you* think?' Clodagh handed the last vestiges of her power over to Yvonne.

'It's hard to say. I don't have much to go on. If you'd consider retraining . . .'

'Maybe,' Clodagh lied.

'If anything comes up, I'll be in touch.'

They both knew she wouldn't be.

Yvonne accompanied her to the door. It gave Clodagh savage pleasure to see that she was slightly pigeon-toed.

Out on the street, in her hateful, ridiculous, expensive suit, she walked slowly to her car. Her confidence was shattered. This morning had been a terrifying lesson in how old and useless she was. She'd hung all her hopes on a job but, manifestly, the world of work was a too-fast place which she didn't have the skills to belong to any more.

Now what was she going to do?

CHAPTER 34

On Tuesday morning, Lisa was pawing the ground and champing at the bit outside Randolph Media, desperate to get in. Never again would she endure a weekend like the one she'd just had. On the bank-holiday Monday, she'd been so bored that she'd gone to the cinema on her own. But the movie she'd wanted to see had sold out, so she'd ended up having to go to something called *Rugrats Two*, sharing the cinema with what seemed like a billion over-excited under-sevens. She really hadn't known there were that many children in the world. And how ironic that the people she was spending so much of her time with lately were children . . .

She glared at Bill the porter, as behind the glass door he jingled his keys to let her in. It was all his fault, the lazy, workshy old bastard. If he'd let her come to work over the weekend she'd never have found out how empty her life was.

'Jayzus, you're early,' Bill grumbled in alarm.

'Nice weekend?' Lisa asked acidly.

'Bedad, I did indeed,' Bill said expansively, and

launched into an account of visits from grand-children, visits *to* grand-children . . .

'Because I didn't,' Lisa interrupted.

'I'm sorry to hear that,' he sympathized, wondering what it had to do with him.

But on the good side, Lisa thought, as she went up in the lift, she'd made some decisions. If she was going to be stuck in this horrible bloody country, she was going to build up a network of friends. Well, maybe not friends *as such*, but people whom she could call 'darling' and bitch about other people to.

And she was going to have sex with someone. A *man*, she hastily specified. Never mind the New Bisexuality which she'd profiled in the March issue of *Femme* – one sheepish snog with a model at the Met Bar had been all she could manage. Like Sensible Chic, having sex with women just wasn't for her.

That terrible weekend urge to call Oliver was a clear sign that she needed a bloke. Jack, if possible. But, with a hardening of her resolve, she decided if Jack wanted to play Burton and Taylor with Mai, she was going to find someone else. Perhaps that would bring him to his senses. Either way, things couldn't go on as they were.

Of course, she mightn't be able to find a suitable boyfriend immediately. But she swore to herself that *at the very least* before the week was out she was going to sleep with someone.

Like who? There was Jasper Ffrench, the celebrity

chef, he'd certainly been up for it. But he was much too much of a pain. There was that Dylan she'd seen with Ashling. He was a babe. Married, unfortunately, so she wasn't really likely to run into him in a nightclub. Spending the weekend hanging around DIY stores would be a better bet.

'Jesus Christ,' she said aloud, coming to a halt when she walked into the office. Champagne bottles, mugs, tin foil and wire were strewn everywhere, and the place stank like a pub. Obviously the cleaner didn't think it was her job to clear up the remains of Friday's beano. Well, Lisa wasn't going to wash anything, she had her nails to think of. Ashling could do it.

To Lisa's jealous contempt, every single other member of staff was late. They'd all had a wild three days. Even Mrs Morley, who, after her couple of mugs of champagne on Friday, had spent the weekend on the sauce.

Now it was payback time – all and sundry were moany and depressed, especially Kelvin, who'd punctured his inflatable orange rucksack with his thumb ring in a tragic looking-for-a-biro accident on Sunday night.

As everyone studiously avoided looking at the dirty cups, comparisons of hangovers abounded.

'It always gets me more in the stomach than the head,' Dervla O'Donnell confided to the general populace. 'Nothing but two rasher sandwiches stops the queasiness.'

'Nah, it's the paranoia that does for me,' Kelvin

shivered, flicking a furtive glance at her, then dipping his head down again immediately.

Even Mrs Morley admitted shyly, 'I feel as though a dagger is being stabbed repeatedly into my right eye.'

Lisa longed to join in and couldn't. The icing on her pissed-off cake was when Mercedes swanned in, laden with bags covered in airline stickers. Apparently she'd gone to New York, of all places, for the weekend. Spoilt bitch, Lisa thought bitterly. *Lucky* bitch. And how come everyone seemed to have known about it except her?

Mercedes had been commissioned to bring back several items: white Levi's for Ashling – apparently they were half the price over there; a Stussy hat for Kelvin, which you couldn't get in Europe; and a consignment of Babe Ruth bars for Mrs Morley, who'd been to Chicago in the sixties and had never been able to settle for Cadbury's since. The lucky recipients fell with glad cries upon their items and money changed hands briskly.

'I was thinking of killing myself,' Kelvin cheerfully sported his new hat, 'but now I'm not going to.'

Lisa watched sourly. She could have asked Mercedes to bring back Kiehl's body butter. Not that she would have. But she would have enjoyed *refusing* to ask her.

As well as the requested items, Mercedes brought generous presents for the office – forty flavours of jelly beans, bags of Hershey kisses and armloads of Reece's peanut-butter cups. But when Mercedes offered her a bag of Hershey kisses, Lisa shuddered, 'Oh no. I always think American chocolate tastes slightly like sick.'

Mrs Morley – her mouth full of a Babe Ruth – gasped at such sacrilege and, momentarily, Mercedes' shark-dark eyes bore into Lisa's. Lisa saw contempt, possibly even amusement in there.

'Whadever,' Mercedes deadpanned. And Lisa nearly combusted. Mercedes had been to New York for two days. Two days! And she had a New York accent.

Last of the non-managerial staff to arrive was Trix, contributing considerably to the strong, aromatic mix.

'Cod above,' Mrs Morley exclaimed, showing an unexpected tendency to play to the gallery. 'This, ahem, *plaice* stinks.'

'Ha ha,' Trix said scornfully.

This triggered a ton of fish puns.

'You smell fish-ious, Trix!' Kelvin exclaimed.

'Oh, don't carp,' Ashling soothed.

'Shoal-ong, best if you go home,' Mercedes surprised everyone with.

Kelvin proved to have quite a gift for it. 'Salmon chanted evening,' he sang, his arms outstretched, 'you might meet a stray – ayne – ger.'

'Here's another song for you!' Boring Bernard got things right, for once. Pulling up the collar of his shirt, and despite his red tank-top and suit trousers, he attempted a little jive. 'Hake, rattle and roll! I said, hake, rattle and roll . . .'

In strolled Jack, hands in pockets, wreathed in smiles. 'Morning all,' he said cheerfully. 'D'you know, this place is a shambles.'

Trix turned to him. 'Jack – yeah, I know, Mr Devine to me – they're all making fun because I smell of fish. They're singing songs about it.'

'What kind of songs?'

'Go on,' Trix instructed a discomfited Kelvin. 'Sing for our glorious leader.'

Kelvin reluctantly obliged.

Jack grinned.

'And you,' Trix said to Bernard.

Bernard did a very half-hearted reprieve of his earlier show-manship.

'That's not very good,' Jack said.

Trix nodded smugly.

'I've a better one,' Jack surprised everyone. Then strutting with surprising grace towards his office, he sang loudly, 'I'm a SOLE man. Bababopbabop. I'm a SOLE mah-han.'

The office door closed, but they could still hear him making faint trumpet noises within.

Everyone exchanged astonished looks. 'What the hell's up with *him*?'

'Am I herring things?' Trix could hardly speak. 'Was he singing –?' She stopped in alarm. 'Shite, even I'm doing it now.'

Ashling's face drained of animation. She'd only just remembered the drunken relationship advice

389

she'd given to Jack on Friday evening. 'Oh God,' she groaned, covering her hot cheeks with her hands.

'Am I that bad?' Trix looked hurt. She expected a slagging from most of the others but not from Ashling.

Ashling shook her head. She could smell nothing now, it had all been wiped out by the tide of mortification. She had to apologize.

'This office is a state.' Killjoy Lisa began to impose order. 'Kelvin, can you gather up the empty bottles, and Ashling, can you wash the cups?'

'Why should I? I always wash them,' Ashling said vaguely, too trapped in the horror of what she'd said to Jack Devi – Christ, she'd even called him JD!

This jolted Lisa into astonished silence. She glowered threateningly at Ashling, but Ashling was miles away, so she turned viciously on Trix. 'Right then, fishgirl, *you* do them.'

Astounded at being spoken to thus by Lisa, who'd treated her up to now as most-favoured, Trix mulishly, resentfully clattered the cups on to the tray, treated each of them to half a second beneath a running tap in the ladies', then pronounced them washed.

Ashling waited for everyone to settle down to work before she trembled across to Jack's office, the nerves around her knees jumping.

'Morning Miss Fix-it.' Jack was almost skittish as he welcomed her in. 'Is it cigarettes you're looking for? Because I'd kind of intended last week's to be a one-off. But if you insist . . .'

'Oh no! That's not why I'm here.' Then she stopped, abruptly snagged by his tie. It was covered with bright yellow Bart Simpsons. He didn't usually wear such frivolous ties, did he?

'So why are you here?' His dark eyes twinkled merrily at her. Funny, his room didn't seem as brooding and gloomy as it usually did.

'I wanted to say that I'm very sorry for giving you advice on your relationship on Friday. There was, ah . . .' she tried for a light-hearted smile, but it came out as a bloodless rictus instead. 'There was drink taken.'

'Not a problem,' Jack said.

'Well, if you're sure –'

'You were right, you know. Mai is a lovely girl. I shouldn't be fighting with her.'

'Well, er, grand.'

Ashling left, feeling – perplexingly – almost worse than before she'd gone in. As she emerged, Lisa stared hard at her.

Shortly afterwards a courier arrived bearing the photos from the Frieda Kiely shoot. Mercedes tried to grab them, but Lisa intercepted her. She tore open the jiffy bag and out fell a heavy, floppy pile of glossy shots of models with turf stains on their faces and straw in their hair, prancing around the bog.

Lisa flicked through them in ominous silence, separating them into two unequal piles.

The smaller pile contained a picture of a dirty,

dishevelled girl wearing a slinky evening gown teamed with muddy wellies, her bare legs streaked with mud. The same girl clad in an exquisitely tailored suit, sitting on an upturned bucket, pretending to milk a cow. And another model in a short, tight, silver dress, allegedly driving a tractor. The larger pile contained airy-fairy shots of girls in airy-fairy frocks dancing about an airy-fairy landscape.

Lisa picked up the much smaller of the two bundles. 'These are just about usable,' she coldly told Mercedes. 'The rest are pants. I thought you were a fashion journalist.'

'What's wrong with them?' Mercedes asked, with menacing calm.

'There's no irony. No contrast. These . . .' she indicated the pictures of the floaty dresses. '. . . should have been shot in an urban setting. The same girls with the same dirty faces and mad frocks, but this time getting on a bus or getting money from a cash-point or using a computer. Get on to Frieda Kiely's press office. We're going to shoot this again.'

'But . . .' Mercedes glowered blackly.

'Go on,' Lisa said impatiently.

Everyone else in the office suddenly found their toecaps very, very interesting. No one could look at the humiliation, it was too horrible.

'But . . .' Mercedes tried again.

'Go *on!*'

Mercedes stared, then grabbed up the photos

and banged to her desk. As she passed, Ashling heard her mutter, 'Bitch,' semi-under her breath.

Ashling had to agree. What was Lisa *like*?

The atmosphere was toxic with tension. Ashling had to open a window, even though the day wasn't warm. Some fresh air was needed to cleanse the ugly mood.

The only person in good form was Jack. Occasionally he emerged from his office, blithely oblivious to the tension, conducted his business, bestowed grins all round, then disappeared again. Slowly the poison dissipated, until everyone except Mercedes felt almost normal again.

At twelve-thirty, Mai arrived. She gave a general greeting then asked to see Jack.

'Go on,' Mrs Morley nodded perfunctorily.

Everyone sat up in glee as the door closed behind her.

'That'll wipe the smile off his face,' Kelvin observed.

Trix almost went around selling hot dogs, so festive and ringside was the air.

But no fighting broke out and they emerged serenely, very much together, Mai smirking beside Jack's bulk as they left the office.

Everyone exchanged startled looks. 'What was *that* all about?'

Lisa, about to leave to inspect the bedrooms at the Morrison for their 'sexiness' factor, was abruptly stricken with privation. She had to sit down and swallow hard to try to dislodge the cold, hard sensation of loss. But what was the problem? She'd known he had a girlfriend. It was just with all the squabbling they'd done, she'd never fully taken it seriously.

Ashling was also a little nonplussed. *What have I done?*

When Lisa booked a taxi to take her to the Morrison, she asked – with mild embarrassment – for Liam. She'd started doing that lately. She could only suppose that she liked Liam, with all his salt-of-the-earth Dublin chat.

By the time she arrived at the hotel she'd taken her upset about Jack and Mai and reconfigured it into something manageable. Hadn't she promised herself only that very morning that she was going to bag herself a bloke? And that it didn't have to be Jack. Not yet, in any case.

'Where do you want to be dropped, Lisa?' Liam interrupted her thoughts.

'Just up here, at the building with the black windows.'

There was a young man, decked out in a beautiful grey tailored suit, loitering by the front door of the hotel.

'Ah, look, love,' Liam's voice softened. 'Your fella's waiting on you. And all done up like a dog's dinner in a whistle and tie. Is it your birthday? Many happy returns of the day. Or is it your anniversary?'

'That's the doorman,' Lisa muttered.

'Is he?' Disappointment made Liam very high-pitched. 'I thought he was your chap. Ah well. D'you want me to wait for you?'

'Yes please, I'll only be about fifteen minutes.'

Briskly, Lisa tested the bounciness of the Morrison's beds, the crispness of the sheets, the size of the bath – it was big enough for two – the amount of champagne in the mini-bar, the aphrodisiac foodstuffs available from room service, the CDs in the room and, finally, the handcuff opportunities. All in all, she concluded, you could have a very nice time here. The only thing that was missing was the right man.

Returning to work, her eye was caught by a huge billboard advertising a new ice-cream called Truffle. She was going to the launch that very evening. Then she noticed the magnificent man on the poster, his ravishing mouth wrapped around a Truffle, his eyes glazed with what was meant to be lust, but could just as easily have been achieved with a couple of Mogadon.

I'd love to have sex with him.

God, she realized, I'm turning into a sad old spinster. Fantasizing about a photograph. The sooner I get laid the better.

CHAPTER 35

The launch party for the new Truffle ice-cream started at six that evening. Because it was basically a choc-ice, it had no Unique Selling Point, in a marketplace crammed to capacity with products boasting USPs. So the manufacturers were pelting money at it, holding the launch in the Clarence and luring journalists there with promises of champagne. It promised to be a fairly glitzy affair.

'Want to come?' Lisa asked Ashling.

Ashling, still uncomfortable after the way Lisa had humiliated Mercedes, was about to refuse, then decided it would kill an hour before her salsa class. 'OK,' she said, cautiously.

Before they left, Lisa went to the ladies' to do her hourly check on her appearance. Sweeping a cruelly appraising eye over her slender, tanned reflection in a white Ghost dress, she was pleased. This was no misplaced arrogance. Even her worst enemy (and competition was stiff) would have acknowledged that she looked good.

She'd want to, she admitted. She worked hard enough at it. She was her masterpiece, her life's work. Not that she was ever complacent about her appearance: she was also her own harshest critic. Long before it was ever visible to the naked eye, she could tell when her roots needed to be done. She could *feel* her hair growing. And she always knew – even if the scales and the tape-measure disagreed – when she'd put on even an ounce of fat. She fancied she could hear her skin stretch and expand to accommodate it.

She paused and narrowed her eyes. Was that a line she saw on her forehead? The merest whisper of a hint of a wrinkle? It was! Time for another Botox injection. She was from the attack-is-the-best-form-of-defence school of beauty therapy. Get it before it gets you.

Touching up her already perfect lip-gloss, Lisa was finally ready. If she didn't pull this evening, it wouldn't be her fault.

It turned out that both Kelvin and Jack were also going along to the Truffle shindig. As Truffle was sponsoring the new drama series on Channel 9, Jack was reluctantly playing the corporate game.

'And what's your excuse? Which of your many magazines are you going to cover it for?' Lisa sarcastically asked Kelvin.

'None. But I'm in the mood to get stotious and I'm skint after the bank holiday.'

Lisa flinched at the mention of the awful, endless bank holiday. Never again.

As soon as they arrived. Lisa disappeared into the well-dressed, rowdy throng, Kelvin made straight for the bar and Ashling circled the room cautiously. She knew no one and couldn't get too drunk because of her salsa class. And she *must* go to her salsa class, it was only the second lesson, way too soon to be skiving off. Occasionally through the crowds she spotted Jack Devine uncomfortably trying to be backslappingly jovial and failing miserably. Lack of practice, she deduced.

Somehow she ended up standing beside him, on the edge of things.

'Hello,' she said nervously. 'How are you?'

'I've a headache from smiling,' he said grumpily. 'I hate these things.' Then he lapsed into muteness.

'I'm very well too,' Ashling said, tartly. 'Thank you for asking.'

Jack pulled a surprised face, then turned to the passing waitress. 'Nurse,' he waggled his empty glass, 'something for the pain.'

The waitress, a young, appealing girl, handed him a glass of champagne. 'One of these every half-hour should do the trick.'

She dimpled prettily and he smiled back. Sourly, Ashling monitored the exchange.

As soon as the 'nurse' was gone, Ashling tried to think of something to say to Jack, any kind of vague conversational gambit at all, and couldn't. And Jack was no better. He stood in silence, shifting from foot to foot, drinking his champagne far too fast.

Another waitress passed, this time carrying a

tray piled high with Truffles, which Ashling accepted eagerly. Nót so much because she loved ice-cream, although she did, but because it would give her something to do with her mouth other than not talking to Jack Devine. She applied herself to it with gusto, twirling her tongue around the top. Abruptly she sensed she was being watched and peeped up to see Jack Devine looking amused and suggestive. A prickly blush crawled up her neck. Still holding his look, she bit the top off her choc-ice with a savage *crunch*. Jack winced and she laughed with serves-you-right wickedness.

'I'm going now,' she said.

'You can't leave me,' he complained. 'Who will I talk to?'

'Well, it hasn't been me so far!' she exclaimed and picked up her bag.

'Oi! Miss Fix-it, where are you off to?' He sounded quite panicky.

'My salsa class.'

'Oh, your dirty dancing. Sometime you'll have to bring me too,' he teased. 'Go on, abandon me to the salary-men, then.'

Passing Dan 'I'll try anything once' Heigel from the *Sunday Independent*, who was making his version of a Brown Cow by putting lumps of ice-cream into his champagne, Ashling departed.

No sooner was she gone than Jack was flanked by Kelvin, holding two glasses of champagne, both of them his.

'Look at Lisa. Is she wearing knickers or isn't

she?' Kelvin asked, studying Lisa's pert bottom through her white dress. 'I can't see any lines but . . .'

Jack wouldn't join in.

'I know what you're thinking,' Kelvin said.

'I doubt it.'

'You're thinking she could be wearing a thong. She might be, of course,' Kelvin reluctantly acknowledged, 'but I'd like to think otherwise.'

Lisa was systematically working her way through the room looking for the best-looking man in it, but already she'd gone up a couple of blind alleys.

First she'd met a mysterious, almost silent man wearing blue, roundy shades. He looked very cool and had a gorgeous, knowing mouth, a wicked smile, lovely hair and great clothes. Then he took off his glasses and Lisa recoiled. Suddenly he was horrific. His eyes were tiny, too close together, and kind of stunned and bewildered-looking. They belonged to a different face altogether, to someone with learning difficulties.

Backing away she bumped into Fionn O'Malley, a self-styled eligible bachelor. He fancied himself as one of Ireland's sexiest men on account of his pointy Jack Nicholson eyebrows.

'Hello there.' Evilly, he smiled at Lisa and raised his eyebrows with demonic intent. 'You're looking particularly luscious this evening.' This compliment was accompanied with further raising and lowering of his eyebrows in a manner contrived to make Lisa feel uncomfortable with sexual stirring.

Bored, she turned her back.

And then she saw him. The model who was on billboards across Ireland. He was text-book gorgeous: pouty, lantern-jawed, dewy-skinned, his shiny, blue-black hair falling in a lick over his tanned forehead. A face so perfect he was a millimetre away from being boring.

Bingo! She'd found her man.

Shorter than she ideally preferred them, but it couldn't be helped.

The great thing about models was that, in her experience, they were dreadful tarts. Because their job entailed almost non-stop travelling, they permanently had that 'on holiday' approach to sex. While this meant he'd probably be easy to pick up, the downside was that he could only ever be a Milky Way man, mere one-night-stand material.

That was OK, Lisa decided, eyeing the long flank of his thigh and muscular hollow at the side of his bottom. Just sex was fine.

It had been quite a while since she'd propositioned someone. And there was only one way to do it. There was no point pussy-footing around, being coy, hoping he'd be the one to notice you. Oh no – you'd got to march up to the man you wanted and dazzle him with your confidence. It was like being around dogs – you couldn't show your fear.

Taking a deep breath and reminding herself that she was fabulous, she widened her shiny mouth into a blinding smile and launched herself into his path. 'Hello, I'm Lisa Edwards, editor of *Colleen* magazine.'

He shook her hand. 'Wayne Baker, the face of Truffle.' Said with utmost seriousness. Oh dear, irony deficiency! Never mind, she didn't have to *like* the bloke. In fact it was probably better if she didn't. This was about sex and very often liking someone got in the way.

She summoned every reserve of confidence, because the next line had to be delivered with conviction. Never let him think he had any choice in the matter. He couldn't reject her. It simply wasn't an option.

Fixing him with her eyes, she cooed, 'Make mine a large one.'

'What would you like?' He inclined his head at the bar.

'I'm not talking about a drink,' she said, with heavy meaning.

Muscle by muscle, an expression of comprehension settled on his face. 'Oh.' He swallowed. 'I see. Wha –?'

'Dinner. First.'

'OK,' he said obediently. 'Now?'

'Now.'

She allowed herself a little exhalation of relief. He'd fallen for it. She'd thought he might, but you never knew . . .

As they left, she sought out Jack with her eyes. He was looking at her, his expression closed. 'See ya,' she mouthed at him, and he responded with a stiff little nod.

Good.

In the restaurant at the Clarence, Lisa and Wayne had a competition to eat the least. Warily watching each other, they skated food around their plates. For one exciting, breathless moment it looked like Wayne was going to put a piece of monkfish into his mouth, and if he did, Lisa would permit herself a corner of artichoke. But at the last moment he changed his mind and Lisa reluctantly lowered her fork back to her plate also.

Wayne Baker was from Hastings and was young – although probably not as young as he claimed. He said he was twenty, but Lisa reckoned it was more likely to be twenty-two or twenty-three. He took his career as a model very, very seriously.

'It's hardly rocket science, is it, sweetie?' Lisa teased.

He looked hurt. 'As it happens, I don't intend to do it for ever.'

'Let me guess,' Lisa said. 'Eventually you want to take up acting.'

Surprise stamped itself on to his almost risibly perfect face. 'How did you *know*?'

Lisa swallowed a sigh. Though it pained her to peddle clichés, he wasn't the brightest and it blunted the edge of his stunning attractiveness. She had nothing against people with little or no education – after all, she'd barely been able to write her name in the ground with a stick when she'd left school. But there was no reason for a person not to know who Meg Matthews was married to.

'Where do you live, handsome?' Lisa asked. Somehow she made 'handsome' sound derogatory, as if he was a piece of meat. Funny, Wayne thought vaguely. That was usually the way he spoke to girls.

'I've an apartment in London, but I'm almost never there.' He couldn't hide his pride in this.

'And how long are you in Dublin?'

'I leave tomorrow.'

'Where are you staying?'

'Here, at the Clarence.'

'Top.' Lisa didn't want to bring him to Pine Cottage. She was afraid that he'd be put off by all that unstylish pine, but there was an even bigger chance that she'd have gone off him by the end of the taxi journey.

As soon as the waiter took the plates of slightly rearranged food away, Lisa decided she'd deferred gratification for long enough. Wantonly she said to Wayne, 'Time for bed.'

'Blimey.' He started at her brazenness and stood up obediently.

Ascending the lift of the hotel, bubbles of anticipation simmered in Lisa. She felt wicked and decadent – sometimes what a girl really needs is fast and furious sex with a total stranger. And what's the point of having a fabulous, starved body if someone doesn't get to see it occasionally?

Wayne's smooth, brown hand shook slightly as he put the key in the door, and though she was really only acting a part, Lisa was thrilled at her power.

Once in, her fizzy expectation built. It was like being on a film set: the modern, stylish room, the man, young and fit and firm and pumped. There was no denying it – he was beautiful.

'Close the door and take your clothes off,' Lisa said, getting more and more into her dominatrix role.

Wayne anticipated her admiration. 'You're going to love this,' he grinned, slowly unbuttoning his shirt. 'I do two hundred sit-ups a day.'

His stomach was a tight marvel of six taut mounds, veeing outwards and upwards at his ribs into a taut, tanned chest. He was so perfect that Lisa's confidence stumbled. He must be used to sleeping with exquisite, skinny models. Good thing she never ate.

'Now you,' he said.

With a minxy, meaningful smile – attitude was important – she pulled her white dress over her head in one fluid movement. Kelvin had been right – no knickers.

'Snap,' Wayne laughed, unzipping his tight, tailored trousers. His erection sprang forth, already semi-tumescent. No underwear.

A thrill passed through her. She was so ready for this.

He wasn't the first person she'd slept with since

Oliver. Shortly after he'd left she'd brought someone home in an attempt to get him out of her head. But it hadn't been a great success, she'd probably tried too soon. This was far nicer.

'You're beautiful,' Wayne remarked, touching her nipple with a professional interest.

'I know. So are you.'

'I know.'

They gorged on laughter, on each other's beauty, and he kissed her, not unsexily.

'Come on,' he tried to lead her to the bed.

'No. The floor.' She wanted it rough and hard and intense.

'Kinky,' he said.

'Hardly.' She was scornful. 'You've led a sheltered life.'

He wasn't bad. He wasn't great either. That was the problem with very good-looking men. They thought that if they just lay there it was enough to trigger a wave of orgasms. Luckily Lisa was very sure of what she wanted.

She shooed him away when he tried to get on top of her. This was her gig.

'Slower,' she warned, when he looked like getting a little too frisky beneath her. It was a bother having to stage-manage events, but at least he was compliant.

Some time later she shoved her hands under his buttocks and said, 'Faster, faster!'

'I thought you liked it slow.'

'Well, I like it fast now,' she gasped, and Wayne

obediently obliged. In the throes of pleasure, she bit his shoulder.

'Don't,' he yelped. 'I'm on a swimwear shoot in two days' time. I can't have toothmarks.'

'Jesus Christ!' she exclaimed. 'Harder!'

Wayne gathered force and speed, bucking his muscular hips up into hers. 'I think I'm going to . . .' he panted.

'You'd better bloody not,' she snapped. And she was so frightening, his imminent orgasm receded obediently.

Afterwards, they lay on the floor, still panting and breathless. Momentarily sated, Lisa idly surveyed the beechwood chair-legs at her eye level. That had been great, she thought. Just what she'd needed.

They continued to lie on the kingfisher-blue carpet until their breathing returned to normal, then Wayne began to make signs of life. Tenderly he stroked her hair and mused dreamily, 'I've never met anyone like you. You're so . . . strong.'

She responded with a curt, 'Is there a mini-bar? Pour me a drink, I'm going to the loo.'

'Righto.'

Righto!

She could barely squeeze into his bathroom because it was so crammed with skin-care products, shampoo, mousse, setting lotions and cologne. This did not endear him to her. *What a girl.* She curled her lip in contempt. On the washstand there were some beautiful shower-gel and body-lotion freebies and Lisa promised herself that she'd nick them before she left.

When she emerged, he guided her to the bed and put a glass of cold champagne in her hand. Climbing in beside her between the cool, cotton sheets he said, 'Can I ask you something?'

His hushed, serious tone gave her to expect it would be one of those wanky questions that lovers ask each other – Do you believe in love at first sight? What are you thinking? Would you be faithful to me?

'Go on,' she said shortly.

He leant on his elbow, pointed to his forehead and asked, 'Does that look like a spot to you?'

There was nothing on his forehead. It was as smooth as a baby's bottom, as the skin of a peach, as a millpond, whatever . . .

'Ooh, yeah,' she frowned. 'Quite a nasty one, isn't it? Looks infected.'

He actually squawked with distress and pulled out a mirror he'd obviously been inspecting himself in while she'd been in the bathroom.

Lisa guffawed, highly amused. 'What's on the in-house movie?' she asked. She didn't want to talk to him while she waited for him to get it up again.

In between bouts of satisfyingly rough sex they watched films and drank champagne from the mini-bar. Eventually, sated and exhausted, they fell asleep. Lisa slept soundly and woke up in a marvellous mood, insisting on one more shag before she prepared to leave.

But in the bathroom, as she squeaked her tooth-paste-covered finger around her teeth, she came across something she hadn't noticed the night before. Mascara and eyebrow pencil. Yuk. She'd *thought* his eyelashes were suspiciously spiky. And she was prepared to bet that his hair was probably dyed too, from some nondescript brown to its current ebony. Suddenly she went right off him.

Wayne, however, was rather taken with Lisa. She was inventive in bed and she wasn't mad about him.

'Will I see you again?' he asked, as she slipped her white dress on. 'I'm in Dublin regularly.'

'Where did I leave my bag?'

'Over there. Will I see you again?'

'Sure.' Lisa tipped a shower cap, four soaps, two little bottles of shower gel and three of body lotion into her bag.

'When?'

'End of August. My photo will be above the editor's letter in *Colleen*.'

Holding the sheet modestly to his chest, Wayne looked so vulnerable and confused that Lisa relented. 'I'll call you.'

'Will you?' he asked hopefully.

'The cheque is in the post. I'll respect you in the morning,' Lisa grinned, running a comb through her hair and checking her reflection. 'No, of course I won't call you.'

'But . . . but why did you say you would if you didn't mean it?'

'How do I know?' Lisa gleefully rolled her eyes. 'You're a man, you lot invented the rule. Bye!'

Swinging down the steps and out on to the street, her elbows and knees pleasantly raw with carpet-burn, Lisa hailed a taxi. Just enough time to run home and change her clothes before going to work.

She felt great. Glowing! Anyone who said that a one-night stand with a complete stranger left you feeling cheap and shitty was wrong. She hadn't felt so good in ages!

CHAPTER 36

Lisa swung into the office after her night of sex in a dynamic mood.

'Morning Jack,' she said brightly.

'Morning Lisa.'

She gazed into his face. Eyes still opaque, expression no different from usual. No obvious signs that he'd minded her going off with Wayne Baker, but she'd seen his face at the time. He'd looked miffed. She *knew*.

So, to work! Fired up, Lisa went into overdrive and decided that she wanted all the nuts and bolts of the magazine in place *now*. Talking about something called a 'dummy copy'. It was shaping up to be a rough week.

'All regular features – film, video, horoscope, health, columns – to be inputted. Then we'll take a look at what we still need.'

Proof copies of books that were due for September publication were flooding in for review, as were videos and CDs. In theory, free stuff sounded exciting, but it was no use if it wasn't the kind of thing you'd normally like. There was a brief but ugly three-way scuffle over an AfroCelt

CD, but no one was interested in any of the others.

'Gary Barlow, I don't think so,' Trix sniffed, clattering it back on the pile. 'Enya, not in this lifetime.' Another clatter. 'David Bowie, nah.' Clatter. 'And who the hell are "Woebegone"? You know, they look all right, your man's good-looking. I'M TAKING THIS ONE,' she yelled to the rest of the office.

'Does anyone mind if I take this?' Ashling held up a clogs-and-shawl blockbuster.

'Hardly,' Lisa hiccuped with scornful laughter.

But it wasn't for Ashling, it was for Boo, who was so bored that he'd read anything.

The great typeface wars raged all week. Lisa and Gerry were locked in an angry stand-off over the appearance of the books page.

'It's all typeface and no content,' Gerry said heatedly.

'No one reads fucking books,' Lisa screamed at Gerry. 'That's why we've got to make the page look sexy!'

Things kept going wrong. Lisa hated the illustration commissioned for Trix's ordinary-girl column. Allegedly it wasn't 'sexy' enough. Gerry crashed a file and lost an entire morning's work. And a piece Mercedes wrote about a beautician got suddenly binned when they over-plucked Lisa's eyebrows on Wednesday lunch-time.

'But I've worked really hard on it,' Mercedes complained. 'You can't drop it.'

'I'm not dropping it,' Lisa snapped. 'I'm *killing* it. If you're going to work in a magazine, can't you at least learn the jargon?'

The atmosphere was fraught and the work kept coming. No one had less than three projects awaiting attention at any one time.

Ashling was keying in the New-Age horoscopes when Lisa dumped an armful of hair-care stuff on her desk and said, 'A thousand words. Make it –'

'I know, sexy.'

Looking for a theme for her page, Ashling surveyed the products piled on her desk. There was a volumizing mousse, a hairspray that promised to 'lift' the roots, and a 'bodifying' shampoo – all paraphernalia for women wanting big hair. But then there was also anti-frizz masque, smoothing complex, and leave-in conditioner. All for those women who liked their hair flattened against their heads. How could she reconcile the two? How could her piece have any consistency? Back and forth she agonized. Was it possible to have big hair *and* flat hair? Or could she try to pretend that your hair needed to be flat before it could be big, thereby inventing a whole new set of worries for big-haired women? But no, that would be too cruel: having this kind of power brought responsibility. She sighed and broke off another piece of her white-chocolate muffin. Then – perhaps it was the sugar rush – she had a brainwave that, after the deadlock, took on the momentousness of the discovery of the law of gravity. Her piece would start off, 'No matter what you want from your hair . . .'

'Eureka!' she declared, giddy with relief.

'What's that then?' Jack called from the photo-copier.

'I've been so worried!' Ashling waved a hand over the tubes and cans. 'All this stuff, there was no pattern to it. But everything fell into place once I realized that different women want different things for their hair.'

'Different women want different things for their hair,' Jack repeated good-humouredly. 'Profound. That's got to be up there with Einstein's theory of relativity . . . Time is not an absolute,' he scoffed, 'but depends on the shininess of the observer's hair in space. And space is not an absolute, but depends on the shininess of the observer's hair in time. What a worthwhile job we do here!'

Ashling wavered, wondering if she should take offence, but Jack beat her to it.

'Sorry,' he said, suddenly humble. 'Only having a laugh.'

'That's what's so worrying,' Trix threw into Ashling's ear.

'Have you finished typing in Jasper Ffrench's piece yet?' Lisa snapped at Trix.

'Yes.'

Lisa came and looked over Trix's shoulder. 'Aphrodisiac is *not* spelt with an "f", there's only one "y" in oyster and it's aspara*gus*, not aspara-*grass*. Familiarize yourself with your spell-checker.'

'I never had to spell-check anything before.'

'Things are different now. *Colleen* is a class act.'

'I thought we were sexy,' Trix challenged mulishly.

'It's possible to be both. Oi! Mercedes! Where are you on the "fuck-me-slingbacks" piece?'

Not exactly challenging work, but necessary. And exhausting.

Ashling was dog-tired. As well as the long, stressful days, she was carrying a niggling worry at how abruptly things had ended with Marcus on Monday night. Why hadn't she gone to bed with him? It wasn't exactly as if she'd been saving it for her wedding night, she acknowledged ruefully. But she'd always resisted change and it was a long time since she'd slept with someone who wasn't Phelim.

With a sing-song sigh, she accepted that life was hard for the modern woman. In the old days, the rule was that you had to hold off sleeping with a man for as long as possible. But now the rule seemed to be that if you wanted to hold on to him you'd better deliver the goods asap.

Marcus didn't ring on Tuesday night or Wednesday night, and though Joy spoke long and loud about something called the three-day rule, Ashling said, 'But what if he never rings again?'

'Let's face it, he mightn't – men work in mysterious ways. But you certainly won't hear from him this evening. Do something else, use the time constructively – any washing to be done? Paint you need to watch drying? Because tonight's the night.'

Ashling promised herself that if Marcus rang again she'd *definitely* sleep with him.

On her chocolate break at work, while flicking desultorily through the paper, his name suddenly jumped out. Mentioned in the context of how well Irish comedians were doing in the UK. The letters danced dizzily off the page at her – MaRcUs. *He's my boyfriend*. Ashling stared hard at the small black letters, uplifted by a warm powerful surge of pride. Which disappeared a second later. *Or is he?*

Lisa suddenly going into overdrive meant that by Thursday everyone was on a very short fuse. Lisa was quarrelling with Mrs Morley when Jack, looking distraught, catapulted from his office.

'Mrs Morley, would you mind booking somewhere for me for lunch today? Two people.'

'The usual?' Whenever any of the number-crunchers came over from London, Jack reluctantly escorted them for rare steaks and blood-red wine in an oak-panelled, leather-lined club.

'Christ, no! Somewhere nice, somewhere a woman would like.' He seemed charmingly help-less. Bashfully he admitted, 'Apparently it's my six-month anniversary with Mai.'

Lisa couldn't hide her dismay. Why was he being nice to Mai? Why hadn't they had a fight when Mai had called into the office earlier in the week? With chilling dread she realized that a pattern might be developing, and the buoyant confidence that she'd cruised on since sleeping with Wayne evaporated without trace.

'Thank God I remembered the anniversary!' Jack grinned.

'How did you manage to?' Mrs Morley asked.

'Actually, she as good as told me,' Jack said vaguely. 'Hey, what was that place you took me to, Lisa? She'd probably like it there.'

'Halo,' Lisa said, but her voice was so strangled that Jack said, 'Sorry? Say again.'

'Halo,' she repeated, only marginally louder.

'That's right!' Jack was cheerful. 'Full of tossers! Tricksy food at outrageous prices, she'll love it. If you give me the number I'll book it.'

'You will not.' Mrs Morley became more bulldog-like than ever. 'That's my job.'

Physically trembling with anger, Lisa left, praying that it was too short notice to get a table.

Half an hour later Mai arrived, looking like Asian Barbie. When Lisa saw her, her anger slumped into hopeless depression.

'Nice suit,' Trix sucked up to Mai.

'Thank you.'

'Dunnes?'

'Er, yeah.'

Mai had assumed a distance that she hadn't had the day of the champagne drinking. Somehow Jack's recent devotion had changed things. She was gracious, pleasant, but very definitely their boss's girlfriend.

Mrs Morley gave Mai the nod and she swayed

her non-existent hips into Jack's office. The door shut firmly behind her and the entire office ceased operations, their ears stretched off the sides of their heads as they hoped, longed, *yearned* for a row. But seconds later Jack and Mai emerged, smugly holding hands. Watched by a hungry-eyed throng they made their Brady-Bunch way to the exit, and then they were gone. Even after it was clear that nothing was going to happen, silence reigned.

'I liked it better the other way,' Trix observed forlornly, articulating everyone's thoughts.

Lisa, about to leave for her love-bombing lunch with Marcus Valentine, tried to swallow away jealousy, hurt – and confusion. She hadn't imagined Jack's interest in her, she was sure of it. So what was he *at?* She couldn't understand it. One minute it was non-stop shouting matches with Mai, the next it was lovey-dovey heaven. Why? *Why?* The fruitless, unanswerable thoughts circled in her head all the way to Mao.

A mere ten minutes late, Marcus arrived. Tall, good body, but . . . ugh, no! How *could* Ashling? Lisa plastered on a welcoming smile but found it uncharacteristically hard to dredge up her usual excess of charm.

'Lunch, right?' Marcus said almost aggressively as he swung into the seat opposite her. 'What I mean is, let's enjoy our food without you going on at me about doing the column.'

'Yeah.' Lisa managed a speedy upturn of her

lips, but her spirits were suddenly dragging across the ocean floor. This job could be terribly humiliating. You had to be disgustingly pushy and have skin as thick as a rhino's hide.

All at once she didn't care if he didn't do the column. What did it matter? It was only for a stupid women's magazine. Apart from a few perfunctory remarks about liking spicy food, she let the conversation fall into gloomy abeyance.

Ironically, the more subdued she became the more Marcus was forthcoming, and about halfway through her main course she finally twigged. Then she started to milk her reticence for all it was worth.

'So what kind of article did you have in mind for me to do?' Marcus asked.

She shook her head and waved her fork. 'Enjoy your food.'

'OK.' But he came back to the subject moments later. 'How many words were you thinking of?'

'About a thousand, but forget it.'

'And did you find out about syndication?'

'One of our Australian publications would love to run it, as would *Bloke*, our men's magazine in Britain.' Then she went for the kill. 'But Marcus, if you don't want to do a column, then you don't want to do it.' She smiled regretfully at him. 'We'll get someone else. They won't be as good, but . . .'

'Tell me how fantastic I am,' he grinned. 'And I'll do it.'

Without missing a beat, Lisa said, 'You're the funniest person I've seen in the last three years. Your comedy is a unique melding of innocence and awareness. Your bond with your audience is rock-solid and your sense of timing is impeccable. Sign here.' She pulled a contract from her bag and thrust it across the table at him.

'A bit more,' he twinkled.

'Despite your act having echoes of Tony Hancock and . . .' Damn! She couldn't think of anyone else.

'Woody Allen?' he prompted. 'Peter Cook?'

'Woody Allen, Peter Cook *and* Groucho Marx,' – she smiled conspiratorially at him. She bet he knew every single one of his reviews off by heart – 'your style is undeniably cutting-edge and modernist.'

She hoped that was adequate. Because if he asked for one further explanation for his funniness, all she'd be able to come up with would be, 'Your face is goofy.'

On her return she ran over to Ashling's desk and said with vicious glee, 'Guess what? Marcus Valentine has said yes to a monthly column.'

'Really?' Ashling stuttered. He'd seemed so against it on Monday night. Hadn't he . . . ?

'Yeah,' Lisa gloated. 'He did.'

Forty minutes later a seething Ashling finally realized what her response to Lisa should have been. She should have said coolly, 'Marcus doing the column? That must have been because of the great blow-job I gave him last night.'

Why couldn't she ever think of these things at the time? Why did it always have to be ages later?

CHAPTER 37

To Ashling's overjoyed relief, Marcus rang on Thursday and opened the conversation by asking, 'Are you busy on Saturday night?'

She knew she should tease, torment, string him along for ages, play hard to get, make him *sweat*.

'No,' she said.

'Right then, I'm taking you out for dinner.'

Dinner. On a Saturday night – what a meaningful combination. It meant that he wasn't pissed off with her for not sleeping with him. It also meant, of course, that she'd really better sleep with him this time. Anticipation flared. So did a little anxiety, but she'd knock that on the head good and fast.

Cautiously Ashling admitted that this was going well. Marcus was treating her nicely, and even though she'd been riddled with obligatory angst, it wasn't really because of anything *he'd* done. Since she'd first seen Marcus on stage a regeneration had begun to creep across Ashling's internal landscape. After Phelim's scorched-earth policy she'd been off romance, more interested in recovering from than replacing him.

But she'd always intended to get back in the game just as soon as she was fit. And Marcus's phone call had nudged through little buds of hope which told her that perhaps that time had come. She was finally out of hibernation.

The funny thing was, there was a lot to be said for hibernation. Once awake she was suddenly seized with an urgency about her age, the ticking of her biological clock and all the usual thirty-something, single-woman angst. The fuck!-I'm-thirty-one-and-not-married! syndrome.

When Joy asked her what she was doing on Saturday night, Ashling decided to try out her new life for size.

'My boyfriend is taking me out for dinner.'

'Your *boyfriend*? Oh, you mean Marcus Valentine? And he's taking you out for dinner?' Joy sounded jealous. 'All men want to do is get drunk with me. They never feed me.' She paused and Ashling knew she was going to say something gross. She wasn't disappointed. 'The only thing my fella feeds me,' Joy said gloomily, 'is his mickey. You realize that if Marcus is taking you out for dinner on a Saturday night, he means business? . . . *Business*,' she repeated with emphasis. 'No more stunts like the last time, saying you have to get up for work in the morning.'

'I know. And the hairs have already started to grow back on my legs.'

Ashling knew exactly what she was going to wear on Saturday night. Everything, right down to her nice underwear. It was all entirely under control. Then suddenly she took violently against her lipstick. She'd worn the same colour for what felt like years, buying the same again when one ran out. And all because it suited her! What tosh!

Mag-hags got through lipsticks like they got through men – speedily. She needed a new lipstick to redefine her. It was imperative that she track down the right one, and until she did everything felt wrong.

Saturday morning was spent obsessively foraging, but nothing suited. They were either too pink, too orange, too frosted, too shiny, too dark, too pale or too shimmering. Experimenting with being someone else, she tried on a vampy dark-red colour and viewed herself in the mirror. No. She looked as though she'd been on a fourteen-hour spree, drinking red wine which had congealed and solidified on her mouth. Attempting a smile, she looked like Dracula. The sales girl came running. 'That's fabulous on you.'

Ashling managed to escape and the hunt continued. The back of her hand, criss-crossed with red stripes, looked like an open wound. And then, just when hope was fading, she found it. The perfect one. It was love at first sight and Ashling knew with a deep warm conviction that everything was going to be all right now.

Marcus was picking Ashling up at eight-thirty, so at seven o'clock she poured herself a glass of wine and let the preparations commence. It had been a long time since she'd gone for dinner with a man. She and Phelim had had a lazy, comfortable routine of takeaways and only ever went to restaurants when they'd had enough of delivered pizzas and curries. Meals out had been strictly utilitarian exercises in nourishment, not seduction – they'd employed other methods for getting each other into bed. When Phelim was in the mood he used to say, 'Beast with two backs, any takers?' and when Ashling was instigating matters she'd command, 'Ravish me!'

And what would sex with Marcus be like? A terrified, excited fizz lit her nerve-endings and she pawed for her cigarettes. Joy couldn't have picked a better time to arrive.

She complimented Ashling on her clothes, pulled down the waistband on her jeans and admired her choice of thong, then asked, 'Did you remember to put conditioner on your pubic hair?'

Ashling winced and Joy looked wounded. 'These things matter! Well, did you?'

Ashling nodded.

'Good girl. How long is it since you had sex? When Phelim went to Oz?'

'When he came home for his brother's wedding.'

'And you're really going for it with Mr Valentine?'

'Why else would I put conditioner on my pubic hair?' Anticipation rendered Ashling irritable.

'Excellento! So you like him?'

Ashling considered. 'I could really come to like him. We get on well, and he's attractive but not too attractive. People like me never get off with male models or actors or the kind of men that people say, "God, he's really good-looking." You know what I mean?'

'You're freaking me out. What else?'

'We like the same kind of films.'

'And they are?' Joy enquired.

'Ones in English.'

Phelim had showed an irritating tendency to think of himself as an intellectual and often talked about going to foreign and subtitled films. He'd never actually gone, but used to distress Ashling by reading aloud reviews and suggesting that they *might* go.

'Marcus is just kind of ordinary,' Ashling explained. 'He doesn't go bungee jumping or protest against motorways or anything mental. No insane hobbies, I like that in a man.'

'What else?'

'I like . . .' Suddenly Ashling turned on Joy and said savagely, 'If you ever tell this to anyone I'll kill you.'

'I promise,' Joy lied.

'I like that he's sort of famous. That he gets mentioned in the paper and that people know about him. Yes, I know, that makes me shallow, but I'm being honest with you.'

'How are his freckles?'

'Freckly.' A pause followed. 'Look, I've one or two myself,' Ashling said defensively. 'There's no shame in them.'

'I'm only saying . . .'

'There's Ted at the door. Let him in, will you?'

Ted came into the bedroom, obviously excited. 'Look at this,' he yelped, and unfurled a poster.

'It's you!' Ashling declared.

It was a picture of Ted's face on top of an owl's body with the words 'Owl Ted Mullins' across the top of the page.

'Wow, that's fantastic!'

'I'm getting them printed, but what do you think?' He unfurled another poster and let one hang from between each thumb and index finger. 'Red background or blue background?'

'Red,' Joy said.

'Blue,' Ashling said.

'I don't know,' Ted mused. 'Clodagh says –'

'What Clodagh?' Ashling barked an interruption. 'Who Clodagh? *My* friend Clodagh?'

'Yes, I called around to her . . .'

'What for?'

'To collect my jacket,' Ted said defensively. 'What's the biggie? I left my jacket when we were babysitting, it's hardly a crime.'

Ashling couldn't explain her resentment. She had no option but to mutter, 'Right. Sorry.'

A tense silence reigned. 'Pass me my new lipstick please,' Ashling said shortly.

She tipped it from its box and twisted up the waxy finger, shiny and new. Gorgeous. But as she admired it, she was afflicted with a sudden, very unwelcome awareness.

'I don't believe it,' she breathed. Quickly she inspected the base of the lipstick, launched a searching scramble in her make-up bag, unearthed another lipstick and checked the base of that also. 'I don't fucking believe it,' she exclaimed, in despair.

'What?!'

'I've bought the same lipstick. I spent all morning looking for a new lipstick and I'm after buying exactly the same one I had already.'

With a passionate rush of *I'm such a failure*, Ashling was all set to hurl herself on the bed, except the bell rang. The alarm clock on her dressing table said half past eight. Which meant it was twenty past.

'That better bloody not be Marcus Valentine at the door,' she threatened.

It was.

'What kind of man arrives early?' Joy asked.

'A gentleman,' Ashling said, not at all convinced.

'A weirdo,' Joy said, not quite under-her-breath enough.

'Out, the pair of you.'

'Make sure you use a condom,' Joy hissed, then they were gone. Seconds later Marcus appeared up the stairs, all smiles.

'Hi,' Ashling said. 'I'm nearly ready. Would you like a beer or something?'

'A cup of tea. I'll make it, don't worry about me.'

While she hurriedly finished preparing she heard him opening cupboards and drawers in the kitchen.

'Cute apartment,' Marcus called in to her.

Ashling wished he'd be quiet. Providing witty repartee while applying lipstick was not one of her strengths.

'Small but perfectly formed,' she called back absently.

'Like its owner.'

Which was nothing near the truth, Ashling thought, but it was nice of him to say so.

And that kind of set the tone. She cheered up, put the lipstick shame behind her, brushed her hair and went forth to meet his admiration.

Before they left Marcus insisted on washing his teacup.

'Leave it,' Ashling said, as he dashed it under the running water.

'Ah no.' He placed it on the draining-board and turned to her with a grin. 'My Mammy taught me well.'

She got that feeling again. More buds poking their heads up.

The place he took her to was intimate and rosy-lit. At a corner table, with their knees occasionally touching, they drank cold white wine so dry it sucked at their teeth, and admired each other, dewy-skinned and flawless in the candlelight.

'Hey, I like your . . .' And he gestured at Ashling's shell top. 'I never know the right word for women's clothes. T-shirt? I've a feeling I could cause grave offence by calling that a T-shirt. But what do I call

429

it? A top? A blouse? A shirt? A vest? Whatever it is I like it.'

'It's called a shell top.'

'So what's a blouse then?'

Ashling took him through the various options. 'You must never, ever say "blouse" to any woman under sixty,' she said gravely. 'You can compliment a woman on her vest if you mean a sleeveless T-shirt. Not if it really *is* a vest. In fact if it really is a vest, I'd advise you to leave immediately.'

Marcus nodded. 'I see. God, it's a minefield.'

'Hold on.' It had just occurred to her. 'Are you pumping me for info for your act?'

'Would I do that?' he smiled.

The food was unobtrusive, the talk was easy, but Ashling had the feeling that it was all a type of prelude. A trailer. With the main feature to come later.

When the bill arrived she made a half-hearted attempt to contribute.

'No,' Marcus insisted, 'I'm having none of it.'

Because you expect to be having plenty of it later?

Out on the street he asked, 'What now?'

Ashling shrugged, then couldn't help giggling. Surely it was obvious?

'My place?' he suggested softly.

He kissed Ashling in the taxi. And again in the hall of his flat. It felt very nice, but when they broke apart, she couldn't help looking around, checking the place out. She fancied him, but she was also keen to see how he lived, to find out about him.

It was a one-bedroomed apartment in a modern block and the grunge factor was surprisingly low.

'But it doesn't smell funny!'

'I told you, my Mammy trained me well.'

She turned into his living-room. 'Look at all your videos,' she gasped. There seemed to be hundreds lining the walls.

'We could watch something if you like,' he said.

She did like. Torn between attraction to him and childish nerves, she welcomed a delay.

'Pick one,' he invited.

But when she began scanning the shelves, she slowly realized something odd. Monty Python, Blackadder, Lenny Bruce, Laurel and Hardy, Father Ted, Mr Bean, The Marx Brothers, Eddie Murphy – they were *all* comedy videos.

She was confused. On their first date they'd had a lively discussion on their favourite films. He'd claimed to like a wide variety of stuff, but you'd never know it from looking at his shelves. Eventually she plumped for *The Life of Brian*.

'An excellent choice, if I may say so, madam!' He produced a bottle of white wine for her, a can of beer for himself, and they tentatively snuggled together in front of the telly.

Ten minutes into the film Marcus touched her bare shoulder with his index finger and began to stroke it slowly. 'Asssh-liiing,' he crooned with an intensity which flipped her stomach. Almost

431

afraid, she looked at him quickly. He was staring at the screen. 'Now watch carefully,' he urged, in the same low tone. 'One of the greatest comedy moments of all time is coming up.'

Mildly disappointed but ever obedient she paid attention and when Marcus dissolved into convulsions she couldn't help laughing herself. Then he swivelled round to her and asked, like a cute little boy, 'Would you mind, Ashling?'

'What!?' *Sleeping with me?*

'If we watched that again.'

'Oh! Not at all.'

When her heart rate had slowed down to normal she decided she was touched that he wanted to share what was important to him.

'So were they pleased about me saying I'd do the column?' he asked, some time later.

'Oh, delighted!'

'That Lisa, she's some piece of work, eh?'

'Very persuasive.' Ashling wasn't sure how smart it would be to start slagging off Lisa.

'You should get the credit for it, though.'

'But I didn't do anything.'

Marcus looked at her with meaning. 'You could tell them you persuaded me when we were in bed together.'

The naked intent in his look made her throat seize up. Then she swallowed as if eating an oyster. 'But that wouldn't be true.'

A long pause, where his eyes never wavered from hers. 'We could make it true.'

432

Her high spirits had worn off. Disappeared, in fact. It felt too soon to go to bed with him, but to resist would seem old-fashioned. She simply could not understand the ridiculous timidity which paralysed her – she was thirty-one years old, she'd had sex with lots of men.

'Come on.' He stood up and tugged gently at her hand. Something was telling her that he wouldn't take no for an answer.

'But the film . . .'

'I've seen it before.'

No kidding.

Shyness wrestled with curiosity, attraction fought with fear of intimacy. She wanted to sleep with him and yet she didn't, but his urgent need was compelling. She found herself on her feet. A kiss went some way to persuading her, and she was in his bedroom. It wasn't a fluid dance where fumbling disappeared and clothes dissolved without clumsiness. He hadn't been able to get the hang of unhooking her bra, and when she saw how large his erection seemed in the narrowness of his hips, she had to look away. She trembled like a terrified virgin.

'What's wrong?'

'I'm shy.'

'So it's not because of me?'

'Oh no.' His vulnerability made her try harder. She gathered him to her, which had the double effect of pleasing him and ensuring she no longer had to see his hardness springing from its nest of hair.

433

The sheets were fresh, the candles a surprising touch, he was thoughtful and attentive and never once remarked on her absence of waist, but she had to admit that no, she wasn't entirely transported. However, he was very appreciative, and she enjoyed that. It certainly wasn't the worst sexual experience she'd ever had. And the best sex had always been slightly unreal, usually taking place during making up with Phelim, when the joy of being reunited added an extra piquancy to an already compatible experience.

She was a big girl now and expecting the earth to move was unrealistic. Anyway, the first time she'd had sex with Phelim it hadn't set the world on fire either.

CHAPTER 38

On Sunday morning Clodagh woke, perched precariously on the six inches at the edge of the bed. Craig had shunted her to the margin of the bed, but it could quite easily have been Molly or both of them. She couldn't remember the last time she and Dylan had slept unchaperoned, and she was so well practised at sleeping hanging over the side that she was sure she could manage a great night's sleep on the edge of a cliff, at this stage.

Something was telling her it was very early. Five o'clock early. The sun was up and the gap where the calico curtains didn't quite meet glowed in a line of acid-bright light, but she knew it was too soon to be awake. The unseen seagulls beyond her window wailed shrill and plaintive. They sounded like babies from a horror film. Beside Craig, Dylan slept heavily, his limbs thrown across the bed in a random tangle, his breath whistling rhythmically in and out, each exhalation lifting his hair from his forehead.

Despondency lay heavy upon her. She'd had a bad week. After the disaster with the employment agency, Ashling had urged her to get a second opinion. So she'd put her expensive suit back on and tried again. The second employment agency treated her with almost as much disdain as the first had. But to her enormous surprise, the third proposed sending her for a two-day trial, making tea and answering the phone at a radiator-supply firm. 'The pay is . . . modest,' the recruitment man had admitted, 'but for someone like you who's been out of the workplace for a long time, it's a good start. They're bound to love you, so off you go. Good luck!'

'Oh. Thanks.' As soon as Clodagh knew she might have a job, she didn't want it. Making tea and answering the phone, where was the fun in that? She did it at home all the time. And a radiator-supply firm? It sounded so dreary. In a strange way, getting a job and then finding she didn't want it was almost worse than being told she was unemployable. Though not much given to introspection, she vaguely realized that she wasn't actually looking for a job – she certainly didn't need the money – she was looking for glamour and excitement. And the reality was she wasn't going to find them at a radiator-supply firm.

So she rang Mr Recruitment and pretended she couldn't start because Craig had got measles. Children had their uses, she reflected. If there was something you didn't want to do, you could say they had a high temperature and that you were worried about meningitis. It had absolved her from attending Dylan's Christmas party last year.

And the year before. And she fully intended to use it this year as well.

She shifted uncomfortably. Something sharp was digging into her back. A forage revealed it to be Buzz Lightyear. Outside the window the seagulls shrieked again, their ugly forlorn cries echoing within her. She felt trapped, painted into a corner, blocked. As though she was locked in a small dark airless box, which was getting ever tighter – she couldn't understand it. She'd always been happy with her lot. Her life had happened exactly as it should and its progress had been ever forward, ever positive. Then, with no warning, it seemed to have stopped. Going nowhere with nothing to look forward to. A horrible thought wormed in – was it going to be like this for ever?

Suddenly she noticed that Dylan's whistling had reached crescendo level. Seized by a frenzy of intolerance she exploded, 'Stop *breathing*!' With a rough shove to his head she changed the angle of his windpipe.

'Sorry,' he mumbled, without waking up. She envied his uncomplicated slumber. Flattened against the mattress, she half-listened to the seagulls until Molly clambered into bed beside her and hit her in the face. Time to get up.

An emergency appendectomy, she thought longingly. *Or a mild stroke*. Nothing too serious. But one that involved a long stay in a hospital that had very restricted visiting hours.

After her shower she dried herself and spoke

briskly to Dylan, who was sitting, yawning, on the edge of the bed. 'Don't give Craig any Frosties, he's asked for them all week, but then he won't touch them. There's a new playgroup opening at the bottom of the road, we're all invited to see it today. I don't know whether or not to disturb Molly with a move, but she's so unpopular with the old boot at her current one that maybe it might be a good idea –'

'We used to talk about more than the kids.' Dylan sounded weird.

'Like what?' Clodagh asked defensively.

'Don't know. Nothing . . . anything. Music, films, people . . .'

'Well, what do you expect?' she said angrily. 'The kids are the only people I see, I can't help it. But while we're on the subject of outside interests, I was thinking we might do some decorating.'

'Decorate what?' he asked tightly.

'Here, our bedroom.' She slapped on some body cream and speedily rubbed it in.

'It's only a year since we did this room.'

'It's at least eighteen months.'

'But . . .'

Clodagh began to pull on her underwear.

'You missed a bit.' Dylan reached over to rub in the blob of cream at the back of her thigh.

'Get off!' she snapped, shoving his arm away. The touch of his hand on her skin enraged her.

'Would you calm down!' Dylan shouted. 'What is *wrong* with you?'

438

Too late, her response frightened her. She shouldn't have done that. Dylan's expression scared her even more – anger twisted and troubled with pain.

'Sorry, I'm just tired,' she managed. 'Sorry. Can you make a start on dressing Molly?'

Trying to dress Molly when she didn't want to be dressed was like trying to put a reluctant octopus into a string bag.

'No!' she screamed, wriggling and writhing.

'Clodagh, give us a hand,' Dylan called, trying to catch a flailing arm and shove it in a sleeve.

'Mummy, nooooooo!'

While Clodagh held Molly still, Dylan crooned in a patient, sing-song voice. Ameliorative nonsense about how Molly was going to look lovely when her shorts and T-shirt were on and how pretty the colours were.

When the final shoe was wedged on to Molly's kicking foot, Dylan smiled in triumph at Clodagh.

'Mission accomplished,' she grinned. 'Thank you.'

When Dylan had said that all they talked about was the kids, it had panicked her. But if she was honest she'd admit it was partly true. They soldiered together, side by side, childcare workers – almost colleagues. And what was so wrong with that, she thought, seeking justification. They had two children, what else were they meant to do?

★　★　★

There was a good turnout at the new playgroup. As Clodagh walked through – and winced slightly at – the day-glo-painted jack-in-the-box doors, the first person she met was Deirdre Bullock, who had a black belt in Mothering. Her daughter, Solas Bullock, was the world's most talented child.

'You'll never believe it!' Deirdre exclaimed. 'Solas is speaking in complete sentences now.' She left a grisly little pause before enquiring, 'Is Molly?' Solas was three months younger than Molly.

'No.' Then Clodagh added airly, 'Molly prefers to communicate with us in writing.'

She'd probably be drummed out of the coffee-morning circuit, but it was worth it to see the horrified look on Deirdre's face.

On Monday, Clodagh came up with a great idea to lift her out of her gloom. She'd go out tonight with Ashling. They'd go on the piss like the old days, maybe even go to a club, and she'd get a chance to wear some of her lovely new clothes. Maybe the palazzo pants and tunic – but what shoes did you wear with them, she wondered. She suspected chunky platforms might be expected of her, but could she go through with it without feeling like a complete dick? Hard to know, it was so long since she'd worn fashionable clothes.

All excited, she rang Ashling at work.

'Ashling Kennedy speaking.'

'It's Clodagh. Oh –' She'd just remembered

something. 'That Ted called round on Friday to collect his jacket.'

'So he said.'

'He's nice, isn't he? I always thought he was a bit of a fool, but he's actually not so bad once you get to know him, is he?'

'Um.'

'He was telling me about being a stand-up comedian. He showed me his posters.'

'Oh.'

'I'd love to go and see him. He said he'd let me know the next time he's on, but will you keep me posted?'

'Ah, right.'

'Now, why don't we go out for a few drinks tonight? Get plastered, maybe even go for a dance. Dylan can babysit.'

'I can't,' Ashling apologized. 'I'm going out with Marcus. My new boyfriend,' she explained.

'Your what?'

'Boyfriend.' The pride in Ashling's voice was startling. 'We've only seen each other a couple of times, but we spent all day yesterday in bed, and he wants to see me tonight.'

A gap in time opened, hurtling a whoosh of nostalgia at Clodagh. The first buzzy flush of love was right with her, surprising her with its crazy clarity. Then, as suddenly as it had come, it receded, leaving inexplicable yearning in its wash.

'Can't you cancel him?' she attempted.

'No,' Ashling said awkwardly. 'I said I'd help

him with his act. He's a stand-up comedian, you see –'

'Another one!'

'And he needs me so he can try out some new stuff.'

'How about tomorrow night then?'

'I've got salsa.'

'Wednesday night?'

'I've to attend the opening of a new restaurant.'

'Lucky you.' The contrast between Clodagh attending the opening of a new playgroup and Ashling attending the opening of a new restaurant wasn't lost on her.

'How's Dylan?'

Clodagh clicked her tongue scornfully. 'Working day and night. He's going to be away on Thursday night. Again! Going to another bloody conference. Will you come over? We could have wine and something to eat?'

'Sure. A girls' night in.'

'That's the only kind of night I ever seem to have. But you'll let me know about Ted?'

CHAPTER 39

A week passed. Then another, and another. The pace of work remained frantic. Even though everyone was working rabidly on the September issue, Lisa had already begun work on the flat-plan for the October, November, even the December issues.

'But it's only June now,' Trix complained.

'Actually, it's the third of July and in the real world magazines have a lead time of six months,' Lisa said loftily.

Obstacles abounded. Although they'd made literally hundreds of phone calls to dozens of agents, Lisa hadn't been able to bag one celebrity for her celebrity letter. It was maddeningly frustrating and she was bitterly aware that that wouldn't be the case if she was still working for *Femme.* Then a hotel in Galway got wind that they were being included in the sexy-bedroom piece and threatened to sue.

Morale soared briefly when freelancer Carina secured an indepth interview with Conal Devlin, a beautiful Irish actor who was all cheekbones and stubble. Then morale plummeted when he cropped up in the July issue of *Irish Tatler*, telling their interviewer all about his childhood abuse – which he was supposed to have given Carina an exclusive on.

'We've been scooped!' Lisa was raging. 'That bastard! No one treats my magazine like second best!' Not only did the piece have to be killed, but it had the knock-on effect of the film page having to be rewritten. They'd given his new movie a glowing recommendation. 'Slate it,' Lisa now ordered. 'Tell everyone it's pants. You, Ashling, you do it.'

'But I didn't even see the film!'

'So?'

Any achievements were hard won. The one thing – probably the only thing, in fact – that everyone agreed on was that Lisa was a total nightmare to work for. She was very definite about what she wanted. Then three hours later, when a piece was half written, she was just as definite that she didn't want it. Until a day later when she was adamant that she wanted it again. Pieces got slaved over, binned and cried over, reinstated, killed once more, then cut in half and stuck back in. Ashling's lovely no-matter-what-you-want-from-your-hair article had been dropped, cropped, rewritten and reinstated so many times that she actually wept when Lisa reprieved it one more time. 'Will you rewrite it?' Ashling hiccuped at Mercedes. 'If I have to look at it ever again I'll set myself on fire.'

'Sure. If you'll ring that maniac Frieda Kiely about Saturday's shoot.'

Lisa had gone ahead with her threat to reshoot most of the Frieda Kiely fashion piece.

'Ashling, Trix and Mercedes, cancel Friday night, we'll all be working on Saturday,' Lisa announced. 'We need bodies to carry the clothes, fetch coffees, that kind of thing.'

There was a shocked clamour of complaint but it didn't do anyone any good.

'She's a slave-driving bitch,' Ashling wailed that night over dinner in Mao with Marcus. 'The biggest bully I've ever met in my whole life.'

'Don't hold back,' Marcus urged, pouring her a glass of wine. 'Go on, have a good old rant.'

'Ah no.' Ashling ran a stressed hand through psychiatric-looking hair. 'It's just that she's such a pushy bitch, she doesn't seem to care that any one of us has a life outside her precious bloody magazine. And when are we supposed to sleep? Or eat? Or wash our clothes? . . .'

By the time Ashling finally stopped she'd drunk most of the bottle of wine and was in much better form. 'Just listen to me, I sound like a nutter!' she exclaimed, her face rosy. 'Oh don't! I've had enough.' She tried to stop Marcus pouring the last of the wine into her glass.

'Go on,' he insisted. 'Get that inside you, you need to keep your strength up.'

'Thanks. *God*, I feel better,' she groaned, slumping

in relief against the banquette. 'Psychotic episode over, I'll act normal now.'

Lingering over coffee, they speculated about the other customers. It was a game they usually played, attributing stories, indeed entire lives, to the people around them.

'How about him?' Marcus indicated a weather-beaten older man, wearing sandals over socks, who had just walked in.

Ashling considered thoughtfully, 'A priest home on holidays from the missions,' she finally concluded.

Marcus was greatly tickled. 'Hmmm, funny girl, arncha?' Admiration softened his voice, then he nodded across the restaurant at two young men drinking hot chocolate and eating cheesecake. 'And what about that pair?'

Ashling wrestled with her opinion. Perhaps she shouldn't voice it, but the wine got the upper hand and eventually she said, 'OK, it's probably not politically correct to say so, but I reckon they're gay.'

'Why?'

'Because . . . well, lots of reasons. Straight men don't eat together, they have pints together. And they don't sit opposite each other, they sit side by side and refuse to make eye-contact. And the eating-cake thing – macho men are too afraid that it looks sissy. Gay men are much less hung-up.'

Then Marcus narrowed his eyes thoughtfully. 'But look Ashling, they're wearing leathers and they've got helmets beside them on the floor. What if I was to say to you, "Dutch or German bikers touring Ireland"?'

'Of course!' Instantly it was all clear to Ashling. 'They're *foreign*. Foreign men can eat cake without anyone thinking they're gay.' A few years back she'd had a one-weekend stand with a visiting Swiss boy who had publicly eaten a raspberry meringue with charming unselfconsciousness.

'It's kind of sad for Irish men,' Marcus remarked.

'Sure is.' And they both laughed, the heat in her solar plexus matched by the warmth in his eyes.

At this precise moment, life isn't so bad, Ashling acknowledged.

At eight-thirty on Saturday morning Ashling turned up at the studio, dragging two huge suit-cases of clothes that she'd collected from the Frieda Kiely press office the night before. She'd never been on a proper fashion shoot before so, despite her resentment, she couldn't help being excited and curious.

Niall the photographer and his assistant had already arrived. So had the make-up girl. Even Dani, the model, was there. Which twisted Lisa's face into a look of scorn – real models were always at least half a day late.

'Who's styling this?' Niall asked.

'Me,' Lisa said.

Mercedes looked like she wanted to kill her. *She* was the fashion editor, *she* should be styling it.

Lisa, Niall and the make-up girl went into a huddle around Dani while Lisa outlined her ideas. Though Niall declared they were 'genius', Ashling and Trix exchanged nonplussed glances when Dani was finally ready. She was dressed in one of Frieda's mad floaty creations, made up with streaks of mud on her face and straw in her long black hair, then positioned on a chrome and white-leather couch. A half-eaten pizza lay beside her and a chrome remote control was placed in her hands. Apparently she was supposed to be watching telly. There was much talk of 'irony' and 'contrast'.

'It looks fucking stupid,' Trix whispered to Ashling.

'Yeh, I don't get it at all.'

The setting up took for ever – the equipment, the lighting, the angle at which Dani was slumped on the couch, the way the folds of the dress fell.

'Dani, love, the remote control's blocking the detailing on the bodice. Hold it lower. No, lower. No, a little bit higher . . .'

Finally, *finally*, they were ready.

'Look bored,' Niall urged Dani.

'I *am*.'

So were Ashling and Trix. They had simply had no idea how tedious this was going to be.

After checking something called 'the level' several more times, finally Niall pronounced the scene satisfactory. But just as he was about to start, Mercedes darted forward and tweaked Dani's skirt.

'It was a bit bunched,' she lied. Mercedes so resented Lisa hijacking the shoot that she kept manufacturing work for herself to pretend that she mattered.

It took another fifteen minutes before Niall was ready again, and just at the point when they thought he was going to depress the button on his camera and *actually take a picture*, he paused and came out from behind his tripod to remove an invisible strand of hair from Dani's face. Ashling bit back a scream. Would he ever, *ever* take the effing photo?

'I'm slowly losing the will to live,' Trix said between clenched teeth.

Eventually Niall took a shot. Then he changed lenses and took some more. Then he changed to a black and white film. Then he changed camera. Then the entire production upped sticks and went to a supermarket for more shots. Where people wheeling their trolleyful of groceries went into convulsions at the sight of the rail-thin, muddy-faced model being photographed bending over the frozen chickens. Ashling was acutely embarrassed – and worried. 'These pictures are going to look ridiculous, we'll never be able to use them.'

It was four o'clock by the time Lisa and Niall decided they were happy with the supermarket pictures.

'We got some good shots,' Niall admitted. 'Great juxtaposing, great irony.'

'Please can we go home now?' Trix said in a low,

desperate mutter. Ashling agreed. Her arms ached from holding Frieda Kiely's godawful frocks, she was tired of answering Dani's mobile phone which rang incessantly, and she was sick of being treated like a skivvy. Run and get batteries for Niall's flash, go and get coffees for everyone, find the suitcase that had the straw in it.

'The street scene,' Lisa reminded Niall.

'I don't think we're going home just yet,' Ashling hissed angrily.

Miserably, everyone trooped to South William Street, where, on the pavement outside an Indian restaurant, Niall set up his equipment for what felt like the millionth time that day.

'How about we have Dani rooting through a litter bin, like a homeless person?' Lisa suggested.

Niall loved the idea.

'No!' Dani was close to tears. 'No fucking way.'

'But it's urban,' Lisa insisted. 'We need strong urban images to balance these clothes.'

'I don't care, I'm not doing it. Sack me if you want.'

Lisa looked sternly at her. Tension thickened the air. If Boo hadn't chosen that moment to pass by with Hairy Dave, Ashling dreaded to think what the outcome would have been.

'Hi, Ashling,' Boo called cheerfully.

'Um, hello.' She was slightly mortified. Boo, with his dirty blanket around his shoulders and Hairy Dave by his side, was very obviously homeless.

'I finished *The Blacksmith's Woman*,' Boo told

450

Ashling. 'Unputdownable, but the end was a right cop-out, I'd never really believed that fella was her half-brother.'

'Great!' Ashling said tightly, hoping that the boys would disappear on their way. When, to her great surprise, she saw that Lisa was studying Boo with hard interest.

'Lisa Edwards.' With a wide smile she stuck out her hand and – fair play to her – barely shuddered when Boo, then Hairy Dave, grasped it. Lisa swept her gaze along the horseshoe of waiting people. 'OK,' she said with a reptilian smile. 'Forget the rubbish bin, I've a better idea.'

She turned to Boo and Hairy Dave. 'How would you two boys like to be photoed with this beautiful woman?' She shunted the sullen Dani forward.

Ashling was rocked by shock. This wasn't right, it felt like . . . like some form of exploitation. She opened her mouth to object, but Boo seemed charmed beyond belief. 'This is a fashion shoot? And you want us in it? Deadly!'

'But . . .' Dani attempted.

'It's this or the litter bin,' Lisa said, steel in her voice.

Dani paused for an angry second, then positioned herself between Boo and Hairy Dave.

'Genius!' Niall declared. 'Love it! No need to smile, er, Dave, just be yourself. And, you, um, Boo, could you give your, eh, blanket to Dani. Terrific! Dani, darlin', could you drape it across your shoulders. Pretend it's a pashmina, love, if that

451

makes it easier. We need a styrofoam cup! Trix, run to McDonald's and get some cups . . .'

Ashling turned to Mercedes and asked, in astonishment, 'Surely these pictures will be unusable?'

'No,' Mercedes admitted, her dark eyes miserable. 'They're inspired. They'll probably win a fucking award!'

It was eight o'clock before they finished. Ashling raced home to get ready and as she bolted in the door, the phone was ringing – Clodagh, who had spent the day having her hair cut and coloured into such a radical restyle that Dylan wasn't talking to her. Then she'd bought a pair of white, skin-tight cut-offs in a slender size ten – which she hadn't been since before she'd got pregnant with Craig. The shoe situation was finally under control (kitten-heeled mules) and she was desperate to go out.

But before she managed to relay any of that Ashling whispered, 'I've never been so tired in my life. I've been on a fashion shoot all day.'

Clodagh paused, her exuberance dying on her lips, then she stirred with black rancour. Ashling was a lucky bitch. A lucky glamorous bitch. She was doing it on purpose, just to rub in how boring Clodagh's life was.

'I can't really talk,' Ashling apologized. 'I've got to get ready, I'm due at Marcus's five minutes ago.'

Clodagh was crushed. She'd have to sit in with

her new hair and her new clothes and her new shoes and watch telly. So foolish did she feel that it was several seconds before she managed to say, 'How's it all going with him?'

Ashling was unaware of Clodagh's bitter disappointment. Her mind was on Marcus as she wondered if she should tempt fate. 'Great,' she answered. 'Fantastic, in fact.'

'It sounds serious,' Clodagh needled.

Again Ashling hesitated. 'Maybe.' Then added because she felt she should, 'But it's early days.'

It didn't *feel* like early days, though. They saw each other at least three times a week and shared an easiness and intimacy that seemed to belong to a much longer relationship. And the sex had greatly improved . . . She barely gave her tarot cards a glance these days, and her little Buddha was sorely neglected.

'Oh, Ted rang. He's on next Saturday,' Clodagh said.

Ashling paused, and tried to push down the eruption of dirty emotion. She did *not* want to encourage Clodagh to get too friendly with Ted.

'So he is.' She tried to sound casual. 'He's supporting Marcus.'

'Call me during the week and we'll fix on times and all that.'

'Will do. Must go.'

As soon as she got to Marcus's she knew something had happened. Instead of kissing her as he usually did, he was sullen and moody.

'What's wrong?' she asked. 'Sorry I'm late, I was working . . .'

'Look at this.' He tossed her the newspaper.

Anxiously she read. It transpired that Bicycle Billy had got a publishing deal. Described as 'One of Ireland's top comedians,' he'd been given a two-book contract and a 'six-figure advance'. A spokesperson for the publishing house described the novel as 'Very dark, very grim, quite different to his stand-up.'

'But you haven't written a book,' Ashling said, keen to soothe.

'They describe him as one of Ireland's top comedians.'

'But you're much better than him. You are,' she insisted. 'Everyone knows it.'

'So how come it's not in the paper?'

'Because you haven't written a book.'

'Go on,' he said coldly. 'Rub it in.'

'But . . .' She was at a loss. She'd seen previous glimpses of insecurity, but nothing on this scale. She couldn't understand it, but was desperate to fix it. 'You're the best,' she repeated earnestly. 'You must know that. Why else did Lisa want you to do the column? She didn't even mention anyone else. Look at how people love you.'

He shrugged moodily, and Ashling knew she was getting through to him.

'I've never seen such devotion at anyone else's comedy gigs,' she laboured on.

'Was Lisa really worried that I wouldn't do the column?' he asked sulkily.

'Out of her mind!'

He said nothing.

'She said you're about to go stellar.'

He took her hand and kissed her for the first time since she'd arrived. 'Sorry. It's not your fault. But comedy is a cut-throat business, you're only as good as your last gig. Sometimes I get spooked.'

After the shoot Lisa was on a high. Her instinct – always reliable – was telling her that these pictures were rather special and likely to cause a stir.

She'd managed to keep phenomenally busy over the past month, and those bizarre bouts of depression that had dogged her early weeks in Dublin seemed to have abated. Any time the blackness began its insidious crawl, she thought up a new article for the magazine or someone else for them to interview or another product to plug. She didn't have *time* to be depressed, and she'd experienced small pockets of satisfaction with how the magazine was coming together. They weren't there yet in terms of advertising revenue, but she suspected that today's pictures would round up the last few cosmetic houses that were still holding out. Jack would be pleased.

Instantly, her clear, clean spirits clouded. Jack and Mai continued to behave like the perfect couple. They hadn't had a public row in a month, and overnight, the sparks of sexual tension between Jack and Lisa had entirely vanished. At least they had on Jack's part. Not that there had been *much* sexual tension, Lisa admitted, ever the realist. But there had been enough to give her hope. When she'd tried to reclaim lost ground with a spot of mild flirting, it provoked no response from Jack. He remained polite and professional and Lisa realized she had to let this thing with Mai run its course. And hopefully it *would* run its course – into the sand.

In the meantime she was on the lookout for a half-decent man. Tonight she was having drinks with Nick Searight, an artist famous more for his good looks than for the artistic merit of his canvasses. Lisa suspected he was more of a Milky Way man than a real one, but sex is sex is sex, and right now, it would have to do.

When Lisa reached home, Kathy was just letting herself out. Her hair was so frizzy it looked like it had been deep-fried.

'Howya Lisa, all done, ironing and everything. Er, and thanks for the nail varnish.' Kathy's life didn't have much call for yellow-glitter nail varnish, but Francine was bound to like it. 'D'you want me to come next week as usual?'

'Yes, please.'

It'd be filthy again by next Saturday, Kathy acknowledged as she walked home. Apple cores rotting under the bed, the bathroom splattered with all kind of gloop, the sink higgledy-piggledy with a week's worth of dishes. Unbelievable really. For such a well-turned-out girl, Lisa kept a very dirty house.

★   ★   ★

In a house in a bleak, sea-facing corner of Ringsend, over the tin-foil cartons and remains of their Indian takeaway, Mai turned to Jack and finally said the unsayable.

'You don't care enough to fight with me any more.'

Jack fixed his still, sombre eyes on her, and waited a long time before delivering the undeniable truth. 'But people who care about each other shouldn't be constantly at each other's throats.'

'Bollocks,' Mai said, spiritedly. 'If you don't fight, you don't get to make up. All the door-slamming and shouting keeps the passion alive for us.'

Jack chose his next words very carefully. With unbearable gentleness, he suggested, 'Or maybe it just disguises that there isn't much there in the first place.'

Mai's eyes filled with angry tears. 'Fuck you, Jack . . . Fuck you.' But her heart wasn't in it.

He wrapped his arms around her and she sobbed a little against his chest, but found she couldn't really get too worked up.

'You bastard,' she accused, breathlessly.

'Yes,' he agreed, sadly.

'Is it over?' she finally asked.

He drew back to look at her. He nodded slightly. 'You know it is.'

She sobbed a little more. 'I suppose,' she admitted. 'I've never had so many bust-ups with anyone.' She made this sound like a good thing.

'We've had more come-backs than Frank

Sinatra,' he agreed, even though he'd never enjoyed the rows.

They laughed shakily, their heads close together.

'You're a superb woman, Mai,' he said, with tender, dark-eyed regard.

'You're not so bad yourself,' she sniffed. 'You'll make some nice girl very miserable. That Lisa, maybe.'

'Lisa?'

'The hard, shiny one? God,' Mai lapsed into inappropriate giggles, 'that makes her sound like an M&M. She should be well able for you. Or if not Lisa, the other one.'

'What other one?'

'The Latina babe.'

'Oh, Mercedes. Apart from anything else, she's married.'

'Huh.' Mai hid her upset behind gruffness. 'You're so contrary you'll probably pick her. Drive me home, will you?'

'Ah, stay a while.'

'No, I've wasted enough time on you.' She flashed him a watery consolation of a grin.

Without words, they drove through the night-time streets, Mai reducing her loss until it became something manageable. Jack was a special man: big and hard and clever and challenging. Initially she'd loved the game-playing. But she'd fallen badly for him and suspected that Jack would have run a mile if he'd known.

The only way she'd felt in control was by keeping

him in a state of perpetual insecurity. She'd never felt at ease except in the short period after he'd apologized for something and was behaving with abject devotion. But that was hard work – and had been getting harder. Since he wouldn't fight with her any more, her only tool was her exotic mystique. And she was *worn out* being exotic and mysterious.

Too soon they were at her flat. Jack stopped his car outside, actually switched off the engine, instead of keeping it idling. But Mai wasn't sticking around.

'Bye,' she gulped, swinging her legs out of the car.

'I'll call you,' he promised.

'Don't.'

With an ache in his stomach, Jack watched her walk away from him, a tough little girl-woman, in her ludicrously high shoes. Scrunching her key into the front door, she let herself in.

She didn't look back.

CHAPTER 40

Coming back from lunch, as Lisa came out of the lift she passed Trix, who was clumping along to the ladies' to apply yet another layer of make-up.

'Howya,' Trix said. 'There's some man waiting to see you.'

Some man, Lisa thought irritably. Couldn't she have found out who he was, and what he wanted?

Natasha, her PA at *Femme*, would have insisted on knowing a caller's grandmother's maiden name before they were permitted an audience with Lisa.

And then it happened.

She turned to pass through the reception area into the office, and sitting on the couch was the last person in the world she expected to see.

Oliver.

She crashed into an invisible wall. Shock turned her inside-out and her ears buzzed with deafness. She'd last seen him on New Year's Day – it was now the thirteenth of July. All their time apart concertinaed into less than a second.

'Hey, babes.' He looked up at her, very comfortable, very at ease.

She began to shake. Several thoughts hit at once. What was she wearing? Did she look good? Thin? Why did he have to come to her work? Did he realize what a small-time, two-bit operation she was heading up?

'What are you doing here?' she heard herself enquire.

She couldn't stop staring, unable to figure out why he was both familiar and a stranger. Her body language was startled and gawky, frozen in the step she'd been taking when she saw him. Belatedly she pulled her legs together and pushed back her shoulders. It took effort.

'We need to talk.' He smiled and glinted; his teeth, his earring, his heavy, silver watch-strap. He shifted his ankle from where it was balanced on his opposite knee, and sat up straight. With every movement he bulged with grace.

'About what?' she mumbled.

Then he laughed. One of his great big belly-laughs that nearly blew out the windows. 'About what?' he exclaimed, grinning without humour. 'What do you think?'

D-I-V-O-R-C-E . . .

'I'm busy, Oliver.'

'Still knocking yourself out, girl?'

'I'm at work, Oliver. If you want to talk to me call me at home.'

'Hey, a number would be nice.'

'I'll meet you after work.' Might as well get this dealt with.

'Good of you . . . I'm staying in the Clarence.'

'That's a bit flash.'

'I'm on a shoot.'

For some reason that hurt. 'So you didn't really come to see me?'

'Let's just call it good timing.'

Trembling, Lisa attempted to work but it was almost impossible to concentrate: she'd forgotten the effect Oliver had on her.

'Delivery for you!'

Lisa jumped as Trix flung a jiffy-bag on her desk. It was the photos from Saturday's shoot and Lisa's instinct had been spot on. They were amazing, but she could hardly focus. It was as though the edges of her vision were damp and grey. All she could think about was Oliver. They'd parted so acrimoniously, with such bitterness. He'd been so nasty. Said such terrible things.

'Hey Ashling.' She made a great effort to regain control. 'Take this photo . . . no, this one . . .' She selected the best picture, a reportage-style shot of Dani looking sulkily beautiful, flanked by Boo and Hairy Dave. 'Get twenty copies from Niall and send them off to all the major houses. Sticker them, saying "Frieda Kiely Autumn collection. *Colleen* September issue" . . . That should cause a stir,' she muttered, missing completely Ashling's appalled expression.

Seconds later she became aware that Ashling was still loitering by her desk.

'What?!'

'Can we . . . I think . . . Boo and Hairy Dave –'

'Who?!'

'The homeless men. In the photo,' Ashling elaborated when it became clear Lisa had no idea who she was talking about. 'Can we give them something?'

'Like?'

'A present or . . . something. For being in the photo and making it so good.'

Under normal circumstances Lisa would just have told Ashling to fuck off and get a grip, but she was too distracted.

'Ask Jack,' she snapped. 'I'm busy.'

Clutching the photograph, Ashling nervously knocked on Jack Devine's door. When he bellowed, 'Come in,' she reluctantly entered and cringingly explained her mission. 'They did it without a word of complaint and they didn't ask for anything and I just thought we should show some sort of appreciation . . .'

'Fine,' Jack interrupted.

'Really?' she asked cautiously. She'd been expecting him to mock her request.

'Absolutely. They make the picture. What d'you think they'd like?'

'Somewhere to live,' she semi-joked.

'I haven't got the budget,' Jack replied. He sounded quite regretful. 'Any other ideas?'

She thought about it. 'Money, probably.'

'Thirty quid each? It's all I can stretch to, I'm afraid.'

'Er, fantastic.' It wasn't much, but it was more than she'd hoped for. At least Boo and Dave would get a couple of hot meals out of it.

'Here,' Jack signed a petty cash slip. 'Give that to Bernard.'

'Thank you.'

He let his dark eyes rest on her face for two or three long seconds. 'You're welcome.'

At seven o'clock, as arranged, Lisa went to the bar at the Clarence. Oliver rose when he saw her.

'What d'you want to drink? White wine?'

White wine was her drink, at least it had been when they'd been together. He'd remembered.

'No,' she said, hoping to wound. 'A cosmopolitan.'

'I might have known.'

She watched him, big and bulky, loud and forthright, cheerfully joking with the bar staff. How come he always occupied more space than he actually filled? Her head tightened and lifted – he was so familiar she almost didn't know him.

Returning with her drink, he got straight to the point. 'Have you got a solicitor, babes?'

'Weeell . . .'

'We both need a solicitor,' he explained patiently.

'For the divorce?' She tried to sound blasé but it was the first time the word had ever been actually uttered as a real likelihood.

''s right.' He was brisk, businesslike. 'Now, you know the deal –'

She didn't, actually.

'Our marriage has irretrievably broken down, but that's not enough to get divorced. We need to give a reason. If we were already separated for two years we could just do it. But until then, one of us has to sue the other. For desertion, unreasonable behaviour or adultery.'

'Adultery!' Lisa bristled. She'd been totally faithful while they'd been together. 'I never . . .'

'And neither did I.' Oliver was equally emphatic. 'As for desertion –'

'Yeah, *you* left *me*.' She was keen to blame.

'You gave me no choice, babes. But you could sue me for that. Only thing is we have to be separated for two years before you can use desertion as grounds, and we want to get this sorted soon?' He threw her a questioning look and waited for her to concur.

'Yeah,' she said snippily. 'Sooner the better.'

'So that leaves us unreasonable behaviour. We need five examples.'

'Unreasonable behaviour? What's that?' She was almost laughing, forgetting briefly that this had anything to do with her. 'Like doing the hoovering at three in the morning.'

'Or working every weekend and bank holiday.' His tone was bitter. 'Or pretending you want to get pregnant and continuing to take the Pill.'

'Whatever.' Her expression was hostile.

'We have a choice. I can sue you or you can sue me.'

'So you admit you were unreasonable too?'

He sighed heavily. 'It's only a formality, Lees, it's not about allocating blame. The person who gets sued doesn't get punished in any way. So which is it to be? You sue me?'

'You decide, seeing as you know so much about it all,' Lisa said unpleasantly.

He gave her a long look, as if trying to make sense of her, then he shifted. 'If that's what you want. Now, costs. We each pay our own solicitor but we split the court costs between us, yes?'

'Why do we need solicitors? If we flew to Vegas for a quickie wedding, can't we fly to Reno for a quickie divorce?'

'Not that simple, babes. Think about it, we own a property together.'

'Yeah, but we each know how much we contributed to . . . OK, I'll get a solicitor.' She couldn't take another second of this, so she rearranged herself in her chair and asked with brittle gaiety, 'How's work been?'

'Loco. Just got back from France and before that I was in Bali.'

Lucky bastard.

'After here, I've got a quietish time until the shows.' He nodded at Lisa's tailored two-piece. 'I haven't seen that suit before.'

She inspected herself. 'Nicole Farhi.' Lifted from

a shoot the previous January, she'd attempted to hang the blame on Kate Moss.

'I don't like it.' Oliver said.

'What's wrong with it?' She'd always valued his opinion on her clothes and hair.

'Nothing. I mean I don't like that I've not seen it before.'

She knew what he meant. She felt an aching affront that his hair was longer, that his watch was new, that since she'd last seen him he'd travelled halfway around the world and she'd known absolutely nothing about it.

'You look different,' he said.

'Do I?'

'No.' He shook his head and laughed with an odd breathlessness. 'I don't fucking know.'

She knew exactly what he meant. Extreme familiarity and empty distance hung together in strange coexistence. Both were present equally, so it felt that two different realities had been sliced and put back together incorrectly.

'Excuse *me*!' He interrupted himself to pick up her wrist and, with his other hand, turn her fingers to him. There was something he wanted to see. He was rough and the angle was painful. 'You don't wear your wedding ring any more?' he accused, his brown eyes contemptuous.

She tugged her hand away and glared. Rubbing her sore wrist she accused, 'You hurt me!'

'You hurt *me*.'

'What's the big deal with the ring?' Her face

was flushed and angry. 'You're the one talking divorce.'

'You were the one who brought it up in the first place!'

'Only because you were leaving me.'

'Only because you gave me no choice.'

They glared at each other, breathing hard as emotion over-spilled.

'Do you want,' he demanded, his expression like thunder, his eyes never leaving her face, 'to come up to my room?'

'Come on.' Already she was on her feet.

The first kiss was a frantic, teeth-clashing grind. Trying to do too much at once he pulled at her hair, tugged at her jacket, kissed her too hard, then tore off his shirt.

'Wait, wait, wait.' Looking exhausted, he laid his naked back against the door.

'What?' she mumbled, numbed by the sight of his hard polished chest.

'Let's start this again.' He reached and pulled her to him with delicate tenderness. She buried her face in his chest. The special Oliver smell. Forgotten, but remembered with such stupefying, sense-filling impact. Peppery, sweet-spicy, and something unique and indescribable that didn't come from soap or a bottle or from his clothes. A smell that was just *him*.

His familiarity brought tears to her eyes.

With unbearable fragility he placed a fluttery kiss on the corner of her mouth. As if it was the first time. Then another butterfly kiss. And another. Moving inwards slowly, creating pleasure that was almost indistinguishable from pain.

Not moving, barely breathing, she let him administer kisses.

Sex with Oliver was the one time in her life when Lisa played passive. When she wasn't controlling or rapacious or proactive or voracious. She always let him be in charge and he loved it.

'I look into your eyes and you're not even there,' he often used to remark. 'You're just this whimpery, helpless little girl.'

She knew he was turned on by the contrast between her usual bolshiness and such bedroom passivity, but that wasn't why she did it. With Oliver there was no need to be in charge. He knew exactly what to do. Nobody did it better.

The kisses moved from her mouth to her neck, her hairline. Her eyes closed, she groaned with pleasure. She could die now, she really could. She heard him whisper, his breath hot on her ear, 'You're gone, babes.'

Like a sleepwalker, she was led to the bed. Obediently she stretched out her arms for her jacket to be removed, lifted her hips for her skirt to come off. The smooth, cool sheets poured across the bare skin of her back. Her whole body was quivering, but she lay without moving. When he grazed her nipple with his mouth, she jerked as if she'd had an electric shock. How could she have forgotten how sensational this was?

The kisses moved downwards, ever downwards. He placed a tiny kiss on her stomach, so gentle it barely lifted the downy little hairs, but it flooded her with swollen sensation.

'Oliver, I think I'm going to . . .'

'Wait!'

The condom was the bum note, the one thing that reminded her that things weren't the way they used to be. But she refused to let herself think about it. So he was probably having sex with others? Well, so was she.

When he entered her, a great peace settled. She exhaled long and clean, all tension fleeing. For a second she savoured her absence of agitation until he began to drive himself into her with long, slow thrusts. She intended to enjoy this. She knew she would.

Afterwards she wept.

'Why are you crying, baby?' He cradled her to him.

'It's just a physical thing,' she said, already regaining control of who she really was. Enough of that passive stuff. 'People often cry when they've come.'

Their earlier anger and discomfort had been burnt off by passion. Instead they lay in bed, talking idly, wrapped around each other in affection that was bizarrely comfortable. It was as if they'd never been apart, never fought acrimoniously, never thought with bitterness of each other. Not that either of them was naïve enough to think that the sex indicated that a reunion was on the cards. Even when their fighting had been at its ugliest, they'd had sex. Amazing sex. It had seemed to provide an outlet for all that excess of emotion.

Absently she swept her hands along the undulation of his biceps. 'Still working out, I see. What can you bench-press now?'

'One hundred and thirty.'

'I'm impressed!'

After midnight, conversation wound down further and further until eventually he yawned. 'Let's go to sleep, babes.'

''K,' she said drowsily. There was no question that she leave, they both knew that. 'I'll just go to the bathroom.'

After she'd washed her face, she used his toothbrush. She did it without thinking and it was only after she'd finished that she noticed.

When she returned from the bathroom she put her chilly feet between his thighs to warm them, the way she'd always done. Then they slept, as they had slept almost every night for four years, spooned together. She curled into a 'C', with him curled into a bigger 'C' around her, hugging her length, his palm warm on her stomach.

'Night night.'

'Night.'

Silence.

Into the darkness, Oliver remarked, 'This is really weird.' She could hear his pain and confusion. 'I'm having an affair with my wife.'

She closed her eyes and pressed her spine into his stomach. The rigid tension that kept her back teeth permanently clamped together loosened, lessened and dissolved. She slept better than she had in a long, long time.

In the morning they slipped with almost alarming ease into their old routine. The pattern of domesticity that they'd shared every morning for four years. Oliver got up first and organized coffee. Then Lisa hogged the bathroom while he seethed outside trying to chivvy her along. When he pounded the door and yelled, 'C'mon babes, I'll be late!' the *déjà vu* was so intense she had a long, dizzy moment when she couldn't remember where she was. She knew it wasn't home but . . .

When she emerged swaddled in towels, she grinned, 'Sorry.'

'You'd better have left me some dry towels,' he warned.

''Course I have.' She scooted across to gulp some coffee. And waited.

She heard the rush of the shower being turned on, then a while later the sudden cessation of its pounding. Any minute now . . .

'Aw, Lisa.' Oliver's echoey complaint issued, as expected. 'Babes! You've only left me a naffing face-cloth! You always do this.'

'It's not a face-cloth,' Crouching with laughter, Lisa came into the bathroom. 'It's *much* bigger.'

Oliver scorned the hand-towel that Lisa demonstrated. 'That's not even going to dry my knob!'

'I'm sorry,' she teased tenderly, and unwound one of her own towels. 'See, I'm going to give you the shirt off my back.'

'You're a trollop,' he grumbled.

'I know,' she nodded.

'You really are un-fucking-believable.'

'Oh, I *know*,' she agreed, with extreme sincerity.

Alternately mocking and soothing, Lisa dried his hard shiny body. It was an activity that she'd always loved, though some parts of his body got more attention than others.

'Hey, Lees,' Oliver eventually said.

'Mmmm?'

'I think my thighs might be dry now.'

'Oh . . . yeah.' They shared a wry look.

As they got dressed, across the room she suddenly noticed something almost as familiar as herself. Before she could stop herself, she'd exclaimed, 'Oi, that's my LV holdall!'

And it was. He'd used it to pack some of his stuff the day he'd left.

Instantly the room was dense with the ugly emotions of that day. Oliver furious – *again*. Lisa angrily defensive – *again*. Oliver objecting that theirs was no longer a proper marriage. Lisa sarcastically telling him to divorce her.

'I'll give it you back.' Oliver proferred the holdall hopefully, but it was no good. The mood was sombre and, in silence, they finished getting ready for work.

When she couldn't stall any further, Lisa said, 'Well, bye.'

'Bye,' he replied. To her surprise she had tears in her eyes.

'Aw, don't cry.' He bundled her in his arms. 'C'mon, Editor-Girl, you'll smudge your make-up.'

She managed a wet giggle, but her throat ached as if a big round stone was stuck in it. 'I'm sorry things didn't work out for us,' she admitted, in a low tone.

'Well,' he shrugged. 'Shit happens. Did you know that –'

'– two in three marriages end in divorce,' they said together. With effort, they managed a laugh, then disengaged.

'And at least it's amicable now,' she said awkwardly. 'Like, we're, you know, talking to each other.'

'Exactly,' he cheerfully agreed. She was distracted by the sheen of his lilac linen shirt against the silky chocolate of his throat. Jesus, that man knew how to dress!

As she pulled the door closed, he called, 'Hey, babes, don't forget.'

Her heart lifted and she opened the door again. *Forget what? I love you?*

'Get a lawyer!' He wagged his finger and grinned.

It was a beautiful sunny morning. She walked through the buttery sunshine to work. She felt like shit.

CHAPTER 41

Lisa suddenly realized that no one had mentioned the shows. Or should she say, The Shows!!! She could never think of them without seeing them lit up in neon. They were the highlight of an editor's job. Twice a year, jetting off to the buzzy hub of Milan or Paris. (She flew everywhere else but the shows were so glamorous that naturally one 'jetted' to them.) Staying at George V or Principe di Savoia, being treated like royalty, getting frontrow seats at Versace, Dior, Dolce & Gabbana, Chanel, receiving flowers and gifts simply for showing up. The four-day circus teeming with egomaniac designers, neurotic models, rock-stars, film-idols, sinister millionaires in gold, chunky jewellery, and, of course, magazine editors – eyeing each other with savage hatred, checking out how high their seat was in the pecking order. Party after party, in art galleries, nightclubs, warehouses, abbatoirs (some of the more cutting-edge designers just didn't know where to draw the line). Where you simply couldn't be more at the centre of the universe if you *tried*, dear.

Of course, it was written in stone that you bitched that the clothes were unwearable nonsense designed by misogynistic wankers, that the post-show presents weren't as lavish as the previous year's, that the best hotel room was always bagsed by Lily Headley-Smythe, and what a huge pain it was having to travel a mile outside the city-centre to see some young hotshot display his ground-breaking collection in a disused bean-canning plant, but it was still unthinkable not to go. And it hit her like an avalanche of Kurt Gieger loafers that there had been no talk of the shows at *Colleen*. Seeing Oliver must have triggered thoughts of them.

It was probably all in hand, she soothed herself. There was likely to be a budget provision for both herself and Mercedes to go. But what if there wasn't? The freelance budget she'd been given couldn't accommodate the costs. Not even close. It could barely have paid for a croissant at George V.

With rising panic Lisa knocked on Jack's door and didn't wait for him to answer before she marched on in. 'The shows,' she said with an involuntary wheeze.

In surprise, Jack looked up, frozen in a hunched pose over what looked like a ton of legal documents. 'What shows?'

'Fashion shows. Milan, Paris. September. I will be going?' Her pounding heart was too big for her chest.

'Sit down,' Jack gently invited, and instantly she knew those words were bad news.

'I always went when I was editor of *Femme*. It's important for the profile of the magazine that we have a presence there. Advertising, all that,' came out in a garbled rush. 'We'll never be taken seriously if we're not seen . . .'

Jack watched her, waiting for her to finish. The sympathy in his eyes told her she was wasting her time, but never say die.

A deep breath steadied her, 'I am going?'

'I'm sorry,' Jack crooned, his voice like Savlon. 'We don't have the budget. Not this year, anyway. Maybe when the magazine is more on its feet, when the advertising has increased.'

'But surely I –?'

Sadly he shook his head. 'We haven't the money.'

It was the pity in his look as much as his words that finally hammered the truth home. The full awful reality slammed into her. Everyone else would be there. Everyone in the whole world. And they'd notice she wasn't, she'd be a laughing stock. Then an even more awful thought filled her head. Maybe they *wouldn't* notice.

Jack was pouring oil on troubled waters like no one's business, promising to buy syndicated pictures from any number of sources, how *Colleen* could still do a fantastic spread, how the readers would never know that their editor hadn't actually been . . .

It was then that Lisa realized she was crying.

Not angry, tantrummy tears, but pure, sweet grief that she was powerless to control. Infinite sadness heaved out of her with each sob.

It's only a few silly fashion shows, said her head.

But she couldn't stop crying and from nowhere came a memory, completely unrelated to anything. Of when she was about fifteen, smoking and mooching around Hemel town centre with two other girls, complaining about how shit it all was.

'Full of spastics,' Carol's slick mouth had twisted with bored disgust as she surveyed the high street.

'And pricks with shit clothes and shit lives,' Lisa had agreed nastily.

'Look, that's your mum, isn't it?' Andrea's blue-mascaraed eyes were catty and amused as, with a nod of her backcombed head, she'd indicated a woman across the road.

With an unpleasant lurch Lisa saw her mother, dowdy and ridiculous in her 'best' coat. 'Her?' Lisa had scorned, exhaling a long plume of smoke. 'That's not my mum.'

Back in Jack's office she was saying something. Over and over, her voice muffled. 'I've worked so hard,' she insisted, into her hands. 'I've worked so hard.'

She was barely aware of Jack, as he pawed around in his pockets. There was the rustle of cardboard, the click of a lighter, the acrid whiff of nicotine.

'Can I have one?' She lifted her tear-mottled face briefly.

'It's for you.' He passed her the lit cigarette which she accepted meekly and sucked on as if it was saving her life. She smoked it in six hungry pulls.

Jack continued pawing. Passively, uninterestedly, she watched him pull a scratchcard from one pocket, a receipt from another. Finally, in his desk drawer, he found what he was looking for. A wodge of paper napkins bearing the SuperMac logo, which he pressed into her hand.

'I wish I was the kind of man who carries a big, clean white hanky for this sort of eventuality,' he said softly.

''s all right.' She rubbed the shiny paper over her salt-tender cheeks. With each hit of nicotine, her weeping lessened, until the only sound she was making was a sporadic tearful gasp.

'Sorry,' she eventually said. Everything had slowed down; her heart rate, her reactions, her thoughts. She could go on sitting in this office for ever, too stupefied to be embarrassed, too sleepy to question what was happening to her.

'Another one?' Jack enquired as she stubbed out her cigarette. She nodded.

'You know that they only picked you for this job because you're the best,' Jack said, passing her a lit cigarette, then lighting one for himself. 'No one else could set up a magazine from scratch.'

'Funny way to reward me,' she said, another wheezy gasp jumping from her.

'You are amazing,' Jack said earnestly. 'Your energy, your vision, your ability to motivate staff.

You don't miss a trick. I wish you could see how much we value you. You'll get to the shows. Maybe not this year, but soon.'

'It's not just the job or the shows.' The words spilled from her mouth.

'Oh?' Jack's dark eyes were interested.

'I saw my husband . . .'

'Your . . . um?' The sideshow of emotions on Jack's face interested her. He was bothered. Though she couldn't feel it yet, she knew this was a good thing. 'I didn't know you were married,' he settled on.

'I'm not. Well, I am, but we've split up.' Painfully, she added, 'We're getting divorced.'

Jack looked deeply uncomfortable. 'Christ! I've never been through it, so I'm not going to patronize you with advice or stuff . . . I mean, I've split up with people, which is rough, but not the same, I'd imagine. But, anyway, well, it sounds . . .' He searched around for the appropriate word and couldn't find anything dramatic enough. 'Rough, it sounds rough.'

She nodded. 'Yeah. Look, I don't know why I'm telling you this.' With a sudden show of control and efficiency, she blew her nose, rummaged in her bag, then flipped open a mirror. 'I'm a horror-show,' she said briskly.

'You look fine to me . . .'

After a quick repair job with Beauty Flash and All About Eyes, she said, 'I'd better get back. Ashlings to shout at, Gerries to row with.'

'You don't have to . . .'

Slowing down, she momentarily took off her mag-hag persona. 'You've been very kind to me,' she admitted. 'Thank you.'

CHAPTER 42

'Him, there, the tall one.' Ashling pointed through the crowds at the River Club.

'That's your boyfriend?' Clodagh asked incredulously. 'He's lovely, a bit like Dennis Leary.'

'Ah, he's not really,' Ashling demurred, *thrilled*.

All of a sudden she felt nearly as good as Clodagh. OK, Clodagh obviously needed glasses, but so what! And wait until she saw Marcus perform!

It was Saturday night and there was a star-studded cast on at the River Club. As well as Marcus and Ted, Bicycle Billy, Mark Dignan and Jimmy Bond were also playing.

'Quick, spread your jacket and your bag across as many chairs as possible.' Ashling threw herself towards a vacant table. The comedians were doing the great honour of sitting with them, and Joy and Lisa were also coming. Even Jack Devine had said he might drop in.

From across the room, Ted had spotted Clodagh and came running. 'Hello,' he exclaimed, pathetically aglow. 'Thank you for coming.'

'I'm looking forward to it,' Clodagh said graciously.

Ted pulled up a chair and sat next to Clodagh in a way that proclaimed they were 'special' friends.

Ashling anxiously watched the interplay. The dogs in the street knew that Ted fancied Clodagh. But what of Clodagh? She *had* insisted on coming without Dylan.

With wild animation Ted chatted away until suddenly he realized that he might have to vomit. His usual nerves were wildly exacerbated by Clodagh's presence. White-faced, he made his excuses and lurched towards the gents'.

Ashling watched. Clodagh did not follow him with her eyes as he zigzagged off. Good. She managed to rein in her ridiculous anxiety. Clodagh and Ted, as if!

'Hiya.' Joy arrived and gave Clodagh a wary nod.

'Hiya.' Clodagh nervously attempted a smile. Joy made her feel even more deficient than usual. But according to Ashling, Joy had recently been dumped by her fella, so was to be treated with tenderness.

Then Clodagh's eye was caught by someone approaching their table. A woman so shiny and gorgeous, trendy and funky that Clodagh tumbled down a well of inadequacy. She'd agonized over what to wear for tonight, this desperately yearned-for treat, and had been rather pleased with the results, but one look at the fabulous clothes and quirky accessories of this woman conspired to make Clodagh feel rather pathetic. As if the way she'd assembled her appearance was naïve and clueless. It looked as if the woman was going to join them. She was taking off her jacket, saying hello to Ashling. Fuck! She must be . . .

'My boss, Lisa,' Ashling introduced.

Clodagh managed a mute bow of her head, then watched with jealousy as Lisa greeted Joy like an old friend. 'Michael Winner, Prince Edward or Andrew Lloyd Webber. And you *must* sleep with one of them!'

'Prince Edward, I suppose.' Joy was rather subdued. 'David Copperfield, Robin Cook or Wurzel Gummidge?'

'Yuk.' Lisa frowned. 'Wurzel Gummidge – *please*! Robin Co– no. David Copperf– no, I couldn't. I suppose it'll have to be Wurzel Gummidge. Ugh.'

Mad keen to fit in, Clodagh turned to Ashling and challenged loudly, 'Brad Pitt, Joseph Fiennes and Tom Cruise, and you *must* sleep with one of them!'

Lisa and Joy exchanged a look. Clodagh just didn't get it, did she?

Too late, Clodagh saw that she'd done something wrong. 'Oh,' she admitted, stung raw by her own stupidity. 'They're meant to be unattractive, aren't they? Who wants a drink?'

'Clodagh, can I introduce you to –' Ashling said. Marcus had arrived at the table. 'Marcus, this is my best friend Clodagh.'

As Marcus shook Clodagh's hand, she felt marginally better. He was nice and friendly, not like those two bitches, Joy and Lisa.

'I'm just buying a round,' Clodagh smiled at Marcus. 'Can I get you something?'

'Only a Red Bull. I don't drink before I go on stage,' he explained kindly.

'OK, I'll get you a proper drink afterwards.' Stiffly, she asked Joy, 'What would you like?'

'Red Square.'

'Red . . . um?' Clodagh had never heard of such a drink.

'It's vodka and Red Bull,' Ashling explained. 'I'll have one too.'

'And me,' said Lisa.

And so will I, Clodagh decided. When in Rome . . . Hey, who was *he*? A tall, dishevelled man had arrived and was hovering uncomfortably on the edge of the group. Gorgeous! Not really her type – a bit *too* unkempt – but all the same . . . Then she noticed Lisa attach herself to him like she had suckers.

'Would, um, Lisa's boyfriend like a drink?' Clodagh asked Ashling.

'Who? Oh, him, he's not Lisa's boyfriend, he's our boss.'

'Well, would your boss like a drink?'

Ashling swallowed a sigh and with bad grace said, 'Mr Devine, this is my friend Clodagh, she's going to the bar.'

Jack smiled at Clodagh, shook her hand and

said, 'Call me Jack.' Then he *insisted* on buying the round.

Ashling couldn't help an eruption of jealousy. Why couldn't he be nice to *her*? Then she switched her focus to Marcus and immediately felt better. Before the gig began he was approached by a steady stream of fans. Female fans, mostly. As she watched the girls go up to him, she swelled with pride that he was her boyfriend. She couldn't help being pleased with herself for bagging him. *He could have had anyone*, she thought, *and he picked me.*

It was Clodagh's night, no doubt about it. The comedians – intimidated by Lisa, sick of the sight of Joy and respectful of Ashling being Marcus's girlfriend – swarmed around Clodagh with her swishy new hair, gorgeous face and tight, white trousers. Ted's dark little face was miserable, but he was hopelessly outnumbered.

Clodagh, blazing a trail through Red Square after Red Square, was having a blast. During one of the breaks, Ashling overheard her saying to a cluster of men, 'I was a virgin before I got married.' With a twinkle in her eye she added, 'A long time before, mind.'

Everyone fell into convulsions and Ashling couldn't help a shameful little thought, *It wasn't that funny.* She pushed it away – it wasn't Clodagh's fault she was beautiful. And it genuinely was nice to see her enjoying herself so much.

Then Clodagh crossed her legs and all eyes flickered to the movement. Unselfconsiously she eased her embroidered mule off her foot and let it swing idly on her big toe. Ashling watched several sets of eyes – all male – scud back and forth in time with it, looking mildy hypnotized.

Ted's act went down a storm and when he came back to the table, alight with triumph, Ashling watched Clodagh rub his shoulder and say, 'You were brilliant!'

Some time later Ashling saw Clodagh smiling at Jack Devine with the tip of her tongue poking out saucily through her teeth. Then Bicycle Billy got the same treatment. Oh no! It was her I'm-gorgeous-and-I-know-it smile, at least that was what she thought. But to quote Phelim on it, it was her scary-old-bat-from-Benny-Hill leer.

The next time Ashling looked, Clodagh had deteriorated markedly. With the slinkiness of an affectionate cat, she was rubbing her face against people's shoulders and explaining with charming bleariness to *everyone*, 'I've two children, so I don't get out much.' She hugged Lisa and said earnestly, 'I'm pissed! You see, I don't get out much.' Then she saw Ashling looking and exclaimed, 'Oh Ashling, I'm pissed. Are you cross with me?'

But before Ashling could demur, Clodagh had turned away and, skimming over the top of her words, was explaining to Mark Dignan, 'I've two chirn, soadoan get out much.'

Marcus was last on the bill and as he took the

stage Clodagh was whispering and giggling with Jack Devine. Ashling was annoyed, she'd really been looking forward to showing off how good her boyfriend was.

'Shush,' she elbowed Clodagh, then indicated the stage.

'Sorry,' Clodagh said loudly – too loudly. Then proceeded to absolutely scream with laughter at everything Marcus said. When, amid rapturous applause, he returned to the table, Clodagh propelled herself into his arms and insisted, 'You were HILARIOUS!'

Marcus gently disentangled himself from her and steered her back to her seat beside Ashling. As he sat down he squeezed Ashling's hand and gave her a secret smile.

'She's right,' Ashling murmured, 'You *were* hilarious.'

'Thanks,' he mouthed, and they shared a moment of warm mutual regard, which went on for far longer than was decent.

'Is that it, then?' Clodagh demanded. 'No more funny stuff. Do we have to go home?'

'Jesus, no!' Jimmy Bond looked aghast. 'Late bar until two.'

'Brilliant!' Clodagh exclaimed and promptly knocked over someone's glass. It clattered against the table and sent a stream of lager rushing over Bicycle Billy's thighs. 'Sorrysorrysorrysorrysorry,' Clodagh insisted, fuzzily. 'God, I'm verr sorry.'

'Ah, the poor thing,' Ted sympathized. In unison,

most of the table chorused, 'She doesn't get out much.'

Mark Dignan had just rejoined them and took in the scene, Bicycle Billy rubbing his soaked legs with the sleeve of his jacket, Clodagh apologizing thickly. Before anyone started to condemn her, Mark had some news for them. 'She's got two children,' he confided and furrowed his brow to urge compassion, 'so she doesn't get out much.'

Next Clodagh started up a long, huddled head-to-head with a woman from another table. They looked as though they were solving the problems of the world, but when Ashling eavesdropped, all they seemed to be saying to each other was, 'If you don't have chirn yourself, you can't understan'.' 'Thass right. If you don't have chirn yourself, you can't understan'.'

Then Clodagh went to the loo, and when she hadn't returned to their table after ten minutes Ashling anxiously scanned the room and saw her in intimate conversation with a trio of girls. The next time she looked, Clodagh was laughing with a man. Shortly after that Clodagh was talking to two boys, making elaborate hand gestures that looked exactly like she was demonstrating how to express breast milk. But she seemed happy – and so did the two boys – so Ashling decided to let her alone. Not long afterwards Ashling went to the bar and as she placed her order she saw Clodagh weaving between tables, then bumping into one, sending a dozen drinks rocking. 'Whoops!' she exclaimed loudly.

Two men leaning on the bar were also watching Clodagh.

'That was close,' one remarked, as the drinks just managed to pull themselves back from toppling.

'Ah, yeah,' the other replied, 'but she has two kids so she doesn't get out much.'

'Excuse me, could you change one of those Red Squares to a Red Bull?' Ashling, on impulse, asked the barman. Clodagh had had enough to drink.

But amazingly, drunk and all as she was, Clodagh knew she'd been fobbed off with an alcohol-free drink, and turned slightly nasty. 'Mus' think I'm a big gobshite,' she complained. 'Mus' think I'm a big, stupid gobshite.'

'Should we get her home?' Marcus murmured.

Ashling nodded, so grateful for him.

'I'm not leaving until I've had another drink,' Clodagh insisted belligerently.

Marcus was sweet, as though explaining to a child. 'You see, Ashling and I want to go home, and it seems like a good idea to drop you off.'

'Well, *go* home,' Clodagh ordered.

'But we'd really like you to come with us in the taxi.'

'I might,' Clodagh said sulkily. 'But it's only because I like you.'

'Do you need any help?' Ted asked hopefully.

'No.' Ashling was firm. 'We're just going to drop her home to *her husband.*'

Clodagh enveloped Ted in a big hug, then

puckered up – Ashling flinched – and kissed him on the forehead. 'You're cute,' she said fondly. 'Don't forget to come and visit me.'

'I won't!'

'Come on.' Ashling took her arm, but Clodagh had turned around and was trying to get to someone else.

'Bye, Jack,' she carolled.

'Bye Clodagh, nice to meet you,' Jack smiled.

'Nice to meet you too.' Clodagh's voice was like cream. 'Hope to see you again soo- Ow! Ashling! You're pulling my arm off!'

Grimly, Ashling tugged her towards the exit.

In the back seat of the taxi, Clodagh complained bitterly and at length about what spoilsports Ashling and Marcus were, how she didn't want to go home, how she'd been enjoying herself, how she had two children and didn't get out much . . . Then, abruptly, mid-rant, silence fell. Her chin on her chest, she'd passed out peacefully.

When Dylan answered the front-door, Marcus said cheerfully, 'Delivery of a drunken woman for you. Sign here.'

With much stumbling and hoisting, Clodagh was helped in, then Marcus and Ashling got back into the taxi to go home.

'Have you a pen?' Marcus asked Ashling, as they whizzed through the dark streets to Ashling's flat.

'Yip.'

'And a piece of paper?'

Already Ashling was seaching.

Out of the corner of her eye she watched Marcus scribble something. It looked remarkably like, 'Delivery of a drunken woman for you. Sign here.' But before she could be sure, he'd folded it away.

The following day, Ashling's phone rang at a quarter past eight. The earliness of the hour meant it would be Clodagh, in the horrors. And indeed it was.

'I've been awake since half six,' she said humbly. 'I just wanted to say sorry for last night. I'm really sorry, I'm so sorry. Did I make a terrible fool of myself? I suppose the problem is that because I've two children I don't get out much.'

'You were fine,' Ashling said sleepily. 'Everyone thought you were great.'

Clodagh? Marcus mouthed at her. Ashling nodded.

'You were lovely,' Marcus called from his pillow. 'Very sweet.'

'Who's that? Marcus? That's decent of him. Tell him I thought he was brilliant.'

'She thought you were brilliant,' Ashling relayed, turning to Marcus.

Clodagh's relief only lasted a moment. 'I can't tell you how much I was looking forward to going out and I enjoyed myself so much, but now you'll never let me come out with you again. It was the nicest night I've had in years and I blew it.'

'Don't be mad, you can come out with us any time you like!'

'Any time,' Marcus echoed.

'Um, Ashling, would you have any idea how I got home?'

'Marcus and I dropped you off in a taxi.'

'Oh yes,' Clodagh said confidently. 'I remember . . . Actually, I don't,' she crumbled. 'I remember the comedians being on stage, but I don't remember much after that. I had a horrible feeling that I'd knocked over someone's pint, but I think I just imagined that.'

'Um, yeh.'

'But it's very bad not to remember how I got home.' Clodagh recommenced flaying herself with guilt. 'Oh my good God,' her voice dropped several octaves into a disbelieving groan. She had suddenly remembered something too awful. 'I have a horrible feeling . . . ah no, I couldn't have.'

'What?'

'These girls I was talking to in the ladies', one of them was pregnant. I think I offered to show her how well my episiotomy stitches had healed. Oh bloody hell, tell me I didn't,' she moaned softly. 'I'm imagining it. I must be.'

'You must be,' Ashling lied stoutly.

'Well, even if I'm not imagining it, I'm pretending I am. I blame that bloody Red Bull,' she exclaimed. 'I'm never touching it again!'

After she hung up, Marcus kissed Ashling and asked softly, 'Was I good last night?'

'Well . . . no.' Ashling was surprised. They hadn't made love when they'd come in.

'No?' His voice was sharp with anguish.

Oh Christ! Too late, Ashling realized what he was on about. 'On *stage*? I thought you meant in bed. You were fantastic on stage, I told you at the time.'

'Better than Bicycle Billy, "one of Ireland's top comedians"?'

'You know you are.'

'If I knew it I wouldn't have to ask.'

'Better than Billy, better than Ted, better than Mark, better than Jimmy, better than everyone.' Ashling wanted to go back to sleep.

'Are you sure?'

'Yes.'

'Jimmy's gag about the football supporters was great, though.'

'It was OK,' Ashling said cautiously.

'How OK?' Marcus pounced. 'On a scale of one to ten?'

'One,' Ashling yawned. 'It was crap. Let's go back to sleep now.'

CHAPTER 43

Oliver's visit had shattered Lisa's fragile equilibrium. At work her eye was off the ball and her bitchy-remark quota was way down. What made things worse was that he didn't ring her. She'd hoped that he would, if only just to leave a jokey 'Thanks for the shag' message. Especially now that he had her number. But the days passed and hope faded.

On day five the yearning got too bad and she rang him, but it went straight to message service. He was out, she deduced, having a good time, living the life she used to live. Full of irritating desolation, she hung up, too raw to leave a message.

She should have known he wouldn't get in touch. It was over, they both knew it, and once his mind was made up, it stayed that way. Subdued and distracted, she couldn't stop dwelling on questions that she should have considered six months, nine months, a year previously. What had happened to her marriage? What went wrong? Like so many relationships, theirs had foundered on the issue of children. But this time there was a twist. He wanted them, she didn't.

She'd *thought* she wanted them. There was a spate when absolutely anyone who was anyone was up the duff: various Spice Girls; a plethora of models; several actresses. A bump was as much of a style statement as a pashmina or a Gucci handbag, and pregnancy was *hot*. She'd even included it in a list – Pregnancy was 'Hot' and Precious Stones were 'Not'.

Shortly after that, the in-thing was to be seen wheeling a tiny little baba in a black jogging buggy – don't leave home without it. Lisa, her gimlet eye registering the infinitesimal rise and fall of all things trendy, took in these developments.

'I want a baby,' she told Oliver.

Oliver wasn't so keen. He liked their stylish, sociable life, and knew that a baby would put the brakes on it. No more partying until dawn, no more white sofas, no more spontaneous, last-minute trips to Milan. Or Vegas. Or even Brighton. Sleepless nights would no longer be courtesy of high-grade cocaine, but of a screaming child instead. All disposable income would be diverted away from Dolce & Gabbana jeans and reapplied to mountains of disposable nappies.

But Lisa got to work, and slowly she convinced him. Appealing to his macho pride, 'Don't you want your genes to be carried on?'

'No.'

And then one day, lying in bed he said, 'OK.'

'OK, what?'

'OK, we'll have a baby.' Before Lisa could

exclaim with pleasure he had plucked her foil card of pills from the bedside shelf and ceremoniously flushed them down the loo.

'No safety net, babes.'

In her fantasies, Lisa was already sporting a delicious coffee-coloured baby on her slender hip. 'It's not a doll,' Fifi pointed out to her. 'It's a human being and they're a lot of hard work.'

'I know that,' Lisa had snapped. But she didn't really.

Then someone at work got pregnant. Arabella, a sharp, slightly dangerous woman, who was as smart as a whip and always immaculately turned out. Overnight she became as sick as a dog. One day she even puked into the wastepaper bin. When she wasn't in the ladies' either weeing or throwing up, she was slumped at her desk, queasily nibbling ginger, too exhausted to work. And the food! Despite her ever-present nausea, she ate mountains. 'The only thing that settles my stomach is food,' she mumbled, shoving another Cornish pasty down the hatch. In no time she looked as if she'd been buried up to her neck in a sandpit. It got worse. Her once-glistening hair became unaccountably frizzy and suddenly she was very prone to cold sores. Her skin yielded flaky patches of psoriasis and her nails split and broke. To Lisa's supercritical eye she looked more like a plague victim than a pregnant woman.

Most disturbing of all, Arabella's concentration disappeared. Mid-interview she forgot Nicole

Kidman's name, and could only come up with the office nickname for her: Nicole Skidmark. She couldn't remember if her wraparound John Rocha velcro skirt was last season's or the one before. And these things were *elementary*, Lisa noted in mounting alarm. The day came when Arabella's ability to make a decision between a White Magnum and a Classic Magnum just went west on her. 'Whi– No, Classi– No, no, wait. White. Definitely White. No, Classic . . .' She could have dithered for England. 'I've become lime-jelly-brain girl,' she moaned.

Thoroughly spooked, Lisa went to see another woman who'd had a baby. Eloïse, features editor at *Chic Girly*.

'How are you?' Lisa asked.

'Psychotic from sleep deprivation,' Eloïse answered.

It got worse. Though it was six months since Eloïse had had her baby, she *still* looked as though she'd been buried up to her neck in a sandpit.

And something else. She no longer cared, she'd lost her hardness. This was the editor formerly known as Attila. She sacked without fear – or at least she used to. But now she was afflicted with a faint but unmissable air of goo.

Lisa began back-pedalling like there was no tomorrow. She didn't want a baby, they destroyed your life. It was easy for models and Spice Girls. They had teams of nannies to ensure you got your sleep, personal trainers to insist you regained your figure, private hairdressers to comb your hair when you hadn't the energy to.

But by then Oliver was well into the idea. And the thing about Oliver was that once he'd decided on something, it was very hard to make him change his mind.

Secretly she began taking the Pill again. No way was she destroying her precious career.

Ah yes, Lisa's career. Oliver had objected to that too, hadn't he?

'You're a workaholic,' he accused, over and over, with mounting frustration and anger.

'Men always say that about successful women.'

'No, I don't just mean that you work too hard, although you do. Babes, you're *obsessed*. All you talk about is office politics or circulation figures, or how the competition is doing. "At least we get more in advertising . . . We did that article six months ago . . . Ally Benn is out to get me."'

'Well, she is.'

'No, she isn't.'

Mad with the irritation of being misunderstood, Lisa glared at him. 'You've no idea what it's like, they *all* want to be me, all those twenty-year-olds. They'd stitch me up and stab me in the back, given half a chance.'

'Just because you think that way doesn't mean everyone else does. You're paranoid.'

'I'm not, I'm telling it like it is. Their only loyalty is to themselves.'

'Just like you, babes. You've got so hard, you've

sacked too many people. You shouldn't have sacked Kelly, she was sweet, and on your side.'

Shame flickered for the tiniest moment. 'She couldn't hack it, she wasn't tough enough. I need a features writer who isn't afraid of doing hatchet jobs. Nice people like Kelly hold the magazine back.' She rounded on Oliver. 'I didn't enjoy sacking her, if that's what you're thinking. I thought she was all right, but I'd no choice.'

'Lisa, I think you're the business. I always did. I . . .' he paused as he searched for the right word. 'I admire you, I respect you . . .'

'But?' Lisa questioned sharply.

'But there's more to life than being the best.'

A scornful laugh. 'No there isn't.'

'But you *are* the best. You're so young and successful, why isn't it enough?'

'That's the trouble with success,' Lisa muttered. 'You've got to keep doing better.'

How could she explain that the more she got, the more she wanted? Every coup left her empty, chasing the next one in the hope that perhaps then she'd feel like she'd arrived. Satisfaction was fleeting and elusive and success simply whetted her appetite for more and more and more.

'Why does it matter so much?' Oliver had asked in despair. 'It's only a job.'

Lisa flinched at that. Oh, he was so wrong. 'It's not. It's . . . everything.'

'You'll change your mind when you get pregnant.'

Instantly, terror bathed her in sweat. She wouldn't

be getting pregnant. She had to tell him. But she'd tried and he'd totally stonewalled her.

'Let's go away this weekend, babes,' Oliver suggested with a brightness that he didn't feel. 'Just you and me, hanging out, the way it used to be.'

'I've got to pop into the office on Saturday for a couple of hours. Got to check the layout before it goes to the printers . . .'

'Ally could do that.'

'No way! She'd screw it up on purpose just to show me up.'

'See what I mean?' he said bitterly. 'You're obsessed and I never get to see you, except at work bashes . . . And you're no fun any more.'

There continued a steady, bitter accretion of let-downs and disappointments, a mounting litany of resentments and blame, of withdrawal and isolation from each other. Two people who had blurred into one gradually became two again, sharply defined and separate.

Something had to give and eventually it did.

On New Year's Day Oliver found a packet of the Pill in Lisa's handbag. After a savage and lengthy exchange of words, they lapsed into silence. Oliver packed his bags (and one of Lisa's) and left.

CHAPTER 44

'Who's doing the lunch run today?' Lisa asked.

'Me,' Trix replied quickly. Too quickly.

Trix loved doing the lunch run, not because she wished to be of service to her colleagues, but because it ensured she got two lunch-hours. It took four minutes to walk to the sandwich shop, another six to order, pay for and collect the sandwiches. Which left forty-five minutes to wander around the shops of Temple Bar before returning to the office and shriekingly condemning the indecisive crowds ahead of her in the sandwich queue, the gobshites who worked there who couldn't tell the difference between chicken and avocado, the man who'd had a heart attack so that she had to loosen his clothing and wait with him until the ambulance came . . .

Even though everyone was snowed under by work, with just over a month to go before the launch of *Colleen*, nevertheless they found themselves looking forward to her progressively more outrageous excuses.

Then she would sit and spend fifteen minutes

eating her sandwich, before looking at the clock and announcing, 'One fifty-seven, I'm going on lunch, see you all at two fifty-seven.'

'I'd like something a little bit different for my lunch today,' Lisa told Trix.

'Ah, Burger King.' Trix understood.

'No.'

'*No?*'

'There's more to lunch than sandwiches and burgers.'

Trix's look was baffled.

'Is it fruit you want?' Her over-made-up forehead puckered in confusion. She knew that Lisa sometimes ate apples and grapes and that kind of gear. Trix never ate fruit. Absolutely never. She prided herself on it.

'I'd like sushi.'

The suggestion was such a revolting one that Trix briefly lost the power of speech. '*Sushi?*' she eventually spat in horror. 'Do you mean raw fish?'

Over the weekend Lisa had read that a sushi emporium had come to Dublin and she hoped that sampling their merchandise might lift her out of her Oliver-triggered depression. But she'd hoped the comedy gig on Saturday night would do the trick too, and it hadn't: although Jack *had* showed up and had talked to her for a lot of the night – when he hadn't been talking to that pain-in-the-arse Clodagh, that is.

'Some of your best friends are fish,' Lisa said wearily.

'How many times do I have to tell you that there are never any fish in the van when I'm in it!'

'Here, I've drawn you a little map,' Lisa said. 'Just ask for a bento box.'

'A bento box? Are you making that up?' Trix snarled, terrified of being made a fool of.

'No, that's how takeaway sushi is packaged. They'll know in the shop what you're talking about.'

'A bento box,' Trix repeated suspiciously.

'Who's getting a bento box?' Jack had appeared in the office.

'She is,' Trix whined, at the same time as Lisa said, 'I am.'

Trix launched into a noisy condemnation of Lisa, how she was forcing her to buy and transport disgusting raw fish across the city, how the very thought made her feel like vomiting . . .

'Someone else can do the lunch run if you'd prefer,' Jack suggested mildly.

'No, it's OK,' Trix said sulkily – but speedily.

Then, to everyone's surprise, Jack said, 'Here, get me one too.'

Open-mouthed, Lisa watched him root around in his trouser pocket for money, his shoulder against his chin as his hand rummaged. For some reason she'd pegged Jack for a meat-'n'-two-veg man, the kind of person who'd say, 'If I can't pronounce it, I won't eat it.' But he had lived in the States . . .

Jack's hand emerged with a car-park ticket and

he looked at it sadly. 'That won't do.' He recommenced the search, this time locating a fiver that had seen better days and handing it to Trix.

'They mightn't take this,' Trix complained. 'What've you done to it? It looks like it's been on a tour-of-duty in some war.'

'That must be the one that got washed,' Jack said. 'I left it in my shirt pocket.'

Trix was disgusted. How could anyone forget that money had been left in a pocket? She knew exactly how much cash she had at any given time, to the nearest ten pence. It was too precious to leave in a shirt pocket.

Jack returned to his office, and Kelvin arrived, in for the first time that day. He'd been at a press do.

'Guess what?' he gasped.

'What?'

'It's all off with Jack and Mai.'

'No shit, Sherlock.' Trix's scorn was corrosive.

'No, I mean it. Really, really off. Not *Who's-Afraid-of-Virginia-Woolf* off. Proper over, no more fighting, haven't-seen-each-other-in-more-than-a-week off.'

'How do you know?'

'I, er, met Mai at the weekend. At the Globe. *Believe* me,' he nodded with heavy emphasis around the office, 'it's off.'

'God, you're pathetic,' Trix scoffed. 'Trying to pretend you slept with her.'

'No, I – Oh, OK, I am. But it's still all off.'

'Why?' Ashling asked.

Kelvin shrugged. 'It just ran its course.'

Lisa was amazed at the transformation this news effected on her. Things didn't seem so bleak all of a sudden. Jack was available and she *knew* she was in with a chance. He'd always liked the look of her, but something had changed on the day last week when she'd cried in his office. Her vulnerability and his tenderness had edged them closer.

And she realized something else. She liked him. Not the way she had when she'd first arrived in Dublin, in that hard, aggressive, I-always-get-what-I-want manner. Back then she'd liked his looks and his job and pursuing him had just been a project to take her mind off her misery.

When he came out to use the photocopier, she sidled up to him and said, her eyes dancing, 'I'd never have thought it.'

'Thought what?'

'You. A sushi socialist,' she teased, swinging her hair.

His pupils dilated, instantly turning his eyes almost black, and a look sparked between them.

Fifty minutes later, Trix clumped back into the office, dangling the handle of the sushi bag on her little finger, holding it as far away from her body as she could manage.

'What happened to you today?' Jack asked. 'Taken hostage in a bank raid? Kidnapped by aliens?'

'No,' Trix complained. 'I had to stop off at O'Neill's for a good puke. Here.' She just about threw the bag at Lisa, then put as much distance as possible between it and herself. 'Ugh,' she shuddered elaborately.

Lisa hoped that Jack would suggest that they ate the sushi behind closed doors in his office. She had ambitious visions of them feeding each other, sharing more than just raw fish. Instead, he pulled up a chair to Lisa's desk and she watched his big, sure hands remove chopsticks, napkins and plastic boxes from the depths of the paper bag. Placing a bento box before Lisa, he popped the crackling plastic lid, presenting the rows of pretty sushi with a flourish. 'Madam's lunch,' he said, high-spiritedly. 'Mind you don't puke!'

She couldn't exactly identify the emotions generated by his actions, they shot away when she tried to put names on them. But they were good ones: she felt safe, special, in a circle of belonging. Watched by the rest of the office, Lisa and Jack ate their sushi, like grown-ups.

Ashling, in particular, was appalled, but couldn't keep away. She kept sneaking looks at them, the way you would at a terrible road accident, then wincing as she saw something she wished she hadn't.

From what she could see, it wasn't just raw fish. There were tiny parcels of rice with the raw fish in the middle, accompanied by an elaborate ritual. A green paste was dissolved into what must be soy sauce, into which the underside of the sushi was dipped. Ashling watched fascinated as, with his chopsticks, Jack delicately lifted a pink see-through sliver and laid it expertly along the shiny rice-and-fish package.

The words were out before she could stop herself. 'What's that?'

'Pickled ginger.'

'Why?'

'Because it's nice.'

Ashling watched for a few more intrigued seconds, before blurting out, 'What's it like? All of it?'

'Delicious. You have the piquancy of the ginger, the heat of the wasabi – that's the green stuff – and the sweetness of the fish,' Jack explained. 'It's a taste like no other, but it's addictive.'

Curiosity stirred Ashling's soul. A part of her yearned to taste it, to try it, but, honestly, *raw fish* . . . I mean, *raw. Fish!*

'Try this.' Jack extended his chopsticks towards her, the sushi he'd prepared balanced between them.

An immediate body-swerve from Ashling and hot, high colour spilled across her face. 'Um, no. No thanks.'

'Why not?' His dark eyes were laughing at her. Again.

'Because it's raw.'

'But you eat smoked salmon?' Jack enquired, unable to hide his amusement.

'*I* don't,' Trix interrupted mulishly, from the safety of the far side of the office. 'I'd rather stick needles in my eyes.'

'Going for the last time. Sure you don't want to

try some?' Jack softly probed Ashling, his eyes refusing to relinquish hers. Stiffly, Ashling shook her head, and returned to her ham and cheese sandwich, feeling relieved, yet curiously deprived.

Lisa was pleased when Ashling pushed off. She was enormously enjoying this intimacy with Jack, not to mention impressed with the way he used his chopsticks. Expertly, stylishly, as though he was born to do it. You could take him to Nobu and he wouldn't embarrass you by asking for a knife and fork. She was quite good at wielding chopsticks herself. She should be. She'd spent many evenings in training in the privacy of her own home, with Oliver laughing at her. 'Who are you trying to impress, babes?'

Thinking of Oliver squeezed her with pain, but it would pass. Jack would help.

'I'll trade you my eel sushi for a California maki,' Lisa offered.

'The eel too gross for you?' Jack enquired.

Lisa began to protest, then admitted with a smile, 'Yeah.'

As predicted, Jack was happy to eat her piece of raw-eel sushi. Raw eel was going too far, even for a sophisticate like her. But men – they'd eat anything, the more revolting the better. Rabbit, emu, alligator, kangaroo . . .

'We must do this again,' Lisa suggested.

'Yeah.' Jack leant back in his chair and nodded thoughtfully at her. 'We must.'

CHAPTER 45

'You'll never believe it!' It was Thursday night and Marcus had just arrived at Ashling's, a video under his arm. His eyes were ablaze with excitement. 'I'm supporting Eddie Izzard on Saturday night.'

'H – how?'

'Steve Brennan was meant to be doing it, but he's gone into hospital with suspected CJD. What a result! It'll be a huge gig.'

Ashling's face darkened with disappointment. 'I can't go.'

'What?' Marcus said sharply.

'Remember, I told you, I've to visit my parents in Cork this weekend.'

'Cancel.'

'I couldn't,' she protested. 'I've put them off for so long that I just can't cancel again.'

They'd been so excited when she'd confirmed that she was finally coming that the thought of telling them otherwise made her break out in a sweat.

'Go next weekend.'

'I can't, I've to work. Another photo shoot.'

'It really matters to me that you're there,' Marcus said evenly. 'It's a big show and I'm trying out some new stuff, I need you there.'

Ashling twisted, trapped by conflicting emotions. 'I'm sorry. But I've psyched myself up to going to see them, and it's been ages . . . I've bought my train ticket,' she threw in.

As his expression became hurt and closed, her intestines snarled themselves into a tight knot. She hated herself for letting him down, but it was either disappoint him or her parents. She liked to oblige, and this was the worst situation she could find herself in, where whichever way she manoeuvred, she was going to displease someone.

'I'm really sorry,' she said, with sincerity. 'But things with my parents are messy enough. If I didn't go it would only damage relations even more.'

She waited for him to ask exactly in what way were things messy with her parents. She'd tell him, she decided. But he just looked at her with wounded eyes.

'I'm sorry,' she reiterated.

''s OK,' he said.

But it wasn't. Though they opened a bottle of wine and settled down to watch the video he'd brought, the mood was plastered flat. The wine behaved as though it was non-alcoholic and Ardal O'Hanlon had never been less funny. Guilt subdued Ashling, so that all her conversation start-ups drove straight into a wall. For the first time since she'd started seeing Marcus, she couldn't think of anything to say.

After a strained couple of hours brought them to ten o'clock, Marcus stood up and did a pretend stretch. 'I'd better get going.'

Terror plopped a rock into Ashling's stomach. He always stayed the night.

A whole new terrifying vista opened up: perhaps this wasn't just a fight, maybe it was The End. As she watched Marcus make his horrifyingly speedy progress to the door, she found herself frantically reconsidering her options. Maybe she could change her visit to Cork. What difference did a couple more weeks make? Her relationship with Marcus was way more important . . .

'Marcus, let me have a think.' Her voice wobbled with panic. 'I might be able to visit them in a few weeks' time instead.'

'Ah, it's all right.' He managed a ghost of a smile. 'I'll cope. I'll miss you, though.'

Relief only lasted an instant. It mightn't be all over, but he was still leaving her flat. 'We could see each other tomorrow night,' she suggested, anxious for the chance to mend things. 'I don't go until Saturday morning.'

'Ah, no.' He shrugged, 'Let's leave it until you get back.'

'OK,' she conceded reluctantly, afraid that if she pushed, it would simply cause a bigger rupture. 'I'll be back Sunday evening.'

'Give me a ring when you get in.'

'Sure. The train is supposed to get in at eight, that's if it doesn't break down, then there's often a queue for taxis, so I don't know what time I'll get home but as soon as I do I'll call you.' The desire to oblige made her voluble.

A quick kiss – not long or passionate enough to calm her down – and he was gone.

Like an alcoholic who goes back on the sauce as soon as they hit a rocky patch, the first thing Ashling did was reach for her tarot cards. She'd sorely neglected them lately and if it hadn't been for Joy's constant consultation in the wake of Half-man-half-badger's departure, they'd have been covered in dust. But the noncommittal selection gave her no comfort.

Edgy and agitated, Ashling was immersed in familiar resentment of her family. If only she'd had a normal one this wouldn't have happened. She thought for a moment about Marcus. She didn't blame him for being insecure. How he got up on a stage and did what he did was beyond her.

Rancour and regret generated insomnia: she had to talk to someone. But Joy wouldn't do, and not just because her current sole topic of conversation was the 'All half-men-half-badgers are bastards' one. It had to be either Clodagh or Phelim, because both of them knew all there was to know about Ashling's family. They'd understand and come through with the desired sympathy. But Phelim's Sydney answering-machine picked up, so, despite

513

the lateness of the hour, Ashling had no choice but to ring Clodagh. After apologizing for waking her, Ashling ranted her way through the sorry story and finished up by exclaiming, 'And I wouldn't mind, but I hate having to visit them.'

However, the required words of comfort didn't issue from Clodagh. Instead she said sleepily, 'I'll go and see Marcus if you like.'

'No, I didn't mean . . .'

'I can go with Ted.' Clodagh's tone woke up, as the idea became a possibility. 'Ted and I will go instead of you, and we'll provide moral support.'

This made Ashling feel much worse. She did *not* want Clodagh and Ted bonding. 'But what about Dylan?'

'Someone has to babysit.'

'I don't even want to visit my parents,' Ashling repeated, keen to get her quota of sympathy.

'But your mum's much better now. It'll be fine.'

There's no one in charge here, nine-year-old Ashling had realized, before the end of that strange, horrible summer. She took to standing on the corner at the bottom of the road on Friday evenings, looking into the distance for her dad's car, a churny sickness in her belly. While she waited, she muffled the terror that he would never come by playing games with herself. *If the next car is a red one, everything's going to be fine. If the second car's reg plate ends with an even number, it'll all be OK.*

Eventually the Monday morning came when she asked her father not to leave.

'I have to.' He was terse. 'If I lose my job, I don't know how we'll manage. Do your best to keep an eye on her.'

Ashling nodded gravely, and thought to herself, *He shouldn't have said that to me, I'm only a little girl.*

'. . . Of course, Ashling's very responsible. Only nine, but very grown-up for her age.'

There was muttered talk amongst the adults. People came to the house, conversed in low tones and fell silent whenever Ashling came near. '. . . his parents are elderly, they couldn't cope with three lively children . . .' Strange new words began to be mentioned. Depression. Nerves. Breakdown. Talk of her mother 'going in someplace'.

Eventually her mother did 'go in', and her dad had to take them with him, as he worked. They drove long distances, car-sick and bored, Janet and Owen sharing the back seat with a display vacuum-cleaner. Ashling sat in the front like an adult as they criss-crossed the country, stopping at small electrical shops in small towns. From the very first appointment she absorbed Mike's anxiety.

'Wish me luck,' he said, as he grabbed his folder of brochures. 'This fellow wouldn't spend Christmas. *And don't touch anything.*'

Through the car window, Ashling watched her

father greet his customer on the forecourt, and saw him mutate from irritable and worried to care-free and chatty. Suddenly he had all the time in the world for a chinwag. Never mind that he still had eight more calls to make that day and was way behind schedule due to their late start. Over he went to admire the man's new car. A lot of leaning back, inspecting from all angles and congratulatory shoulder-slapping. As he talked animatedly to his customer, full of smiles and good-natured slagging, Ashling was visited with an awareness that she was much too young for. *This is hard for him.*

As soon as Mike got back into the car, the airy smiles dissolved and he changed back to being abrupt.

'Did he order stuff, Dad?'

'No.' Mouth tight, reversing fast, getting the car back on the road, screeching to his next appointment.

Sometimes people ordered goods, but it was never as much as he'd hoped, and every time he climbed back into the car and drove away, he seemed further diminished.

By the end of the week, Janet and Owen were crying almost constantly, agitating to go home. And Ashling had managed to pick up an ear infection. Something which continued to recur at times of stress throughout her life.

After three weeks of incarceration, Monica re-emerged devoid of any obvious improvement.

The anti-depressants she'd been prescribed made her irritatingly dopey and slow, so she changed to another type, which didn't agree with her either.

And despite her on-going interaction with pharmaceuticals and Ashling's increasingly elaborate rituals, things never really got better. Monica's grief could be triggered by *anything*, from a natural disaster to a small random act of cruelty. A schoolboy being bullied out of his pocket-money could unleash the same torrent of weeping as an earthquake in Iran which killed thousands. But the days of silent, mostly bed-bound weeping were punctuated by fits of screaming, violent rage, directed at her husband, her children, and most of all herself.

'I don't want to feel this way!' she used to shriek. 'Would anyone want to feel like this? You're lucky, Ashling, you'll never suffer like me because you've no imagination.'

Ashling held on to this fact as though it were a shield. Lack of imagination was a great thing, it stopped you from turning into a nutter.

So volatile was Monica that Ashling spent large parts of her teenage years practically living at Clodagh's.

Occasionally, amid the torpor and hysteria, there were pockets of normality. Which weren't really normal at all. With each shirt that Monica ironed perfectly, with every meal that she served up on the dot of six, Ashling's nerves stretched that little bit more, waiting for the time when it would all slip again. And when it came it was nearly a relief.

At seventeen, Ashling left home and moved into a flat. Three years later, Mike got a job over a hundred miles away in Cork, and their subsequent move meant Ashling rarely saw her parents. During the last seven years Monica had stabilized: the depression and rage departed as unexpectedly and as unheralded as they had arrived. Her doctor said it was linked to the end of her menopause.

'She's not so bad now.' Clodagh's voice brought her back to the present.

'I know.' Ashling exhaled wearily. 'But I still don't really want to be near her. That's an awful thing to say, I know. I love her, but I find it hard to see her.'

CHAPTER 46

Ashling was due to arrive in Cork at lunch-time on Saturday, and she was getting the five o'clock train home on Sunday. So the 'weekend' was really only twenty-eight hours long. And she'd be asleep for eight of those hours. Which only left twenty hours to talk to her parents. No bother to her.

Twenty hours! Clutched by panic she wondered if she had enough cigarettes. And magazines? And her mobile? She must have been insane to say she'd come.

As she watched the countryside rickety-rack past, she prayed that the train would oblige and break down. But no. Of course not. That only happened if you were in a desperate hurry. *Then* the train would spend several unexplained half-hours loitering in sidings. *Then* you'd all have to change to a different train, *then* you'd all have to get off the new train and on to a waiting, freezing bus, and the original three-hour journey would end up taking eight hours.

Instead Ashling's train arrived in Cork a galling ten minutes early. Naturally her parents were already there, waiting, looking determinedly normal. Her mother could have passed for any Irish mother of a certain age: the bad perm, the nervous, welcome-home smile, the acrylic cardigan draped about her shoulders.

'You're a sight for sore eyes.' Monica was about to burst into proud tears.

'You too.' Ashling couldn't help feeling guilty.

Then came the hug – Monica's uncertain cross between ladylike cheek-to-cheeking and full-on body-slamming ended up being more like a scuffle.

'Hi, Dad.'

'Er, welcome, welcome, welcome!' Mike looked uncomfortable – would he too be required to indulge in affection? Luckily he was able to grab Ashling's bag and busy all available arms with that.

The drive to her parents' house, the discussion about what Ashling had eaten on the train, and the debate over whether she'd have a cup of tea and a sandwich or just a cup of tea, took up a good forty minutes.

'Just a cup of tea is fine.'

'I've Penguins,' Monica tempted. 'And butterfly buns. I made them myself.'

'No, I . . . oh . . .' The talk of home-made butterfly buns poleaxed Ashling. Monica opened a biscuit tin, displaying small misshapen buns, each with two sponge 'wings' arranged in a blob of cream on top. The cream was sprinkled with hundreds and thousands and as Ashling swallowed a bite – a wing, actually – she discovered she was also swallowing a lump in her throat.

'I've to go into town,' Mike announced.

'I'll come with you.' Ashling catapulted up.

'Oh, will you?' Monica looked disappointed. 'Well, make sure you're back in time for your dinner.'

'What are we having?'

'Chops.'

Chops! Ashling almost sniggered – she hadn't realized that such a foodstuff still existed.

'Why are we going into town?' she asked her father as they backed out on to the road.

'To buy an electric blanket.'

'In July?'

'It'll be winter soon enough.'

'Nothing like being prepared.'

They exchanged a smile, then Mike had to go and ruin it by saying, 'We don't see you much, Ashling.'

Oh, for fuck's sake.

'Your mother's delighted to see you.'

Some response was called for, so Ashling settled on, 'How, um, is she?'

'Marvellous. You should come and see us more, she's back to being the woman I married.'

Another silence, then Ashling heard herself ask a question that she had no memory of ever asking before. 'What was it all about, that terrible time? What made it happen?'

Mike took his eyes off the road to look at her, his expression a grisly mix of defensiveness and determined innocence – he had *not* been a bad father. 'Nothing happened.' His joviality seemed unexpectedly pitiful. 'Depression is a sickness, you know all this.'

As children, they'd had it explained to them that it wasn't their fault that their mother was a basket case. Naturally, none of them had believed it.

'Yes, but how do you get depression?' She struggled for understanding.

'Sometimes it's triggered by a loss or a – what d'you call them things? – trauma,' he muttered, the car full of his ghastly discomfort. 'But it doesn't have to be,' he continued. 'They say it can be hereditary.'

That cheery thought knocked all talk out of Ashling. She rummaged for her mobile phone.

'Who are you ringing?'

'No one.'

He watched Ashling continue to press buttons on her mobile phone. Affronted, he demanded, 'Do you think I'm blind?'

'I'm not ringing anyone, I'm checking my messages.'

Marcus hadn't rung her since he'd departed her flat on Thursday night. In the two months that they'd been going out – not that she was counting – they'd slipped into a routine of ringing each other every day. She felt his absence of contact keenly. Holding her breath, she yearned for a message from him but, once again, there was none. Disappointed, she snapped her phone away.

That evening, after her time-warp dinner – chops, mash and peas from a can – she decided to ring him. She had a good excuse: wishing him luck with the Eddie Izzard gig. But she got his answering machine – again. She had a horrible vision of him standing in his flat, listening to her message but refusing to pick up. Unable to stop herself, she tried his mobile: it went straight to message service. *Mercury is in retrograde*, she told herself. Then she reluctantly admitted, *or maybe it's just that my boyfriend's pissed off with me.*

Plainly, he was hurt by her visiting her parents, but just how bad was the damage? For a moment she considered the possibility that it was irreparable, and the accompanying squeeze of terror left her weak. She really, really, *really* liked Marcus. He was the closest to Mr Right she'd met in a long time. She was dying for Sunday evening, because he'd *asked* her to call him then. But what if he still didn't answer the phone . . . ? Christ!

'We usually watch a video on a Saturday night,' her mother informed her.

From Here to Eternity – how appropriate, Ashling thought, as the evening stretched like chewing gum. Chilled by exclusion, she ached to be in Dublin, with her boyfriend. All the while Burt Lancaster romped with Deborah Kerr, Ashling was wondering how Marcus was getting on, and if Clodagh and Ted had gone to the gig. It shamed her that she hoped they hadn't, that it would make her feel even more left out.

Her parents tried very, very hard. Producing a bag of pick'n'mix that had been bought specially for her, tentatively offering her a 'drink' while they drank tea, and, when she went to bed at a shamefully early ten-twenty, her mother insisting on filling a hot-water bottle for her.

'It's July, I'll roast!'

'Ah, but the nights can be cold. And it'll be August in two days' time, officially Autumn.'

'Oh no, nearly August already.' Ashling squeezed her eyes shut in breath-shortening fear. *Colleen* was due to be launched on the last day of August and there was still a titanic quantity of work to be done – on the bloody launch party as well as the magazine. While it was still July, she'd been able to reassure herself that they had plenty of time. August felt way, way, *way* too close for comfort.

Grasping a dog-eared Agatha Christie from the shelf, she read for fifteen minutes, then switched off the peach-shaded lamp. She slept as well as could be expected beneath a peach duvet and in the morning the first thing she did was switch on her mobile, praying there would be a message from Marcus. There wasn't – this was her darkest hour. Which wasn't helped by the peach and white stripy wallpaper moving in on her. Reaching for her cigarettes, she upended a little bowl of pot-pourri. Peach flavoured, wouldn't you know it.

She couldn't ring him *again*. He'd think she was

desperate. Of course, she *was* desperate, but she didn't want him to think it. Instead she rang Clodagh, half-looking for information, but half-hoping that Clodagh wouldn't be in the position to offer any.

'Did you go to see Marcus?' She clenched her spare fist and willed her to say no.

'Yes –'

'You went with Ted?'

'Sure did.' This plunged Ashling further into dread. She didn't *really* think there was any chance that Clodagh would touch Ted with a bargepole, it was just . . .

Clodagh chattered on. 'We had a great time and Marcus was fantastic. He did this *hilarious* thing about women's clothes. About the difference between a blouse, a top, a vest, a T-shir–'

'He *what*?' Never mind Ted and Clodagh! Ashling was suddenly concerned with herself.

'He even knew what a shell-top was,' Clodagh exclaimed.

'I bet he did.' Ashling knew she should be flattered, but instead she felt used. Marcus hadn't even told her he was thinking of including their conversation in his act.

'It beats me how he thinks of these things,' Clodagh frothed.

That's because he doesn't.

'And afterwards?' Ashling asked jealously, not sure if she could take any more unwelcome news. 'You went home?'

'Not at all, we went backstage, met Eddie Izzard, got jarred. Fantastic!'

The farewell to her parents, draining at the best of times, was worse than usual.

'Do you have a boyfriend at all?' Mike asked jovially, unintentionally rubbing salt into Ashling's very raw wound. 'Bring him the next time too.'

Oh, don't.

Every carriage was jam-packed and she was weary and Sunday-evening depressed when, three hours later, the train pulled into Dublin. She pushed towards the taxi-rank, hoping the queues wouldn't be too insane, when through the crowds milling about on the concourse she saw someone she knew . . .

'Marcus!' Her skin sparked with joy at the sight of him standing near the exit, wearing a sheepish smile. 'What are you doing here?!'

'Collecting my girlfriend. Often there's a long queue for the taxis, I'm told.'

A delighted laugh bubbled from her. Suddenly she was wildly happy.

He took her bag in one hand and slung his other arm around her. 'Hey, I'm sorry about . . .'

'It's OK! I'm sorry too.'

Our first argument, she thought dreamily, as he steered her to his car. Our first proper row. Now we really *are* a couple.

CHAPTER 47

The pile of discarded clothes on Clodagh's bed grew higher. The tight black dress? Too sexy. The palazzo pants and tunic? Too glam. The see-through dress? Too see-through. What about the white pants? But he'd seen them already. The combats and trainers? No, she just felt silly in them. Of all the fashionable clothes she'd bought over the past two months, they'd been her biggest mistake so far.

For a moment the cloud of clothing anxiety cleared and she was inflicted with a sudden, unwelcome overview. *What am I doing?*

Nothing, she thought defensively. She was doing nothing. She was meeting someone for a cup of coffee. A friend. A friend who happened to be a man. What was the problem? This wasn't some Muslim country where she'd be stoned for being seen in public with a man who wasn't her husband or brother. Anyway, he wasn't even her type. She was just having fun. Harmless fun.

But she shook back her swishy hair, feeling exhilarated, buzzy, tingly.

Black trousers and a tight candy-pink T-shirt

were what she eventually decided on. She looked into the mirror and she saw herself through his eyes. His regard for her was endearingly obvious and she felt beautiful and powerful.

Coffee, she reminded herself firmly, as she swung out into the street. That's all. Where's the harm in that? And she pushed away the guilt and anticipation that swirled nauseously in her belly.

Ashling raced into the pub. She was late. Again.

'Marcus,' she gasped. 'I'm so sorry. Bitch-face Lisa decided at the last minute to make me input my horse-riding feature. She wants to get a "feel" for the November issue.' She rolled her eyes contemptuously and luckily Marcus joined in. So he couldn't have been too pissed off at being left sitting in the Thomas Reid for nearly half an hour.

'I'll just have a quick quadruple vodka-and-tonic, then we'll go for a bite, OK? Are you ready for another pint?'

Marcus got to his feet. 'Sit down, the hardest-working woman in magazines, I'll get the drinks. Do you really want a quadruple?'

Ashling slumped gratefully into a chair. 'Thanks. A double will do.'

When Marcus returned with the drink, he swung back into his seat and said, 'Listen, I just wanted to remind you that I'm going to Edinburgh on the sixteenth. For the Festival.'

'Sixteenth of *August*?' Ashling was horrified. She had some vague memory of him having mentioned it ages ago. 'But that's only two weeks away . . . Look,' she was craven and frantic, 'I'm terribly sorry, Marcus, but I'm not going to be able to go with you. Really, you wouldn't believe what work is like. We're flat out and there's so much work to be done on the launch party *alone*, never mind the magazine . . .'

Marcus assumed a wounded expression.

'I could try to swing a weekend,' Ashling offered breathlessly. 'Even though Lisa says we'll be working every weekend, if I ask nicely she might say . . .'

'Don't bother.'

She hated when he got like this. He was lovely most of the time, but whenever he felt insecure or unsupported he became cold and aggressive, and she couldn't bear confrontation.

'I'll try,' she said desperately. 'Really, I will.'

'Don't bother.'

'Look,' her voice quavered, 'after the end of August, work will totally quieten down for me. Maybe we could even go away together, grab a late-availability week in Greece or something.

'Cheer up,' she softly urged his stony face. Still no reaction. 'Ah, come on, funny-man,' she cajoled. 'One of Ireland's top comedians, tell us a joke.'

Marcus almost catapulted from his seat. 'Tell you a joke!' he demanded, in shockingly unexpected rage. 'It's my fucking night off. I don't ask you to write a magazine article about faking orgasms when *you're* out for the night, do I?'

Ashling froze.

Then Marcus leant his forehead on his hand. 'Hey, I'm sorry,' he said wearily. 'I'm really sorry.'

'I see,' Lisa said, with icy politeness. 'Yes, I'll call back.' Then she slammed down the phone and screamed, 'Fuckers, fuckers, fuckers!'

Bernard tutted, 'Language,' but no one else even blinked.

'Ronan Keating's manager,' Lisa yelled to an uninterested office, 'is in a fucking meeting. For the quazillionth time. Nearly three weeks to D-Day and we still have no celebrity letter.'

In despair she lay across her phone, then noticed Jack watching her. He raised his eyebrows with are-you-OK? concern. He did that a lot. Ever since she'd cried in his office, a solid, silent support wafted from him. A kind of our-little-secret intimacy that no one else received.

But exactly what good were raised eyebrows to her? she thought irritably. It was other parts of his body she'd like raised for her, thanks very much. Fair enough, he was just out of a relationship and perhaps he needed time to recover. But he'd had, oooh, at least *two weeks*, how much longer did he need?

She smiled sadly to herself. She hadn't been in great shape either, after the Oliver episode. She'd wanted to run back to London, get into bed with him and never leave again. He still hadn't rung her, he clearly wasn't going to, but life must go on . . .

'The pressure getting to you?' Jack came and sat on her desk.

She was mortally offended. 'No, just, you know,' she sighed. 'Bastard celebrities.'

'You never give up.' His admiration could have been photographed. 'D'you need some time out? How about we have sushi for lunch? On me.'

'I wish.' The words were out before she could stop them, prompted by the vision of eating sushi from his naked body.

'Um, excuse me?' His laugh was pleasantly dirty.

'Nothing.' She wall-eyed him, but couldn't help a knowing smirk. For a long moment they locked eyes, then simultaneously the flirty tension dissolved into laughter.

'You mean you're going to take me out?' she asked.

'Aw, no, sorry, I can't spare the time. But how about a take-away, like the last time?'

'Get someone else to do your dirty work,' Trix snapped.

'I'll go.' Jack surprised everyone. 'Anyone else want some? How about you, Ashling?'

'No, thanks,' Ashling said huffily, suspecting she was being patronized.

'Sure?'

'Quite.'

'Not even if I get you some of the less scary pieces, and take you through it all?'

'No.'

'Right, I'm off,' Jack announced. 'And take it easy,'

he advised Lisa. 'Everything's coming together nicely.'

Though she told everyone that their work was crap and that the magazine looked like 'a piece of shit', Lisa couldn't deny that progress was being made. The books, film, music, video and net pages were in place. As were the horoscopes, Trix's ordinary-girl article, the sexy-hotel-bedrooms piece, Ashling's salsa spread, a gorgeous food page from Jasper Ffrench, a profile of an Irish actress who'd starred in a controversial erotic play, a warts-and-all 'My Day' from the novelist, and Marcus's 'It's a Man's World' article, which everyone *loved*. Plus, of course, *that* fashion spread.

Eight pages at the front of the mag were devoted to showcasing four achingly hip, up-and-coming Irish stars – a handbag designer, a DJ, a personal trainer and an articulate, sexy eco-warrior who was king of the soundbite. The 'What's Hot and What's Not' list was nearly ready. Lisa knocked most of it up in five minutes and gave it to Ashling to finish. According to Lisa's list, hillwalking was 'Hot' and Hilfiger was 'Not'.

'*Is* hillwalking hot?' Ashling enquired, in surprise.

Lisa shrugged. 'Haven't a clue. But it goes nicely with Hilfiger.'

As well as the content, the magazine *looked* great. The colours, images and typesetting were slightly different to those of other women's magazines and *Colleen* looked somehow edgier and funkier.

Lisa had pushed Gerry to the outer limits of his patience before she got a look she was happy with.

'Where do you sail?' Lisa asked, as Jack arrayed sushi on her desk.

'Dun Laoghaire, where the boats come in.'

'Dun Laoghaire,' she mused meaningfully. 'I've never been there.'

'You'd like it.'

'I must get out there sometime.'

'You must.'

Oh, for crying out loud! How heavily did a girl have to hint around here?

Perhaps he was wary of her combination of dynamism and good-looks, she acknowledged. It wouldn't have been the first time. And there was the added complication of them working together. And of her being married. And of him being on the rebound . . .

OK! She realized she had no choice but to open her mouth and say, 'You could take me the next time you're going.'

'Would you like to?' His eagerness was so – well – *eager*, that Lisa knew instantly that she'd been right to take control. 'How about Friday evening?' he offered. 'We could walk the pier and I'll show you the boats. It's good stuff after being stuck in the office all day.'

Hmmmm. Walk the pier. *Walk* the pier. She wasn't really a 'walks' kind of woman. 'I'd love to!'

CHAPTER 48

Clodagh dug her heels into his buttocks, banging him ever deeper into her. Every time he stroked himself up into her, a word was dragged in a hoarse whisper from her chest.

'God!'

He slammed into her again.

'Harder!'

Another slam.

The bedhead slapped rhythmically against the wall and her hair was tangled and soaked with sweat. She clutched him ever closer, as the ripples of pleasure built and built. Into the vortex she spiralled. With each pulsation, she thought that that must be it, until another, even more beautiful, throbbed from her. She quivered on the top note, and she felt it in her fingertips, her hair follicles, the soles of her feet.

'God,' she gasped.

He must have come too because, panting and drenched, he lay upon her, his weight pinning her to the bed. They lay still, gasping and spent, until she felt their sweat begin to cool, then she buckled beneath him and roughly pushed him off.

'Get dressed,' she ordered. 'Hurry, I've to collect Molly from playgroup.'

This was their third time together and she was always abrupt – cold, almost – when the sex was over.

'Do you mind if I have a shower?'

'Be quick about it,' she answered curtly.

When he emerged from the bathroom she was dressed and refusing to meet his eye. Then she froze, sniffed the air and exclaimed in disbelief, 'Is that Dylan's aftershave I smell?'

'I suppose,' he mumbled, furious at the mistake.

'Isn't it enough that you're fucking his wife in his bed? Have you any respect?'

'Sorry.'

In contrite silence, he put on the clothes that she'd torn from his body only an hour previously. 'When can I see you again?' He hated himself for asking, but he had no choice. He was besotted.

'I'll ring you.'

'I can take time off work whenever you want.'

'I've got neighbours.' She was tight-lipped. 'They're bound to notice.'

'Well, you can come to my place.'

'I don't think so.'

A silence followed.

'You act like you hate me,' he accused.

'I'm married.' She raised her voice, 'I have children. You're ruining everything.'

At the front-door, as he bent to kiss her, she said angrily, 'For God's sake, someone might see.'

'Sorry,' he muttered.

But as he turned away, she grabbed his shirt front and pulled him back to her. They kissed hungrily, desperately. When they broke apart, his hand was inside her shirt, kneading a breast. Her nipples were as swollen and firm as cherries and he was once more erect.

'Hurry,' she urged, fumbling with his fly, pulling him out and holding him silky and erect in her fist. She sank to the hall floor, clawing down her jeans, pulling him on top of her. 'Quick, we haven't much time.'

She flexed her buttocks, rising to meet him, desperate for him. He entered her and thrust with short, intense stabs. Instantly the ripples began to flood through her, rising in intensity, spreading outwards and inwards, peaking into almost unbearable pleasure.

After he came, he wept into her golden hair.

CHAPTER 49

On Friday evening, dressed in trainers, silk cargo pants and her Prada sleeveless viscose top, Lisa loitered by her front-door. She was going on a date with Jack, and an unfamiliar warmth twinkled within her.

A car pulled up, the man within leant over and opened the door for her and, feeling mildly like a prostitute being picked up by a kerb-crawler, Lisa got in. Closing her ears to the singsong shouts of 'Woooooooooh!' and 'Seck-*zee*!' and 'Lee-sa's got a boyfriend!' from Francine and all the other kids, she and Jack drove away.

'Hey, you turned up,' Jack grinned.

'Looks that way.' She stared out the window, biting back a smirk. He'd been nervous. Well, perhaps that made two of them.

During the drive, the sky, which had been peachy-clear in town, transformed itself to heavy, lowering grey-blue. When they got out of the car at Dun Laoghaire pier Jack felt the air doubtfully. 'It might rain. Do you want to skip the walk?'

But Lisa was filled with skittish optimism. It wouldn't dare rain. 'No, let's go.' And off they set.

The too-bright rays of the sun filtering through the swollen clouds had the effect of making everything look almost super-real. Stray clumps of grass were lit to a green so bright it was nearly hallucinogenic. The grey stone of the pier bounced a purple colour back at her. Any fool could tell it was about to piss down, but Lisa was determined that it wouldn't.

So this was walking, she thought, as they strode along. Well, it wasn't so bad. The air smelt funny, though.

'Fresh.' Jack cleared the matter up for her. 'See that there,' he pointed proudly to a boat. 'That's mine.'

'*That* one?' All excited, Lisa gestured at a sleek, shiny-white gin palace.

'No, that one.'

'Oh.' It was only then that Lisa noticed the tatty craft beside it. She'd thought it was a piece of driftwood. 'Fabulous!' she managed. Well, he liked it, why not pretend? *Blimey*, she thought, *I* must *like him.*

Before they were halfway down the pier, the rain started with delicate patters. Lisa had dressed for many eventualities, but rain wasn't one of them. Goose-pimples puckered her bare arms.

'Here, put this on.' Jack was shrugging off his hip-length leather jacket.

'I couldn't.' Of course she could – and would – but it couldn't hurt to be fluffy-coy.

'You can.' Already he was arranging the crackly

jacket on her shoulders, the heat from his body wrapping itself around her. She slipped her arms into the still-warm sleeves, the cuffs covering her hands, the shoulders swamping her. The jacket was miles too big and it felt good.

'We'd better go back,' he said, and as the rain began to pelt down they started running. It seemed the most natural thing in the world to hold hands. 'You'll never come here with me again,' he gasped as they sprinted.

'Too right.' She flashed him a grin, savouring the dry warmth of his palm and his big-man's fingers laced into hers.

When they reached the car, Jack was soaked. His hair was shiny-black and plastered to his skull and his drenched shirt was semi-transparent and stuck to him, tantalizingly showing a covering of chest-hair. She wasn't much drier.

'Christ!' With a screech of outraged laughter he surveyed himself.

Spilling over with good humour, Lisa panted, 'Open the car fast!'

She ran round to the passenger side, expecting him to wrench the key into the lock, but then she glanced up at him . . .

Afterwards, when she thought about it, she couldn't be sure which one of them had made the first move. Did he? Or did she? All she knew was they were suddenly swinging into each other and she found herself up against the hardness of his front, his wet thighs against hers. His face was spattered with drops and his hair had gone into little points which were dripping into his dark eyes. And he lowered his mouth to hers.

Lisa was aware of many things: the salty smell of a rain-soaked sea, the cool drops on her face, the warmth of his mouth and the fish-leap in her knickers. Pretty sexy stuff. She felt like something from a Calvin Klein ad.

The kiss wasn't a lengthy one, coming to an end before it really got going. Quality rather than quantity. Gently unpeeling his lips from her yielding ones, Jack guided her to the car and whispered, 'In you get.'

They drove back into town and went to a café-bar where she dried her hair under the hand-drier. Then she fixed her make-up and went back out to the bar, smiling widely. Over a glass of wine and a pint, they talked in low, comfortable tones, mostly gossipy chat about the people at work.

'Tell me, is Marcus Valentine going out with our very own Ashling?' Jack asked.

'Mmmm. And what do you reckon to Kelvin and Trix?'

'Don't tell me they're an item!' Jack looked quite shaken at the thought. 'I thought she was going out with a – what does she call him? – a fish-mongrel?'

'She is, but I just have a feeling she and Kelvin might end up together.'

'But don't they kind of hate each other? – Oh, I get it.' Jack nodded. 'One of those.'

'You sound as if you don't approve.' Lisa was extremely curious.

Jack was embarrassed. 'Whatever floats your boat. But,' he was alluding to his public rows with Mai and now he was *really* embarrassed, 'I'm not actually keen on routine shouting matches with a partner. Though I know that's probably hard to believe.'

'So why did you and Mai . . . ?'

Jack shifted. 'Dunno, really. Habit, I reckon. It was fun at the start and then I think we didn't know any other way of truly relating. Anyway!' He didn't want to dissect it any further because he still felt a type of loyalty to Mai, so he turned to Lisa with a smile. 'Another drink?'

'No, I don't think so —'

But just as she was about to lay her hand meaningfully on his thigh and say, 'Will you come back for coffee?' Jack said, 'Right then, I'll drop you home.' And she knew that that was all he meant. But never mind, she thought, ever the optimist, he liked her. He *must* like her: he'd kissed her. He couldn't have been nicer. And she closed her mind to the little voice that replied. *He could have been nicer, he could have shagged you.*

Dreamily, Clodagh floated around the kitchen, thinking about the sex earlier that day. It had been beyond belief, the best yet . . .

As she put the sugar in the microwave and the milk in the washing machine, Dylan watched her.

And wondered. Horrible thoughts. Unspeakable thoughts.

'Don't want my dinner.' Craig threw down his spoon with a violent clatter. 'I want SWEETS.'

'Sweets,' Clodagh hummed, foraging in the cupboard and producing a bag of Maltesers. 'Sweets it is.'

She seemed to be moving to music that only she could hear.

'I want sweets too,' Molly snarled.

'I want sweets too,' Clodagh mewed tunefully to herself, locating another packet.

Dylan watched, aghast.

With a playful flourish, she ripped open Molly's bag of sweets and extracted one between her thumb and finger. 'For you?' she sparkled at Molly. 'No, for me.' Ignoring Molly's tantrummy objections, she held the Malteser between her pursed lips, sucking slightly at it, then inhaled it into her mouth where she rolled it around in a way that manifestly gave her enormous pleasure.

'Clodagh?' Dylan's voice cracked.

'Hmmm?'

'Clodagh?'

Instantly she snapped to attention and disposed of the Malteser with a savage crunch. 'What?'

'Are you OK?'

'Fine.'

'You just seem a little bit distracted.'

'Am I?'

'What are you thinking?' he heard himself ask.

Quick as a flash, she replied, 'I was thinking how much I love you.'

'Really?' Dylan asked warily. He was torn. He suspected he shouldn't really believe her, but he so badly wanted to . . .

'Yes, I really, really love you.' She forced herself to put her arms around him.

'Honestly?' He'd managed to make eye-contact with her.

She met his gaze calmly. 'Honestly.'

CHAPTER 50

August advanced and the pressure built. There were still gaps in the first issue, and any attempts to fill them were thwarted. An interview with Ben Affleck had to be cancelled after he contracted food-poisoning, a review of a shoe-shop had to be killed after the shop suddenly closed down, a piece about sexually active nuns was deemed to be too risky, legally.

One particular day was so frustratingly obstacle-ridden that both Ashling and Mercedes cried. Even Trix had a suspicious brightness about her eyes. (Then she stormed from the office into a nearby shop, where she stole a pair of earrings and returned in much better form.)

What added to everyone's grief was that they didn't have the luxury of giving the first issue their undivided time and attention. They were also working on October and November. Then, in the midst of all the mayhem, Lisa called an editorial meeting for the December issue.

But she wasn't – despite the bitter resistance – being a 'slave-driving bitch'. December films were previewed in August. If the star of the film was

544

in town, the interview had to be conducted there and then, and not in a couple of weeks when *Colleen's* workload had lessened and the star had long departed for another country.

Then, of course, there was the launch party, which Lisa obsessed about. 'It's got to make a statement, cause a splash. I want people to *cry* if they haven't been invited. I want a spectacular guest-list, gorgeous gifts, genius drinks and great food. Let's see,' she drummed her fingers on the desk, 'what food shall we do?'

'How about sushi?' Trix suggested, sarcastically.

'Perfect.' Lisa exhaled, her eyes glittery. 'Of course, what else?'

Ashling was charged with the task of assembling a list of a thousand of Ireland's movers and shakers.

'I'm not sure Ireland *has* a thousand movers and shakers,' Ashling said doubtfully. 'And you want to give presents to all of them. Where are we going to get the budget?'

'We get someone to sponsor it, probably a cosmetic house,' Lisa snapped.

Lisa was even more bad-tempered than usual. Three days after the mini-snog from Jack, he'd gone to New Orleans for the worldwide Randolph Communications conference. For ten days! He'd apologized for abandoning them at such a busy time, but Lisa was more pissed off that his absence would disrupt the momentum of their romance.

'Have a look at the party invite.' Lisa tossed Ashling and Mercedes a plain silver card.

'Er, lovely,' Ashling said.

'Words would be nice,' Mercedes sneered.

Lisa sighed irritably. 'They're on it.'

'Well, how about having them visible to the naked eye?'

Ashling and Mercedes bent and turned the card until the light caught it in a particular way, then the words were revealed – also silver, tiny and crammed into a corner.

'That'll intrigue them,' Lisa said grimly.

Ashling was worried. It all seemed a bit clever. If it had arrived through her letter-box she'd have thrown it in the bin.

Lisa flew to London for the day to discuss party drinks with a 'mixologist'.

'What's a mixologist?' Ashling asked.

'A barman,' Mercedes said drily. 'Something there's hardly a shortage of in this country.'

Mercedes suspected she'd overheard Lisa making an appointment to have a Botox injection done while she was in London, and that that was her real reason for going there. Sure enough, when Lisa returned the following day, there was an armour-plated rigidity to her forehead. But she also had an elaborate list of too-cool-for-school drinks. The guests were to be greeted with a champagne cocktail, then served lemon martinis, followed by cosmopolitans, manhattans, go-go rums and, finally, vodka espressos.

'Oh yeah, and I've also sorted the gifts,' Lisa accused. Was she the only one who did any work around here? 'As each guest leaves, we'll present them with a bottle of wee.'

'A bottle of *what*?' Ashling was weary and perplexed – if this was Lisa's idea of a joke, it was an extremely poor one.

'Wee. A bottle of wee.'

'You're going to give a thousand of Ireland's movers and shakers a bottle of wee?' She didn't have the energy to laugh. 'That's an awful lot of wee. Where are you going to get it? Do we all have to make a contribution?'

Open-mouthed, Lisa surveyed Ashling. 'From Lancôme, of course.'

Immediately Ashling's head flashed with an image of hundreds of Lancôme employees urinating into bottles, especially for Lisa. 'That's very decent of them.' What was Lisa *on* about?

'It's only the fifty-ml bottle.' Lisa persisted with her parallel-universe chat. 'But it looks big enough, no?' She held up a little bottle of Oui.

'Oh,' Ashling breathed in enlightenment. 'You mean *Oui*!'

'Yeah, wee. Why, what did you think I said?'

I need a break, Ashling realized.

She rang Marcus, who greeted her with, 'Hello, stranger.'

'Um, yeh, hahaha. Meet me for lunch?'

'Can you spare the time? I'm honoured.'

'Half-twelve at Neary's.' She couldn't be doing with this.

★   ★   ★

'C'mere till I tell you something hilarious.' Ashling was all set to launch into her wee/Oui story, when Marcus retorted, 'Look, I'm the funny one, right?'

Astonished, Ashling gaped at him. 'What is *wrong* with you?'

'Nothing.' Marcus was suddenly humble. 'God, I'm sorry.'

'It's because I'm working so hard, isn't it?' Ashling grasped the nettle. They'd been having a few too many little spats of late, generated by his feeling ignored. 'Marcus, if it's any consolation, you're the only person I see. I haven't seen Clodagh, Ted, Joy or anyone else and I haven't been to salsa in ages. But in two weeks this magazine will be launched and life will go back to normal.'

'Right,' he said quietly.

'Come over tonight,' she urged. 'Please. You're going to Edinburgh in a few days and I won't see you for a week. I promise not to fall asleep.'

He conceded a half-smile. 'You have to sleep at some stage.'

'I'll stay awake long enough for, um – I'll stay awake long enough,' she promised, with innuendo.

She *had* been neglecting him. She couldn't actually remember the last time they'd made love. Probably only a week or so ago, but that was too long. She couldn't help it though: she was so stressed, and knackered. It was actually a relief that he was going away.

'If you're too tired I don't want to put you under pressure.' His eyes were concerned.

'I'm not too tired.' She could manage one night, couldn't she?

Roll on August the thirty-first. After that, everything would be back to normal.

Red-eyed and agitated, Clodagh surveyed the kitchen table. There was nothing left to iron. She'd done everything: Dylan's T-shirts, his shirts, his underpants, even his socks.

The guilt, the guilt, the horrible corrosive guilt. She could hardly bear herself, she wanted to tear her skin off with self-hatred.

She was going to make it up to all of them. She was going to be the most devoted wife and mother there ever was. Craig and Molly were going to eat everything on their plates. She moaned softly – what kind of mother had she become? Giving them biscuits on tap, letting them stay up as late as they wanted. Well, no more. She was going to be so strict. Borderline dangerous, in fact. And poor Dylan. Poor devoted, hardworking Dylan, he didn't deserve this. The betrayal, the terrible cruelty, the cold withdrawal of her love: she hadn't been able to let him touch her since she'd started this affair.

Affair. Her breath spasmed in her chest – she was *having an affair*. She swayed with vertigo at its enormity. What if she got caught? What if Dylan found out? Her heart nearly seized up at the thought. She was going to stop this now. Right now.

She hated herself, she hated what she was doing,

and if she stopped before anyone found out, she could make everything all right, almost as if it had never happened. Fired by resolve, she picked up the phone. 'It's me.'

'Hi, me.'

'I want this to stop.'

He sighed. 'Again?'

'I mean it, I'm not going to see you any more. Don't ring me, don't call to the house. I love my children, I love my husband.'

After a crackly pause, he said, 'OK.'

'OK?'

'OK. I understand. Goodbye.'

'Goodbye?'

'What else is there to say?'

She replaced the phone, unexpectedly cheated. Where was the warm reward for having done the right thing? Instead she felt dissatisfied and empty – and stung. He hadn't put up much of a fight. And he was supposed to be crazy about her. Bastard.

Earlier, she'd entertained a daft notion that she was going to darn the holes in Dylan's socks in another desperate attempt to demonstrate her love for him. But as she desultorily returned to the kitchen, all her housewifely resolve melted. Fuck it, she thought listlessly, Dylan could buy new socks.

Almost against her will she ran back to the hall, snatched the phone and pressed the redial button.

'Hello,' he said.

'Get over here now.' Her voice was tearful and angry. 'The kids are out, we have until four o'clock.'

'I'm on my way.'

It was eight-thirty before Ashling left the office. Nauseous with exhaustion, she couldn't face the ten-minute walk home, so she got a taxi. Slumping back, she checked the messages on her mobile. Only one. From Marcus. He wouldn't be coming over tonight, something about having to go to a gig. Thank God, she exhaled. Now she could ring Clodagh, then go straight to bed. And in two weeks' time, when all this was over, she'd make it up to Marcus . . .

As she got out of the taxi she met Boo, who was sporting a black eye.

'What happened to you!'

'Saturday night's all right for fighting,' he quipped. 'A few nights ago. Bloke, drunk, looking for aggro. Oh, the joys of life on the streets!'

'That's awful!'

The words were out before Ashling could stop them. 'Do you mind me asking, but why are you, er, homeless?'

'Career move,' Boo deadpanned. 'I make two hundred quid a day begging, all us homeless people do, didn't you read about it in the papers?'

'Really?'

'No,' he scoffed sarcastically. 'I'm lucky to net two hundred *pence*. It's the old story. No job without an address, no address without a job.'

Ashling was familiar with the concept, but she'd never really believed it actually happened.

'But don't you have a, you know, um, family to help you? Like parents?'

'Yes and no.' With a slight laugh he expounded, 'My poor ma isn't in the best of health. Mentally speaking. And my da did a very good impression of the invisible man when I was five. I was brought up in foster homes.'

'Oh God.' Ashling was sorry she'd ever opened the discussion.

'Yeah, I'm a walking cliché,' Boo said ruefully. 'It's very embarrassing. And I couldn't really settle in any of the foster homes because I wanted to be with my ma, so I managed to make my way through the educational system without passing a single exam. So even if I got an address, I probably still wouldn't be able to get a job.'

'Why don't the corporation house you?'

'Women and children first. If I could get pregnant I'd stand a better chance. But childless men are meant to be able to take care of themselves so we're their lowest priority.'

'What about hostels?' Ashling had heard such things existed.

'No room at the inn. More homeless people in this city than you can shake a stick at.'

'Oh. Oh, that's terrible. All of it.'

'Sorry, Ashling, I've ruined your day now, haven't I?'

'No,' she sighed. 'It wasn't going very well anyway.'

'Hey, I finished *Sinister Days*,' Boo called after her. 'Those serial killers sure do know how to mutilate. And I'm halfway through *Sorted!* and I counted the word "shag" thirteen times on one page.'

'Imagine that.' She hadn't the energy for Boo's book 'reviews'.

Ashling trudged up the stairs, poured herself a glass of wine and listened to her answering machine. After a lengthy absence, the messages from Cormac were back. Apparently, the hyacinth bulbs would be delivered next weekend, but the tulips would take a bit longer.

Then, sheepishly, Ashling rang Clodagh. She hadn't spoken to her in a couple of weeks, since the weekend she'd been in Cork, actually.

'I'm really, really sorry,' Ashling prostrated herself. 'And I'm probably not going to be able to see you until after this fecking magazine is launched. I'm there most nights until nine and I'm so tired I hardly know my own name.'

'That's all right, I'm going to be away anyway.'

'Holiday?'

'I'm going away by myself for a few days next week. Health spa in Wicklow . . . Because I'm stressed and overworked,' Clodagh finished, with grisly defensiveness.

Suddenly Ashling remembered with ghastly clarity Dylan's concern about Clodagh, the conversation they'd had earlier in the summer. All at once she was visited with a very, very bad feeling. A presentiment of disaster. Clodagh was in some sort of trouble and was hovering on the verge of a great unravelling.

Guilt and fear savaged Ashling. 'Clodagh, something's up, isn't it? I'm so, so sorry I haven't been around. Let me help, please let me help, it's good to talk about these things.'

Clodagh began to cry softly, and then real fear took hold of Ashling. Something genuinely *was* wrong.

'Tell me,' Ashling urged.

But Clodagh just sobbed, 'No, I can't, I'm horrible.'

'You're not, you're fantastic!'

'You don't know, I'm so bad, you've no idea, and you're so good . . .' She was crying so hard her voice became incoherent.

'I'll come over,' Ashling offered wildly.

'No! No, please don't do that.' After sobbing some more, Clodagh sniffed and announced, 'It's OK. I'm fine now. Really.'

'I know you're not.' Ashling felt her slipping away.

'Yes, I am.' She was almost firm.

As soon as she hung up the phone, Ashling began to shake. Ted. Fucking Ted. She just had a feeling . . . With trembling fingers she dialled his number and accused, 'I haven't seen a lot of you lately.'

'Whose fault is that?' He sounded hurt. Or was it defensive?

'Yeh, look, sorry, it's the job. Why don't we go out on the piss?'

'Great! Tonight?'

'Er, how about next week?'

'No, I can't.'

'Why not?'

Don't say it, don't say it. . . .

'I'm going away for a few days.'

Oh God. Her breath disappeared as if she'd had a blow to the stomach. 'With who?'

'No one. I'm going to the Edinburgh Festival to do some stand-up.'

'Are you, indeed?'

'Yes, I am, actually.' Hostility poisoned the phone lines.

'Well, good luck on your trip to *Edinburgh* with no one,' Ashling said, sarcastically, and hung up. She'd ask Marcus to keep an eye out, to report back on any sightings of Ted and Clodagh, or even more tellingly, no sightings of Ted at all.

CHAPTER 51

In a blur of fraught, hysterical days and sleepless nights, the thirty-first of August, the day of the *Colleen* launch, rolled around. Far, far too soon.

Ashling was woken by the familiar agony, stabbing in and out of her ear like a hatpin. She might have known. Her bargain-basement ear could always be relied upon to play up at the most inopportune times – the initial exam of her Leaving Cert, her first day at a new job. If it hadn't let her down today – 'The most important day of your working life,' according to Lisa – she'd almost have been disappointed.

Almost, but not quite, Ashling thought grimly, as she swallowed four Paracetamol and shoved a lump of cotton wool into the side of her head. This shagged everything. She couldn't wash her greasy hair herself in case she splashed water into the ear, she'd have to go to the doctor before work, then she'd have to cram a hair appointment into the lunch-hour she hadn't planned on taking.

She had to plead with Dr McDevitt's receptionist to get an early appointment, then she had

556

to *implore* the doctor to give her some decent painkillers. 'The antibiotics take a couple of days to work,' she begged. 'I can't think straight with the pain.'

'You shouldn't have to think at all,' he scolded. 'You should be at home in bed.'

As if! As soon as she'd picked up her prescriptions she had to race to a film preview, where everyone she met conducted their conversations with her greasy hair. The film lasted three endless hours, during which she fidgeted irritably, thinking of all the work she could be getting through at the office. Imagine that she'd once thought this sort of thing was glamorous!

As soon as the credits began to roll, she snatched the press release from the publicist and hit the ground running. A record-breaking ten minutes later she burst into *Colleen*'s almost deserted office, tripping over party sandals and walking into dresses hanging from doors and filing cabinets. Lisa's phone was ringing, but by the time she got to it, the person had hung up. She threw herself upon her own phone, only to discover there wasn't a hope of getting a hair appointment on a Thursday lunchtime. Not even when she tried the salons that were beholden to *Colleen*.

The first one said, 'Emergency? Yeah, we know about tonight. Lisa is here.'

Well, that was the end of that one. Lisa would be getting a Freebie Deluxe, using up the entire quota. Calls to further hairdressers established that Mercedes, Trix, Dervla, even Mrs Morley and Honey Monster Shauna had all used the *Colleen* name to bag themselves appointments.

Excuse me? What kind of fucking eejit am I?

But she couldn't spare the time to berate herself – she was starting to panic. Her hair felt *rancid*. She'd have to wash it here. Luckily the office was overrun with hair-care products – there was even something as basic as shampoo. But she needed help and literally the only person in the office was Bernard, decked out in his best diamond-patterned tank-top in honour of the occasion.

'Bernard, will you be my lovely assistant and help me wash my hair?'

He looked terrified.

'I've an ear infection,' she explained patiently. 'I need help to make sure water doesn't get in.'

He squirmed in agony. 'Get one of them girls to help you.'

'Look around, there's no one here. And I'm interviewing Niamh Cusack in less than an hour, it has to be now.'

'When you come back?'

'I've to go straight to the hotel to help set everything up. Please, Bernard!'

'Ah, no,' he writhed. 'I couldn't, it wouldn't be right.'

Christ! The day and a half from hell! But what could she expect? Bernard was forty-five and still lived at home with his mother.

'Anyway, I've to go out to the credit union,' he lied. And off he raced.

Ashling slumped at a desk and tears were way too close for comfort. Her ear hurt, she was exhausted, she'd have to go to the party with flat, filthy, greasy hair and everyone else would look fantastic. She cupped a hand over her throbbing ear and let a few exploratory trickles run down her face.

'What's wrong?'

She jumped. It was Jack Devine, studying her with what was almost concern.

'Nothing,' she mumbled.

'What's wrong?'

'The party's tonight,' she recited resentfully. 'My hair is dirty, I can't get a hairdresser's appointment for love nor money, I can't wash it myself because I have an ear infection and no one will help me do it here.'

'Who's no one? Bernard? Was that why he was leaving at such high speed? He nearly knocked me over coming out of the lift.'

'He's gone to the credit union.'

'No, he's not. He only goes to the credit union on a Friday. God, you must have really spooked him.'

Jack had a good old laugh at that while Ashling regarded him sullenly. Then he laid down his pile of documents and abruptly snapped into action. 'Right then, come on!'

'Come on what?'

'Come on to the bathroom till we wash your hair.'

She turned her dismal face up to his. 'You're busy,' she accused. He was always busy.

'It won't take long to wash your hair. Let's go!'

'Which bathroom?' she finally asked.

'The gen–' he started, then stopped. They locked eyes in a silent struggle. 'But –'

'Not the gents', she said, as firmly as she could.

'But –'

'No.' Bad enough for Jack Devine to be washing her hair, but to have to eyeball a wall of urinals into the bargain – I don't think so.

'All right then,' he sighed, defeated.

'It's not a bit like our one.' Jack hovered on the threshold, looking into the innocuous washroom as if it was something remarkable, frightening even.

'Come on,' Ashling said snippily, trying to hide her awkwardness. She took the rubber shower-hose that had been a freebie from a shampoo company and tried to suction it on to the tap. But it concertinaed up into bendy uselessness. 'No-good pile of shite.' Her jaw was clenched. Could this day get any worse?

'Give it here.' He leant over her, and she stepped smartly out of the way. With one upward yank he thrust it on to the faucet.

'Thanks,' she muttered.

'Now what?' He watched her dash her hands

under the pin-pricks of water, adjusting the tap until she got the right temperature.

Tipping her head forward she leant into the white porcelain basin. 'Get it wet first. And mind my ear.' God, she could have done without this!

Uncertainly he picked up the hissing shower-head and buzzed an experimental trail of water over her head. Her brown hair changed instantly to a black slick.

'You've to get it *all* wet,' she called, her voice upside-down smothered.

'I know!' She felt him start at her left ear – the good one – lifting the hair, systematically separating it into hanks, soaking it all, moving around to her hairline, then down to her neck. It tickled, not unpleasantly.

As he stretched to reach it all, he was bent over her yielding back and his thigh was near against her side. At the same time that she realized she could feel the heat of him, she became very aware that the door was shut. They were alone. She started to sweat.

But as the trail of water tickled its way towards her right ear, she was diverted by fear. 'Careful!'

'All right!' Jack was disappointed. He'd thought he was doing quite well for a man who'd never washed anyone's hair other than his own before.

'Sorry.' Her voice was muffled. 'But if any water gets in, the eardrum will perforate. It's happened twice already.'

'Right, I get the picture.' He made himself slow

right down and, with his fingers, stroked gentle furrows to sluice water away from the danger area. To his surprise there was something about the arc of skin at the back of her ear that bizarrely touched him. That little line of clean tenderness before her hair sprang into vibrant life. It looked so pitiful and sweet and inexplicably brave. And the big, idiotic-looking lump of cotton wool which blossomed from the side of her head . . . He swallowed.

'Shampoo,' she interrupted. 'Put a blob on the hair, then lather it –'

'Ashling, I know how shampoo works.'

'Oh. Of course.'

Slowly he began to circle his fingers on her scalp, working the shampoo through. It was unexpectedly pleasurable. She closed her eyes and let herself lapse into it, letting the last exhausting month, her enormous workload recede.

'How'm I doing?' he asked.

'Fine.'

'I always wanted to be good with my hands,' he admitted. He sounded wistful.

'You couldn't be a hairdresser,' she murmured, half-resenting having to speak, so much was she enjoying this. 'You're not camp enough.'

Her skull tingled with ecstasy as he worked his hard, sure hands along her. She was going to be dead late for Niamh Cusack and frankly, she didn't give a shite. Little shivery thrills crawled along her hairline, the tension departed her over-stressed body and the only sound in the shady room was that of Jack's breathing. Slumped over the sink, she was sleepily cocooned in his warmth. Bliss . . . But then, as she felt an ache opening way down in her, she became frightened. He was not giving her a normal shampoo. She knew it. *He* must know it. It was far too intimate.

And there was something else. A presence. An upright hardness that was hovering around her liver, just about where Jack Devine's groin was. Or was she imagining it . . . ?

'Perhaps you could rinse it now,' she said in a little voice. 'And put some conditioner in, but do it quick, I'll be late.'

This was Jack Devine. Her boss's boss. She didn't know what was going on, but whatever it was, it was too freaky.

The very second he finished, she squeezed out the excess water, then saw him approaching with the towel. 'I can dry it myself, thanks.' She was breathless.

In the mirror their eyes collided. Instantly she swung away from his sloe-black look. She was embarrassed, confused . . . the way she always felt around him, but to the power of ten.

'Thank you,' she managed politely. 'You've been a big help.'

'No problem.' Then he smiled and the mood altered totally, so much so that she later wondered if she'd imagined the unspoken something buzzing around them. 'I'm not the big ogre you all think I am.'

'No, we don't –'

'I'm just a bloke doing a tough job.'

'Er, right!'

'Now, how much do you bet me that Trix will catch me coming out of here?'

It took Ashling a moment to reply, 'A tenner.'

CHAPTER 52

When Jack arrived at the Herbert Park Hotel, the party was well underway. The place was thronged, copies of *Colleen* lay on tables in thick, lustrous piles, and the girls had a highly efficient human conveyor-belt in place to process the anticipated movers and shakers.

First port of call was Lisa, who, lacquered and glittery-shiny, had probably never looked more beautiful. Then Ashling, awkward in a dress and spindly heels, was checking invitations against a list. Mercedes, snake-thin in black wet-look, was affixing name-badges to arrivees, then Trix, attired in nothing much at all, was directing people towards the cloakroom. Beautiful young men and women circulated with trays of grown-up-looking cocktails – not an umbrella in sight.

'Madam editor,' Jack stopped in front of Lisa.

'Hi, I'm the greeter!' she grinned.

'Well, greet me then.'

She kissed his cheek and in a mag-hag parody exclaimed, 'Darling, so fabulously fantabulous to meet you! Er, who exactly are you?'

Jack laughed and moved on to Ashling, who

looked up from her print-out. 'Oh, hello,' she exclaimed, unexpectedly skittish. 'Devine. Jack. Can't see you on my list. Which are you, a mover or a shaker?'

'Neither.' He acknowledged her black shift-dress. 'Looking good.' But what he really meant was, 'Looking different.'

'I hardly ever wear dresses,' Ashling confided. 'And I've already laddered one pair of tights.'

'How's the hair working out for you?'

'Judge for yourself.' She did a tipsy twirl.

On other women a swingy bob would look sleek and feline; on her it had an endearing plainness which he found vaguely heartwrenching.

'And your ear?'

'What ear?' Ashling demanded gaily, then raised her champagne cocktail. 'Cheers! Feeling no pain. Now, move along, please.'

Lisa spent the night receiving congratulations. The party was a triumph: they'd all come. A thorough search had uncovered only six hundred and fourteen Irish movers and shakers, but it seemed as if every single one of them had turned out. Praise and goodwill swirled around the room in great uplifting gusts. It was fabulous!

And despite disasters right up to printing, *Colleen* was a dazzling achievement. Its cutting-edge heat practically hopped from the glossy pages. Lisa had even, at the eleventh hour, secured a celebrity letter. The new boy-band Laddz had just broken through and Shane Dockery, their lead singer, the nervous youth who Lisa had met all those months ago at the Monsoon launch, had managed to mutate into a *bona fide* heart-throb, who had teenage girls swarming like monkeys up the walls of his house.

Shane remembered Lisa. How could he forget the only person who'd been nice to him during the wilderness months? If he could just evict the teenage girls from his stationery drawer he'd be happy to write the letter. And everyone agreed that his article had an engaging freshness and exuberance that hoarier old rockers wouldn't have been able to simulate.

Lisa couldn't stop smiling: proper, ear-splitting beams. Who would have thought, four months ago, that she'd have pulled it off? And that she'd feel so good about it?

Even the advertising situation was sorted – swung by the Frieda Kiely homeless pictures. Press officers in all the major fashion houses had realized that *Colleen* was no provincial free-sheet, but a force to be reckoned with. Not only had they placed big, expensive ads, but they'd actually asked for their collections to be included in forthcoming issues.

'Hiya, Lisa.' Lisa turned to see Kathy, her neighbour, holding a tray of sushi.

'Oh, hi, Kathy.'

'Thanks for getting me this gig.'

'No problem.'

'Thing is, a few people have been asking where the sausage rolls are?'

Lisa actually laughed. 'Then they shouldn't be here.'

'I tried that sushi stuff myself,' Kathy confided. 'And, d'you know, it's not bad.'

Marcus Valentine, looking the worse for wear, lurched past. Automatically, Lisa gave him a blinding smile. And Jasper Ffrench, looking even more the worse for wear, tottered after him. And here came Calvin Carter, who'd flown in from New York specially.

Calvin was all meaty handshakes and first-name usage.

'Terrific, Lisa.' He surveyed the good-looking crowd. 'Terrrific. All righty, Lisa, let's make speeches!'

He bounded up to the little stage and kicked off with an Irish phrase he'd made Ashling write out for him phonetically.

'Kade Meela Fall-che,' he bellowed, which seemed to go down very well, judging by the storm of laughter that rose. Although, of course, Calvin had always found it hard to distinguish between people laughing *with* him and people laughing *at* him.

Then he gave a speech about Dublin, about magazines and about how fab *Colleen* was.

'And the woman who's made it all possible . . .' he extended his arm to encompass Lisa. 'Ladies and gentlemen, I give you the editor's editor, Lisa Edwards!'

As the room erupted into drunken applause, Lisa took the podium.

'Clap,' Ashling hissed at Mercedes, 'or you'll be sacked.'

Mercedes laughed darkly and kept her arms folded. Ashling gave her an anxious look, but couldn't tarry. She was on bouquet duty. She was also trolleyed drunk – a combination of exhaustion, painkillers and alcohol, of course – and hoped she could stay on her feet long enough to carry the flowers up the little flight of steps.

As Lisa made her pretty speech, her glance alighted on Jack – or to use her own secret name for him, The Icing on Tonight's Cake. He was leaning against the wall, his arms folded, his slight smile wrapping her in great warmth and appreciation.

The high she was on lifted even further. Tonight was the night. Since he'd come back from New Orleans they'd all been too busy for enjoyment, she'd barely had time to flirt with him. But they could rest on their laurels after tonight and she fully intended to have him resting alongside her. She scanned her audience with a transcendental smile. Where the fuck was Ashling? Ah, there she was. Lisa gave the nod – time for the bouquet.

After the speeches, the partying moved up several gears. Calvin looked quite alarmed – they didn't drink like this in New York. And where had Jack disappeared to?

Jack, worn out from glad-handing, had found a quiet seat in a corner and fallen gratefully into it. On the table there were some abandoned pieces of sushi – which someone had clearly been too perplexed by to eat.

Then, shattering his calm, the nearby swing doors burst violently open and, completely in time to the music, in danced Ashling, holding a glass and a fag. She was a surprisingly good dancer, every part of her body moving like a rhythmic sackful of puppies. Possibly because she was very, very drunk, he realized.

She made her way over to Jack, flung down her bag with drunken force, then noticed something on her knee. 'Ladder alert!' she announced. 'Pass me my bag.' Her fag thrust in her mouth, her eyes narrowed against the smoke, she fished out a can of hair-spray and briskly and efficiently ran it from mid-shin to thigh.

Jack watched, mesmerized. 'What's with the hairspray?'

'Should stop the ladder.' Her mouth did a kind of peristalsis, holding her fag steady in a corner, while she spoke and exhaled further along it. He was strangely in awe.

As he watched her put the canister back in her bag, he fixed upon the certain notion that he could trust her with his life.

She gave a sharp exclamation, as if she'd just thought of something great, then dived back into her bag and, seized by a spasm of laughter, emerged with a little glass bottle. In the grip of great mirth, she sprayed it on her wrist, which she then extended to Jack. 'Guess what? I smell of wee.'

The way she gave at the middle indicated that she thought this was *hysterical* and he found himself laughing also, though he didn't get the joke.

She demonstrated the bottle of *Oui*. 'Oui, wee, geddit? Tonight's free gift. Pity it's not being given out until the end, else we could go round saying to everyone "You smell of wee" . . . Hey look,' she'd noticed something. 'You bite your nails.' She picked up his hand and examined it.

'Um, yeah,' he admitted.

'Why?'

'Dunno.' He wanted to come up with a reason but couldn't seem to.

'You worry too much.' With fuzzy compassion, she patted the tender quick of his ragged fingers. 'Here,' she looked at him with sudden urgency. 'Have you any cigarettes? Jasper Ffrench stole mine.'

'I thought you'd have a spare pack.' He was striving for a jokey tone, but his mouth felt mumbly-numb, as though he'd been at the dentist.

'I had, but he stole them too.'

Across the room Jack noticed Lisa raising her glass to him. Everything about her body-language was an invitation. As he fumbled for his cigarettes, his head felt full of cotton-wool and he couldn't think straight. Lisa was beautiful. She was smart and sassy and he was full of admiration for her vision and energy. More than that, he genuinely liked her. He must do – hadn't he kissed her? Even if he still wasn't sure exactly how it had happened.

Lisa had plans for him tonight, but with a sudden cold certainty he knew he didn't want to fall in with them. Why not? Was it because Lisa was married? Because they worked together? Because he wasn't over Mai? Or could it be because he wasn't over *Dee*? But it wasn't for any of those reasons. It was because of Ashling. The woman formerly known as Little Miss Fix-it.

What on earth was happening to him? Could it be jet-lag? he wondered swimmily. But he'd been back twelve days, it couldn't be jet-lag.

Well, there was only one other conclusion he could draw. One sole, unavoidable conclusion.

He was having a nervous breakdown.

CHAPTER 53

Ashling woke up and felt as if she'd been run over by a juggernaut in the night. Her ear throbbed, her bones hurt, weariness gripped her, but who cared? Last night had been great. The party had not only been a huge success, but lots of fun too.

For a moment she didn't know whether or not she was alone in the bed. Then she remembered that she'd mislaid Marcus at some point in the evening and that she'd come home by herself. No problem. Now that the magazine was up and running, life could return to normal.

Aching all over, she dragged herself to the couch, where she smoked and watched morning telly. Her brain felt bruised. She was heinously late for work, but she didn't care. The unspoken consensus was that everyone could roll in at whatever time they liked today. Eventually she reluctantly washed and dressed herself and it was eleven o'clock by the time she hit the street. It was raining. Dirty low September clouds hung over the city and the light was greeny-grey. A few yards from Ashling's door Boo was sitting on the wet pavement. He was huddled into himself, his hair flattened against his skull, rivulets of rain running down his face. But as Ashling got nearer she noticed, with a hard bang to her heart, that it wasn't the rain that was making his face wet. He was crying.

'Boo, what's wrong? Has something happened?'

He looked up at her, then his mouth gaped wide as a silent bawl overtook him. 'Look at me.' Covering his eyes with one hand, he used the other to indicate himself, his soaked dirty clothes, the absence of shelter over his head. 'It's so fucking degrading,' he shuddered.

Ashling froze. Boo was usually so cheerful.

'I'm hungry, I'm cold, I'm soaked, I'm dirty, I'm bored, I'm lonely and I'm scared!' His face was contorted as he wept. 'I'm tired of being hassled by the police, I'm tired of being pissed on by drunk stag parties, I'm tired of being treated like a piece of shit. They won't even let me into the café across the road to buy a cup of tea. A *take-away*.'

Ashling had never actually thought Boo enjoyed being homeless, but she hadn't realized he hated it so much.

'I get so much abuse. People tell me I'm a lazy bastard, that I should get a job. I'd fucking *love* a job. I hate begging, it's so humiliating.'

'Has something happened?' Ashling asked. 'That triggered all of this?'

'No,' he said thickly. 'I'm just having a bad day.'

As Ashling wondered what to do, rain dripped

off the spokes of her umbrella and dotted the back of her jacket with cold, wet blobs. She experienced a burst of frustration. Boo shouldn't be her responsibility. She paid her taxes, the government should take care of people like him. How about letting him shelter in the lobby of her apartment block? But she couldn't: she'd done that during a heavy thunderstorm earlier in the summer and some of the other residents had kicked up a fuss. So should she let him into her flat? She really ought to, yet fond of him though she was, she was nevertheless resistant. But he was so miserable . . .

She gave in. 'Come on up to my place. Have a shower and a bite to eat. And you can stick your clothes in the washing machine.'

She was hoping he'd refuse and she could go on her way with a clear conscience, but he looked at her with forlorn gratitude. 'Thanks,' he gulped, then burst into tears again.

'I won't make a habit of this,' he promised, as she led him up the stairs.

As soon as she saw him contrasted against her cleanish flat she realized just how filthy he was. His grimy jeans were flappy-loose against his pathetic, skinny frame, his pale impish face was smeared with filth and his knuckles were cracked with dirt.

'I smell,' he admitted, shamefaced. 'I'm sorry.'

Something burst in her heart. A grief, a rage.

'Towels.' Her back teeth were clamped against each other as she plumped a soft bundle into his arms. 'Shampoo, spare toothbrush. In here, the washing machine, washing powder. Over here, the kettle, tea, coffee. If you find anything edible in the fridge, you're welcome to it.' She palmed him a fiver. 'I've got to go to work, Boo. I'll see you later.'

'I'll never forget this.'

She closed the door on the sight of him standing in her hall, the knees of his sodden jeans Charlie-Chaplin-bandy, the bouffant bundle of towels dazzlingly white and marshmallow soft.

When Ashling arrived at the office, Jack Devine said, 'Someone's waiting for you.' He indicated the man sitting punch-drunk at her desk.

The moment Ashling saw Dylan she knew something appalling had happened. Something truly dreadful. His features were so altered by shock that she almost didn't recognize him, this man she'd known for eleven years. He looked faded, his skin and hair and eyes bleached of all life. He fastened his stunned, wounded gaze on to hers and announced for all to hear, 'Clodagh's having an affair.'

Realization slammed into Ashling with force. She believed him. A thought reeled through her consciousness: *What terrible things people do to those they love.*

She was honour-bound to go through the motions. There was no earthly way she could say to Dylan, 'Actually I thought she might be playing away.' Instead she had to pretend there was a possibility that he might be wrong. So she asked, 'What makes you think that?'

'I caught them.'

'When? Where?'

'I came home from work at ten o'clock this morning. I've been worried about her,' he said defensively.

Suspicious of her, more like. But Ashling understood.

'And I caught them in bed.' Dylan's voice charted into sudden soprano and for the second time in a morning Ashling watched a grown man weep like a child. 'And I know who he is,' Dylan admitted. 'You know him too.'

Dread and knowledge built in tandem. Ashling knew who Dylan was going to say.

'It's that comedian fucker.'

I know.

'That friend of yours.'

Ted!

'Marcus wankhead,' Dylan gulped. 'Whatever his fucking name is. Valentine or something – Marcus Valentine.'

'No, you mean Ted, little dark Ted.'

'No, I don't, I mean that lanky friend of yours, Marcus Valentine.'

Ashling's nightmare suddenly swerved off in a different direction.

'He's not my friend,' her voice said from a distant room. 'He's my boyfriend.'

★   ★   ★

The few people who were in – Jack, Mrs Morley, Bernard – were immobile with amazement. The only sound was of Dylan's sobs.

'I suppose it's not that surprising,' he said thickly. 'It's not the first time she's stolen a boyfriend from you.'

He looked at her long and hard and asserted, 'I should have stuck with you, Ashling . . . I'd better get going.' He picked up a holdall.

'What's that?' Ashling mumbled.

'Clothes, stuff.'

'You've *left* her?'

'Fucking right I have.'

'But where will you go?'

'My mother's, for a while.'

Numbly, she watched him leave.

A weight arrived on her shoulders. An arm. Belonging to Jack Devine. 'Come into my office.'

Lisa woke up, afflicted by the hollow anticlimax that follows a high. All the sparkling stardust of the night before had gone. Yeah, the magazine was great, yeah, the party was a triumph, but it was only a thirty k circulation in a backwater. What was the big deal?

Her anticlimax was laced with a bigger disappointment. It was Jack. She'd been sure he'd come home with her. She felt she'd deserved it, her reward for working so hard and making everything happen.

Though they hadn't gone out together since he'd

returned from New Orleans, she'd assumed that they shared an unspoken agreement that they'd wait until the launch was underway. But last night when she'd gone to claim her prize, he'd disappeared.

At midday, her mood scraping the pavement, she arrived at work. She made straight for Jack's office, partly to do a postmortem on the launch, partly to check the vibe from him. She opened the door . . .

And saw the most amazing scene. In an instant, primeval knowledge shot through her and rooted her to the spot.

It wasn't that Ashling and Jack were alone in his office, it wasn't that Jack was cradling Ashling like the most precious of china dolls. It was the look on Jack's face. Lisa had never seen such an expression of tenderness.

She backed out, her disbelief turning the office into a dreamscape.

Trix approached with a scrap of paper. 'There's been a phone call for you —'

'Not now.'

Some minutes later, Ashling emerged, putty-grey and avoiding eye-contact. She left the office.

Then out came Jack, looking weary. 'Lisa!' he exclaimed. 'Ashling's had a bad shock, I've sent her home.'

Speaking to him required effort. 'What's wrong with her?'

'She's, ah, discovered that her boyfriend is having an affair with her best friend.'

'What? Marcus Valentine and that Clodagh?'

'Yes.'

Lisa had a hysterical urge to laugh.

'Could you come into my office?' Jack asked. 'I need to talk to you about something.'

Was he going to apologize? Explain that he'd only been comforting Ashling and that it was Lisa he really cared for? But all he wanted to talk about was work.

'First, I'd like to congratulate you on last night, and on the first issue. What you have achieved is above and beyond what we'd hoped for and the entire board offer their congratulations.'

Lisa nodded, aware of an undertow of loss. All their easiness was slipping away, being tugged from under her feet. Jack was clearly uncomfortable with her.

'I'm sorry to do this when you should be enjoying your success,' he went on. 'But I have bad news.'

You're in love with Ashling?

'Mercedes resigned this morning.'

'Oh. Oh. Why?'

'She's leaving Ireland.'

Bitch, Lisa thought viciously. She hadn't even had the decency to say it was because Lisa was a power-crazed tyrant whom she could no longer work for.

'She's got a job in New York,' Jack elaborated. 'Apparently her husband's been seconded there.'

'New York?' Lisa was reminded of the trip Mercedes had taken in June. The most horrible thought in the world hit her. 'Her new job, it's not . . . not . . . at *Manhattan*?'

'I don't know which magazine, she didn't say.'

'Where is she?' Lisa snarled, suddenly feral.

'Gone. She was due a week's holiday, which she took in lieu of notice.'

Lisa put her face in her hands. 'Do you mind if I go home?'

She called a cab, and fifteen minutes later, still feeling like she was dreaming, she found herself at home. Scratching the key in her front door, she let herself in. The post had come – one big manila envelope was lying in the hall. Absently she picked it up and, as she kicked off her shoes, tore it open. She unfolded the stiff paper within while tossing her handbag on to the kitchen counter. Then, finally, she turned her attention to the pages she held in her hand.

A one-second glance was all it took. She sank to the floor, jack-knifed with disbelief.

It was a divorce petition.

Clodagh opened her front door and recoiled as 'You bitch!' was flung at her.

'Ashling!'

'Weren't you expecting me?'

She hadn't been. All she'd been able to think about was Dylan, that he'd found out and that he'd left her. Somewhere at the back of her head she knew she'd have to talk to Ashling, but she hadn't been able to think about it yet.

'So, my best friend,' Ashling pushed into the kitchen. 'Did you think of me at all when you were fucking my boyfriend?'

Clodagh was in agony. How could she explain the guilt, the torture? 'I did think of you, Ashling,' she said humbly. 'I did, it's been so difficult. But you think only people in soap operas have affairs. Ordinary people do, it just happens.'

'But to me? How could you do it to me?'

'I don't know. But you hadn't been going out with him long, it's not like you were married or anything, and I've been so unhappy, I've felt so trapped and like I was going mad –'

'Don't try to make me feel sorry for you. You have fucking everything,' Ashling said wildly. 'Why did you have to go and take him? You have every-thing.'

All Clodagh could say was, 'Sometimes every-thing isn't enough.'

'When did this start with Marcus?'

'When you were in Cork,' Clodagh said stiffly. 'He gave me a note with his phone number –'

'"Bellez-moi."' Ashling was pleased at the surprise on Clodagh's face. 'You and most of Dublin got one of those notes. So why did he collect me from the train that weekend?'

Clodagh gave a dismal shrug. 'Maybe he felt guilty.'

'Then what happened?'

'He called here to the house on the Monday after. Nothing happened. He just had a cup of tea, then when he was leaving, he washed his cup. It was just a small thing but –'

'He said "my Mammy trained me well",' Ashling chimed in with. 'Yes, I was fucking charmed by that too.'

'He loves me.' Clodagh was defensive.

He probably does, Ashling realized, shards of agony piercing the protective lagging of anger. 'Then what happened?'

'He invited me out for a cup of coffee . . .'

'And then?'

'And then . . . he showed up here again the following day.'

'When he did more than wash his cup?' *We're not having this conversation. I'm hallucinating.*

Clodagh nodded, avoiding eye-contact.

'Did you go to Edinburgh with him?'

Once again Clodagh nodded humbly.

'I wouldn't have thought he was your type,' Ashling accused, aware that her face was twisted and ugly with pain. How she longed for a smooth, dignified mask.

'I wouldn't have thought he was my type either,' Clodagh admitted. 'But from the first night I saw him at that comedy place I really liked him. I didn't want to, but I couldn't help it.'

'And what about Dylan?'

Clodagh hung her head. 'I don't know, I just don't know . . . Look, I've betrayed you, our friendship, and that must hurt more than the end of your, um, romance.'

'You're wrong,' Ashling corrected nastily. 'I mind losing my boyfriend much more.'

Clodagh gazed at Ashling's pale, angry face and admitted uncertainly, 'I've never seen you like this before.'

'What? Angry? Well, it's long overdue.'

'How d'you mean?'

'You've done this to me before,' Ashling said quietly. 'Dylan was my boyfriend first.'

'Yes, but . . . he fell in love with me.'

'You stole him.'

'Well, why didn't you say anything before now?' Clodagh said, with sudden savagery. 'You were always such a victim.'

'So this is my fault?' Ashling was unpleasant. 'Let's get one thing straight. I forgave you for Dylan. But I will never forgive you for this.'

CHAPTER 54

'*Dammit,*' she realized. '*I think I'm having a nervous breakdown.*'

She looked around at the bed she was flung in. Her well-overdue-for-a-bath body was sprawled lethargically on the well-overdue-for-a-change sheet. Tissues, sodden and balled, littered the duvet. Gathering dust on her chest of drawers was an untouched arsenal of chocolate. Scattered on the floor were magazines she'd been unable to concentrate on. The television in the corner relentlessly delivered daytime viewing direct to her bed. Yip, nervous-breakdown territory all right.

But something was wrong. What was it?

'*I always thought . . .*' *she tried.* '*You know, I always expected . . .*'

Abruptly she knew. '*I always thought it would be nicer than this . . .*'

CHAPTER 55

Clodagh thought she was cracking up, she was certain she was. But she had to get dressed and collect Molly from playgroup. Once back, she returned to bed and attempted to take up where she'd left off, but Molly began agitating that noodles be microwaved for her. With resignation, Clodagh got up again.

She hadn't been enjoying it anyway – which had come as a big surprise. As a child, she'd watched Ashling's mother take to her bed and thought that it looked gloriously abandoned. But in practice, lying down feeling unable to cope, riddled with self-hatred and confusion, wasn't half as much fun as she'd expected.

Since ten o'clock this morning – was it *really* only this morning? – her entire life had become an out-of-body experience. From the moment she'd heard Dylan's key in the door, she *knew*. The gig was up.

She'd paused from her frantic bucking beneath Marcus and cupped an ear to listen. 'Sssh!' In a fluid movement he'd rolled off her: frozen and bug-eyed, they'd listened to Dylan mounting the stairs.

She'd had every opportunity to jump from the bed, fling on a robe and hustle Marcus into the wardrobe. Indeed, Marcus had tried to skid out of bed, but she'd arrested him by gripping his wrist tightly. Then she'd waited with horrible calm, the scene set to change her life.

For the last five weeks she'd endured sleepless nights wondering where her affair with Marcus would end up. She'd vacillated between ending it with him and resuming a normal life with Dylan, or fantasizing about a situation where Dylan was magically absent, but without her having actually told him it was over.

But as she listened to Dylan's footsteps get ever closer, she'd realized that the decision had been taken for her. Suddenly she wasn't sure she was ready.

The door to the bedroom opened, and even though she knew it was Dylan, his presence shocked her into a stupor.

His face. The expression on his face was so much worse than she'd ever imagined it could be. She was almost surprised at the amount of pain there. And his voice when he spoke was not Dylan's. There was an *Oof* to it, as though he'd been slammed in the abdomen. 'At the risk of sounding like a song lyric,' he'd struggled for breath with pathetic dignity, 'How long has this being going on?'

'Dylan . . .'

'How long?'

'A month.'

Dylan turned to Marcus, who was clutching the sheet to his chest. 'Would you mind leaving? I'd like a word with my wife.'

Cupping his genitals coyly, Marcus edged crab-like from the bed, snatched up some clothes and muttered to Clodagh, 'I'll call you later.'

Dylan watched him leave, then turned back to Clodagh and asked quietly, 'Why?' A hundred thousand questions were contained in that one word.

She struggled for the right words. 'I don't really know.'

'Please tell me why. Tell me what's wrong. We can fix it, I'll do anything.'

What could she say? With sudden certainty, she knew she didn't *want* him to fix it. But she owed him honesty. 'I think I was lonely . . .'

'Lonely? How?'

'I don't know, I can't describe it. But I've been lonely and bored.'

'Bored? With me?'

She hesitated. She couldn't be that cruel. 'With everything.'

'Do you want to fix this?'

'I don't know.'

He studied her in long, painful silence. 'That means no. Do you love this . . . him?'

A miserable nod. 'I think so.'

'OK.'

'OK?'

But Dylan didn't answer. Instead, he slid a holdall off the top of the wardrobe, bounced it on to the bed and, slamming drawers open and closed, began flinging in underwear and shirts. Nothing had prepared her for how shocking it was.

'But . . .' she tried, her eyes flicking back and forth, seeing ties, his shaving stuff, then some socks hop into the bag. Everything was happening very quickly.

Suddenly the bag was bulging-full. Then Dylan was zipping it with a high-pitched whizz. 'I'll be back for the rest later.'

He swung from the room, and after a panicky second Clodagh dragged on a dressing-gown and ran down the stairs after him.

'Dylan, I still love you,' she implored.

'So what was that all about?' He jerked his head upstairs.

'I still love you,' she repeated, her voice more subdued, 'but . . .'

'You're no longer *in* love with me?' Dylan finished harshly.

She hesitated. But she had to be honest. 'I suppose . . .'

He shuttered his face. 'I'll be back tonight to explain things to my children. You can stay here in the house for the time being.'

'For the time being?'

'The house will have to be sold.'

'*Will it?*'

589

'I can't afford to pay the mortgage on this place and another. And if you think you're staying on here while I'm in some smelly shoebox in Rathmines, you're very much mistaken.'

And then he was gone.

She reeled from shock, from the speed it had all happened at. She'd fantasized about Dylan removing himself from her life, but now that it had actually come to pass it was ugly. Eleven years wiped out in half an hour, and Dylan in such agony. And talking about selling the house! Yes, she was wild about Marcus, but things weren't that simple.

Too stunned to cry, too frightened to grieve, she sat in the kitchen for a long time. A ring at the front door jolted her back to the real world. It might be Marcus.

But it wasn't. It was Ashling.

Clodagh hadn't been expecting her. She certainly wasn't ready for her. And Ashling's uncharacteristic angry hostility compounded the whole horrible mess. Clodagh had always been surrounded by love, but suddenly everyone hated her, including herself. She was a pariah, a scumbag, she'd broken every rule in the book and wouldn't be forgiven.

After Ashling left, *then* she cried. She crawled back into bed, between the sheets with their smell of abandoned sex. She'd never laundered so much bed-linen as she had in the past five weeks. Well, no need to do it today, nothing to hide any longer.

She reached for the phone and rang Marcus, so he could remind her that they hadn't really done anything wrong. That they were mad about each other, that they couldn't help it, that theirs was a noble entanglement. But he wasn't at work and he wasn't answering his mobile, so she had to endure her anguish alone.

This isn't my fault, she repeated again and again like a mantra. *I couldn't help myself.* But, like a fissure into hell opening, she caught a glimpse of the atrocity she'd perpetrated. What she had done to Dylan was unforgivable. *Unbelievable.* With shaky speed she grasped the nearest magazine to hand and tried to forget herself in an article about stencilling. But the fissure opened again – worse this time. It wasn't just Dylan she'd fucked over. It was her children. And Ashling.

Her heart beat faster and with a hand slidy with sweat she pressed buttons on the remote control until she found Jerry Springer. But he wasn't enough to distract her from herself – normally the people he had on seemed like cartoon characters with their ridiculously convoluted private lives, but today she didn't feel any different from them.

She flicked to *Emmerdale,* then *Home and Away,* but nothing worked. She trembled with shock and disbelief at her own actions, at the devastation she'd wrought. Then she remembered she'd have to collect Molly from playgroup and had a panicky seizure of paralysis. She couldn't go out. She really couldn't. It was impossible.

She couldn't be on her own and she couldn't be with anyone else and for a horrible moment she wondered if she was cracking up. This beyond-the-pale thought held her in its grip for a nightmarish while, then she struggled from the embrace of the bed. Cracking up was even more unpleasant than having to face the outside world.

Marcus rang in the afternoon and, in spite of everything, every cell in her body sang as soon as she heard his voice. She was mad about him, in a way that she hadn't felt about Dylan in years. If ever. Love would conquer all.

'How're you doing?' he asked, his voice full of concern.

'Shit!' she half-laughed, half-cried. 'Dylan's moved out, everyone hates me, it's all a disaster.'

'It's going to be fine,' he soothed.

'Promise?'

'Promise.'

'Hey, I rang you earlier and your phone was off.'

'Keeping a low profile.'

'Ashling knows. Dylan told her.'

'I figured he might.'

'Will you talk to her?'

'I don't think there's any point,' he said, trying to disguise his shame. 'I want to be with you. What can I tell her that she doesn't already know?'

Marcus had spent the past five weeks justifying his involvement with Clodagh by saying that Ashling was neglecting him. But, in truth, his feelings were more complex. He hadn't been able to credit his luck with Clodagh. She was so beautiful and he certainly preferred her to Ashling. But he'd been very fond of Ashling and was needled by his shitty behaviour. The last thing he wanted to do was confront his own cavalier carry-on by having a question-and-answer session with Ashling.

Far better to focus on the positive. His voice intense with desire, he asked Clodagh, 'Can I see you?'

'Dylan's coming after work. To talk to the kids. Christ, it's hard to believe . . .'

'But how about when he's gone? I could spend the night. After all, there's nothing to be afraid of now, is there?'

Her heart soared. 'I'll call you when he's gone.'

'Right, ring me at home. Ring three times, then hang up, then ring back. That way I'll know it's you.'

Dylan arrived after work. He was different. No longer obviously in pain, but angry.

'You wanted to be caught, didn't you?'

'No!' *Did she?*

'Yes, you did. You've been behaving really weirdly.'

Maybe she had been, she acknowledged.

'Have my children seen you in bed with that prick?'

'No, of course not!'

'Well, they better not. Not if you want any access to them.'

'What do you mean?'

'I'm going to get custody of them, you don't stand a chance. *In the circumstances*,' he added, unpleasantly.

His words and the hard expression on his face suddenly brought home to Clodagh how deadly serious this situation was. It was a side to Dylan that she wasn't familiar with.

'Jesus Christ, Dylan,' she exploded, 'why are you being such a –!' She stopped short of calling him a bastard. Why wouldn't he be a bastard, all things considered?

He seemed amused by her frustration – if it was possible for someone to laugh and sneer simultaneously.

She was reminded that Dylan was a businessman. A very successful one. A man who played hardball. Maybe he wasn't going to roll over and play dead just because she wanted him to. Dylan had always treated her with tenderness and love, she was finding this abrupt change hard, even if she was responsible for it.

'I'm going to get custody,' he repeated.

'OK,' she said humbly. But even as her face was meek, her head was whirring. *He's not getting my children, no way.*

'Right, I'm going to talk to them.' Dylan went into the room where Craig and Molly were watching telly. They obviously sensed something was wrong because they'd been bizarrely subdued all afternoon.

When Dylan emerged he said coldly, 'I've just told them I have to go away for a while. I need time to think what the best way to deal with this long-term should be.' He rubbed his hand over his mouth and suddenly he looked *exhausted*.

But Clodagh's aching compassion for him vanished when he added, 'I *could* tell them their mother is an adulterous bitch who's ruined everything, but it would do more harm than good, I'm told. Right, I'm going. I'm at my parents'. Ring me –'

'I will –'

'If there's anything up with my children.'

She watched him hug them fiercely, his eyes clenched shut. This was so fucking awful. This time yesterday things couldn't have been more normal. She'd made stir-fry for dinner, Craig had spat it all back out on to his plate, she'd watched *Coronation Street*, she'd nagged Dylan into changing a light-bulb, Molly had smeared her bedroom wall with peanut butter. In retrospect it seemed like a golden era, untouched by pain or worry. Who would have thought that so quickly their lives would be thrown up in the air and utterly rearranged, mired in bitterness?

'Bye.' Dylan closed the front-door behind him. She'd seen him pack his bag, he'd told her he was leaving, but she hadn't been able to imagine it until presented with it as a *fait accompli*.

This isn't happening, she thought as she stood in the hall. *This isn't happening.*

She turned away from the door and found Craig and Molly standing gazing at her in silence. Shamed, she turned away from their questioning eyes and reached for the phone.

She listened to Marcus's phone ring and ring, then click into answer-machine mode. Where was he? Then she remembered that he'd asked for her to ring, hang up, then ring again. Reluctantly she did so – it made her feel like a type of outlaw.

On the second set of rings, Marcus answered and instantly her pain lessened and was replaced by a soaring, giddy sensation.

'Is Dylan gone?' he asked.

'Yes –'

'OK, I'm on my way.'

'No, wait!'

'What?' His voice was suddenly unfriendly.

'I'd love to see you,' she explained, 'but not tonight. It's too soon. I don't want to confuse the kids. You see, Dylan's talking about all kinds of terrible things like making sure I don't get custody of them.'

All was still, then in a low voice Marcus asked, 'Don't you want to see me?'

'Marcus, I would give anything! You know I would, but I think it's better if we leave it until tomorrow. Hey, I bet you're sorry you ever got involved in this,' she sniffled, with a little laugh.

'Don't be mad,' he insisted, as she'd known he would.

'Call over tomorrow afternoon,' she invited shyly. 'There's a couple of people I'd like you to meet.'

The following afternoon Marcus arrived with a Barbie for Molly and a big red truck for Craig. Despite the presents, the children greeted him with suspicion. They both sensed that their world was horribly askew and were further unsettled by this newcomer. Battling their resistance, Marcus patiently played with them both, solemnly brushing Barbie's hair and shoving the truck back and forth, back and forth along the carpet to Craig. It took an hour of full-on dedication and the production of a bag of Percy Pigs before Molly and Craig began to slip into unselfconsciousness.

Sick with hope, Clodagh watched, hardly daring to breathe. Maybe things would get better. Maybe everything would work out. Her head reeled off into the future. Perhaps Marcus could move in here, he could pay the mortgage, she'd get custody of the children, Dylan would be unmasked as a paedophile or a drug-dealer so that everyone would hate him and forgive her . . .

While Craig and Molly were briefly distracted, Marcus took advantage of the gap to gently touch her. 'How are you?' he asked softly. 'Bearing up?'

'Everyone hates us,' she laughed tearfully. 'But at least we have each other.'

'That's right. How soon can I get you into bed?' he murmured, sneaking a hand under her T-shirt and cupping the breast furthest from the children. He pinched her nipple and her mouth went slack with desire.

'Muuuummmeee,' Craig set up a wailing, clambered to his feet and tried to push Marcus off his mother. He flailed wildly with his new red truck and managed to catch Marcus on the outer reaches of his left testicle. Not near enough to cause any real damage but enough to send eddies of nausea through his abdomen.

'Darling, you're going to have to learn to share,' Clodagh said softly.

'Don't want to!'

After an awkward pause, Clodagh said, 'Marcus, I was actually talking to Craig.'

CHAPTER 56

Lisa crouched on the floor, clutching her divorce petition. The wave of depression that had lapped and receded, lapped and receded since she'd first arrived in Dublin had finally broken over her head.

I'm a failure, she acknowledged. *I'm a big, fat failure. My marriage is over.*

Crazily, she'd never really thought it was going to happen. She saw that now with painful clarity. It was why she'd never got herself a solicitor. Throughout the entire break-up with Oliver she'd behaved uncharacteristically: she'd always been proactive and dynamic. She got things done, and quickly. But, for whatever reason, not this.

Well, she'd better get herself a solicitor now.

But if she'd been in denial, then so had Oliver, she insisted, keen to stop feeling so . . . so . . . *foolish*. He'd left her in January and was paying rent elsewhere but continued to pay his half of their mortgage. That wasn't the behaviour of a man keen to sever links.

She caught a glimpse of herself crouched on the floor in all her pathos. Feeling silly, she clambered to her feet – then immediately ran out of steam. She made it as far as her bedroom, fell into bed and dragged her duvet over her.

Something about the way the duvet wafted and softly wrapped itself about her burst open her swollen emotions, and she cried tears of loss, of failure and – yes! – of self-pity. She was entitled to feel sorry for herself, dammit. Look at all the shitty things that had happened. Being rejected by Jack – though it wasn't up there with the pain of losing Oliver – contributed to the mix. And Mercedes, if she's got a job at *Manhattan*, I'll, I'll . . . Well, what could she do? Precisely nothing. She'd never been so keenly aware of her own powerlessness. And though she'd got Trix to make a thousand phone calls to the shop, her wooden blind still wasn't ready. Would probably *never* be ready, at this rate.

This was the emetic she needed. The ladylike weeping escalated until she was bawling like a baby.

'. . . *In sickness and in health . . .*'

'. . . *Ashling's had a bad shock . . .*'

'. . . *Yew may kiss the braaaaade . . .*'

'. . . *she's got a job in New York . . .*'

'. . . *the factory is closed for their summer holidays . . .*'

Howling, she stretched out a hand and toppled a box of tissues into the bed with her.

As the hours passed the light outside her bedroom window faded into pink. Charcoaly blue darkened her room, then night-black tinged with city-violet. She was still treating herself to the occasional squall when the muffled pearly grey of dawn crept in. This eventually dispersed and sharpened into a hard blue September sky. Noises began outside as the day got going, but Lisa elected to remain where she was, thanks very much.

Sometime, in what might have been the afternoon, there was an intrusion into her cotton-wool reality. A noise in her hall, footsteps, then she jumped as Kathy stuck her shredded-wheat head around the bedroom door.

'What are you doing here?' Lisa gazed with red-rimmed eyes.

'It's Saturday,' Kathy said. 'I always clean for you on Saturday.'

The tissue balls strewn over the duvet cover, the unmistakable miasma of despondency and the fact that Lisa was in bed and seemed to be still dressed, greatly alarmed Kathy. 'Are you OK?'

'Yeah.'

Kathy clearly didn't believe her. Then Lisa had a wearily inspired idea. 'I'm ill, I've got the flu.'

Instantly Kathy was all sympathy. Would she like some flat 7-Up, a Lemsip, a hot whiskey?

Lisa shook her head and got back to staring at nothing. A full-time job.

Flu? Kathy wondered. She hadn't heard of anyone else coming down with it. But was it any wonder Lisa had caught something, living in this filth? She started her clean-up operation in the kitchen, wiping sticky surfaces – how did Lisa *do* it? – then shifted a document out of the way. Naturally she cast a glance over it – what was she, a saint? – and in an instant everything made sense. Flu? Lisa didn't have flu. God love her, flu would be far nicer.

An indeterminate amount of time later and Kathy was back in the bedroom. 'I'll just clean in here.'

'No, please don't.'

'But those sheets are manky, Lisa.'

'It doesn't matter.'

Kathy exited, then Lisa heard the slam of the front-door. Good. On her own again.

But a short few minutes later the front-door opened once more and Kathy reappeared with a plastic shopping-bag. 'Fags, sweets, a scratch-card and the *RTÉ Guide*. If there's anything you want from the shop, just give us a shout. If I'm not there Francine will go, and she says she'll do it for free.'

Francine normally charged a pound every time she went to the shop for Lisa.

'I'm off to work now,' Kathy said. 'Before I go, would you like a cup of tea?'

Lisa shook her head. Kathy made it anyway.

'Strong, sweet tea,' she said meaningfully, as she placed it beside Lisa.

Lisa found herself looking at Kathy's runners. They were worn-down, grey-white plastic and on the instep bend they were cracked. Quickly she ripped out another hank of tissues and pressed it to her eyes.

After Ashling threw down the final gauntlet that she would never forgive Clodagh, she left, still burning with righteous anger. Next stop Marcus.

Her face set, she walked speedily, almost tripping, heading for town and Marcus's office. Zipping through the crowds of Leeson Street, a man going the other way, also moving at high speed, bumped against her, his shoulder smacking hard against hers. He was already gone, but in slow motion Ashling staggered back, feeling the bang reverberate through her again and again. Suddenly fragmented, all her anger smashed like a glass bauble, reduced and useless. The noise of the city hit her in a roar. Cars beeping; hard, snarling faces. Abruptly, nowhere was safe.

Her body quivering to the rhythm of fear, the showdown with Marcus was forgotten. She couldn't have a showdown with a marshmallow.

What was she doing being angry anyway? Anger had never been her style. It was only twenty minutes since the confrontation with Clodagh and right now it was impossible to believe it was she who had done it.

She hastened towards home, cradling her fragility. The world had turned into a Hieronymus Bosch painting: dirty travelling children singing songs they didn't know the words to; couples snarling at each other for not filling their own emptiness; a toothless alcoholic woman shouting the odds at invisible enemies; homeless men in doorways, their mouths maws of despair.

Homeless men!

Please let Boo have gone. And please let him not have robbed me blind.

She didn't really think he would have, but after the day she'd had, she was braced for anything.

He hadn't. The place was pretty much as she'd left it, except for a thank-you note on the table. She climbed into bed. She'd just have a little rest to get over the shock.

But she was still there when, sometime on Friday evening, Joy let herself in with Ashling's spare key. She burst into the room, her face bruised with concern. 'I rang you at work and spoke to Divine Jack. He told me what happened. I'm so sorry.' Joy gathered her in her arms while Ashling lay as unresponsive as a rolled-up carpet.

Half-an-hour later Ted made a wary appearance. He and Ashling hadn't spoken in over three weeks, since Ashling had quizzed him on his Edinburgh trip.

'Ted, I'm sorry,' Ashling said wearily. 'I thought you were having an affair with Clodagh.'

'You did?' His dark narrow face lit up in delight. Then hastily he wiped it and assumed an expression of gravitas. 'I've brought you some tissues,' he offered. 'They say "Groovy Chick" on them.'

'Leave them there. Beside the tissues Joy brought me.'

At the sound of the key in the door, Lisa semi-emerged from torpor. Kathy again. But it wasn't Kathy, it was Francine.

'Hiya.' Francine swung her roly-poly body into the bedroom. 'My ma says I've to keep you company.'

'I don't want company.' Lisa could hardly lift her head from the pillow.

'Can I try this on?' Francine had her eye on a pink feather boa.

'No.'

She draped it around her anyway and admired herself in the full-length mirror, a stout little figure in flowered leggings and a yellow T-shirt.

'Shouldn't you be at school?' Lisa asked wearily.

'Nah.' Francine did a scornful swagger. 'It's Sunday.'

Blimey, Lisa thought in idle wonder. *I've lost track of the days.*

'Though even if it wasn't Sunday and I didn't want to go to school, I wouldn't go,' Francine boasted.

'But you won't get an education and then you won't get a good job.' Lisa didn't care whether or not Francine got an education, but she wanted to annoy her so that she'd leave.

'Don't need an education. I'm going to be in a girl-band and my da says they're all as thick as

605

bottled shite. Here! Will I show you my dance routine?'

'No. Just piss off and leave me alone.'

'D'you've a stereo?' Francine stalwartly ignored Lisa's hostility. 'No? OK, I'll hum. Right, you've to imagine that I'm in the middle and that there are two girls on this side of me and two on that side. Hold on.' Quickly Francine rolled up her T-shirt into a makeshift crop top, displaying her childish, rotund belly.

'What's that gold mark on your stomach?' Lisa asked, interested, despite everything.

'My belly-button ring.' Francine was defensive.

'No, it's not.'

'Look, I *had* to draw it,' Francine insisted. 'My ma says I can get a real one when I'm thirteen – though I'll be dead by then,' she added gloomily.

Then she rallied. 'Two, three, four.' She tapped her foot on the floor and counted herself in, then launched into her routine. Right elbow 'chickened' to the side twice, then left elbow. Two jerky hops on the right foot, two jerky hops on the left, then with a sharp smack to her plump buttock, she turned her back on Lisa. Humming all the while, she swung her hips, getting lower and lower to the floor. An exotic dancer couldn't have been more explicit. She undulated back to normal height, then did an ungainly jump to the front again, her expression a fist of grim concentration. 'This is the best bit,' she promised. 'Shimmmmmeeee.' Stretching both arms out as far as they would go, she wriggled her shoulders and did a bosom-free shimmy at Lisa. 'Da-dah!' She finished by attempting to do the splits. She got nowhere near the floor.

'Amazing,' Lisa acknowledged. It had certainly been that.

'Thanks.' Francine was breathless and red with pleasure. "Course I'll be singing as well. I'll be the lead singer. You get paid more for that. And I'll write the songs too. You get even more money for that.'

Lisa nodded at her enterprise.

'And merchandising, I'll be in charge of that too,' Francine promised. 'That's where the real money is.' She gave Lisa a sharp look. 'How's your flu now? Better?'

'No. Go away.'

'Are you eating that KitKat?'

'No.'

'Can I have it?'

It was only when Lisa couldn't get out of bed to go to work on Monday morning that she suddenly realized she was losing it. Apart from skiving off early on Friday, she couldn't remember when she'd last missed work. Had she ever? She'd gone in when she had period pains, head colds, hangovers, bad-hair days. She'd gone in on her holidays. She'd gone in when her husband had left her. So what was she at now?

And why wasn't it nice?

She'd always been such a control freak that she'd never been able to understand those who'd cracked up, who'd been led sobbing from their desks and had never returned. But she'd entertained a perverse curiosity about losing it, suspecting that there must be some comfort therein. Wouldn't it be liberating to be utterly incapable, to have no choice but to let others take charge?

Well, apparently not. She was unable to function and she hated it.

She should go to work. She was needed there. The *Colleen* staff was too small to accommodate absenteeism, especially with Mercedes gone and Ashling laid low also. But she didn't care. *Couldn't* care. Her body was too heavy and her mind was too weary.

Eventually she became aware that she had to pee. She battled it, pretending it wasn't happening, but eventually the discomfort got so great she had to go to the bathroom. Passing the kitchen on her return she noticed the divorce petition lying on the counter. She hadn't looked at it since Friday, she never wanted to see it again, but she knew she had to.

She took it back to bed and forced herself to study it. She should hate Oliver. The fucking nerve of him, divorcing her! But what did she expect? Their marriage was over, 'irretrievably broken down' if you wanted to be technical about it, and let's face it, he did.

The language on the petition was pompous and

impenetrable. Again she realized how badly she needed a solicitor, how frighteningly out of her depth she was. She skimmed the stiff pages, trying to understand, and the first thing that actually made sense was that Oliver was seeking a divorce on the grounds of Lisa's 'unreasonable behaviour'. The words jumped out and stung her. She hated being accused of doing something wrong. The marriage breakdown wasn't her fault, she fumed. They'd just wanted different things. Fucking bastard. She could come up with some unreasonable-behaviour accusations of her own, if she put her mind to it. Wanting her barefoot, pregnant and manacled to the kitchen sink – that's pretty unreasonable.

But the anger cooled as she remembered the unreasonable-behaviour accusation was only a formality. He'd explained all that when he'd come to Dublin – they had to have a reason to give to the court and she could just as easily have sued him.

Reading on, there were five examples, just as he'd told her there had to be. Working nine weekends in a row. Missing his parents' thirtieth wedding anniversary due to work commitments. Cancelling their holiday in St Lucia at the last minute because she had to work. Pretending she wanted to get pregnant. Owning too many clothes. Each instance cut through her like a knife. Apart from the owning-too-many-clothes one. She presumed that by example five he'd run out of real complaints. Costs would be shared and neither would be seeking maintenance from the other.

Apparently she had to sign something called an Acknowledgement of Service and send it back to Oliver's solicitor. But she was signing nothing. And not just because she hadn't the will to pick up a pen. Her instinct for self-preservation went very deep.

There was a knock at her door. She actually managed a silent laugh. The thought of her leaving the bed to answer it was so unlikely as to be funny. Another knock. It didn't bother her in the slightest. No chance she'd respond. Voices outside. Another knock – more of a pounding, really. Then a creak as the letter-box flap was lifted.

'Lisa?' a voice asked.

She barely registered it.

'Lisa,' the voice called again.

It was *so* not a problem to ignore it.

'LEEEEEESSSSAAAA,' the voice bellowed. She realized she recognized it. It was Beck. Well, that wasn't his real name, but he was one of the Man-U-loving little boys who lived on the road. The one with the very loud voice. 'I KNOW you're in there. I'm on the MITCH too. There's a BIG packet of flowers here, d'you want them?'

'No,' Lisa called feebly.

'WHAT?'

'No.'

'I can't hear you. Did you say yes?'

Angrily, Lisa dragged herself from the bed. For fuck's sake! All her life she'd been strong. She'd never given in to PMT or mental-health days or *anything*. And the one time she decided to have a nervous breakdown, people kept interrupting it. She flung open the front-door and roared into Beck's face, 'I SAID NO!'

'Right you are.' He crackled a big, cellophane bouquet into her arms and slipped past her into the hall. 'Quick, before someone sees me. I'm meant to be at school.'

Lisa gazed dully at the flowers. They were good ones. No carnations or any of that cheap-skate unimaginative shit, but lots of weird stuff – purple thistle and orchids that looked as though they came from another planet. Who were they from? Suddenly her hands were shaking and she was ripping open the envelope. Could they be from Oliver?

They were from Jack.

All the note said was, 'We think you're great. Please come back to work.' But, with a flash of insight, Lisa recognized it as an apology. Jack had known she'd had her sights set on him, and he wasn't interested. He knew that she knew. And she knew that he knew that she knew and all at once it didn't matter anyway. Though good-looking and hard-bodied, Jack would have driven her loco. He didn't care enough about the things that were vital to her. She'd only been diverting herself with fantasies of him – Oliver was the man she was really upset about.

Beck was agitating for her attention. 'I want to ask you something.'

'What?' The word was dragged up from her toes.

'Help me put this in my HAIR?' He produced a packet from his sweatpants. It was Sun-in.

'Don't tell me, you want to be in a boy-band,' Lisa said.

Beck's face was a picture as he searched for the right words. Eventually he located them. 'Would you ever fuck OFF?' he exclaimed. 'I'm going to be a winger for Man U.'

'So you need blond highlights?'

'Duh,' he scorned her stupidity. ''Course I do!'

'Not now, Beck, I've the flu.'

'No, you haven't.' Already he was on his way into her bathroom and he turned and gave a one-skiver-to-another wink. 'But if you won't grass on me, I won't grass on you.'

She leant against the wall and toyed with screaming, then simply yielded to her fate.

An hour later Beck departed, his hair striped with blond. 'Thanks Lisa, you're a COOL girl.'

After his departure, she sat at her kitchen table, smoking. She was cold and kept meaning to get a top, but every time she finished a cigarette, she lit another one.

In the silent room the phone rang and her heart nearly jumped out of her chest – her nerve-endings were frayed to pieces! The answer-machine picked up: she wasn't so much screening calls as stonewalling them. But every cell in her body went on red alert as Oliver's voice filled the room.

'Babes, it's me. Uh, Oliver, that is. Thought I'd give you a bell about the –'

She snatched up the phone. 'It's me. I'm here.'

'Hey,' he said warmly. 'Thought you might be. I called you at work, they said you were at home. Did you get the, um . . . ?'

'Yes.'

'I tried calling you Thursday and Friday at work to let you know it was coming, but couldn't get you. Left a message with your PA to call me, didn't you get it?'

'No.' Or maybe she did. She had a vague memory of Trix trying to press some message on her on Friday morning.

'And I would have called over the weekend but I was working. Mental shoot in Glasgow with psychotic models. Twenty-hour days.'

'It's OK.'

'So, um . . . even though we knew this was going to happen, it doesn't feel too hot, no?'

'No,' she gulped.

'But one of us had to do it.' He sounded very uncomfortable. 'To be honest, babes, I thought it'd be you. I was wondering what was taking you so long.'

'Busy,' she swallowed. 'New mag and all that.'

'Right! But, hey, I felt a total toe-rag putting those five things on it. I don't mean to bad-mouth you, you know that, right? Like, I was pissy at the time but not now, know what I'm saying? But they're the rules. We've not been separated two years and adultery wasn't the reason we split, so we have to give some reason to the court.'

Lisa wasn't quite ready to speak. She was waiting for the storm of crying that was happening in a locked place within her to pass. If she opened her mouth now it would all come out.

'Lees,' he pressed. He sounded concerned.

'I . . .' she managed.

'He*yyyy*,' he cooed.

'It's very sad,' she shook.

'I know, I know. Tell me about it!' After a pause, Oliver seemed to be thinking aloud. 'Why don't I visit you? We can sort it, put it to bed and all that.'

'You're loco.'

'I'm not loco. Look at it this way, we can both save ourselves a wedge in solicitor's fees if we sort out things like the apartment face to face. Any idea how much it'll cost each time my brief writes a letter to yours? Lots, Lees, I'm telling you.

'C'mon babes,' he coaxed. 'We can do this totally, like, amicably. One on one. *Mano a mano.*' When she didn't speak he cajoled further, '*Hombre a hombre.*'

With the tiniest of laughs, she managed, 'OK.'

'Yeah? For real? When?'

'This weekend?'

'You won't be working?'

'No.'

'Well, well, well,' he said, in a tone she wasn't quite sure of. Then he lightened up. 'I'll try and get a flight on Saturday and I'll bring all the bumpf.'

'I'll meet you at the airport.'

Just one night, she promised herself. One night pressed up against him, then she'd get over it.

She hung up the phone, unsure of what to do next. She could go back to bed, but instead, on a wild whim, decided to ring Jack.

'Thank you for the flowers.'

'Don't mention them. They were just to say that we . . . I . . . have the greatest respect for you and that –'

'Jack, apology accepted,' Lisa cut in.

'Ehm, what are you talking ab–' Then Jack stopped and sighed. 'OK, thank you.'

'So what's been happening?' She almost managed to sound interested.

Jack's tone cheered. 'Lots of good stuff, actually. The magazine's gone into reprint. I don't know if you saw them but pictures of the party were in five papers over the weekend and we've had requests for you to go on national radio during the week. We've had four unsolicited applications to replace Mercedes. Dublin's a very small place. And I found out which magazine Mercedes has gone to. It's not *Manhattan*, it's a teen weekly called *Froth*.'

It could have been because Oliver was coming, it could have been the good reports about *Colleen*, it certainly could have been the news about Mercedes, but something had shifted in Lisa, because when Jack then asked, 'Any chance of you coming back to work?' she was able to answer, 'S'pose.'

'Good.' he said. 'That means I can stop writing this article on men's skincare.'

'???'

'Trix made me do it. With yourself and Ashling out and Mercedes gone, she's the most senior member of *Colleen's* editorial staff who's in. The power has gone to her head. She's talking about sending Bernard for a facial just to see if she can make him cry.'

'I'll be in in an hour.'

En route to the bathroom for a much-needed shower, Lisa passed her bedroom and was shocked at the state of it. What had she been thinking of? She just wasn't the kind of person who lost it. Other people did, and good luck to them. But not Lisa – like it or not she was a survivor. Not that she didn't feel raw and wretched. She did. But nervous breakdowns were like coloured contact lenses – fine for other people, but they weren't really *her*.

CHAPTER 57

Ashling shifted in the bed and located the phone from underneath her. She'd been sleeping with it for four days. For the millionth time she pressed Marcus's home number. Answering machine. Then his work number. Voicemail. Finally his mobile.

'Still no reply?' Joy asked sympathetically as she and Ted clustered on Ashling's smelly bed.

'No. God, I wish he would. I'd just like some answers.'

'He's a dirty coward. Call around to his work. Hassle him at gigs. That'd be good, actually,' Joy said fiercely. 'In the guise of heckling, you could really wreck his head. Shouting up at him that he's hopeless in bed and that his mickey's –'

'– really small,' Ashling finished wearily for her.

'Really freckly, I was going to say,' Joy said. 'But I'll accept "small".'

'No. No way. To either of them.'

'OK, forget the heckling. But why don't you call around to him? If you want him back you should fight for him.'

'I don't know if I want him back. Anyway, I don't stand a chance. Not against Clodagh.'

'She's not that beautiful,' Joy said savagely.

Automatically they both turned to Ted, who blushed. 'Not at all,' he lied atrociously.

'See?' Ashling flung at Joy. 'He thinks she is.'

In the awkward silence that lowered on to them, Ashling took a dispassionate look around. She'd been in this room since Friday afternoon. It was now Monday evening and she'd left her bed only for brief visits to the bathroom. Her intention had been to have a sleep to get over the shock, then find Marcus and see what she could salvage. But somehow she'd never managed to get back out of bed. She liked it here now, she thought she might stay.

Her empty stare alighted on a bundle of tissues. All unused. Why wasn't she crying? With the weight of sadness she was carrying she felt she should be in perpetual convulsions. But she remained resolutely dry-eyed. Not even a hint – no catch to her voice, no achey swelling in her throat, no fullness in her face bones.

Not that she was numb. Oh, if only.

She spoke slowly, more to herself than the other two. 'I keep wondering what I did wrong, and I don't think it's my fault. I let him try out new material all the time. I went to all his gigs. Well, nearly.' Look at what happened the one time she didn't go. He'd picked up her best friend. 'I agreed with him ten times a day that

618

he was the best and that all the other comedians were crap.'

'Even me?' Ted asked uncertainly. 'Did he think I was crap?'

'No,' Ashling lied. The first night she'd met Marcus he'd enthused madly about Ted, but only – she realized with hindsight – because he didn't take him seriously. When it became clear that Ted had garnered a small but devoted following, Marcus began subtly to slag him off. Smart enough to know that Ashling wouldn't permit full-blown insults, he contented himself with remarks like, 'Good on Ted Mullins. We need one or two light-weights in this game.' By the time Ashling noticed that he was actually denigrating Ted, she was too set in her helpmeet role to object.

'It was all about Marcus Valentine,' Joy observed. 'He sounds like a selfish fucker.'

'It wasn't like that. It was fun helping him. We were close, we were pals.' That was what hurt so much. But he'd met someone he liked better, it happened all the time.

'Did you sense that something was going on?' Joy asked. 'Has he been behaving any differently?'

It was painful to think of the recent past in the light of her discoveries, but Ashling had to admit, 'The last few weeks, while I've been so busy, he's been narky. I thought it was just because he missed me. Imagine!'

'Did the, um –' Joy was making a half-hearted attempt to frame the question delicately and realized she couldn't. 'Did the riding continue as normal?'

Ted put his hands over his ears.

'No,' Ashling sighed. 'It slowed down a lot. Again I thought it was my fault. But we did have sex since I was in Cork. So for a time he was doing us both.

'Why did Clodagh stand for it?' she wondered, as if she was talking about a character in a soap opera.

'Maybe she didn't know,' Joy suggested. 'He could have lied to her. Or maybe he was using you as leverage to try to get her to leave Dylan.' Too late, Joy realized how cruel she sounded. 'Sorry,' she said humbly. 'I wasn't thinking . . . And what about Clodagh? If I had my choice between Marcus and Dylan I know which one I'd choose! Oh Christ. Sorry again. Listen, would you like some chips?'

Ashling shook her head.

'Anything to eat? Chocolate? Popcorn? Anything?' Joy demonstrated the wide choice of confectionery on Ashling's chest of drawers.

'No, and don't bring me any more.'

'Are you planning to get up ever again?'

'No,' Ashling said. 'I feel so . . . humiliated.'

'Don't give them the satisfaction,' Joy said stoutly.

'I feel that everyone hates me.'

'Why? You've done nothing wrong!'

'I feel like the whole world is against me, that nowhere is safe. And I'm very sad,' she added.

'Of course you're sad.'

'No, I'm sad about the wrong things. I keep thinking about Boo and how sad it is. And all the other homeless people, being cold and hungry. The loss of dignity, it's so dehumanizing . . .'

She stopped. She'd caught the she's-totally-flipped look that had passed between Joy and Ted. They thought the shock had unhinged some part of her. How could she care about homeless people, people she'd never met, when she had such a real-life tangible disaster of her own? They didn't understand. But there was one person who would understand.

If she hadn't been so catatonic, she'd have shuddered in horror. *This is how my mother felt.* And it was then that she made the shocking connection. *Dammit, I think I'm having a nervous breakdown.*

Flowers or no flowers, when Lisa got into work and saw Jack she couldn't help a burst of anger at his rejection of her.

'How are you?' He watched her carefully.

'Fine,' she said touchily.

'We missed you.' His eyes were kind – but not pitying – and her ire evaporated. She was just being childish.

'Want to see my skincare piece?' He proffered a print-out, which claimed that the Aveda stuff was 'nice', the Kiehl stuff was 'nice' and the Issey Miyake stuff was 'nice'.

Lisa fluttered the page back on to the desk and,

with an advisory wink, urged, 'Don't give up the day job.' They must have been really panicked about the *Colleen* staff if the likes of Jack had attempted an article. 'And Ashling's still out?' She couldn't contain her smugness. Hey, she was getting *divorced*, and she'd come to work.

It was only now she was back that she realized what a big buzz there was about the magazine, and how all her efforts to put it on the map had borne fruit. While she'd been lying in bed convinced she was the greatest failure of all time, she'd become a bit of a star – only in Ireland of course, but still.

There had already been one job offer from a rival Irish magazine and several journalists had rung, some interested in doing a serious profile on her, more of them interested in using her for 'filler' pieces, like 'My Favourite Holiday' and 'My Ideal Date'.

She permitted a certain warmth to creep through her, but more important than any magazine success was the coming weekend with Oliver. She had to look utterly spectacular – she'd have to organize a haul of fabulous clothes and get her hair done. And her nails. And her legs. She'd eat nothing, of course, so that she could eat normally with him . . .

'It's the *Sunday Times*,' Trix waved the phone at Lisa. 'They want to know what colour knickers you're wearing.'

'White,' Lisa said absently, and Kelvin almost came.

'I'm only joking,' Trix bleated. 'They just want to ask about your hair-care . . .'

But Lisa wasn't listening. She was on the phone to the DKNY London press office. 'We want to do a spread for our Christmas issue, but we need the clothes *by Friday.*'

'Lisa, can we talk about Mercedes' replacement?' Jack asked.

Mercedes leaving them in the lurch burst another firework of rage in her, which she had to work to disperse. 'Trix, ring Ghost, Fendi, Prada, Paul Smith and Gucci! Tell them we'll run some pages on them for the December issue but only if they get the threads to us by Friday. Come on.' She beat Jack to his office.

'She's up to something,' Trix observed – to thin air. She missed Ashling and Mercedes, it wasn't nice having no one to play with.

Jack and Lisa looked at the four unsolicited applications for fashion editor and decided to interview all of them.

'And if they're pants, we'll run an ad,' Lisa said. 'Can I ask you something? How do I find a solicitor?'

Jack thought for a moment. 'We have a legal firm on retainer. Why don't you go and see them? If they can't do your, um, stuff, they'll recommend someone who can.'

'Thanks.'

'And I'll do whatever I can to help you,' Jack promised.

Lisa eyed him suspiciously. There was no getting away from it. She liked him. He was continuing with the warm, supportive relationship he'd been offering since the day she'd cried in his office over not going to the shows. It wasn't his fault she'd chosen to over-interpret it.

On Tuesday afternoon Ashling's phone rang. She snatched it up. *Be Marcus*, she prayed. *Be Marcus*.

But her heart sank when she heard a woman's voice. Her mother. 'Ashling love, we were wondering how your launch went and I rang you at work. They said you were out. What's wrong, are you sick?'

'No.'

'What then?'

'I'm . . .' Ashling hovered over the taboo word, then gave in, feeling both fear and relief. 'I'm depressed.'

Monica knew immediately that this was not a simple case of 'I'm depressed because I forgot to record *Friends* last night.' Ashling had taken great care never, *ever* to use the word depression with regard to herself. This was serious. History repeating itself.

'My boyfriend got off with Clodagh,' Ashling explained weakly.

'Clodagh *Nugent*?' Monica sounded furious.

'She's been Clodagh Kelly for the past ten years. But anyway, it's more than just that.'

Monica considered anxiously. 'How had are you?'

'I'm in bed. It's my fifth day. I have no immediate plans to leave.'

'Eating?'

'Nope.'

'Washing?'

'Nope.'

'Suicidal thoughts?'

'Not yet.' Goody, she had that to look forward to.

'I'll get the train up tomorrow morning, love, and I'll mind you for a while.'

Monica waited to be told to fuck off, as usual. But instead all she got was a weary, 'Fine.' Fear clutched its cold hand around her heart. Ashling must be very bad indeed.

'Don't worry, love, we're going to get help for you. I won't let you go through what I went through,' Monica promised vehemently. 'Nowadays things are different.'

'Less of a stigma,' Ashling said through unresponsive lips.

'Better drugs,' Monica retorted.

Joy and Ted were trying to tempt Ashling with a fresh consignment of chocolate and magazines on Tuesday evening when her doorbell rang. They all froze.

For the first time in days, Ashling's listless face became illuminated. 'It might be Marcus!'

'I'll go and tell him to fuck off.' Joy was already moving to the door.

'No!' Ashling said fiercely. 'No. I want to talk to him.'

Within seconds Joy was back. 'It's not Marcus . . .'

she hissed. Ashling immediately eddied back into the mire.

'It's Divine Jack.'

This bizarre visit jolted Ashling a little from her torpor. What did he want? To sack her for missing work?

'Wash yourself, for Christ's sake!' Joy urged. 'You smell dodgy.'

'I can't,' Ashling said heavily. So heavily that Joy knew she was wasting her time. As a compromise she insisted that Ashling put on a clean pair of pyjamas, comb her hair and brush her teeth. Then Joy considered two bottles of perfume. 'Happy or *Oui*? Happy,' she decided. 'Let's try the power of suggestion.' She drenched Ashling in a haze of Happy then pushed her, as though she was a wind-up toy, in the direction of the living-room. 'Off you go.'

Jack was on her blue sofa, his hands hanging between his knees. It was the weirdest sight. Depressed as she was, that thought burrowed through her stupor. He belonged to the world of work, yet here he was, making her flat look even smaller than it already was.

His dark suit, messy hair and askew tie gave him the aspect of a careworn and distracted man. She hovered in the doorway, watching him exchange thoughts with her maple laminate floor. Then he cocked his head to one side, saw her and smiled.

The light in the room changed as he stood up.

'Hi,' Ashling said. 'I'm sorry for missing today and yesterday.'

'I only came to see how you are, not to hustle you back to work.'

Then Ashling remembered. Jack had been unexpectedly gentle and kind after Dylan had delivered his terrible news.

'I'll try and come in tomorrow,' she offered. There was as much chance that she'd climb Kilimanjaro.

'Why don't you take the week?' he suggested. 'Try and come back on Monday?'

'OK. Thanks.' The relief that she didn't have to attempt to face the world was so great that she didn't even argue. 'My mother is coming to stay for a few days. If anything will drive me back to work, that will, I'm sure.'

'Oh yes?' Jack's smile was empathetic. 'You'll have to tell me all about it sometime.'

'Yes.' She couldn't imagine having the energy to even tell the time.

'And how are you now?' he asked.

She hesitated. It wasn't exactly the kind of thing you discuss with your boss, but fuck it, what did it matter? What did anything matter? 'I feel very sad.'

'That's to be expected. The end of a relationship, the loss of a friendship.'

'But it's more than that.' She was trying to make sense of her overwhelming grief. 'I feel a sadness about the whole world.'

She watched Jack. Did he think she was a nutter?

'Go on,' he urged gently.

'All I can see is the sad stuff. And it's every-where. We're the walking wounded, the entire human race.'

'*Weltschmerz*,' he said.

'Bless you,' she said absently.

'No,' he laughed softly. '*Weltschmerz*. It's German for "world sadness".'

'There's a word for this?'

She knew she wasn't the first person to feel like this. She knew her mother had too. But if a word had actually been invented to describe the feeling, lots of others must have felt it. It was a comfort. Jack rustled a white paper bag. 'I, ah, brought you something.'

'What? Tissues? I could open a shop. Or grapes? I'm not sick. Just, just . . . humiliated.'

'No, it's . . . well, actually it's sushi.'

She paused, stung. 'Are you having a laugh?'

'No! It's just that you seemed interested when we got it in the office.' When Ashling remained mute he laboured on, 'I thought you might enjoy it. There's nothing scary, not even raw fish. It's mostly vegetarian – cucumber, avocado, a little bit of crab. A sushi-for-beginners kit. I could take you through it . . .'

But at Ashling's suspicious expression he backed off. 'Ehm, fine, I'll just leave you to it then. Hope you feel better. See you on Monday.'

After he'd gone Ted and Joy appeared in the living-room.

'What's in the bag?'

628

'Sushi.'

'Sushi! That's a weird thing to bring.'

They circled the white paper bag warily, as if it was radioactive.

'Will we take a look?' Ted eventually asked.

At Ashling's, ''f you want,' he slid out the lacquered black box and stared, fascinated, at the little rice rolls arrayed in pretty ranks.

'I didn't think it would look like this,' Joy remarked.

'And what are all these other things?' Ted poked at a silver sachet.

'Soy sauce,' Ashling said uninterestedly.

'And this?' Ted peeled the lid off a short styrofoam container.

'Pickled ginger.'

'And this?' He indicated a mound of green putty.

'I forget what it's called,' Ashling admitted sullenly, 'but it's hot.'

After more time was spent in cautious exploration, Ted took the bull by the horns. 'I'm going to try some.'

Ashling shrugged.

'This looks like a cucumber one.' He popped it into his mouth. 'Now I'll cleanse my palate with a slice of ginger, then I'll –'

'That's not how you do it,' Ashling said irritably.

'Well, show me then.'

CHAPTER 58

The gentle knock on her window made Clodagh jump to her feet. Happiness flooded through her. He was here. She flew to the front-door and opened it quietly.

'The cock crows at dusk,' Marcus said in a thick Russian accent.

'Sssshhh.' She put her finger to her lips in an exaggerated gesture but they were both bubbling over with laughter and delight.

'Are they asleep?' Marcus whispered.

'They're asleep.'

'Halleluiah!' He almost forgot the need for quiet. 'Now I can have my wicked way with you.' He stepped into the hall, grabbed her and, both of them giggling and bumping against the coat-stand, he began to remove her clothes.

'Come into the front-room,' she invited.

'I want to do it here,' he said wickedly. 'On the wellingtons and the schoolbags.'

'Tough, you can't!' She went into convulsions at his fake-sulky face. 'You look like Craig.'

He thrust his bottom lip out further and she laughed even more.

'But seriously,' she whispered, 'what if one of them gets out of bed to go to the bathroom and sees us in the throes on the hall floor? Go on, into the front-room with you!'

Obediently, he picked up his shirt and followed her in. 'It reminds me of being a teenager, all this sneaking around. Kinda sexy.'

Dylan had terrified Clodagh with his threats about custody, so she was determined that Molly and Craig wouldn't see her in bed with Marcus. But this week Marcus was very busy at work, so daytime sex was out. The only time they could hope to do it was when Molly and Craig were asleep. A daily period of approximately twenty minutes.

On the couch, they pulled the clothes from each other's bodies and, in a brief pause to stare into each other's eyes, Clodagh sighed up at him, 'I'm so happy to see you.'

The five days since Dylan had left had been a strange, night-marish time. Guilt was ripping her asunder, especially because the children kept asking when Daddy was coming home. She was increasingly isolated: even her own mother was furious with her. And she felt frighteningly out of control – appalled at the destruction that she had unleashed.

The only time the horror let up was when she was with Marcus. He was a diamond in the rubbish tip of her life. She'd read that phrase somewhere – in the novel where the woman opens a second-hand designer-clothing shop – and it had leapt out at her.

'Not as happy as I am to see you.' Marcus scanned her naked body, then placed his hands under her and turned her on her stomach. Before he entered her he waited a moment, almost reverently. It was nearly a week since they'd actually had sex. There hadn't been a hope of it on Saturday afternoon. After Craig had hit Marcus with the red truck, he wouldn't let him within three feet of Clodagh.

'Come on,' Clodagh implored, her voice muffled.

Marcus worked himself once, twice with his hand, then positioned himself accurately at her entrance. Nothing could beat the first thrust into her. Because their time together had always been short there was a fired-up violence to their sex: he liked to get all the way to the hilt on the first go, shoving through that semi-resistant yielding, straight into head-lifting ecstacy. And if he could elicit from Clodagh a stifled gasp that was midway between pleasure and pain, it spurred him even more.

But this time his long, perfect stroke was halted about halfway when Clodagh tensed, semi-sat up and hissed, 'Ssshh.' She turned her head to the ceiling and froze. 'I thought I heard . . . No,' she relaxed again. 'I must have been imagining it.'

He got all the way in on the second go, but couldn't help feeling he'd been deprived of something. After a short, furious shag, they had another slightly less frantic one with her on top.

Dipping with sweat she lay on him and murmured, 'You make me happy.'

'You make me happy too,' he replied. 'But do you know what would make me even happier? Going upstairs to bed. This couch is doing my back in.'

'We shouldn't really. What if they see you?'

'You could lock the bedroom door. Come on,' he grinned, 'I'm not finished with you yet tonight.'

'Yes, but . . . Oh, OK, but you can't stay the night. Deal?'

'Deal.'

Dr McDevitt was alarmed by the woman marching into his surgery and demanding Prozac with menaces. 'And we're not leaving without it!'

'Mrs –' he consulted his appointment sheet, 'Ah, Kennedy, I can't just go handing out prescriptions . . .'

'Call me Monica, and it's not for me, it's for my daughter.' Monica directed his attention to Ashling.

'Oh Ashling, I didn't see you there. What's up?' He liked Ashling.

She shifted helplessly and, aided by her mother's elbow, eventually came up with the goods. 'I feel awful.'

'Her boyfriend left her for her best friend,' Monica elaborated when it became clear that Ashling wasn't going to.

Dr McDevitt sighed. Being jilted by a boyfriend, well, it's life, isn't it? But people wanted Prozac for *everything* – if they lost an earring, if they knelt on a piece of Lego.

'It's not just the boyfriend.' Monica pressed Ashling's case. 'She's had family problems.'

Dr McDevitt could well believe it. Overbearing mother, perhaps?

'I suffered from depression for fifteen years. Been hospitalized several times –'

'No need to boast,' he muttered.

'– and Ashling's acting the way I did. Flung in the bed, refusing to eat, obsessed with homeless people.'

Dr McDevitt perked up. This was more like it. 'What about homeless people?'

Another prod and a hissed, '*Tell him!*' from Monica before Ashling raised her pale, stiff face and mumbled, 'There's a homeless boy I know. I was always bothered about him, but now I'm sad about every single one of them. Even the ones I haven't met.'

This was enough to convince Dr McDevitt.

'Why do I feel like this?' Ashling wondered. 'Am I going mad?'

'No, you're not, but, ehm, depression is a peculiar beast,' he dissembled. In other words, he hadn't much of a clue. 'But at a guess, it sounds from your, eh, mother's testimony that you could have inherited a tendency towards it and that the trauma of losing your earri– I mean boyfriend, triggered it.'

He gave her a prescription for the lowest dose, 'On the proviso,' he scribbled something on a pad, 'that you also go for counselling.'

He approved of counselling. If people wanted to be happy let them put their backs into it a bit.

Outside the surgery Ashling said, 'Can I go home now?'

Monica had only been able to inveigle her to the doctor by getting a taxi. 'Just walk to the chemist with me, then we'll go back.'

Disconsolately, Ashling let Monica link arms with her. She kept being made to do things she didn't want to and was too subdued to resist. The problem was that Monica had made Ashling's happiness her project, because she was so over-joyed to get an opportunity to make up for years of unavoidable neglect.

It was an early-autumn afternoon and, as they walked slowly through the benign sunshine, Ashling leant against her mother's elbow, thick and soft from layers of clothes.

After the chemist, Ashling found herself being walked through Stephen's Green, where she was forced to sit on a bench and watch the lake through slanting sunshine. Birds splish-splashed on the water and Ashling wondered when she could go home.

'Soon,' Monica promised.

'Soon? Good.' Then she recommended watching the birds. 'Ducks,' she observed leadenly.

'That's right! Ducks!' Monica was as animated as if Ashling was two and a half. 'Getting ready to fly south for the winter . . . For the warmer weather,' she added.

'I know.'

'Packing their bikinis and sun-tan lotion.'

Silence resumed.

'Ordering their traveller's cheques,' Monica elaborated.

Ashling continued to stare straight ahead.

'Painting their toenails,' Monica suggested. 'Buying sunglasses and straw hats.'

It was the sun-glasses that did it. The image of a duck wearing shades and looking like a mafioso was comical enough to elicit a half-smile from Ashling. Only then was she allowed to go home.

On Saturday morning, when Liam picked Lisa up in his taxi to drive her to the airport, his admiration was blatant.

'God above, Lisa,' he exclaimed paternally. 'But you're looking fantastic!'

*Scam*tastic, actually. 'I should do, Liam. I've been preparing since seven.'

She had to admit that she'd pulled it off. Everything was perfect: her hair, skin, eyebrows, nails. And clothes. On Wednesday and Thursday couriers had delivered some of the most magnificent garments on the planet, she'd cherry-picked the choicest pieces and was now wearing them.

On the drive, Lisa explained a little of what was happening, which upset Liam.

'Getting divorced,' he muttered. 'Your man must be mad. And blind.'

To get near the door, Liam parked in a spot that was both illegal and dangerous. 'I'll be waiting here for you.'

Lisa was already breathless, even before she ran into the arrivals hall. Although the monitor said that Oliver's flight had landed there was no sign of him, so she stood at the meeting point, trained her eyes on the double glass doors and waited. Her heart was pounding and her tongue kept sticking to the roof of her cotton-wool mouth. She waited some more. People appeared in regular spurts, traipsing self-consciously through those who were waiting, but no sign of Oliver. After a while she jumpily rang home to check that he hadn't left a message saying he was delayed, but there was nothing.

She was almost convinced that he wasn't coming when finally she saw him moving gracefully towards the glass doors. Her head went light and the ground see-sawed slightly. He was all in black. A long-line black leather jacket over a black polo neck and lean black pants. Then he saw her and smiled his thousand-yard smile. The only man-made object they could see from space, she used to say to him in another life.

She rushed forward. 'I'd almost given up on you.'

'Sorry, babes,' his lips curved around his shockingly white teeth, 'but I was stopped by Immigration. Only person on the whole plane to be.' He put his hand on his hip and said with exaggerated curiosity, 'Now, I wonder why *that* was.'

'Bastards!'

'Yeah, just couldn't seem to convince them I was a British citizen. Despite having a British passport.'

She clucked with concern. 'Are you upset?'

'Nah, I'm used to it. The same thing happened the last time I visited here. You look great, babes.'

'So do you.'

Kathy was just finishing a mighty clean-up when Liam dropped them home. She tried to slip away discreetly but Lisa stopped her.

'Oliver, this is Kathy, she lives across the road. And Kathy, this is Oliver, my hus – friend.'

'How do you do,' Kathy said, wondering what a husfriend was. Perhaps it was something like a gal pal.

When Kathy left, they lapsed into extra-nice, super-jovial awkwardness – although they were well disposed to each other, there was no doubt but that this was a very strange situation with no clear code of behaviour. Oliver over-enthusiastically admired the house and Lisa grandiosely outlined her plans, with specific reference to a wooden blind.

Eventually they both calmed down and began behaving more normally. 'We should get started, babes,' Oliver said, and unloaded from his bag something that, for a heartbeat, she thought was a present for her, then realized was a box-file of documents: deeds, bank accounts, credit-card statements, mortgage bumpf. He put on a pair of silver-framed glasses and, though he looked deliciously professional, all her fluttery, nervy, girly anticipation abruptly vanished. What was she thinking of? This wasn't a date, this was a meeting about their divorce.

Her spirits suddenly slithered to the bottom of the pole. Heavily, she took a seat at the kitchen table and set about the severing of their two financial lives, in order to restore them, functioning and complete, to their single status. It was as delicate and complicated a process as separating Siamese twins.

Playing paperchase with bank accounts that went back five years, they tried to list all the different payments they'd both made on their flat. Between deposits and endowment policies and solicitor's fees, the two distinct strands were regularly obscured.

A couple of times it got jagged and ugly, as things often do over money. Lisa insisted quite forcibly that she'd paid all the solicitor's fees, but Oliver was certain that he too had contributed.

'Look here,' he rustled and located a stiff-paged invoice from their solicitor, 'a bill for five hundred and twelve pounds, sixteen pence. And here,' he jabbed at his bank statement, 'a *cheque* for five hundred and twelve pounds, sixteen pence, issued three weeks later. A coincidence? I don't think so!'

'Show me that!' She examined them both, then muttered, 'Sorry.'

The doorbell rang and Francine waltzed in. 'Hiya Leeeeesa. Er, hiya,' she nodded at Oliver, shyness eclipsing her confidence. She turned back to Lisa. 'We're having a slumber party tonight. Me and Chloe and Trudie and Phoebe. Will you come?'

'Thanks, but I've already got plans.'

'OK. Um, have you any spare face-packs we could use?'

Lisa bit back annoyance. 'Sorry Oliver, just a sec. Come into my bedroom, Francine.'

'Bless!' Oliver exclaimed, when Francine departed with a plastic bag full of face-packs, nail polishes, exfoliants and other slumber-party paraphernalia.

Lisa twitched irritably. 'She only called to get a look at you.'

They returned to the paperchase and kept stumbling over memories.

'What the hell did we buy at Aero that cost so much?'

'Our bed,' Oliver replied shortly.

Stillness descended, dense with unexpressed feelings.

'A cheque to Discovery Travel?' Lisa asked later.

'Cyprus.'

That one word hurled a bomb of emotions at her. Dazzling warmth, limbs tangled while late-afternoon sunshine slanted shadowy patterns across their sheets: she was intensely in love, on her first 'married' holiday, unable to imagine ever being without Oliver.

Look at them now, coming across the cheque as they prepared for their divorce. Wasn't life weird?

A couple of hours on, the doorbell rang again. This time it was Beck. 'Lisa, do you want to come OUT? We're just kicking a BALL around.'

'I'm busy, Beck.'

'Hiya.' Beck tried a man-to-man nod at Oliver, but couldn't hide his manifest awe. 'How about yourself?'

'He's busy also.' Lisa was getting increasingly pissed off. They were treating Oliver like a freak-show.

'Actually,' Oliver put down his pen and took off his glasses, 'I could do with a break. This is doing me in. Half an hour?' He unfolded himself fluidly and Lisa watched his muscular grace.

'You coming, LISA?'

'Might as well.'

'At the start she used to play dirty,' Beck confided to Oliver, 'but she's stopped now.'

'She plays football with you?' Oliver sounded astonished.

''Course she does.' Now it was Beck's turn to sound astonished. 'She's not bad. For a girl.'

Open-mouthed, Oliver said – almost accusingly – 'You've changed.'

'I haven't.' Lisa's voice was level.

The thirty minutes spent skidding and scuffling after a ball around the cul-de-sac was a good idea. They were breathless and elated when they returned to the kitchen table strewn with documents.

'Oooo-weee,' Oliver winced when he saw it. 'I'd forgotten.'

'Hey, let's leave it for tonight.'

'Best not, babes. A lot to get through.'

Knocked back but hiding it well, Lisa rang for a couple of pizzas and they started work again. It was midnight before they stopped.

'What's the time-scale on all this?' Lisa asked.

'As soon as we're in agreement over the finances we lodge it in the court, and the decree nisi will be delivered two to three months later. Then the final decree comes six weeks after that.'

'Oh. That quickly.' And Lisa couldn't think of anything else to say.

The day had left her exhausted, sullied and sorrowful. Her neck hurt, her heart hurt and now it was bedtime and she so didn't want to have sex.

Neither did he. They were both much too sad.

He undressed unthinkingly, wearily, letting his clothes lie where they fell, then climbed into Lisa's bed as though he'd been there a million times. He held out his arms to her and she went to him.

Skin against skin, they assumed their normal sleeping positions – spooned together, her back pressed tightly against his chest, her feet between his thighs. More intimate, more tender than sex. In the darkness she cried. He heard her and could find nothing within him to comfort her with.

The following day they took up their positions at the table once more and worked until three o'clock, when it was time for Oliver to leave. She took a taxi with him to the airport and when she returned to her cavernously empty house, her bed beckoned lasciviously. She was so depressed. But she resisted climbing back in and checking out of things again. Life must go on.

CHAPTER 59

On Monday morning, Monica walked Ashling to work. 'Good girl, off you go.' It was like her first day at school. Ashling walked through the front-doors, then half-turned back and Monica gesticulated *Go on!* through the glass. Reluctantly she traipsed towards the lift.

When she took up her position at her desk everyone looked funny at her, then suddenly they became humiliatingly extra-nice.

'Would you like a cup of tea?' Trix offered awkwardly.

'Trix, you're freaking me out,' Ashling replied, then tried to look at the things on her desk. When she looked up a second later Trix was shaking her head at Mrs Morley and mouthing *She doesn't want tea.*

Jack came flying in, a huge bundle of documents under his arm. He looked stressed and narky but when he noticed Ashling he slowed down and lightened up. 'How are you?' he asked gently.

'Well, I'm out of bed,' she offered. But her plaster-of-Paris rigid face was an indication that all wasn't exactly jolly either. 'Look, the day you came round to my flat . . . Thank you for the sushi, I was a bit, um, touchy.'

'No problem. How's the *Weltschmerz*?'

'Alive and well.'

He nodded in encouraging, but impotent silence.

'I'd better do some work,' she said.

'This sadness you feel?' Jack asked slowly. 'Is it free-floating or does it take a particular form?'

Ashling considered and after a while spoke. 'A particular form, I suppose. There's this homeless boy I know. Boo, the one in the photos, remember? He's made homelessness real for me and it's breaking my heart into pieces.'

After a silence Jack said thoughtfully, 'You know, we could give him a job. Start him on something basic like being a runner at the TV station.'

'But you can't offer a job to someone you haven't met.'

'I know Boo.'

'How?'

'I saw him in the street one day. I recognized him from the photos, so we had a little chat. I wanted to thank him, those photos made a huge difference to the profile of *Colleen*. I thought he seemed very bright, very keen.'

'Oh, he is, he's interested in everythi – Wait a minute, are you serious?'

'Sure. Why not? God knows, we owe him. Look at all the advertising those pictures generated.'

Ashling lifted momentarily, then she slid back

645

into the pit. 'But what about all the other home-less people? The ones who didn't get into the photos.'

Jack laughed sadly. 'I can't give them all jobs.'

With a loud clatter the door opened and a dapper-looking young man beamed around the office. 'Morning campers!' he declared.

'Who's that?' Ashling wondered, taking in his streaked hair, tailored magenta pants, see-through T-shirt and the tiny leather jacket he was peeling from his body.

'Robbie, our new boy. Mercedes' replacement,' Jack said. 'He started on Thursday. Robbie! Come and meet Ashling.'

Robbie fluttered a hand to his almost-naked chest and affected surprise. 'Little old moi?!'

'I think he's gay,' Kelvin hissed.

'No shit, Sherlock,' Trix said with withering sarcasm.

Robbie solemnly shook hands with Ashling then, with a gasp, fell on her handbag. 'Very Gucci! I think I'm having a fashion moment.'

Ashling actually managed to work – which came as a surprise. In fairness, she wasn't given anything remotely taxing. And the one thing that resolutely didn't appear on her desk for her to edit, sub-edit or input was Marcus Valentine's monthly article.

At the end of the day, her mother collected her from work and permitted her to go straight to bed when she got home.

On Tuesday morning, with much prodding, poking and motherly encouragement, she managed to get up and go to work again. Same on Wednesday morning. And Thursday.

On Friday, Monica returned to Cork. 'I'd better. Your father will probably have burnt the house down in my absence. Now, keep taking the tablets – never mind if they make you feel dizzy and like puking – then sort out some counselling and you'll be grand.'

'OK.' Ashling went to work and felt she was doing quite well – until midday, when Dylan walked into the office. Immediately, her low-level nausea increased. He'd have information. Information she was hungry for but which would inevitably cause pain.

'Free for lunch?' he asked.

His arrival sent a thrill through the office. Those who didn't know what Marcus Valentine looked like mouthed excitedly to those who did, *Is that him?* Were they going to be witness to a romantic passionate reunion? So they were very disappointed when those in the know mouthed back, *No, that's the friend's husband.*

As Ashling got her bag, Dylan's and Lisa's eyes met in a flare of one-beautiful-person-to-another interest.

Dylan looked different. He'd always been handsome, if a mite bland. But overnight, he'd acquired a glittery hardness, a dissipated magnetism. With his hand on Ashling's waist, he guided her out, the eyes of the entire office burning the backs of the two cuckolds.

They went to the pub next door and found a table in a corner. Though Ashling would only have Diet Coke, Dylan ordered a pint of lager.

'Hair of the dog,' he exhaled. 'On the serious razz last night.'

'Still at your mother's?' Ashling asked.

'Yes.' A bitter little laugh.

So that meant Clodagh and Marcus were still together. It hadn't all blown over and revealed itself as a brief madness. She had a very real, visceral desire to vomit. 'What's been happening?'

'Not much yet, except that we've decided I'll see the kids every weekend and stay in the house on Saturday nights.' Shame-faced he admitted, 'I've told Clodagh I'll wait for her, so hopefully she'll cop on. Though she's actually told me she loves this wanker. God knows why.' A pause of realization. 'Sorry.'

''s OK.'

'How are *you* doing?' He turned the spotlight of his concern on to her and momentarily he was like the old Dylan.

She hesitated. What was she going to say? *I hate the world, I hate being alive, I'm on anti-depressants, my mother has to put the toothpaste on my tooth-brush in the morning and now that she's gone back to Cork I don't know how I'll manage to brush my teeth.*

'Fine,' she said.

He didn't look too convinced, so she promised him, 'Really, I am. Go on, tell me more of what's been going on.'

Dylan exhaled miserably. 'It's the children I'm really worried about. They're so confused, it's desperate. But they're too young for the whole story. And I shouldn't be turning them against their mother anyway, even if I hate her.'

'You don't hate her.'

'Oh, believe me Ashling, I do.'

Ashling found his truculence pathetic. He only hated Clodagh because he loved her so much.

'It might all blow over,' Ashling said, with as much hope for herself as for Dylan.

'Yeah. Let's wait and see. Have you spoken to either of them?'

'I saw Clodagh two weeks ago today on the . . . that Friday. But I haven't been able to get hold of . . .' She hesitated. Saying his name hurt. '. . . Marcus. I've tried ringing him, but he's stopped answering his phone.'

'You could call to his house.'

'No.'

'Good on you. Keep your dignity.'

Ashling shifted forlornly. It wasn't really that. She simply hadn't the heart.

When Oliver returned to London he didn't ring Lisa, and she didn't ring him either. There was nothing to say. They were both going to get approval from their solicitors over their financial situations, then the decree nisi was only a matter of months.

Lisa got through the week but, although she was functioning, she wasn't anything like OK. She'd managed to put the October issue to bed, but it had been like pushing a ball of glue up a hill. Especially with Ashling going round like a zombie.

Robbie was good, though. Full of wild ideas for future issues. A lot of them *too* outré, but at least one – for a shoot styled like an S&M session – was pure genius.

When everything had gone to the printers on Friday evening, several people invited her for after-work drinks. Trix and Robbie and even *Jack* had suggested they go somewhere to celebrate 'closure on October'. But she'd had enough of them all and she went straight home.

No sooner was she in than Kathy called to the door. Kathy seemed to be around a lot. Or if it wasn't Kathy it was Francine. Or several others from the road.

'Come over to us for your dinner this evening,' Kathy invited.

Lisa almost laughed at the thought, then Kathy said, 'We're having roast chicken,' and suddenly Lisa found herself agreeing. Why not? she thought, trying to justify it. She could start the Scarsdale diet, she hadn't done it in ages and roast chicken would fit in perfectly.

Ten minutes later she walked into Kathy's kitchen and was hit by steam and the noise of the telly and children fighting. Kathy looked frazzled. 'We're nearly ready. Stir the gravy, you useless eejit.' This was directed at John, her benign lump of a husband. 'Drink, Lisa?'

Lisa was about to ask for a glass of dry white wine when Kathy elaborated, 'Ribena? Tea? Milk?'

'Erm, oh, milk, I suppose.'

'Get Lisa some milk.' Kathy levelled a passing kick at Jessica, who was rolling on the floor with Francine. 'In a good glass. Sit at the table, everyone.'

Lisa noticed that she was given about three times as much as anyone else. Kathy had heaped at least four roast potatoes on to her plate before she could protest that she didn't eat them. She tried to pretend they weren't there but they looked and smelt so delicious . . . She fought it a little harder, then yielded, and for the first time in ten years, a piece of roast potato crossed her lips. *I'll start the diet tomorrow.*

'Stop kicking the table leg!' Kathy yelled at Lauren, the youngest. Lauren made a face, stopped and started again three seconds later.

'You're sticking your elbow into me,' Francine complained to Lisa.

'Sorry.'

'Don't say sorry,' Francine was instantly contrite. 'You should say that at least you don't make noise when you eat.'

'Right, got it.'

'Or that you're not a big fat greedy guts,' Jessica offered helpfully.

'Or that I'm not the one who keeps farting,' Lisa said.

'Yeah!'

Crammed around the small kitchen table, the telly blaring, milk moustaches on everyone, including herself probably, Lisa had a flash of *déjà vu*. Of what? What did this remind her of? And a dreadful realization lunged at her. It was just like her own home in Hemel Hempstead. The crampedness, the noise, the good-natured bickering, the whole *feel* was the same. *How on earth did I end up back here?*

'Are you OK, Lisa?' Kathy asked.

Lisa nodded. But she was fighting the desire to catapult vertically from her chair and run from the house. She was a working-class girl who'd spent her life trying to be something else. And despite years devoted to the gruelling treadmill of networking, sucking up, doing down, always paying attention, never relaxing, she'd been brought inexorably back to where she started.

It knocked the power of speech from her.

She'd never really considered what she was sacrificing as she'd rocket-launched herself away from her roots. The rewards had always seemed worth it. But sitting in Kathy's kitchen, she could see no evidence of the glamorous life she'd constructed for herself. Instead she was walloped by what she'd forfeited – friends, family, worst of all Oliver, and for nothing.

CHAPTER 60

It was midnight and Jack Devine was exhausted and dispirited. He'd been pacing the streets of Dublin for a couple of hours, looking for Boo and having no joy. He felt like a particularly bad gumshoe. Apart from checking the doorways in the streets around Ashling's flat, he had no idea where to look. Where were good homeless haunts?

The street people he'd asked had denied all knowledge of Boo. Perhaps they really didn't know him, but Jack suspected that it was more to do with protecting him. Should he have slipped them a tenner, blown smoke in their eyes and said, 'Maybe this'll help your memory'? Wasn't that what happened in Raymond Chandler books?

Cursing his dearth of street smarts, he continued walking. Off the main streets, along dark laneways, into loading bays . . . maybe this was him! A flesh-less bundle of limbs was huddled under a coat on a flattened cardboard box.

'Excuse me,' Jack crouched down beside him, and a small, thin, *very* young face looked up at him. Defensive and frightened. It wasn't Boo. 'Sorry.' Jack backed away. 'Sorry to have disturbed you.'

653

He made his way back out on to the main drag and just ran out of steam. He'd had enough for one night, he'd try again tomorrow. Heading for his car, he suddenly heard someone call, 'Jack! Over here.'

And there, sitting on a hairdresser's step, reading a book was, of all people, Boo.

'Out on the piss?' Boo enquired, with his gappy grin.

'Er, no.' Jack was stunned that it was Boo who had found *him*. 'I've been looking for you for the past couple of hours.'

'So it was *you*.' Earlier JohnJohn had warned him that some chap was asking about him. He'd suspected he was a plainclothes – because what else could he be? – but he wasn't entirely sure.

'It was me.' Jack crouched down beside Boo and suddenly, as though crossing an invisible line, the smell hit him like a blow from a lump-hammer. With enormous effort of will, he forced his face not to register it.

'So what's up?' Boo was wary. He'd liked Jack that time he'd stopped and chatted about those fashion photos with him. But generally people did not seek Boo out unless he was in some sort of trouble.

Tuning out the reeking air. Jack searched for the right words, unwilling to sound patronizing. He wanted Boo to come away from this with some dignity.

'I have a problem,' Jack began.

Muscle by muscle, Boo's face began to shut down.

'I have a vacancy at the television station I work at and I'm looking for the right person to fill it. Your name was suggested to me by a colleague.'

'What do you mean?' Boo's eyes were narrow with suspicion.

'I'm offering you a job. If you'd like it,' he added quickly.

Boo's face was a study of incomprehension. This was outside the breadth of his experience. 'Why?' he finally managed. People being nice to him was a rare event and he wasn't inclined to trust it.

'Ashling thought you would be suitable and I respect her opinion.'

'Ashling . . .' If she had something to do with this, maybe it wasn't a total put-on. But what else could it be? Sharply, he said, 'You're taking the piss, are you?'

'No, I'm really not. Why don't you come and see us over at the station and you might believe me then.'

'You'd let me in?'

At that Jack thought his heart might cave in. 'Of course we would. How else would you do any work?'

It was then that Boo went against his every natural instinct and began to believe Jack. 'But why . . . ?' His eyes glistened and he looked terribly young, so like a child. Jack felt his own face fill with emotion. 'I've never had a job before.' Boo swallowed.

'Well, isn't it about time you started?'

'Can't be a layabout all my life!'

'Er, yeah.' Jack wasn't sure whether or not to laugh.

'Oh, lighten up,' Boo elbowed him with a watery grin. 'And will it be just book reviews I'll be doing, or will you be needing other stuff done as well?'

'Erm –' Jack was entirely wrong-footed. 'Other stuff as well, I'd say.'

The next morning at work, Jack offered his news to Ashling as if it was a present. 'I found Boo and told him about the job over at the TV station. He seemed keen.'

'Great!' Her enthusiastic voice didn't match her whey-face.

'He's short of clothes, so I've told him to come in and see Kelvin. There's a lot of men's clothes in the "fashion department" that no one wants, he might as well get togged out.'

Ashling became very still. She still hadn't shed one tear, but this was almost enough to dissolve her. 'That's very nice of you,' she said to her chest.

'The thing was,' Jack sounded confused, 'at first Boo seemed to think that we wanted him to do book reviews for *Colleen*. Why's that?'

She lifted and released her shoulder bones. 'Search me.' Suddenly she wished she hadn't said that. The words had caused something to dart across Jack's face and it froze her mid-shrug. Whatever it was made her feel alive. And afraid. 'Book reviews?' She tried to focus, then remembered. 'I've been giving him proof copies. Of books no one else wanted,' she added hastily. 'And he always gave me his opinion.'

'Oh right. Well, he starts as a runner at the station on Monday. The book reviews on *Colleen* are Lisa's call. But we can always ask her,' he concluded cheerfully.

In floods of tears, Clodagh opened her front-door.

'What's wrong?' Marcus gasped.

'It's Dylan. He's a bastard.'

'What's he done?' Marcus demanded, following her into the kitchen, his face bruised with fury.

'Oh, I deserve it,' Clodagh sat at the table and wiped her leaking eyes. 'I'm not saying I don't. But it's so hard. Whenever I see him he has more bad news and he makes me feel awful.'

'So what's he done?' Marcus demanded again.

'He made me give back all my credit cards. And he's closed our joint account and instead he's going to give me an allowance every month. For guess how much?'

Sobbing again, she named a sum so low that Marcus exclaimed, 'Allowance? That's more like a forbiddance!'

She rewarded this with a trembly smile. 'Well, I've been a bad girl, what do I expect?'

'But he has a duty to look after you, you're his

wife!' Marcus's vehemence wasn't matched by his actions. He was fumbling in the containers along the window-sill.

'But I suppose he doesn't feel he should take care of me . . .' She paused. 'What are you doing?'

'Looking for a pen.'

'Here.' One was located in Craig's pencil case. 'What are you doing?'

'Just . . .' He scribbled something on a scrap of paper. 'Something. Let's go to bed,' he murmured into her neck.

'I thought you'd never ask.' She summoned a less watery smile and led him to the front-room. But Marcus paused and wouldn't go in. The novelty of having teenage sex on a couch had begun to pall.

'Let's go upstairs.'

'We can't.'

'How long is this cloak-and-dagger stuff going to go on for? C'mon Clodagh,' he cajoled. 'They're only kids. They don't understand.'

'You brat,' she giggled. 'You'd *better not* make noise.'

'In that case you'd *better not* be so fucking sexy.'

'I'll try,' she grinned.

The sex was fantastic, as always. She managed to lose herself and her shame and her new-found penury with each stroke that Marcus banged into her. Until she felt his rhythm falter.

'Go faster!' she hissed.

But he went even slower, then stopped altogether.

'What's wrong?'

'Cloooodaaaagh.' His voice was full of warning, his eyes were focused elsewhere and she was hurriedly excavating herself from under him. *I forgot to lock the door.*

It was both a shock and not a shock to see Craig framed in the doorway, staring at Marcus.

'Daddy?' he asked in tremulous confusion.

'Mum, it's Lisa.'

'Hello, love,' Pauline said warmly. 'How lovely to hear you.'

'You too.' Lisa's throat ached at the love she heard in her mum's voice. 'Hey, I was thinking of coming to see you and Dad next weekend. If it's good for you,' she added hastily.

'Do you know?' Pauline mused. 'We couldn't possibly think of anything we'd rather do. We'd absolutely love to see you.'

When Lisa had left Kathy's house on Friday night she'd felt raw, naked and exposed, as though everything which made her who she was had been stripped away. And out of nowhere she'd wanted her mum.

It was an unexpected reaction, and so was what followed next – the first shock of realization passed and it no longer seemed so dreadful. *You can take the girl out of the council house, but you can't take the council house out of the girl,* she half-laughed to herself. She wasn't exactly happy about it, but she wasn't exactly unhappy either.

In the immediate aftermath she'd been engulfed with the desire to run away. But that had left her and instead she wanted to return to the source.

'I'm so looking forward to seeing you, Lisa. It's cheered me right up.' Such was Pauline's delight and warmth that Lisa wondered how much she'd imagined her parents' uncomfortable awe of her. Had it all been projected by herself?

The days stacked up for Ashling. The world remained a griefscape and when she woke up every morning, she felt as though she'd been drinking really heavily the night before. Even on the nights when she hadn't. But after a couple of weeks she realized that the small things, like brushing her teeth and having a shower, no longer seemed ridiculously onerous.

'That'll be the anti-depressants taking hold,' Monica said, in one of her many phone calls. 'Those Selective Serotonin Reuptake Inhibitors are a godsend. Much better than those old-fashioned Tricyclic whatever-they're-calleds.'

Ashling was surprised. She hadn't expected the anti-depressants to work and she realized she'd had no faith in anything. After all, her mother hadn't got well. At least not for a very long time.

As well as keeping herself clean, she managed to work, so long as it wasn't anything too tricky. She'd always been embarrassed about her conscientiousness but now vaguely recognized that it had probably been her salvation.

'The November horoscopes are in,' Trix waved pages. 'Gather round everyone and I'll read them out.'

The entire office crashed to a halt. Any excuse. Even Jack hovered, aware he should be reading the riot act. He would, he decided, just as soon as they'd done Libra.

'Read Scorpio,' Ashling urged Trix.

'But you're Pisces.'

'Go on. Scorpio. And then Capricorn.'

Clodagh was Scorpio and Marcus was Capricorn and Ashling wanted to know how they were going to fare in November. Jack Devine caught her eye and flashed her a tricky look – a mix of censoriousness and sorrow. He knew what she was up to. Haughtily she turned her head away. She could read whoever's horoscopes she liked and there were far worse things she could be doing. After all, Joy had suggested putting a curse on Marcus and Clodagh.

According to their horoscopes, Clodagh's and Marcus's month was going to be up and down. Ashling could well believe it.

'What are you, JD?' Trix asked.

'Mr Devine to you . . .

'Libra,' he sighed, when it became clear she was still waiting. 'But I don't believe in any of that star-sign stuff. Librans never do.'

Ashling found that sort of funny. She peeked out from under her hair and looked at Jack. He was already watching her. They exchanged a little smile, then quickly she found herself diving beneath her desk. She emerged with her handbag but, confused, she wasn't sure she needed anything from it. Had she only got it in order to stop looking at Jack Devine? Then she realized it was nearly lunch-time anyway, and time for her appointment with Dr McDevitt.

The ten-minute walk to the surgery was like walking through sniper-fire. She was afraid of being out and seeing something that might cause her pain. Her eyes, as much as possible, were downcast and she didn't see much of people above knee-level. This guaranteed a safe passage until a Bosnian refugee tried to sell her an out-of-date *Big Issue*. Immediately she was slapped by a wave of hopelessness.

And there was worse to come – from Dr McDevitt himself.

'How're you getting on with the Prozac?' he asked.

'Fine.' With a wan smile she said, 'Please sir, can I have some more?'

'Side effects?'

'Just some nausea and trembling.'

'Loss of appetite?'

'It was gone anyway.'

'And you know you're not supposed to mix this medication with alcohol?'

'Um, yeah.' Asking her not to drink was going too far.

'How's the counselling going?'

'Er, I haven't gone.'

'But I gave you a number to call.'

'I know, but I can't ring them. I'm too depressed.'

'Ah now!' He sounded cross, picked up the phone, made a call, then made another. He put his hand over the mouthpiece and said, 'What time do you finish work on a Tuesday?'

'It depends . . .'

'Five?' he asked irritably. 'Six?'

'Six.' If she was lucky.

He hung up and handed her a page. 'Every Tuesday at six. If you don't go, there'll be no more Prozac.'

Bastard!

Returning listlessly through Temple Bar she heard a shout of 'Hey Ashling!' A young fashion-victimy man in absolutely ludicrous shoes was clumping after her and it took a second to recognize him as Boo. His hair was shiny, his face had colour and, unexpectedly, she laughed.

'Look at you,' she said, in delight.

'I'm on my way into work, I'm on the two-till-ten shift.' He promptly lapsed into convulsions. 'Can you believe I just said that?!'

Then he launched into breathless, effusive thanks. 'Everything's going great at the telly station. They've even given me an advance on my wages so I can stay in a hostel.'

'And the work's not too difficult?' Ashling had been vaguely worried that after a life without boundaries, Boo wouldn't be able to adapt to the disciplined, responsible world of work.

Boo scoffed. 'Being a runner? Piece of piss! Even in these shoes.'

'Cool clothes,' Ashling remarked, taking in his over-tailored jacket, his frantic shirt and his *very* peculiar shoes. They looked like the *Starship Enterprise* times two.

'I look like a tool.' Boo started laughing again. 'The shoes are the worst. Kelvin at your office gave me all the mad things he didn't want, but at least they're clean, and I can buy normal clothes when I get paid. Hang on! I'm just going to say those words again.' Smacking his lips he repeated with relish, 'When I get paid.'

His glee was contagious. 'I'm delighted everything's working out for you,' Ashling said, with sincerity.

'Well, who do I thank? Only you.' Boo gave his gappy grin. Kelvin hadn't got round to kitting him out with a new tooth, it seemed. 'And thanks to Jack too. He's great!'

Boo's face was alight with anticipation as he waited for Ashling to agree.

'Great.' But she was confused. When exactly did Jack Devine get so nice?

'Did you hear about me thinking I was going to be reviewing books for him?' Boo yelped.

'Er . . .'

'I had it all arseways. I don't even want to review books any more.'

'Um . . .'

'I want to be a camera-man. Or a sound-man. Or a news-reader!'

Back in the office, Ashling had to brace herself to tackle Lisa about leaving early on Tuesday evenings. 'The doctor won't give me any more Prozac unless I go for counselling.'

Lisa was clearly annoyed. 'I'll have to OK it with Jack and you'd better come in early to make up the time,' she said resentfully.

But then it passed. Ashling was a good girl really.

And she could afford to be charitable. *At least I don't have to go for counselling*, she thought smugly. *Or take Prozac.*

CHAPTER 61

One Saturday night, about a month after everything had fallen apart, Ted did a comedy gig. Marcus was also on the bill.

'I hope you don't mind,' Ashling said with ton-weight gaiety, 'but I won't be going along to support you.'

'No problem, no bother, not at all, who'd expect you to!'

'But you will have to start going out again sometime,' Joy urged.

Ashling shuddered. The very thought.

'There are no strangers,' Ted wheedled, 'just friends you haven't met yet.'

'Better still,' Joy said, 'there are no strangers, just *boy*friends you haven't met yet.'

Sullenly Ashling said, 'There are no strangers, just *ex*-boyfriends I haven't met yet.'

She remained clenched with tension until she next saw Ted on Sunday afternoon. She tried very hard not to ask, but eventually gave in. 'Ted, I'm sorry, but was he there?'

When Ted assented, Ashling asked in an even more subdued voice, 'Did he ask about me?'

'I wasn't talking to him,' Ted said quickly. Why did he feel he was advancing through a minefield?

Ashling was annoyed. Ted *should* have talked to him, so that Marcus could have asked about her. Although if he *had* talked to him, she'd have felt betrayed.

In a voice even more diminished she forced herself to enquire, 'And was she there?'

Feeling somehow to blame, Ted nodded confirmation.

Ashling slid into morose muteness. Even though she'd hoped otherwise, she'd known Clodagh would be at the gig because Dylan spent Saturday nights with the kids, thus providing a built-in babysitter. Ashling cursed her memory, which had managed to retain every little detail Dylan had provided her with about the lovebirds. She was better off knowing nothing. But it was irresistible, like picking at a scab.

In forlorn silence she imagined Clodagh staring adoringly at Marcus and Marcus staring adoringly back at Clodagh. The stillness extended so long that Ted began to think that he was in the clear and that there would be no more questions. Little by little he began to let himself relax – too soon! In a choked voice, Ashling asked, 'Did they look mad about each other?'

'Ah, not at all,' he scoffed, electing not to mention that at the start of his act Marcus had said, 'This is for Clodagh.'

★   ★   ★

After they'd been caught in bed by Craig, Marcus had persuaded Clodagh that she might as well be hung for a sheep as for a lamb. He now stayed almost every night, and things had worked out better than expected. The children seemed to have accepted him and there were times – like now – when Clodagh felt everything was in harmony.

They were all gathered around the kitchen table, Molly drawing flowers (actually *on* the table), Craig doing his homework, assisted by Clodagh, and Marcus working on some gags.

The air was benign with unity and honest endeavour.

'Hey, Clodagh, can I run this piece by you?' Marcus asked.

'Give me ten minutes. I just want to finish helping Craig.'

Some time later Marcus cut in as Clodagh demonstrated for the umpteeth time how to do a big letter Q. 'Can I show you now, Clodagh?'

'Ten more minutes, darlin', then I'll be right with you.'

Next the kitchen door slammed shut and Clodagh's head jerked up. What had happened?

A quick scan of those who remained in the kitchen indicated that Marcus had stormed out!

It was seven-thirty on a Thursday evening in late October, and Ashling and Jack were the only people still remaining in the office. Jack switched off his light, closed his office door and stopped at Ashling's desk.

'How're you getting on?' he asked tentatively.

'Grand. Just finishing this article on prostitutes.'

'No, I meant . . . in general. With the counselling and that? Is it helping?'

'I don't know. Maybe.'

'As my mother says, time is a great healer,' he reassured. 'I remember when my heart was broken I felt I'd never be right again –'

Ashling cut in. 'You've had your heart broken?'

'And there was you thinking I had no heart at all!'

'No, but . . .'

'Go on, admit it, you did.'

'I didn't.' But she had to look away as a smile curved her hot face. 'Was it Mai?' she asked curiously.

'The woman before Mai. Dee. We were together a long time and she left me, and I eventually got over it. You will too.'

'Yes, but Jennifer – she's the counsellor – says it's not just a broken heart I'm dealing with.'

'So what are you dealing with?' And he asked so gently and kindly that she heard herself telling him about her mother's depression and the mechanisms she'd developed to try and cope with it.

'Little Miss Fix-it,' she finished with.

Jack looked utterly stricken. 'Sorry,' he said quickly. 'I'm sorry I ever –'

''s OK. It's the truth.'

669

'Is it? Why you carry all that stuff in your bag, why you're so obliging?'

'Jennifer seems to think so.'

'What do you think?'

'I suppose I agree,' she sighed.

She didn't add that Jennifer had also suggested that that was why Ashling had always picked men whom she could organize. And that after an initial burst of angry denial, Ashling had actually agreed with her: she'd been useful to most of her boyfriends from long before Phelim the sweet goofball, right up to Marcus the needy comedian, and she'd enjoyed it.

'And what does this Jennifer say about your *Weltschmerz*?'

'She says it's better than it was, even if I can't see it myself. And she says I might get bouts of it in the future, but I can do things to keep it under control. Like doing some voluntary work to help all the other Boos . . . The ones who weren't lucky enough to have a Jack Devine!' she added jokily.

'Shucks.' Jack played coy and peeped up from under his lashes at Ashling – then they locked eyes.

Their high spirits faded abruptly, leaving obsolete smirks still loitering on their confused mouths.

Jack recovered first. 'Christ, Ashling,' he declared over-jovially, 'I'm feeling quite emotional! Boo is doing really well over at the station, you know.'

'You're good to sort all that out.' She realized she'd been so fogged up for the past couple of months that she'd never properly thanked him.

'Don't mention it!' They were in danger of another intimate eye-meet. When in doubt, talk about the weather. 'It's pissing down outside. D'you want a lift home?' He placed his palms on her desk and suddenly she remembered him washing her hair. His touch on her skin, the gorgeous, squirmy feelings administered by those big hands, the hard warmth of his body pressed up against hers . . . *Mmmmmm.*

'Er, no,' she hurriedly recovered herself. 'I'd better finish this.'

To her surprise he asked, 'Do you ever go to salsa any more?'

She shook her head. She had no appetite for it. 'Maybe I'll go again, you know, when things are . . .'

'Could you show me the basics sometime?'

In all honesty, she couldn't think of anything more unlikely. 'We'll have a sushi-and-salsa night,' she joked.

'I'll hold you to it.'

As Jack moved off, Ashling asked, 'How's Mai doing?'

'Good, I see her occasionally.'

'Tell her I said hi. I thought she was great.'

'I will. She's going out with a landscape gardener now.'

'Called Cormac?' Ashling was flip.

Jack's face was a picture of awe and horror. 'How do you know?!'

In the middle of the night Lisa's phone rang. She bolted awake, her heart pounding. Could something have happened to her dad or her mum? Before she got to the phone, the answering machine picked up and someone began to leave a message.

Oliver. And he sounded even louder than usual. 'Excuse me, Lisa Edwards,' he called stroppily, 'you *have* changed.'

She picked up the phone. '*What?*'

'And hello to you too. That day in Dublin when you were playing football with those kids, I said you'd changed and you told me you hadn't. You lied to me, babes.'

'Oliver, it's twenty to five. *AM.*'

'I knew it didn't add up and it's been bugging me ever since. It's just clicked. You're different, babes – not working so hard, being so sweet to those kids – why tell me you're not?'

She knew why, she'd known the day it had happened, but should she tell him? Oh, why not, what difference could it make?

'Because it's too late . . . To save us,' she elaborated, when he didn't speak. 'Better to say that I'm still the same old control-freak I've always been, right?'

Oliver processed this strange logic. 'Is that your final answer?'

'Yes.'

'OK, babes. It's up to you.'

Ted and Joy were in the video shop.

'*Sliding Doors*?' Ted suggested.

'No, doesn't someone have an affair in it?'

'How about *My Best Friend's Wedding*?'

'The name alone is looking for trouble,' Joy pointed out.

They eventually settled on *Pulp Fiction*.

'Good choice.' Joy was pleased. 'No! Bad choice. *Very* bad choice. Someone is unfaithful! Uma Thurman?'

'You're absolutely right,' Ted said shakily. That had been close. 'Maybe we should just get *The Best of the Teletubbies* and be done with it.'

'No, this is our man.' Joy yelped with pleasure and swooped down on *The Exorcist*. 'This won't upset *anyone*.'

'Good,' said Ted. 'I couldn't take a repeat of the last time.'

With the benefit of hindsight, Joy had to admit that making Ashling watch *Damage* had been a mistake. Though two months had passed since she'd found out about Marcus and Clodagh, people having affairs still weren't exactly her cup of tea.

Back in Ashling's flat, the three of them clustered in front of the telly, surrounded by wine bottles, corkscrews, sacks of popcorn and acre-slabs of chocolate. To the relief of all, Ashling seemed quite distracted by the film – until the doorbell rang. Immediately her face sparked with involuntary anticipation: she was still hoping for Marcus to make his long-overdue appearance.

'I'll go.' She clambered to her feet and opened the door.

To her surprise, the person who fell in was Dylan. She'd had lunch with him on average once a week for the past couple of months, but this was a first.

'Hope you don't mind me calling unannounced.' He smiled, but something about the volume of his voice and the laziness of his eyes made her realize he was drunk. 'Look at you, lovely girl.' He ran a hand over her hair and left a trail of heat from the crown of her head to the nape of her neck. 'Nice,' he drawled.

'Thanks. Come on in, Joy and Ted are here.'

He poured himself a glass of wine and Ashling watched as he effortlessly charmed Joy. That he was dissipated and unravelly made him no less attractive. Just different.

When the video ended, Dylan flicked through the channels until he found something he liked. 'Spectacular! *Casablanca*.'

'I'm not watching any romantic shite,' Ashling said firmly and Dylan laughed.

'Aren't you gorgeous?' he said warmly.

'Maybe, but I'm still not watching it.'

'Gorgeous,' he repeated. He'd always been full

of compliments, but Ashling was aware that tonight's mood was slightly loaded.

'Still not watching it.'

'Well, I'm the holder of the remote!'

'Not for long, buster.'

In the ensuing scuffle over the remote control, a bottle of red wine got up-ended.

'Sorry. I'll get a cloth,' Dylan said. But when he got to the kitchen, he called, 'I can't see any.'

'I've got some old towels in the bathroom.' Ashling left the room and was rummaging in the bathroom cupboard when his voice right behind her made her jump. Startled, she turned around.

'Ashling,' he said.

'What?' But already she knew something was up. The look in his eyes, the tone of his voice, his extreme nearness was dense with sex.

'Sweet Ashling,' he almost whispered. 'I should have stayed with you.' This was nothing like the avuncular way he'd treated her for the past eleven years. He touched a finger to her cheek.

I could have him now, she realized. Eleven years on, he could be mine.

And why not? He made her feel beautiful. He always had, even when he was marrying her erstwhile best friend. And she thought he was glorious. She had a curiosity about him, about what it would be like to sleep with him. A hunger which had been stimulated a long time ago and never satisfied.

Her head shuffled a few scenarios. She'd had

her legs waxed. She was heartbreak-skinny. She'd love some affection. Some sex would be nice too.

Then, all at once, she didn't care.

She shoved a towel at him. 'Get mopping.'

The eyes under the floppy blond hair were surprised, but he did as he was told, then sat beside Joy telling her what was going to happen in the film before it did.

'Shut up,' Joy giggled, and when the film ended, she turned to Dylan and said, 'I'm going home to bed now. You're welcome to join me.'

His hazel eyes flicked over her then, with a slightly hard smile, he got to his feet. 'Delighted to.'

Ted and Ashling watched in amazement. Ashling almost thought it was a joke. But when they didn't appear back around the door after a few minutes she realized it wasn't.

The following morning Ashling rang Joy at work.

'Did you sleep with Dylan?' She thought she'd asked it quietly but everyone in the office instantly jerked their heads up.

'Too right I did.'

'I mean, did you have sex with him?'

'Yes, of course!'

Ashling swallowed hard. 'What was it like?'

'Brilliant. He's *gorgeous*. Bitter as anything about women, mind, and there's no way he'll be ringing me –' Joy abruptly changed tack. She sounded horrified. 'Jesus Christ, you don't *mind*, do you? I never thought for a second . . . I thought you were devvo about Marcus and because I hate Clodagh so much . . .'

'I don't mind,' Ashling insisted.

Do I?

Do you? Most of the office wondered.

Actually, I don't think I do.

In early December a buyer was found for Lisa and Oliver's London flat. As the furniture was included in the purchase, all Lisa had to remove were her personal things.

Oliver was away on a shoot the weekend she chose to do so. She could have waited until he was around, but she'd made a deliberate decision not to. She had to let go of him.

Sifting through the remains of their life together was a painful process. But her mum and dad came from Hemel Hempstead to help her. Frankly they weren't much use, but their bumbling warmth made her feel better. When they were finished they bundled Lisa and her possessions into their twenty-year-old Rover and drove back to Hemel. That night, as a special treat, they booked a table at their local Harvester. In one way, Lisa would have preferred to gnaw off her own head than go there, but in another way, she really didn't mind.

Ashling arrived at the pub and Ted was already there.

'Hiya,' he said. 'He was there. She was there. They didn't look mad about each other.' He'd been at a comedy gig the night before and because Ashling always asked about Marcus and Clodagh, he tried to spare her dignity by delivering a news bulletin.

'He did some new stuff about children. I reckon he's only riding Clodagh for the material,' Ted swaggered. And it was such a patent lie that Ashling was touched to the heart.

'And apparently,' Ted warmed to his theme because Ashling seemed to be enjoying it, 'reading between the lines, I think Dylan is giving Clodagh almost no money, 'cos Marcus did a gag about his girlfriend's – sorry.' He paused to let Ashling wince. 'About his girlfriend's ex-husband giving her an allowance that was more of a forbiddance.'

Joy arrived. 'What are we talking about?'

'Marcus's gig last night.'

'What a dick.' Joy curled her lip, then put on a goofy voice. 'I want to dedicate this to Craig and Molly. How wanky is that?'

Ashling's face bloomed a pale-green colour. 'He's dedicating his act to her *children*?'

In confusion, Joy looked at Ted. 'I thought that was what you were telling . . . oh fuck! I'm always putting my foot in it.'

Ashling felt a wash of humiliation, as fresh as the first one. 'Happy families,' she observed, trying to sound wry.

'It can't last,' Joy said stoutly.

'No, they'll stay together,' Ashling insisted. 'Men always stay with Clodagh.'

Then Joy asked a funny question. 'Do you miss Marcus?'

Ashling considered. She felt many emotions, all of them unpleasant, but in amongst them there was no longer a yearning for Marcus. Anger, yes. And sadness, humiliation and a sense of loss. But she didn't actually miss *him*, his company, his physical presence, the way she once had.

'Of course I care about your children!' Marcus insisted. 'Didn't I dedicate my act to the two of them last night?'

'Well why won't you read Molly a bedtime story then?'

'Because I'm *busy*. I've two full-time jobs.'

'But I'm knackered. It's impossible to cope with two children entirely on my own.'

'But you said Dylan was never here anyway, that he was always working.'

'He wasn't always working,' Clodagh said sullenly. 'He was often here.'

She handed Marcus an illustrated copy of *Little Red Riding Hood*, which he refused to take. 'Sorry, but I've got to put in an hour on my novel.'

She stared at him long and hard. 'My marriage has broken up because of you.'

'And my relationship with Ashling broke up because of *you*. So we're quits.'

Clodagh was raging. She didn't even believe that Marcus had liked Ashling that much, but he insisted he had, so what could she do?

CHAPTER 62

And then, taking everyone by surprise, as it did every year, Christmas arrived. All and sundry drank their heads off for most of the month and on the twenty-third of December *Colleen's* office closed for eleven days. 'Compassionate leave,' Kelvin called it.

Phelim came home from Australia and expressed mild surprise when Ashling wouldn't sleep with him. Nevertheless he took it well and still gave her the didgeridoo he'd brought for her. Ashling went to her parents for Christmas – an event worthy of comment, as she'd stayed in Dublin with Phelim's family for the previous five years. Ashling's brother Owen came home from the Amazon basin and made his mother's Christmas by not having a plate in his lower lip. Ashling's sister Janet flew in from California. She was taller, slimmer and blonder than Ashling remembered. She ate a lot of fresh fruit and refused to walk anywhere.

Clodagh spent the day alone. Dylan took the children to his parents and she boycotted her own parents when they said Marcus couldn't come with her. But at the last minute Marcus decided to spend the day with *his* parents.

Lisa went to Hemel and was grateful for the fuss her mum and dad made of her. She'd signed and posted the final divorce papers a few weeks before Christmas and still felt ridiculously fragile. The next part of the process was the decree nisi.

The night Ashling returned from Cork, she found she had a new neighbour. A blond, wiry boy was huddled in her doorway, tucking into a sandwich and a can of Budweiser.

'Hiya,' she said. 'I'm Ashling.'

'George.' He noticed her looking at the can of Bud. 'It's New Year's Eve,' he said, defensively. 'I'm having a drink like anyone else.'

'I don't mind,' she said softly.

'Just because I'm on the streets doesn't mean I have a problem with booze,' he explained, relenting slightly. 'I'm just a social drinker.'

She gave him a pound and went inside, where despair threatened to overwhelm her. Homelessness was like a many-headed monster – cut off one head and two more appear in its place. Boo was sorted, with a job, a flat and even a girlfriend, but he'd been one of the few lucky ones: intelligent, present-able-looking and still young enough to have the capacity to adapt to a mainstream life. There were so many others who had nothing, and who never would – beaten by the life which had catapulted them on to the streets in the first place and further beaten by hunger, despair, fear, boredom and other people's hatred.

Her doorbell rang. It was Ted, proudly sporting a small, tidy girl. 'You're back,' he announced, then turned to encompass the girl by his side. 'This is Sinead.'

Sinead extended a neat little hand. 'Pleased to meet you,' she said, with prim self-confidence.

'Come in.' Ashling was surprised. Sinead didn't look like your usual comedy groupie.

In Ted swaggered, then smoothed the couch cushions before solicitously inviting Sinead to sit down.

She placed herself daintily on the couch, her knees and ankles aligned, and graciously accepted Ashling's offer of a glass of wine. All the while Ted watched her like a soppy hawk.

'You, um, met Ted at a gig?' Ashling tried to make conversation, as she scouted on the floor for the corkscrew. She was sure that's where she'd left it the night before she went to Cork . . .

'A gig?' Sinead sounded as though she'd never heard the word before.

'A comedy gig.'

'Oh no!' Sinead tinkled.

'She's never seen my act, says she never wants to.' Ted gazed at her with isn't-she-great? fondness.

It transpired that Sinead and Ted worked together, toiling shoulder to shoulder in the department of agriculture. At their Christmas party, as they had drunkenly jived to 'Rock Around the Clock', their eyes had met and that was it – love.

Ashling entertained a strange suspicion that Sinead's advent signalled the beginning of the end of Ted's stand-up career. But as he'd only ever become a comedian to get a girl, perhaps he wouldn't mind. He certainly didn't *seem* upset.

'Tonight? You want to go out again?' Clodagh asked. 'But you were out last night and the night before and Wednesday night.'

Patiently Marcus explained, 'I've got to keep an eye on the new comics out there. This is my career, I have to go.'

'Which is more important to you? Me or your career?'

'You're both important.'

Wrong answer.

'Well, I won't be able to get a babysitter, it's too short notice.'

'OK.'

And that, Clodagh thought, was that. Until at nine o'clock Marcus stood up and said, 'I'll be off. It'll be a late one, so I'll go home instead of coming back here.'

Clodagh was astonished. 'You're *going*?'

'I said I was.'

'No. You said it was OK that I couldn't get a

babysitter. I thought you meant you weren't going to go without me.'

'No, I meant I *was* going to go without you.'

'Ashling, I've something to tell you,' Ted said.

'What?' It was a freezing January evening and Ted and Joy had showed up deputation-like, with sleet on their collars.

'You'd better sit down,' Joy advised.

'I *am* sitting down.' Ashling thumped the couch she was on.

'That's good. I don't know if you're going to be upset,' Ted said.

'*What?*'

'I've worried about whether or not you should be told.'

'Tell me!'

'You know Marcus Valentine.'

'I might have heard of him. Duh, Ted, *please.*'

'Yes, sorry. Well, I saw him. In a pub. With a girl. Who wasn't Clodagh.'

All was still, then Ashling said, 'So what? He's allowed to be seen in the company of another woman.'

'I take your point. I take your point. But is he allowed to stick his tongue down her throat?'

A strange expression lit Ashling's face. Shock – and something else. Joy glanced at her anxiously.

'You've met the girl,' Ted elaborated. 'Suzie. I was talking to her at a party in Rathmines one night and I left with you. Remember?'

Ashling nodded. She remembered a neat, pretty little redhead. Ted had called her a comedy groupie.

'So I, er, asked around,' Ted went on.

'And?'

'And he's sticking more than his tongue into her, if you take my meaning.'

'Oh, my good God.'

'For a freckly bastard he sure is a big hit with the goils,' Joy observed drily.

'Oh my good God,' Ashling repeated.

'Don't go all compassionate and start to feel sorry for Clodagh,' Joy begged. 'Please don't go rushing round there to hold her hand.'

'Don't be so stupid,' Ashling said. 'I'm fucking delighted.'

'I'm coming over to get my stuff,' Marcus said.

'It'll be ready,' Clodagh confirmed heatedly.

Fuming, she banged around the house, shoving his personal effects into a black bin-liner. She couldn't believe how quickly it had all splintered. They'd gone from mutual obsession to near-hatred in a matter of weeks, eddying in a downward spiral from the moment it had stopped being just about sex and started being about real life.

She'd thought she loved him, but she didn't. He was a boring bastard. The boringest of boring bastards. All he wanted to talk about was his act and about how none of the other comedians were as good as him.

And he needed so much attention. She found it distasteful the way he resented it whenever she focused on Craig and Molly. Sometimes it was just like having three children.

Not to mention that bloody novel he'd started. Garbage! *Unbelievably* depressing. He took criticism so badly, even constructive suggestions. All she'd said was that maybe the woman in it could set up her own business, baking cakes or making pottery, and he'd gone *mad*.

And lately he wanted to be out every night. Simply refused to understand that she couldn't keep leaving her two children. It was hard to get babysitters. It was even harder to *afford* babysitters on what Dylan was giving her. But more than that, she didn't *want* to be out every night. She missed Craig and Molly when she was away from them.

Staying in at home was nice. There was no shame in watching *Coronation Street* and having a glass of wine.

And the sex. She no longer wanted to do it three times a night. She shouldn't be expected to. *No one* did after the first crazy passion had passed. But he was still on for it, and it was exhausting.

But all that was small potatoes compared to the bombshell he'd just hit her with – that he'd 'met someone else'.

She was boiling with anger and deeply humiliated. Especially because in some remote corner at the back of her head she'd always entertained a suspicion that she was doing him a favour, that it was the luckiest day of his life when she'd fallen out of a stultifying marriage and into his arms. She minded desperately that she'd been dumped. It hadn't happened since Greg the American jock had lost interest in her a month before he went back to the States.

She was shoving the last pair of underpants into the bag when the doorbell rang. She marched out, opened the door and thrust the bin-liner at Marcus. 'Here.'

'Is my novel in there?'

'Oh yes, *Black Dog*, the masterpiece, is in there all right. Bin-liner's the right place for it,' she said in an undertone, which wasn't really an under-tone at all.

His thundery face indicated he'd heard and he prepared to retaliate.

'Oh, by the way,' he threw over his shoulder as he turned to go, 'she's twenty-two and she's had no children.' He accompanied this piece of infor-mation with a wink. He knew Clodagh had a thing about her stretch marks.

Scalded, she thumped back in. Eventually the first rush of bilious rage passed, and she tried to talk herself into something positive. At least she was rid of Marcus and his jokes and his novel and his moods – that had to count for something.

And it was then that she realized she was in a bit of a bind. No husband, no boyfriend.

Oh fuck.

⋆   ⋆   ⋆

The Jack Devine fanclub were in full flow. Robbie, the Honey Monster and Mrs Morley were clustered together outdoing each other in their bid to wax lyrical.

Jack had recently passed through the office, looking better turned out than usual. Which, as Trix said, wouldn't be hard.

'I wonder,' she often mused, 'if anyone has ever come up to him in the street, given him ten pence and told him to buy himself a cup of tea?'

But this morning he was spruce and glossy, his dark suit pressed, his cotton shirt snowy. Even his tumbled hair wasn't too bad – he sometimes came to work with only the sides of his hair combed and the back still a complete bedhead.

He scrubbed up well, no doubt about it. But when he stopped to pick up his messages from Mrs Morley, his shirt gaped where a button was missing midway down his chest.

This inflamed the fanclub further.

'A tormented man who can save the world but who needs a good woman to take care of him,' Honey Monster Shauna declared. She'd been at the Mills & Boons again.

'Yeah, like he's got that boho chic thing going on,' Robbie concluded.

'He does to be sure,' agreed Mrs Morley, who wouldn't have known boho chic from a bar of soap.

'Wouldn't you ride him as soon as look at him?' Robbie asked. 'Ashling?'

A frantic mouthing session of *Don't ask her* began.

But it was too late. Obedient Ashling was already imagining riding Jack Devine, and several emotions galloped across her face, none of which served to reassure her anxious colleagues.

'She was badly let down,' Mrs Morley hissed. 'I'd say she's off men.'

'I shouldn't have gone there!' Robbie exclaimed. 'I feel a valium moment coming on.' Any excuse. He was always popping valium; librium and beta-blockers, for his 'nerves'.

'D'you want one?' he asked Mrs Morley. 'I've had three already today.'

Her eyes gleamed. 'I suppose it couldn't do any harm.'

Then she spent the rest of the day lurching around like a zombie, banging into desks, catching her fingers in the keyboard, while Robbie had built up such a tolerance he was blithely unaffected.

Meanwhile, Ashling was nearly as stunned as Mrs Morley. Robbie's question had knocked her for six and she couldn't stop thinking about Jack Devine. Her heart swelled up like a balloon as she thought about his narkiness and his kindness, his crumpled suits and his sharp mind, his hard bargains and his soft heart, his high-powered job and his missing button.

He'd washed her hair when he didn't have time. He'd treated Boo, a piece of human detritus, as the person he actually was. He'd refused to sack

Honey Monster Shauna after she'd mistakenly included an extra zero in *Gaelic Knitting* and people ended up knitting christening shawls that were seventeen feet long instead of three.

Robbie's right, she realized. *I would ride Jack Devine as soon as look at him.*

'Ashling!' Lisa cut in irritably. 'For the fifth time, this intro is too naffing long! What is *wrong* with you? Have you been dipping into the valium too?'

They both automatically looked at Mrs Morley, who was slumped on a chair, dreamily painting her thumb-nail with Tippex.

'No.'

Lisa sighed. She should be kinder. Ashling hadn't been like this for ages, not since the first few weeks after Marcus had left her. Perhaps she'd just found out something new and unpleasant – like Clodagh being up the duff. 'Has something happened with Marcus and your mate?'

Ashling made herself focus on something other than Jack Devine. 'Actually, yes. Marcus is knobbing someone else.'

'That comes as no surprise,' Lisa said scornfully. 'You know that type of man.'

Lisa had the ability to make Ashling feel very gauche.

'What kind of man?'

'You know – not a bad bloke but insecure. Addicted to being loved, but only reasonably good-looking.' Blimey, she was being polite.

'Suddenly women like him because he's famous and he's like a child let loose in a candy-store.'

But these words of wisdom did little to snap Ashling back to alertness. If anything, they had the opposite effect. She seemed to slide further away from the world and mumbled, 'Oh, my good God,' in a startled kind of way. Then her face cleared.

'Revelations are like buses, aren't they?' she asked in wonder. 'None for ages, then several come at once.'

Lisa gave a smothered scream, and swung away.

Meanwhile, Ashling fidgeted wildly until it was time to leave work and meet Joy. She wanted to share her mind-blowing insights. Well, one of them anyway. The other would have to wait until she'd made sense of it herself.

The minute Joy arrived at the bar in the Morrison, she was subjected to a hail of words from Ashling.

'. . . Even if Marcus hadn't met Clodagh he would still have done a legger sooner or later, he's too insecure and needy and I should have seen the signs.'

'Oh. And they were?' Joy was tugging off her coat and doing her best to rally.

'I knew he'd given a Bellez-moi note to another girl. Tell me, what kind of man goes around handing out his phone number? If he's interested in you, he asks for your number, right? Instead of trawling for . . . for . . . what's the word? A positive reaction,

I suppose, by giving out his number and seeing who'll bite.'

'Anything else?'

'Yes, I gave him my number twice and he didn't ring the first time. It's clear now he was playing some sort of game. Seeing if I liked him enough to give him the number. He wasn't really interested in me – he was interested in what I thought of him. It was only when I went to his gig that he deigned to ring me.

'And when I wouldn't sleep with him the first night. Sulky or what! Such a baby. And all that "Am I the best? . . . Who's the funniest of them all?" And you know something else, Joy? I wasn't exactly without sin, either. Part of the reason I went out with him was because he was famous. So if it backfired, I've only got myself to blame.'

'But you're making it sound like a total disaster,' Joy objected. 'You both got on really well. I know you liked him and you could see how much he liked you.'

'He liked me,' Ashling admitted. 'I know he did, but he liked himself more. And I liked him but for partly the wrong reasons.' Quietly she admitted, 'Clodagh said I was a victim.'

'Bitch!'

'No, I am. Or rather, *was*,' she corrected. 'Not any more.'

'But just because it's all down to Marcus being insecure doesn't mean you're going to be friends with Clodagh again?' Joy asked anxiously. 'You still hate her, don't you?'

A short, sharp throb of loss had to peak and disperse before Ashling was able to shrug, 'Of course.'

CHAPTER 63

O n Valentine's Day a big, impressive envelope skittered from the letter-box into
Lisa's hall. A card? Who from? Her blood
racing with excitement she ripped open the envelope, then faltered . . . Oh.

It was notification of her decree nisi.

She wanted to laugh, but couldn't quite pull it
off. The speed with which it had been dispatched
by the courts to her solicitor had caught her right
out. It had taken just over two months and in her
subconscious she'd been sure it would be at least
three.

With panicky clarity she realized that she and
Oliver were on the home stretch. The way was
free and, straight down the track, she saw the end
of her marriage rushing towards her.

Only six short weeks to go before the final decree
was issued.

Then she'd feel better. Closure and all that.

That night she went out with Dylan. He'd been
asking her out for the last couple of months –
every time he came into the office to see
Ashling – and she thought it might cheer her

up. Especially as she'd heard not a syllable from Oliver.

Dylan collected her after work and drove her to a pub in the Dublin Mountains, where the lights of the city were arrayed below them, twinkling like jewels. She awarded him top marks for location. He also scored seven out of ten for nice hair and eight out of ten for good looks. And technically, he was very charming and full of observant compliments, so he got seven or eight for that. But she couldn't warm to him, she found him smooth and hard and beneath his gallant conversation she detected a jaundiced cynicism that would put hers to shame.

Or maybe the problem stemmed from her. She couldn't shake off the residue of loss that had shrouded her all day.

She drank a lot, but couldn't get drunk, and the encounter, far from lifting her spirits, only served to depress her. And when Dylan made it very clear how much he wanted to sleep with her, it depressed her even further.

She mumbled something about not being 'that kind of girl'.

'Oh, really?' Dylan quirked his mouth in a manner that conveyed both regret and contempt, and all of a sudden, she wanted to be at home.

In silence, Dylan drove her back to the city, screeching too quickly along narrow mountain roads.

Outside her house she managed to politely thank

him, but couldn't get out of his car fast enough. Once in the sanctuary of her kitchen she ate a walnut whip (she was on a 'W' diet and had found a loophole) and wondered, what was the world coming to when even one-night-stands no longer held appeal?

Sitting down, Clodagh crossed her legs and agitatedly bounced up and down on the ball of her foot. Dylan had taken the kids out for the afternoon and was due back any minute, and though he didn't know it yet, they were going to *talk*.

Every time they met, things were civil but unpleasant. He was bitter and she was defensive, but all that was about to change.

How could she ever have thought that Marcus would do? Dylan was *wonderful*: patient, kind, generous, devoted, hardworking, *much* more attractive. She wanted her old life back. But she expected a certain amount of rancour and resistance from Dylan and she wasn't looking forward to having to eat humble pie to win him over.

A racket of childish voices at the front-door indicated that they were back. She hurried to let them in, and gave Dylan a friendly smile which fell on stony ground.

'Could I have a quick chat with you?' She forced her voice to remain bright.

When he shrugged a flinty 'All right,' she put

Craig and Molly in front of a video, closed the door and came into the kitchen where Dylan was waiting.

She swallowed hard. 'Dylan, these past months . . . I was wrong, I'm very sorry. I still love you and I'd like you to –' she choked, 'I'd like you to come home.'

She watched his face and waited for the golden light of happiness to wash over it and cleanse away the glittery hardness that had taken up residence there since all this started. He gazed at her incredulously.

'I know it'll take a while to get back to normal and for you to trust me again, but we can go for counselling and all,' she promised. 'I was out of my mind to do what I did to you, but we can make everything all right again . . . Can't we?' she asked, when still he didn't reply.

Eventually he spoke and he said only one word. 'No.'

'No . . . what?'

'No, I'm not coming back.'

She had not anticipated this. Not in any of her scenarios. 'But why?' She didn't really believe him.

'I just don't want to.'

'But you've been devastated by what I . . . um . . . did.'

'Yeah, I thought it was going to kill me,' he agreed thoughtfully. 'But I suppose I must have gotten over it, because now that I think about it, I don't want to be married to you any more.'

She began to shake. This wasn't happening. 'What about the children?'

That got him. 'I love my children.'

Good.

'But I'm not going to get back with you because of them. I can't.'

She was losing. All the power she'd thought she possessed was being revealed as a mere façade. And then something so unlikely as to be almost laughable occurred to her. 'Have you . . . you haven't . . . met someone else?'

He laughed unpleasantly. *I did that*, she thought, suddenly ashamed. *I've made him like this.*

'I've met lots of someone elses,' he said.

'Do you mean . . . are you saying . . . you've *slept* with women?'

'Well, not much sleeping gets done.'

She belly-flopped, feeling betrayed, jealous, cheated on. And his knowing, taunty tone roused a horrible suspicion. 'Do I know any of them?'

His smile was cruel. 'Yes.'

Her stomach flopped again. 'Who?'

'What a question to ask a gentleman,' he scorned.

'You said you'd wait for me,' she said quietly.

'Did I? So, I lied.'

It was when Lisa was offered a job by Randolph Media's main rivals that she began to think about her future. In her ten months at *Colleen* she'd brought it to where she wanted it in terms of circulation and advertising revenue. It was time to go.

Already she knew she was going to return to London – it was where she belonged and she wanted to be near her mum and dad. But when she considered her options, she realized she wasn't quite sure she had the stomach for editing a monthly glossy any more. Clambering up the greasy pole, humiliating others and taking credit for their work no longer held the appeal it once had. Nor did the vicious rivalry between magazines. Or the savage internecine warfare which existed within the ranks of a title. Once she'd been excited, fuelled even, by such a competitive environment. But not now, and at this realization she experienced panic – had she become a weakling, a sap, an also-ran? But she didn't feel weak. Just because there were some things she didn't want to do any more didn't mean she was weak, it just meant she was different.

Not too different, obviously, she acknowledged wryly: she still *loved* the shallowness of magazines. The clothes, the make-up, the relationship advice. So the obvious career move was to look for consultancy work.

Something weird was going on, Ashling realized. At first she hadn't noticed, she'd just thought it was an isolated incident. Followed by another isolated incident. Then another. But when does a series of isolated incidents stop being a series of isolated incidents and start becoming a *pattern*?

She'd been afraid to read too much into it because she so badly wanted it to mean something. It was Jack Devine. He'd taken her out for a drink to celebrate her coming off Prozac. Then, a week later, when it became clear that she wasn't going to go mad again, he'd taken her for another drink to celebrate that too. Then he'd taken her for a drink *followed by a pizza* to celebrate her starting her salsa lessons again. Then he'd taken her for a full-on dinner at Cookes to celebrate Boo moving into his first flat. But when Ashling had suggested that it would be appropriate if Boo joined them, Jack didn't seem at all keen. 'I'm going out for a few pints with him and some of the other lads from the station tomorrow night,' he'd added.

And now he'd sidled up to her desk and suggested going out again.

'What are we celebrating this time?' she asked suspiciously.

He paused. 'Er, that it's Thursday?'

'OK,' she said. Because it *was* Thursday. But she was confused. Why was he being so nice to her? Did he still feel sorry for her after all the drama? But that was in the past. And any other reasons for his attention seemed preposterous.

It was Lisa who enlightened her.

'So you and Jack have finally got it together?' she said as airily as she could manage. She still wasn't entirely zen about being overlooked, it just wasn't her way and probably never would be.

'I beg your pardon?'

'You and Jack. You like him, don't you?' she teased. 'As in *like* him.'

The hot high colour that spilled across Ashling's face was her answer.

'And he likes you,' Lisa pointed out.

'No, he doesn't.'

'Yes, he does.'

'No, he doesn't.'

'Oh, don't be so naïve, Ashling,' Lisa snapped.

Ashling looked at her in alarm, then after a period of stillness, she said faintly, 'OK, I won't.'

That evening in the restaurant, Ashling attemped to address the situation. She so didn't want to, but she suspected she had to. To give her courage, she lit a cigarette which Jack watched her smoke as if she was doing something remarkable.

Stop looking at me like that. I can't think straight.

'Jack, can I ask you something? We're out, having our dinner. Is this a . . .' She froze. Maybe she shouldn't say it, what if she was wrong?

'Is this a . . . ?' he prompted, his expression keen to oblige.

She exhaled heavily. Fuck it, might as well. 'Is this a date?'

He considered her intently. 'Do you want it to be?'

She pretended to give it some thought. 'Yes.'

'Then it's a date.'

They both let their eyes wander around the restaurant. 'D'you want to go on another one?' Jack asked over-casually.

'Yes.'

'Saturday night?'

Yikes. First outing not on a week day. New ground being broken.

'Yes.'

Once again their gazes set off roaming around the room, looking at anything except each other.

Ashling heard her voice once more. 'Jack, can I ask why you want to go on a . . . you know . . . with me?'

She raised her eyes to him at the same moment that his gaze returned to her, and their looks collided with force. Her breath left her and excitement leapt, like tiny fishes nibbling beneath her skin. 'Because, Ashling,' Jack said softly, 'you're interfering with my plans for world domination.'

But what did *that* mean?

'I can think of nothing else apart from you,' he said. He sounded quite matter-of-fact. 'It's affecting everything.'

Her head filled up, up, up with air and she couldn't speak. Couldn't locate a single suitable syllable. She'd suspected he liked her, but now that he'd said it . . .

'Say something,' he urged anxiously.

She mumbled, 'How long has this been going on?' *I sound like Dr McDevitt.*

'Ages,' he sighed. 'Since the night of the launch.'

'That long?'

'Yes.' Another sigh.

'But that's months!'

'Six of them.'

'All that time . . .' She was raking over the past half-year, her version of her life falling into an entirely different arrangement. Did he mean it? Well, he'd *said* it, but she was afraid to believe him. Yet.

'No wonder you were so nice to me,' she managed to say.

'I would have been nice to you anyway.'

'Would you?'

'Sure,' he smiled sheepishly. 'Well, maybe. Probably . . . And you?'

'Me?'

'How do you, er, feel?'

Still the words wouldn't come, and the best she could manage was, 'I feel like going on a date with you on Saturday night.'

'OK,' he nodded, reading between the lines. 'Maybe you'd come over to my house? You said you'd show me how to dance.'

She'd never actually said she would, but she let it go.

'And I still think you'd like sushi, if you'd only trust me,' he added wistfully.

'I do trust you.'

The following day, when Lisa handed in her notice and announced her intention to return to London

703

in a month, Jack had the good grace to say, 'We were lucky to get you for as long as we did.' But she was sharp enough to realize he wasn't giving her his full undivided.

'And you could replace me with Trix,' she suggested innocently.

'We'll certainly give it some thoug –! Ahahaha, nice one!' he laughed nervously.

CHAPTER 64

In a house in a bleak, sea-facing corner of Ringsend a man and a woman nervously greeted each other. Through the uncurtained windows the still, black sea watched him lead her into a room that he'd spent several hours cleaning earlier that day. The sea had known Jack Devine a long time and it had never seen such a frenzy. Mind you, he could have ironed his flannel shirt and put on a pair of untorn jeans while he was at it.

The woman sat on the recently hoovered couch and touched a hand to the hair she'd had specially blow-dried. She rearranged herself slightly, feeling the crisp lace and cotton of her new underwear remind her of their presence.

'Hungry?' Jack asked, handing her a glass of wine.

'Starving,' she lied.

On a small table, Jack arranged chopsticks and soy sauce and ginger and other sushi parapher-nalia, then, with painstaking care, he prepared the little rice parcels for Ashling. 'It's nothing too out there,' he promised. 'It's sushi for –'

'– beginners, I know.' And she was touched to the soul, in a way that had been impossible six months previously, when her soul had been out of order.

'Perhaps if I don't have wasabi with the first one? Break myself in gently?' she suggested.

'Fine.' But she saw a whisper of disappointment scoot across his face and it made her sad. He was trying so hard.

'I'll chance it,' she amended. 'It's best to have them all together, isn't it? The different tastes complement each other.'

'Only if you're sure,' he said. 'I don't want to scare you away.'

Delicately he placed a tiny, transparent sliver of ginger perfectly centre. With his chopsticks he daintily tidied up the ragged edges and she marvelled that he was going to all this trouble, for her.

'Ready?' he asked, lifting the sushi towards her.

For a moment she panicked. She wasn't sure she was. Feeling as though she was opening more than just her mouth, she let him place the tiny bundle on her tongue.

Anxiously he watched her reaction.

'Yum,' she finally said, with a smile. 'Scary but yum.' *Not unlike yourself.*

She tried a cucumber one, a tofu one, a crab and avocado one, then pushed the boat out altogether by having a salmon one.

'You're fantastic,' Jack enthused, as though she'd

just done something really worthy of note, like passing her driving test. 'You're just great. So whenever you're ready for the salsa . . .'

Oh no.

'Well, it's kind of hard for me to show you,' she said quickly, 'because the man is supposed to lead.'

'Try anyway,' he urged.

'But . . .'

'Just a rough idea,' he grinned.

'We don't have the right music.'

'What do we need? Cuban stuff?'

'Yeeeesss,' she said slowly, realizing her error. She'd thought there wasn't a hope he'd have such obscure music, but she was forgetting that he was a man.

She was going to have to go through with this.

'OK, never mind the music. The stuff on the stereo will do. Right, we both stand up.'

Immediately he got to his feet and she felt threatened by his height looming over her.

'And we face each other.'

They turned to each other. Except they were about ten feet apart.

'Perhaps slightly further in,' Ashling suggested.

He took a step, then she did. Eventually she arrived at his front, reluctant to get too close. But she was near enough to smell him.

'You put your arm around me. If you want,' she added hastily.

He slid his arm along the small of her back and, briefly, she hovered her hand above his shoulder, then with a small surrender lowered it. She could feel the heat of him through his shirt.

'And this hand?' He demonstrated his free one. 'You hold mine.'

'Right.' He was so matter-of-fact that when his big, dry hand grasped hers, she decided to relax. She was showing him how to dance, it was perfectly acceptable that they touch each other.

'When my leg goes back, yours follows it, right?'

'Show me.'

'OK.' She slid her leg out behind her and his leg came forward in tandem.

'Now the other way,' Ashling said. 'You move your leg back and I follow it. And again.'

They practised it several times, increasing in speed and grace, until mid-move Jack stopped and Ashling kept going and suddenly she found herself pressing her thigh hard against his. She jerked to a halt, but didn't pull away. They were perfectly still, frozen in the dance. Eye-level with his chin, she thought vaguely, *he needs to shave*. It was important to think normal things at a time like this. Because in other corners of her consciousness, other thoughts were going on.

'Ashling, would you please look at me?' Jack's voice against her hair was anguished.

I can't.

Then suddenly she could. She turned her face upwards, his sloe-black eyes blazed down and their mouths met in a hard kiss. Many months of

708

waiting went into it. The low-down opening sensation yielded in Ashling: normally it burgeoned gradually, but this time it arrived with an abrupt thrust of desire.

His hands on her face, they kissed until they hurt each other. Hungry and desperate, they couldn't get enough of each other.

'Sorry,' Jack whispered.

''s OK,' she murmured back.

Gradually the kisses calmed, becoming dreamier and gentle until his lips were like feathers as they sucked against her tender mouth. The music was still on the stereo and they seemed to be circling slowly.

The sea looked in and thought, Slow-dancing in his front-room, well I've seen it all now.

Ashling slid her hands under Jack's shirt and up along the delicious newness of his back. Their bodies were pressed up against each other, his palms on her bottom were pulling her even closer and she felt syrupy, floaty, blissful. She had no idea how long they spent like that. It could have been ten minutes or two hours, but suddenly Ashling had taken off Jack's shirt. Well, it only involved opening one button.

'You hussy,' he said. 'I'll see you a shirt and I'll raise you a pair of boots.'

'OK.' Her heart was banging in her chest. 'What exactly does that mean? I take off my boots?'

'And your shirt. I can see you're not a poker player, I'll have to teach you the rules. Off with your shirt.' Already he was helping her out of it. 'Now you say, I'll raise you a pair of jeans.'

'I'll raise you a pair of jeans.' She swallowed with nerves and excitement, as slowly Jack popped the buttons on his fly. Her hands trembling, she waited a tantalizing moment before unzipping her black trousers and wriggling out of them.

'Socks!' he declared, but his jokey tone was not mirrored by the intent expression in his eyes. Her throat was closed and she felt trickly and achey with longing, as they stood before each other, Jack in white Calvins, Ashling in her new high-cut all-in-one (with waist effect).

'Got the rules?' Jack asked thickly.

She nodded slowly, taking in his perfect legs, the sculpted arms, the flat area of black hair on his chest that snaked down to his stomach. 'Think so. And what's wild?'

'You?'

She surprised herself with a laugh. Waist or no waist, she was more confident than she'd ever been without her clothes.

She reached out her hand and touched the thick column that was straining against the white cotton and was rewarded with a shudder from him. Then she put her finger inside the waistband and pulled. No need to speak. It was perfectly clear what she wanted.

He reached in and freed himself. Revealing black pubic hair, he slid off his Calvins while holding his erection in his fist. Ashling was transfixed by how erotic it was.

Upstairs on Jack's freshly laundered bed, he peeled her underwear off in slow motion. Inching it down and away from her with such tiny, languid movements that she thought she'd shriek. Finally there were no more obstacles.

'Are you sure you want to do this?' Jack asked anxiously.

'What do you think?' She smiled lazily at him.

'You might be on the rebound.'

'I'm not on the rebound,' she said gently. 'Honestly.'

Suddenly he froze. 'You're not doing this for a bet?'

She laughed hard, genuinely entertained.

'No? I just had a vision of Trix running a book on you and me.'

They slid themselves along each other and every touch, every gesture was inquisitive and gentle. Their breath grew shorter and, with gathering speed and desire, they stopped being gentle and became wild and wanton and rough. She dug her nails into his buttocks and he bit her breast. They rolled over each other, welded together as he thrust into her, then she slid tightly down on him.

Afterwards, they lay tangled together, glowing with unity. But suddenly Ashling was gripped with uncertainty. What if he changed his mind? What if, now that he'd slept with her, he went off her?

Then Jack said softly, 'Ashling, you are the nicest

711

thing that has ever happened to me,' and all her doubts went away.

'Of course the question is,' Jack spoke into the darkness, 'will you respect me in the morning?'

Sleepily Ashling said, 'Don't worry. I didn't respect you anyway.'

He pinched her.

'Of *course* I'll respect you in the morning,' she reassured. 'I might disparage you a bit in the afternoon, mind,' she added. 'But I can guarantee my undivided respect in the morning.'

CHAPTER 65

On the first Monday in April, a week before she returned to London, Lisa received notification of her final decree in the post. Before she even opened the envelope she knew what it contained – silly though it was, she was sure she sensed a slightly unpleasant air emanating from it.

Her instinct was to recoil from it, to shove it under the phone book and pretend it had never come. Then, with a sigh, she quickly tore it open. She'd had to do lots of unpleasant things in her life. If she didn't face them head-on she'd never get anything done. But they had to be done *fast*, like ripping off a plaster.

Her head was amazingly clear. She noted the way her fingers shook as she pulled out the pages, then watched the sentences scroll away from her eyes, too quickly to be read. When the words slowed down and stopped moving she forced herself to study the hard black letters on the white page. One at a time, until the message she already knew revealed itself – it was over. No more living half-in-half-out of a marriage, instead it was all tidied neatly away. The end. *Fin*. That's all folks.

With ongoing crystal clarity, she observed that she hadn't suddenly started skipping around the hall with the liberation of closure. Instead she noted that her temperature had soared – was she *sweating*? – and that she didn't feel joyous and free.

All through the divorce process, she'd hoped that the next part of the procedure would be the one where she'd magically feel healed. But now they'd reached the end of the line and she still wasn't restored to her former happiness. If anything she actually felt *worse*.

Perhaps the sadness of a divorce doesn't actually disappear, she realized. Instead you have to incorporate it, learn to co-exist with it – which seemed like such a slog, she felt like going back to bed.

Fifi had thrown a party when her divorce had become final, so why didn't she feel like doing the same? The difference, she reluctantly admitted, was that she didn't hate Oliver. Shame she didn't, she mocked herself. There was a lot to be said for acrimony.

She folded away the document in her hand and she forced hope upon herself. It would all be OK. Some day. London was the place. She'd meet another man there. Even if sometimes it really depressed her how crap other men were. *By comparison*, she conceded. It might help if she stopped using Oliver as a yardstick.

Once back in London she'd do her best to avoid him. Their paths might cross occasionally in the course of work and they would smile civilly at each other. Until the time came when they could meet, work and not think of what might have been, the other life they might have lived. Time would pass and one day, some day, it wouldn't matter any more.

But I've failed, she admitted, in a wash of excoriating honesty. I've failed and it's my fault. I can't fix this, I can't make it go away and I will have to live with it for the rest of my life.

She'd always been the sum of her triumphs. One success stacked on top of another had made Lisa who she was. So where did this failure fit in? And it would have to, because she was visited with the understanding that our lives are a succession of experiences and that the broken ones count as much as the perfect ones.

This pain has changed me, she admitted. This pain that is not going to go away for a very long time has made me a nicer person. Even if I don't want to be, she acknowledged wryly. Even if I consider it a fate worse than death, I am softer, kinder, better.

And I'm *glad* I was married to Oliver, she thought defiantly. I'm sorry and sad and pissed *off* that I messed it up, but I'll learn from it and I'll make certain it won't happen again.

And that was the best she could do.

She sighed heavily, picked up her bag, then left for work like the survivor she was.

When she reached the office it was abuzz – with preparations for Lisa's leaving party on Friday. It was almost as elaborate an operation as the launch party. Lisa planned to leave Dublin in a blaze of glory. She'd already told Trix she was holding her personally responsible for the leaving present and that if they got her a Next voucher she'd maim her.

'Lisa,' Trix held the phone out. 'It's Tomsey from the curtain department at Hensards. Your wooden blind is finally ready!'

At close of business that day, Lisa cornered Ashling as they got the lift down to the lobby. She was anxious to clear something up with her.

'I want you to know,' Lisa emphasized, 'that I put your name forward to be editor and I sang your praises to the board. I'm sorry you didn't get it.'

'It doesn't matter, I'd hate to be editor,' Ashling insisted. 'I'm one of life's second-in-commands, and we're just as important as leaders.'

Lisa laughed at Ashling's blithe self-possession. 'The girl they've appointed seems fine. Could have been worse, it could have been Trix!'

Lisa had no doubt that one day Trix would edit a magazine – and so ruthlessly she'd make Lisa look like Mother Teresa by comparison. But at the moment Trix had other things on her mind. The fish-mongrel had been shown the door to make way for Kelvin and a wild office romance was underway. It was a 'secret'.

As the lift doors opened Lisa sharply nudged Ashling and sneered, 'Well, look who it is.'

It was – of all people – Clodagh, looking extremely nervous.

'What does she want?' Lisa asked aggressively. 'Come to try and nick Jack from you? Cow! Want me to tell her that her husband tried to pork me?'

'That's a lovely offer.' Ashling heard her voice from far away. 'But no need, thanks.'

'Sure? See you tomorrow then.'

Clodagh stepped forward when Lisa left. 'Just tell me to get lost if you want, but I was wondering if we could talk.'

Ashling was helpless with shock and it took a while to find words. 'We'll go to the pub next door.' They located a seat and ordered drinks and all the while Ashling couldn't stop staring at Clodagh. She looked good, she'd had her hair cut much shorter and it suited her.

'I've come to apologize,' Clodagh said awkwardly. 'I've grown up an awful lot over the past few months. I'm different now.'

Ashling nodded stiffly.

'I see how selfish and self-obsessed I was and how cruel I've been,' Clodagh spilled. 'My punishment is having to live with all the damage I've caused. You hate me and I don't know if you've seen Dylan lately, but he's ruined. He's so angry and . . . hard.'

Ashling agreed. She didn't like being around him any more.

'Did you know that I asked him to come back and he wouldn't?'

Ashling nodded. Dylan had almost taken out an ad on national television to publicize it.

'Serves me right, huh?' Clodagh managed a weak smile.

Ashling didn't answer.

'We've sold the house in Donnybrook and me and the kids are living in Greystones now. Miles out, but it was all we could afford. I'm a single mother now since Dylan decided he couldn't cope with custody. It's a steep learning curve –'

'What was it all about?' Ashling interrupted sharply.

Clodagh twitched anxiously at the anger in Ashling's voice. 'Something I've been asking myself a lot.'

'And? Any conclusions? Bad patch in your marriage? They all have them, you know.'

Clodagh swallowed nervously. 'I don't think it was just that. I should never have married Dylan. This is probably hard to believe but I don't think I ever really fancied him. I just thought he was the kind of man you married – he was so good-looking and charming and had a good job and was responsible . . .' She glanced anxiously at Ashling, whose set, thunderous face wasn't exactly encouraging. 'I was twenty and selfish and I didn't have a clue.' Clodagh longed to be understood.

'And what about Marcus?'

'I was desperate for some fun and excitement.'

'You could have taken up bungee-jumping.'

Clodagh nodded miserably. 'Or white-water rafting.' But Ashling didn't laugh. She'd honestly thought she would. 'I was unfulfilled and frustrated,' Clodagh attempted. 'At times I used to feel like I was being suffocated –'

'Lots of mothers are bored and frustrated,' Ashling snapped. 'Lots of *people* are. But they don't have affairs. Especially not with their best friend's boyfriend.'

'I know, I know, I know! I can see that now, but at the time I was clueless. I'm sorry, I just thought I should have anything I wanted because I was so miserable.'

'But why Marcus? Why *my* boyfriend?'

Clodagh reddened and looked at her lap. She was taking a real risk admitting this. 'Probably anyone would have done.'

'But it was *my* boyfriend you picked. Because you didn't have any respect for me.' Ashling cut to the heart of the matter.

Shamefaced, Clodagh admitted, 'Not enough. Which I hate myself for. I've spent the past months feeling guilty and shitty about it. I'd give my left tit for you to forgive me.'

After a long, sweaty pause Ashling sighed heavily. 'I forgive you. Like, who am I to judge? I've hardly lived a perfect life. As you pointed out, I was a total victim.'

'Oh, I'm sorry!'

'Don't be, you were right.'

Clodagh's face lit up. 'Does that mean we can be friends again?'

Another long pause as Ashling thought about it. She and Clodagh had been friends since they'd been five. *Best* friends. They'd lived through childhood, adolescence and early adulthood together. They shared a common history and no one would know her the way Clodagh knew her. That sort of friendship is rare. But . . .

'No,' Ashling broke the tense silence. 'I forgive you, but I don't trust you. To lose one boyfriend to your friend is misfortunate, but to lose two is careless.'

'But I've changed. I really have.'

'It doesn't matter,' Ashling said sadly.

'But . . .' Clodagh objected.

'No!'

Clodagh realized it was pointless. 'OK,' she whispered. 'I'd better go. I really am sorry, I just want you to know that . . . Bye.'

As she left, she found she was shaking. It hadn't gone the way she'd hoped. The last few months had been nasty in the extreme for Clodagh. She was shocked and indeed *surprised* by how painful she found her life. Not just her new, grim, single-mother circumstances, but the insight she'd been given into her own self-seeking behaviour.

Contrition was a new emotion for her, and she'd expected that if she explained the understanding she'd had into her selfishness, and stressed how very sorry she was, she'd be forgiven. That instantly everything would be perfect again. But she'd underestimated Ashling and she'd learnt yet another lesson: just because she was sorry didn't mean people were ready to forgive her and just because people forgave her didn't mean she'd feel any better.

Sad and lonely and still burdened with the fruits of her destruction, she wondered if she'd ever be able to fix all that she'd broken. Would anything ever be normal again?

As she passed Hogan's a crowd of boys noticed her and began whistling and shouting compliments. At first she ignored them, then on a whim tossed her hair and gave a dazzling over-the-shoulder smile which elicted whoops of wild appreciation from them. All at once her heart lifted.

Hey, life goes on.

Meanwhile, when Lisa had left Ashling and Clodagh in the office lobby, she'd made herself walk home. She'd started doing that to counteract all the dinners Kathy made her eat. As she walked along she worked hard at keeping the sadness at bay. *I am fabulous. I have a fabulous mum and dad. I have a fabulous new job as a media consultant. I have fabulous shoes.*

When she turned into her street, one of her neighbours was sitting on her doorstep waiting for her. What amazed her was that they hadn't got the key from Kathy and just let themselves in, she thought drily.

She'd miss them all when she returned to London. Although Francine kept telling her she wouldn't have to, that Lisa would have so many visitors it would be almost as if she'd never left.

Who was on her step, anyway? Francine? Beck? But they were the wrong sex to be Francine, and they were too big to be Beck and . . . Lisa's step faltered as she realized they were the wrong colour to be either of them. It was Oliver.

'What are you doing here?' she called in astonishment.

'I've come to see you,' he called back.

She reached her front-door and he stood up with a big, white grin. 'I've come to win you back, babes.'

'Why?' She put her key in the lock and he followed her into the hall. She was confused – and oddly resentful. She'd put a whole day's effort into 'moving on' and he'd scuppered it.

'Because you're the best,' he said simply. Another dazzling smile.

She clattered her keys on the kitchen table. 'You've left it a bit bloody late,' she said snippily. 'We've just got divorced.'

'You know,' he said, thoughtfully, 'I feel so shit about that. It has messed with my head like you just would not believe! Anyway, nothing to say we can't get married again,' he grinned.

'I'm serious,' he insisted when she gave him a you-mad-bastard look.

She threw him another one but all at once her thoughts got a bit frisky and out-of-control. The idea of marrying Oliver again was ludicrous but seductive. Extremely seductive – for about a nano-second, then she got real.

Briskly she asked, 'Don't you remember how horrible it was? At the end we rowed all the time and it was *bitter*. You hated me and my job.'

'Right,' he admitted. 'But I've got to take some of the rap. I was too arsey. When you changed your mind about having a baby, I should have listened to you. I know you tried to tell me, babes, and I did *not* want to know. That was why finding you were still on the Pill blew me away. But if I'd listened, well . . . 'And you are *so* not as hard as you were. Sorry, babes,' he said as she bristled, 'but you're not.'

'And this is a good thing?'

'*Sure.*'

At her sceptical face he said softly, 'Lisa, we've been apart more than a year, and it still hasn't got any better for me. I've never met anyone who even comes close to you.'

His expression was enquiring, waiting for some encouragement or endorsement from her, but she gave neither. All the buoyancy he'd had on arrival drained away and he was suddenly anxious. 'Unless you've met someone else. I'll just naff off if you have,' he offered graciously. 'And forget about trying to win you back.'

Her face inscrutable. Lisa eyed him and considered shooting him a sly little maybe-I-have-maybe-I-haven't smirk. That would bring to a halt this crazy, dangerous situation. Then abruptly she decided against it. She'd never played games with him, so why start now? 'No, Oliver, there's no one else.'

'Right,' he nodded slowly and carefully. 'Well, I might as well finish ripping my guts out here.' After a nervous pause he continued, 'I still love you. Now that we're older and wiser,' – uncertain little laugh – 'I can see it working out.'

'Can you?' Her question was cool.

'Yes,' he said stoutly. 'And if you were interested I could base myself in Dublin.'

'You wouldn't have to, I'm moving back to London at the end of the week,' she muttered.

'Then, Lisa,' Oliver said, his face deadly serious, 'the only question is, *are* you interested?'

A long, tense silence followed until Lisa eventually spoke. 'Yeah, I suppose.' She was suddenly shy.

'Are you sure?'

'Yeah.' A nervous giggle spilled from her.

'Babes!' he exclaimed, in mock outrage. 'So what are you doing, making me sweat like this?'

Still shy, she admitted, 'I was afraid. I *am* afraid.'

'Of what?'

She shrugged. 'Of hope, I suppose. I didn't want to, in case you were just being mental. I had to be sure you were sure until I could even think about it. The thing is,' she admitted bashfully, 'I love you.'

'Then there's no need to be afraid,' he promised.

'When did you get so wise?' she grumbled.

He laughed hard and loud, a proper Oliver laugh, and suddenly her thoughts were like greyhounds who'd been let out of a trap. They just *took off*.

How lucky was she to get a reprieve? The full extent of her sheer, jammy, good fortune revealed itself to her and she was soaring, almost weightless with happiness. Not everyone gets a chance like this, she realized, savouring – for once – the value of the present moment.

I'll do it differently this time, she vowed fiercely. They both would. And there was something else, the icing on the cake, as it were: if two weddings to the same person were good enough for Burton and Taylor, they were good enough for her. Unable to stop her joyous, runaway head, she was already planning the second wedding, a fabulous extravaganza. No sneaking away to Vegas this time – no, they'd do it properly. Her mum would be *thrilled*. And they'd get *Hello!* to photo it . . .

As if he could read her thoughts, Oliver exclaimed anxiously, 'Easy tiger!'

EPILOGUE

Jack and Ashling were strolling on the pier. It was a May evening, still bright. Arms linked, they ambled along.

'Toffo?' Ashling offered.

'And there I was thinking that things just couldn't get any better,' Jack said.

Ashling lucky-dipped in her bag. 'Where are they?' She brought forth a card of Anadin and a bottle of rescue remedy before finding the Toffos.

'You still have all that stuff in there?' Jack sounded sad. 'The plasters and everything?'

'Habit, I suppose.' But for the first time ever she felt slightly silly for carrying around so much disaster-prevention stuff.

'You wouldn't consider throwing it all away? You don't need any of it now. Everything is different.'

Ashling looked at him for a long time. He was right, everything *was* different. 'OK, I'll lose it all when we get home.'

'Why not do it now? Go on, fling your bag into the sea.'

'Fling my bag into the sea? Yeah, right.'

'I mean it. Let it all go.'

'Are you mad? What about my credit cards? What about the bag itself, for that matter?'

'Take out your credit cards and I'll buy you a new bag, I promise.'

'Oh my God, you're serious.' Ashling gave him a look, semi-wary, semi-excited. She was strangely tempted by the idea, even if it did make her feel sick.

'Let it all go,' he repeated, his face animated.

'I couldn't.'

'You could.'

Could I?

'If this was my python-skin bag, I wouldn't even consider it,' she stalled.

'But this one's old and mank,' Jack urged. 'And the handle's coming apart. I'll get you another one. Oh, go on!'

The symbolism of it was seductive. But then again, throwing away a handbag, full of all the stuff she needed, how could she? But *did* she need any of it . . . ? Perhaps she didn't . . . The image sharpened up, becoming possible, probable, doable.

'All right then, I will! I will! Hold those.' She palmed him her wallet, her mobile, her cigarettes and her packet of Toffos.

'I can't believe I'm doing this.' With an exhilarated shout, she twirled the bag over her head once. Twice. And then, in terror and exultation, simply let it go. It hurtled in a jubilant arc up into the darkening sky, a dense little cargo of

safety-pins and plasters and biros. And gracefully, it followed its path downwards, where,
with the smallest of splashes, it was received by
the sea.

APL		CCS	
Cen		Ear	
Mob		Cou	
ALL		Jub	
WH		CHE	
Ald		Bel	
Fin		Fol	
Can		STO	
Til		HCL	